A
GATHERING
of FINCHES

Other books by Jane Kirkpatrick:

Homestead (nonfiction)

A Sweetness to the Soul
(winner of the Wrangler Award for Outstanding Western Novel of 1995)

Love to Water My Soul

A Burden Shared

Mystic Sweet Communion

A GATHERING *of* FINCHES

A NOVEL

Jane Kirkpatrick

MULTNOMAH PUBLISHERS
Sisters, Oregon

A GATHERING OF FINCHES
© 1997 by Jane Kirkpatrick
published by Multnomah Fiction
a division of Multnomah Publishers, Inc.

Cover design by D^2 Designworks

International Standard Book Number: 1-57673-082-4

Printed in the United States of America.

For information:
Multnomah Publishers, Inc.
Post Office Box 1720
Sisters, Oregon 97759

Library of Congress Cataloging–in–Publication Data
Kirkpatrick, Jane, 1946–
    A gathering of finches/Jane Kirkpatrick.
        p.cm.
    ISBN 1-57673-082-4 (alk. paper)
    I. Title
PS3561.I712G3   1997
813'.54–dc21   97-27682
                                                                          CIP

99 00 01 02 03 04 05 06 — 10 9 8 7 6 5 4 3

This book is dedicated to my sister, Judy Hurtley.

A C K N O W L E D G M E N T S

While the words of *A Gathering of Finches* are mine and reflect my choices, many people contributed to whatever quality they reflect. I am especially indebted to L. T. "Bud" and Peg Day of North Bend, Oregon, nephew and niece of Cassie Simpson's daughter, for their access to family photographs, stories, and memorabilia; for their trust and confidence and encouragement of me personally in telling this story; and for their consent both to place Louie Simpson's poems in print and for the use of a photograph from Louie's album for the cover of this book. Their love of history and reading, their faith in me, and their graciousness and friendship are treasures beyond measure.

I thank Hoquiam, Washington, resident and historian Harold Schmidtke, whose interest in the Washington side of the Simpsons and Stearnses led to newspaper accounts and to an opportunity to speak with Cassie's great-nephew in Aberdeen, Washington, and other Stearns relatives in Washington and California. Harold's good humor and generosity to a total stranger are appreciated gifts. I also thank historian Cecil Herrington of Hoquiam for locating and sharing newspaper accounts including those about the tragic story of Robert Hunt.

Fred Foster of Aberdeen, Washington, Cassie's great-nephew, provided critical documentation from the Hendrick family Bible of birth dates and marriages. He related stories of his grandmother, Cassie's sister, and shared his memories of "Uncle Joe" and the story of Cassie leaving Hoquiam and the circumstances of her later marriage. He led me to Elizabeth Lambie, granddaughter of both George Emerson and John Soule, who confirmed the circumstances from her memory. I am deeply indebted to Mr. Foster and Mrs. Lambie for their contributions.

Dick Wagner of North Bend, Oregon, author of *Louie Simpson's North Bend,* not only inspired several walking tours around the city but provided details about public gifts Louie Simpson made and recorded the inscription to a special gift Louie gave his wife. Dick was gracious in his conversations and generous in his willingness to let me speculate about and use his research. He also read and commented on an early draft of the manuscript for which I am deeply indebted.

Stephen Dow Beckham's nonfiction work *The Simpsons of Shore Acres* provided important information about Louie's family and about the Simpson lifestyle. Despite his busy schedule, Dr. Beckham allowed me to review a 1997 report on Shore Acres submitted to the Friends of Shore Acres and the Oregon Parks and Recreation department and provided me with lengthy answers to questions and suggested I contact the Days for photographs—advice that proved invaluable. I thank him.

At Shore Acres itself, I thank George Guthrie, landscape maintenance superintendent, who gave of his time and memory to lead me on a tour of the gardens, and the Friends of Shore Acres, whose publication *Gardens above the Waves,* with its photographs and plant identification, along with the accompanying video, offered a rich glimpse into the garden. The Friends' support of this Oregon treasure is vital, and I am grateful to them, to the Oregon State Park Commission, and to Oregon's citizens for public access to this site.

Thanks go to the following local people: Ann Koppy, director of the Coos Historical Museum in North Bend, who inspired me with her interest in the Simpsons, Cassie in particular; Dow Beckham, author of *Stars in the Dark* and *Swift Flows the River,* who provided substantive information about the history of the mining, logging, and shipping industries in Coos County; Anna Beckham, Dow's wife, who lived as a child at Shore Acres during the rebuilding and provided additional insights about early life at the estate; Dan Collver, descendant of the owners of the farmland that became a part of Shore Acres, who shared several pages of his ancestor's journal describing life along the coast in 1890. I am grateful for his generosity in making introductions and referring me to helpful people.

Melody Caldera, editor and author of several pieces in *South Slough Adventures,* shared stories of the Coos Indians and their early lives along with other historical information. With good humor and enthusiasm, she guided us around South Slough on a foggy morning and shared the *wit-litz* (crossing-over place) at the Winchester Arm. I am grateful to her and to all the authors included in *South Slough.*

A Century of Coos and Curry by Emil R. Peterson and Alfred Powers and *Pioneer History of Coos and Curry Counties* by Orvil Dodge, the latter published in 1898, were exceptional references, as were *Seeking Pleasure in the Old West* by David Dary and *Hatchet, Hands and Hoe, Planting the Pioneer Spirit* by Erica Calkins.

Many individuals shared remembrances with me and helped in ways they may have thought insignificant but were not: Irene Pittam, Kathleen Larsen, Alice Archer, Judy Hurtley, Normandie Phelps, Kay and Don Krall, Nan Chambers, Jewell Minnick, Lynn Catchings, Blair Fredstrom, Jeannie Eddings, Barb Rutschow, Carol Tedder, Millie Voll, Patty Burnet. They gave richness and color as well as encouragement to this story. I hope I will be forgiven for names I have neglected.

I am grateful to the Oregon State Historical Society and to its librarians for assistance in research; to the Wasco County Library for locating works for me; to the North Bend Library for access to microfilm of early newspapers and to Agnes Sengstacken's 1942 book *Destination West!*; to the Burlingame Historical Society and especially to Marilyn Short for efforts to research issues surrounding Cassie's death and for the invitation to ride the train down the peninsula as Cassie and Louie might have done.

Special thanks are reserved for Ken and Nancy Tedder of Coos Bay. They introduced us to Shore Acres State Park and then gave us the use of their home for research trips. Their kindness and support of my writing are priceless and links them ever closer to our lives.

The confidence of my editor, Rod Morris, in this third book in the series and the encouragement of my publishing family at Multnomah Publishers continue to amaze me as does the support of my agent, Joyce Hart.

Finally, I am grateful to my husband, Jerry, for his map making, his tolerance of my scheduling, and his unending faith in me. I am pleased he walks beside me with unconditional love.

LIST OF CHARACTERS

Corning, New York

Annabelle, an African Grey parrot
- Annie, Cassie Hendrick's friend
- Burr and Anna Hendrick, Cassie's parents
- Cassie Hendrick, a young woman and future wife of Joe Stearns
- Margaret Hendrick, Cassie's younger sister
Marjorie, an Ojibway woman
Granny Stearns, grandmother of Josiah
- Josiah (Joe) Stearns, engineer

Hoquiam, Washington

- George Emerson, partner of Asa Simpson in North-Western Lumber Company
- Fred Foster, husband of Margaret Hendrick and entrepreneur
- Robert Hunt, troubled resident
Mary, a Quinault midwife
Melody, a Quinault businesswoman
- Louis J. Simpson, mill manager and entrepreneur
Beatrice Smith, lumber baron's wife and suffragette
- Francis (Fanny) Soule, daughter of John Soule and second wife of Joe Stearns
- Ida Soule, sister of Francis Soule and friend of Cassie's
- John Soule, mill manager
- Isabelle (Belle) Stearns, daughter of Cassie and Joe
Willard Stems, secretary to Josiah Stearns

San Francisco and Oakland

- George Elliot, a drayman
- Roy Pike, husband of Edith and brother-in-law of Louis Simpson
- Asa Simpson, father of Louis Simpson, shipping, lumber, mining magnate
- Edgar (Captain) Simpson, brother of Louis Simpson
- Edith Simpson, sister of Louis Simpson

- Henry "Harry" Simpson, youngest brother of Louis Simpson
- Sophie Simpson, mother of Louis Simpson

Coos Bay and North Bend

Gus Anders, farmer and husband of Annie
April, Marvin, and Maddie, Gus and Annie Anders's children
- Chauncey Byler, friend of Louie and Cassie and partner of Louis Simpson
- Laura Byler, friend of Louie and Cassie, wife of Chauncey
Ellen, Coos Indian woman
- Jake Evans, pack handler and former owner of Shore Acres
Ming Ho, cook's assistant
- Maj. L. D. Kinney, owner, Coos Bay Rapid Transit Company
- Lung Lem and Lee Ling, Chinese cooks for the Simpsons
Lottie, Coos Indian woman and employee of the Simpsons
Rachel and Benjamin, Lottie's children
- Issac (Russ) Tower, owner of The Gunnery and the Ford dealership, and later, husband of Isabelle Stearns
- Charlie Winsor, manager, Bank of Oregon, and business partner of Louis Simpson
- Kate Winsor, friend of Cassie, wife of Charlie, and a Presbyterian organist
- "Joe" and Helen, Charlie and Kate Winsor's children

Shore Acres

- Mike Bastendorf, dairyman and farm manager
- Donald James, gardener at Shore Acres in later years
- David Masterton, first gardener at Shore Acres
- Alpha Wicklund, employee of the Simpsons
- James Withycombe, governor of Oregon

- denotes actual historical person

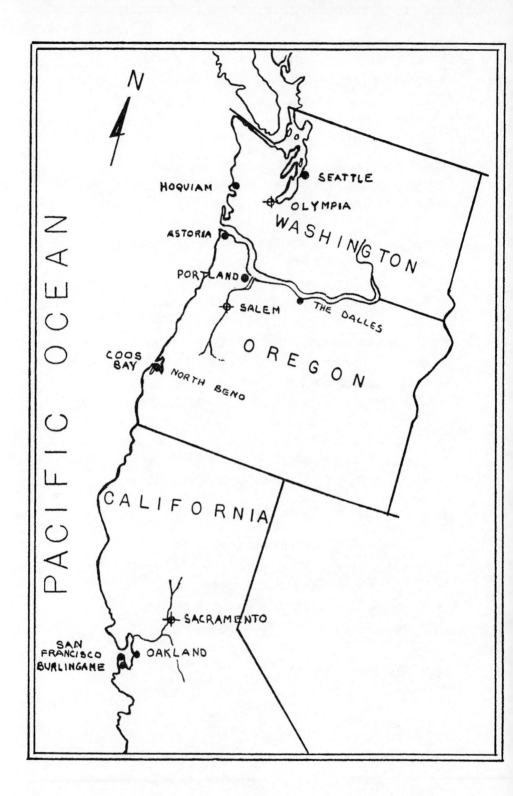

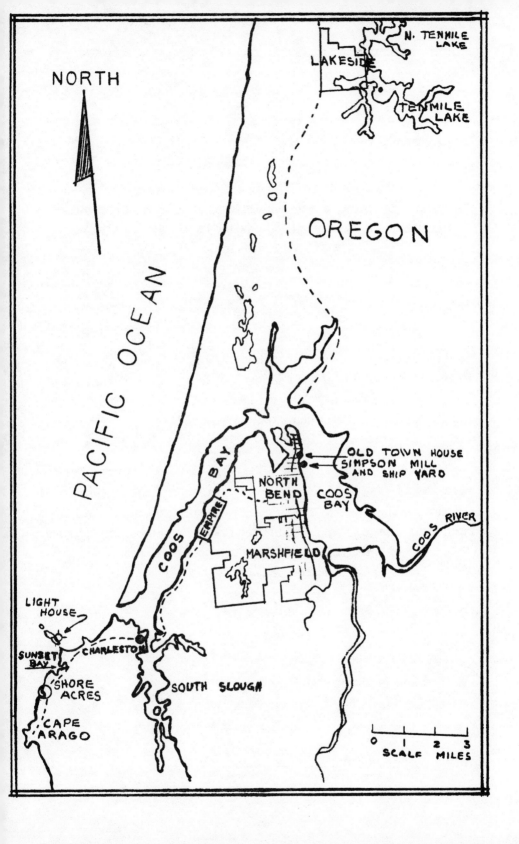

"For whoever wants to save his life will lose it, but whoever loses his life for me will find it. What good will it be for a man if he gains the whole world, yet forfeits his soul?"
Matthew 16:25–26

"So if you faithfully obey the commands...to love the LORD your God and to serve him with all your heart and with all your soul...you will eat and be satisfied."
Deuteronomy 11:13–15

Charm, *n.* The power or quality of pleasing, attracting, or fascinating. From Latin *carmen*, song, incantation; archaic: a confused sound of voices or bird calls. A gathering or company of finches.
American Heritage Dictionary

PROLOGUE

❁

I remember that first *wit-litz* with my Coos Indian maid in the autumn of 1899. Sea gulls screeched against the threatened squall as the wind pushed at our wedge-split canoe breaking choppy water on Oregon's South Slough. As morning sank into afternoon, pileated woodpeckers cackled and flirted with Douglas firs marching like silent warriors down steep banks to sand. I remember that crossing-over, that *wit-litz*. Loaded with people and baskets of berries and bread, the shallow crafts took us from shore to shore and just one mule ride short of the Pacific. The scent of oil burned to smooth and widen the cedar crafts lingered on my fingers and my linen skirt.

We could have crossed on the rickety bridge north of Valino Island. It still stood then. But such a journey lacked the proper adventure. Adventure ought never be thwarted. Adventure and novelty, change and variety, that's what kept boredom at bay, and any price paid proved worth it, even when it bordered on the foolish, even when it circled the insane.

I never imagined Lottie and I would share a friendship, a finished woman and her employee. But we did, though I sensed even then how those brown Miluk eyes judged my lavender love. She might have called it self-indulgent if she'd known the word and I had bothered to ask. I called it a grand love, passionate and providing, despite its being fringed with suffering and anguish...perhaps *because* it was.

So much had happened: the lies, the choices whose consequences now skipped before me like flat stones on ponds. I saw no need to face them, barely gave them a fleeting glance. I sought an invitation to avoid them instead, to celebrate my independence, my intention formed separately from the family and faith I'd been born to.

The *wit-litz* and my friends gave me that chance.

"Harder, Lottie!" I shouted over my shoulder. I heard her wheeze as she dug her paddle deeper, maneuvering us around nasty snags. We led the competition by only a canoe length. The double-pointed cedar dugout swooshed against the tidewaters splashing salt spray onto my face and wilting the plume of my hat that drooped now over my eyes. I pushed my lower lip out and blew air to watch the feather flutter. Covered baskets seeping the aroma of fresh bread sat like clusters of lily pads beyond my knees toward the prow.

"A going-over place," Lottie shouted from behind me, her voice crisp above sea gulls' screeching. "Mmm. My people call it *wit-litz. Wit-litz.*"

"What's that?" I turned enough to see her and the other canoes piercing the distance between us like well-shot arrows.

"Crossing over," she said.

"We're surely doing that!" I said, turning back. The little sound that preceded some of her words reminded me of a hummingbird quietly announcing its arrival.

She said something more, but the slap of water and wind drowned her out. I twisted again to hear her, and when I did, a gust pulled at the plume and ripped it and the hat from the roll of hair piled atop my head. I gasped as I grabbed for the hat and missed. The violet felt and feather took flight like a frightened bird, twisted and rose, then plunged and sank. I swallowed hard as the current sucked it under, leaving behind empty space. Something seemed familiar in the motion.

It wasn't that I needed that hat. I had a dozen others and could buy a dozen more. It wasn't much of a fashion accessory at all. But the pearl hatpin I thought would hold it to my head carried meaning for me and was something that, though not needed, had been wanted.

"Oh, misery," I said.

Lottie back-paddled with the oar now, her muscles brown and bulging as she turned us toward the hat's resting place.

"No!" I said. "Keep going! They'll beat us!"

We were the lead canoe by only half a length now. Five more filled with family, some friends, and one dog broke the water behind us. We could have launched a rowboat and crossed by ourselves or hired one large scow to do the work or even used the hand-drawn ferry at Charleston Beach. But Louie had wanted this first trip with me to be in cedar log dugouts with Indian paddlers. Something "a bit above the ordinary," he'd said, "the way they used to do it."

"Don't worry your lip," Louie said then as his canoe pulled alongside ours. I jerked my hand to my lap. Ellen, his rower, rested the paddle across her knees, and Louie grinned at me. "Sun makes your hair look like sable," he said. "Stunning."

"We could drop a line for it," Ellen offered. One hand shaded her eyes against the afternoon sun as she peered at the dark water. She lowered her hand to control her canoe against a push of wind.

"It's nothing. Silly to wear one anyway out here. I won't again. The pin was special, though. Mother gave it to me when Belle was born."

"We'll get another, Case," Louie said, "soon as we get back. Your mother will never know we replaced her pearl returned this day to the deep."

He had an orator's voice, full of vision and passion and promise of adventure. The sounds of it washed over me, the deep tones as mesmerizing as the pounding of the waves or the soft hiss of the wind through cedars. Or perhaps it was the depth and size of his dark eyes that I sank into, had changed my whole life for.

His wide hands pulled our canoes together. The crafts thunked, unsettled me with the quick movement. The poodle barked from inside her basket nestled between Louie's feet. I grabbed at the canoe's sides to balance. Louie took the moment to kiss me, in front of everyone, his warm lips lingering for just a moment on mine before the wind shifted our crafts. His hands on my cheeks smelled of salt air and charred cedar.

In the distance, I heard a few shouts from his brothers and others as they passed us, but at that moment my heart and ears and eyes belonged only to him, Louis Simpson.

"I love you, Cassie-Casey," he said.

"I love you, Louis-Louie."

He bent his head to my forehead and sighed contentedly. Then quick-changing as a summer squall, he released me, sat alert, faced west, and shouted, "Onward, Ellen!"

She pushed off with a quick thrust, and his hand shot into the air as though holding a sword and leading a military charge. "We've a pack string waiting and a picnic lunch promised." Then over his shoulder to me he issued a challenge he knew I'd not resist. "Beat you to the shore, Babe."

Ellen paddled toward the tangle of dense timber and vines and the sand dunes and ocean beyond. Her arms dug deep, and despite her passenger

17

being the largest of all, she gained on the others. They exchanged shouts and laughter.

Lottie and I were last.

My eyes followed Louie's dark hair and the back of his ivory suit. He sat well above his paddler and waved his hand in a circular motion as he passed the others, urging all to the shore. "Harder, Lottie!" I ordered. She was a bulldog of a woman, short and squatty and square and a powerful rower, but I knew victory would elude us.

Louie passed them all and reached the shore. He busied himself bending low to step out, then stood, pounding his chest in victory. The others beached their crafts, laughing, talking to Jake Evans, the mule-string handler waiting for our group.

A blue wedge chased the squall from the sky and exposed the sun, bright overhead. I grabbed at my skirts and stuffed the bulk between my knees and set my boots firmly on the bottom.

"That is danger!" Lottie shouted. "Think about it!"

A wind gust seized my hair then tangled and twisted it like mist over eyes. Water and sky and audience on the beach disappeared for the moment.

"Sit down!" Lottie shouted, loud enough to cause those beached to turn their eyes toward us.

Through the strands of my hair I saw how they stared. Concern clouded their faces and then admiration as they watched our craft approach through the white chop. It was the latter look I liked.

I took a deep breath and let loose my hands.

"You will make both of us sink!" Lottie warned.

I inhaled the Oregon sea air and stood, spreading my arms wide, embracing the looks of wonder gazing back from the shore.

"I will cross into this new time standing up!" I shouted.

Lottie grunted into her paddle and brought us straight into sand.

I'd ignored the danger my actions placed us in. Instead, my arms surrendered to water, wind, my choice, and the moment, and I got just what I thought I wanted: applause and though fleeting, satisfaction.

PART I

FIRST CHOICES

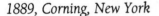

1889, Corning, New York

My friend Annie and I sat in our family's closed Victoria carriage peering out through the round, isinglass window. Pale leaves of oaks and maples drifted down from the tall canopy of trees. The carriage-horse stomped impatiently, shaking harness and hames, while aromas of rose-scented geraniums and monarda from the dooryard gardens made my nose twitch and took my thoughts to dried tea and refreshment.

"He's such a straight-laced one," Annie said. "Looks cocky, though, holding his chin like that." She mimicked the look of the man standing outside the carriage talking with my father on the cobblestone street. They belonged to the same lodge, which was somewhat peculiar given that Josiah Stearns was not yet thirty and my father was already fifty-six and quite particular about his clubbing chums. The owner of a mercantile and a partner in a glassworks company, my father couldn't afford to associate with just anyone. There were "appearances to keep," he often said, and he knew just how to keep them.

"Blond hair'll turn white on his wedding night."

"Oh, Cassie!" Annie said. "How you talk."

I settled back into the leather. Autumn light without warmth streamed in through the window. I hugged myself against the chill. My stomach growled into the silence. I wondered if we'd have fresh croissants for lunch.

"What kind of man do you think I'll marry?" Annie said.

She untied the bow that held her bonnet and fingered her sunrise hair. Freckles made a trail across her nose by late summer growing darker as her hair became lighter. We were both eighteen and had been friends forever.

"Someone warm and wonderful with wide hands."

"Why would I care about his hands?" Annie said, looking at her own. She wore fawn-colored gloves smudged with the city and soot of industrial smoke that lingered over the carriage.

"Because you love to be held," I said. "A man with wide hands'll do that."

Annie turned her hands over and back then looked at me. "Oh, la! You're teasing, aren't you?"

I shrugged. "It's been my experience," I said.

"And what better teacher?" she said and grinned.

The leather pillow I leaned into proved too hard to be comfortable. I sat up, straightened my suit jacket over a silk blouse, and smoothed the linen skirt across my knees. As I did, my eye caught those of Josiah Stearns through the window. One eyebrow rose in acknowledgment of my gaze.

"What about your husband?" Annie asked. "Do you ever dream how he will be? How wide his hands?"

"Never." I fluttered my fingertips at her in dismissal. "I like the passion of surprise. Wonder what they're talking about."

Josiah bent stiffly at his middle, his whole body attentive to my father. We came from short but sturdy Dutch stock, and my father stood five feet, four inches and was almost as round as he was tall. Josiah stood over him by three or four inches.

"It's something to consider," Annie persisted.

"I don't plan to."

"You've never said that before."

"Why should I?" I said, turning back to face her. "Lots of other things to do. Look at Abigail Duniway Scott or that reporter woman, Nellie Bly."

"You're interested in doctoring?" Her eyes got big.

"It's an example of what a woman can do if she doesn't marry, seeks her own way instead."

"That Oregon woman's married," Annie said. "So is Caddie Stanton. My mother says it's where women truly shine."

"In Oregon, maybe," I said, "not necessarily in marriage."

Annie pulled the tips of her gloves from her fingers and fanned herself with the soft leather. She fluffed at the curls of her hair. Other Saturday carriages rolled on by, their rattle proving a welcome pause in our conversation.

"You're just afraid of the harness," she said. "A team can pull harder and go farther than just one horse alone."

"Oh, I suppose I might marry eventually," I said. "But I get enthralled with the possibilities if I don't. Maybe study music for a time or travel. Stroll through art museums outside of New York, go to Kiev and visit castles and cathedrals. Taste a pastry from every country."

"And how do you intend to do that? Your father'll balk."

"Maybe I'll find a rich benefactor," I said. I wiggled my eyebrows at her.

"What about that one?" Annie said pointing with her chin again toward Josiah Stearns. "My mama says he's of the first family of New Hampshire, those railroad people." She looked with me through the window then leaned back. "But he plans to settle in Washington State. Probably take himself a western wife."

It certainly sounded like a challenge.

"We'll see about that," I said and reached to open the latch to Annie's startled "Oh!"

I carried no feeling for him. Had never even met him. But Annie said I couldn't, and my mother later said I shouldn't, forming two ultimatums to my mind.

Maybe it happened because I was bored. I'd had my coming-out party months before and no end of stolen kisses while strolling arm and arm with wide-eyed beaus who offered no real sense of adventure. Another school waited for me in the fall: upstate, Episcopal, tense and tight. I longed for encounters, the rush of pleasure found in newness and intrigue, in hot cheeks and hunger met.

My earliest memory, in fact, was of longing. I stood at the trundle-bed, arms outstretched, crying for attention. Adults like shrouded clouds misted around a room swaddled by the scent of lavender. The room was predawn dark, chilled against a New York winter, 1875 or so. I felt the presence of my parents but couldn't turn them into forms to grasp. Beyond me, a child wheezed and gasped, and I smelled tobacco that was my father speaking. I heard tender words, but not for me—for my sister, Margaret, three years younger. Salty tears traced their way along my face and touched my tongue. I was hungry, oh, so hungry.

I swallowed, listened for the sound of hands through air reaching out to hold me next, to feed me. "Wait, Cassie!" a voice hissed. I seemed to wait forever. Then inside that empty space I took another breath and with my voice and stomping feet tried to bring them to me, those adults who leaned to Margaret's bed. I screamed. They moved. Anticipation preceded joy! But I wasn't lifted. Instead, my mouth was struck. Pain arrived. And I learned then that life is made of that, whether you wait or act.

Perhaps some lingering of longing made me speak the words that day with Annie, made my feet take action.

I pushed the carriage door open, careful to show enough above my ankles to gain interest without inviting reproach. I lifted my skirts to step out. Like a stunned animal facing the locomotive's catcher, Josiah Stearns watched me coming.

An October breeze chilled my nose and brushed against my gopher cheeks to sass the day.

I kept my eyes on the taller man. He had a clock master's hands, tapered fingers without tension. "Papa," I said, my words dripping with maple syrup as I eased up beside him. "You'll catch your death out here without your cape. Perhaps you could invite Mr. Stearns for tea and biscuits where we could all be warmed."

My words had the oddest effect on my father. He turned to me as though he'd forgotten I was even in the neighborhood let alone waiting with my friend in his carriage. He stared as though not certain who I was.

It was rare that I was even with my father on a Saturday afternoon. My sister Margaret usually attended him as she was quiet and attentive and undemanding. But I was eager for an outing and had pushed my way into his day. Margaret didn't pout. Why should she? After all, I was the older sister.

It was my father I had to win over.

"We'll make it a fun time, Papa," I'd said.

He had grunted his displeasure, but he hadn't said no, and when Margaret didn't object, he relented. He'd been thoughtful most of the morning as though something weighed heavily on his mind. When I'd suggested we stop by for Annie he seemed relieved, as though his obligation to entertain me vanished in the presence of my friend.

At the butcher shop, he'd shifted from foot to foot, waiting for the meat. That, too, was the oddest ritual, I thought, for him to run this errand himself instead of sending the maids or the cook. He'd observed the shopkeepers less and his watch more, pulling it often from his vest pocket. Then he'd rushed Annie and me along to the carriage, shooing us like chickens when we paused to pat an approaching dog.

"Later, later," Papa said. It was as though he meant to keep an appointment though I didn't know where or with whom.

We were already in the carriage and moving when he had spied Josiah Stearns propelling himself forward with his walking stick swinging and his brown cape flowing behind him. Papa'd ordered the driver to stop and stepped out on a run, halting Mr. Stearns by shouting his name. I'd thought it odd when he'd been in such a hurry earlier.

Now here I stood, face to face with Papa's reason for stopping and my father acting confused, as though his men's club had been invaded by ants.

Josiah looked down at me through round glasses. I couldn't tell if his gaze resulted from poorly fit lenses or a twinge of arrogance that kept his nose up like an English setter sniffing the wind.

"Josiah Stearns," my father said, finally, introducing us even though I'd already used the man's name.

My ostrich-plume hat barely reached Josiah's chin as I lifted myself from the curtsy I knew would make my mother angry for its quick and shallow show.

"And this," Josiah said in well-modulated words, his eyes washing over me, "this must be the lovely daughter you speak of so often, Burr." He tipped his bowler brim at me, and his cyan-blue eyes held mine.

I hadn't imagined my father *ever* spoke of me to others. He was a hardworking Dutchman who expressed praise daily that he had immigrated—"I thank the Lord He gave me a merchant's and not a miner's mind"—relieved to be in the city surrounded by the soft hushed hues of his club. I assumed he rarely spoke to others about us, his children, who had come along late in his life. I had even wondered if his awkwardness at home stemmed from his being accosted at the end of each day by the high voices and swishing skirts of women after being surrounded by finance and trade and the converse of fine gentlemen.

That thoughts of me had formed inside my father's mind and had then been expressed to another man, this man, in a generous way, was beyond my greatest hope and warmed me to my hidden boots.

A smile edged its way up Josiah's smooth face. It was the start of something pleasant, I thought.

Then my father spoke.

"Nay," he said. He stared at me. "This be Cassie. Cassandra, I'm prone to call her when needing correction. She is my oldest. I doubt I spoke o' her to you. No, woulda been my Margaret." His voice softened with my sister's name. "She's the beauty."

I felt more than saw Mr. Stearns's eyebrows lift with recognition of the heat I could feel rising up my neck to flood my cheeks. I could hardly catch my breath, barely heard Josiah's words of rescue.

"Listen," he said, "you've been keeping your loveliest from us. Miss Cassandra," he nodded to me, "has quite a beauty of her own."

To his credit, my father did examine me as though seeing his oldest daughter for the first time. I thought he might be considering whether he'd erred in his judgment. I swallowed and hoped to catch my stride but before I could my father spoke again.

"You're mistaken, Stearns."

"Sometimes hard to see a treasure when you live with it each day." Josiah kept my gaze. "Loses freshness."

"Nay," my father insisted, still watching me. "Margaret's much finer featured. Has fairer skin. Bears a warmer spirit too."

"The eldest in a family often has to endure the immature fragrance of youth," I said.

"She's a shade better manners, your sister has," Papa said. "Knows how to be a lady."

Pain poured out my nose as a snort.

"Back to the carriage with you," my father said, his words blustery but firm. "Children," he said, shaking his head.

"Manners!" I began, my voice breaking, "Papa, you—"

"You are greatly blessed, then, Hendrick," Josiah said, "to have two such spirited females to call your own."

My father snorted now. "A matched team they aren't. One so much more headstrong than the other."

"Listen, Burr," Josiah said, "I'd be inclined to meet their mother."

"You would?" my father asked.

"She must share your pride in such gracious children."

My father's irritation diffused. He moved the package he carried to his other arm, fidgeted with the lapel of his jacket suddenly consumed with lint, removed his hat and brushed at the brim, switched the package again. I waited for him to answer or at least to move me out of hearing range.

"She does, yes," my father said. "Well then, we'll have you in once, soon enough. Margaret makes a fine spread though she's just fifteen. If your schedule's not so full, with your leavin' soon, we could say Thursday next, to have a dinner?"

"I'm free this afternoon." Josiah said, still staring straight at me.

"Are you then?" my father said. He coughed.

"If you've room for another, we can all go in your carriage." Josiah nodded to the Victoria. "It's my Saturday walk time so I'm without a cab." Then he offered me his arm.

I slipped mine through his, swung Josiah and myself around, and turned my back on my father.

My father's smooth leather shoes made scurrying sounds on the stones behind us. I looked into Annie's brown eyes staring from the Victoria as we approached, and I grinned, stood a little straighter. I chattered to Josiah with no idea what I was saying, my gloved hand resting on his cashew-colored sleeve. Behind us, I heard my father clear his throat as if to speak, perhaps to take a deep breath to interrupt or protest. I spoke louder. I remember I wasn't hungry in the least. Eyes forward, I relished for just a moment the discomfort my father must have felt and anticipated some ruffling for my mother when I swung through the door on the arm of this prominent, blond-haired man.

"Won't Mama be delighted," I said over my shoulder. "She so loves surprises."

I patted Josiah's arm with my gloved fingers and hoped my father would feel the bite in my words, the contradiction of confidence chiseled into my tone.

But he never answered, never said any words to either chastise or forgive. Instead, he cleared his throat again as though negotiating with a cough.

A quiet sound it was, and foreign, so foreign that I turned. I didn't see him scowl at my misbehavior. Instead, he looked perplexed, confused. And then a wash of wonder crossed his eyes as he collapsed in a heap on Corning's cobblestoned street.

CHAPTER 2

REDEMPTION AND REGRET

❋

Regret, unmitigated, molds inside the soul like an untreatable disease set to flourish. In me, as I began to master masking pain, regret materialized at first as frivolous, cavalier perhaps, as though my mind remained indifferent to important matters when what I wished for was to keep the grief from piercing armor, to stop it from covering me head to toe.

"Papa!" I said, bending to lift his head. His hat had rolled toward the gutter of the street. I heard Annie crying, Josiah ordering our driver to help him lift my father to our carriage.

"Papa! Can you hear me?"

His eyes stared with disgust. His cheeks hung more jowly on one side, raining wrinkles. But he breathed, however raspy.

I bumped Annie as Josiah and our driver lifted Father to the carriage, laid his head on my chest. His breathing drowned out even the horse clopping a fast beat on the street. The air took on a foul scent.

"What's wrong with Mr. Hendrick?" Annie said, her eyes as big as biscuits.

"We don't know," Josiah said, patting her hand with his narrow palm.

I stroked my father's face, felt the smallness of his ears beneath my hands, so aware of the foreignness of this gesture and yet so sure I wanted him to feel my presence even if he couldn't see me through those distant, vacant eyes.

The doctor Josiah rushed him to called it a "pulmonary consumption" as he listened with his long tube and said he heard water like the ocean in my father's chest. He had pushed Annie and me aside and placed Papa in a hospital where my mother and sister arrived soon after, Josiah having sent the cab for them.

"Nothing I can do for him, Mrs. Hendrick," the doctor told my mother while she dabbed at her eyes. "His heart's given out, perhaps done something already to his brain so now his speech is lost. Did you know he had a bad heart?"

She shook her head. "Worked since he was a small boy."

"Can't you do something?" I said. "He's awake. He's breathing."

"It's difficult, I know," the doctor said, his thin mustache moving at the same time his hands patted my head like a child. "Especially for children to understand."

"What good are you then?" I said, pulling away.

"Cassie!" my mother said. "No need to be rude."

"No need to be hopeful either," I said and swung my skirts before me out of the room.

Josiah followed me out. "Listen, let me be of assistance."

"Take Annie home," I said, "then come back. Keep me company. This place is a misery."

Papa's breath rattled like an ancient weather vane in ever-changing wind. Margaret's crying accompanied it as I slipped back into the room. My sister held one of Papa's cool, stiff hands; Mama held his other. I stood at the foot of the white-draped bed, smoothing the sheets across his feet and finding myself thinking of how small they were, his feet. His toes reached toward the pressed-tin pea-green ceiling, perhaps never to hold him up again.

I wanted to think of his feet or his hands or his eyes, even of the incompetent doctors, anything but his heart or my words or actions that might have affected how it beat now, slowly, without power enough to give him voice or even to keep his eyes awake for long.

A wooden cabinet beside his bed held three Old Cardinal roses still pressed into bloom. Margaret must have thought to cut them to bring along.

The deep red of the blossoms stood as stark contrast to the quiet ice of my father's face.

"A bloom for each of us, Papa," I said.

Papa's eyes blinked, and he looked into Mama's with a kind of recognition. She cried then and reached for his hand while his gaze shifted to Margaret. His look softened on her, and she began to whimper.

Then his eyes found me. They followed me around the room, accusing me as I poured fresh water into the vase, then fussed at the curtain, smoothed the bedsheets again, always being stared at when I chanced to look.

"Grandpa lived a long life," Margaret said, her voice catching. "Almost seventy when he died."

"Papa's not dying," I snapped. "He's just regaining his strength, aren't you, Papa?"

Margaret's lower lip popped out, pouting, but I wasn't sorry.

I stepped beside her then. My eyes pleaded for a word from my father, a look, something that said he knew this was not my fault. I took his hand from Margaret's. It lay lifeless in mine, and for the first time since he'd collapsed, I knew he would not make it, that what words he'd already spoken had been his last. I tried to remember exactly what he'd said.

With her fingertips Margaret patted drool from the corner of my father's open mouth.

"Not sick a day in his life," Mama said. She shook her head. "Cassie? Tell me again."

My throat grabbed at my words, turning them to tears. I told it truthfully, yet each time I knew I grew further from my part in it, painting unpleasantness with a coral color even then.

"We were walking and Papa collapsed," I said, wiping at the pool in my eyes. "Mr. Stearns happened along. We were just talking, having a fine time of it. He was even going to come to tea. Then Papa coughed. Or maybe he tripped or something. He might have hit his head. We planned to come on home."

It was how I would remember it for years. I didn't want to think of just how low a place I occupied in my father's world just moments before he died.

Mama nodded, turned back to rub my father's limp hand between hers, brushed the side of his muttonchops already dusted with flakes of gray. "Oh, Burr," she said. "We had such plans."

I prayed, I did. Not just for my father's recovery but selfishly for myself, to have one last chance to talk with him while he was still larger than life for me and not the thin, fragile being he became during the weeks he lay there, pale whiskers appearing daily on his chin like an early frost.

My father disappeared into the bed and then, silently, into another world. The doctors shook their heads. My prayers went unanswered. Then my father died.

The service, just before Christmas, happened in a haze of uncertainty and soft words. The Presbyterian ritual comforted my mother. She spoke of the fine smorgasbord of food the ladies had provided, commented on the pastor's words, said how good it was to know she'd meet Papa again. Margaret, too, seemed buoyed by the messages of Scripture, which to me sounded hollow, more challenging than kind, raising questions they then refused to answer. Numbness overtook my body and left me dredging bottom.

The routine of standing vigil beside my father had ceased. Anxiety sniffed at me like a dog left behind in an empty house when people packed their bags and moved away. After the funeral we returned to our two-story townhouse. Friends and guests had been fed and left. We Hendrick women met in the small parlor draped in black.

"Girls," my mother said. With her lace hanky, she dabbed at her wax makeup turning shiny in the heat from the parlor stove. "No sense waiting with more bad news. Tell you now and be done with it. Your father's solicitor tells me there are financial constraints far more involved than your father led me to believe." She straightened her skirt then sat stiff as a starched collar against the mahogany twists of the chair.

"What kind of constraints?" I said. Margaret slipped her fingers through the cage to wiggle them at the gray parrot perched within.

"Maybe he wanted to protect us," Margaret offered.

Mama cleared her throat. "Your father was looking for investors. I knew that. I didn't know the extent to which finding them was critical." She rubbed at the black satin-covered buttons on her sleeve. "Apparently, he did not succeed. I'm advised to sell the business for what I can and for each of us to learn to live more frugally."

"Will we starve?" Margaret asked, eyes wide.

"Of course not!" Mama said. "I've baked bread before, and I can do so again, to eat or to sell. We have a choice here. It must be made with care, is all I'm saying."

I was about to suggest foregoing my college year when we were interrupted by Josiah.

He had attended the service, his blond hair shining against the candles that lit the foyer where he stood, disappearing before the casket bearers preceded us down the aisle. I'd not expected to see him again this soon.

Mama sighed. "Don't want to be ungrateful, but I'm not a'tall sure I want visitors."

She turned the card he'd sent in over in her hand, then laid it back into the silver calling basket, letting it linger there. She wiped at her nose with her black hanky.

"Papa would have wanted it," Margaret said. She spoke in small, precise words pronouncing every *d* and *t*. "Mr. Stearns was special to him. I heard him say that once or twice."

"He did at that," Mama sighed. "He had such plans." She was lost to a memory hidden somewhere in the transom above the door.

"Plans," Annabelle, the parrot, mimicked.

With a pang of envy I wondered when Margaret and Mama and Papa had talked about his life or the likes of Josiah Stearns or when their "plans" had been discussed and why they hadn't included me. For just a moment I wondered if our meeting Josiah that day might not have been by chance.

"We'll offer tea," Margaret said, standing to the bellpull. A sausage curl hung on either side of her face, covering her dainty ears.

Mama shook herself into the present. "Only three cups out, though," she said, scanning the tray on a small table nearby. "Should have been four to warn of an unexpected guest. Hope that doesn't bode poorly. Well, bring him in."

Josiah passed through the parlor door without bending and sat on the chair my mother offered, his knees held tightly together. His blue-green eyes stared brighter through the small glasses he wore, his ears appeared larger, and I noticed he combed his hair over the top of them on either side of a center part. His nails were white and shiny, perfectly trimmed.

Josiah sipped from the teacup, smiled at us, and spoke about the lovely service, a description I found peculiar. We waited, the man's gentle slurp breaking the silence. China cups clinked against saucers. I struggled to find something engaging to say. Josiah said it for me.

"I came," he said, "to ask for your daughter's hand in marriage." He set his cup into the saucer and lifted his gaze to the very wide eyes of my mother.

"Why, we…that is…I don't know what to say!"

"I realize it's sudden and she's young," he said. "But—"

"Margaret would be proud of such an offer," my mother cooed, recovering her surprise. She primped at the snood on the back of her neck, a pink color flushing her cheeks. We turned together toward Margaret, and I caught the slightest hint of wonder on my mother's face.

"Call the solicitor," said the parrot. "Call the solicitor."

Josiah laughed. "I'm sure Margaret'll receive many offers, charming as she is. However, it's not Margaret I refer to. It's Cassie."

"O mis-er-y," Annabelle answered, sounding just like me except she gave the word three parts.

"She's Cassie's bird," Margaret said in fluttered explanation.

"Would have expected something flashier than an African Grey," Josiah said.

"She has a flashy tongue," I said, happy to change the subject.

My mother coughed, brushed imaginary crumbs from her dress. "Let's think about this," she said. "You'll want a woman able to encourage and support you in your work." Josiah nodded. "Margaret, though young, well, she's quite capable and could run a household with very little help."

"Margaret's too young," I said.

"Of course she is, right now," my mother said. "But Burr and I thought, if you were interested at all, that when you returned from Washington you could marry. He did talk with you, then?"

"Not directly," Josiah said. "And then I met Cassie."

"Who isn't all that interested in marriage, are you, dear?"

"I can give you eighteen reasons why you should look elsewhere," I said, "one for every year of my life."

"Yes," Mama said. She sat up straighter in the chair. "And Margaret's willing, aren't you, dear?"

Josiah raised his palm to silence my mother.

"It's Cassandra I'm asking for, eighteen reasons and all." He spoke with soothing tones, well modulated, precise. "It is sudden, I know. But listen. You're a widow, now, with two daughters. Perhaps you've been left with ample supplies. Perhaps not. You'll still need someone to manage them."

"We'll do it ourselves," I said. "Any woman can."

"Any woman can," mimicked the bird.

Josiah's eyes twinkled. "Not property," he said.

"So, we'll hire you," I said. "Make you do the work while we reap the interest."

Josiah said, "Not practical. I'll be in Washington State. Though I suppose there are solicitors more than willing to manage your affairs right here. Still," he said, crossing his knees, bumping the lavender table fringe that wiggled now as we spoke. He flicked lint from his pant leg. "Why give them their commission when you could keep it in the family?"

All teacups settled into saucers.

"Fascinating place, the West," Josiah offered into the silence.

"Fascinating," said the African Grey. Her reddish tail feathers flicked as she gripped and released her feet along the perch.

"Mr. Roosevelt speaks nothing but the best of it, it's true," Mama said. "I just can't imagine you and Cassie…"

"Any Congressman would find sagebrush and snakes more to their liking than the sidewinders in Washington, D.C.," I said.

Josiah laughed. It was a high-pitched laugh, not deep from his belly.

"And does my opinion on this subject even matter?" Margaret said, "because if you asked me, I'd say neither—"

"Not now, dear." A look crossed my mother's face. "You're right, of course. It wouldn't be seemly for either of my daughters to marry so soon. And to such an older man at that though we are grateful for your interest."

"With your husband's death, what's left here worthy of your interest? The West's the perfect place for Cassie's high spirit, and I intend to make a fortune there, and she can help me spend it once we have it in hand. I'll take you all with me. I can be a generous man.

"My private car leaves for Hoquiam, Washington, mid-January," he said, looking at his pocket watch as though the date instead of the time rested there. "Travel to San Francisco for a few weeks then north. Act as a honeymoon trip. Eventually, a fine home, gatherings, readings, and such. It's a life of leisure I'm promising. I suggest we set the wedding date for January fifteenth." He made movements to leave.

I surveyed the lace curtains, the carpet spots where Queen Anne chairs sat to cover strands of dark threads I'd failed to notice before. I just wanted him to go.

"Go to Washington State and send for us when you're settled," I told him as he stood at the door. "Give me more time to prepare."

Josiah laughed loudly. "Fish while they're feeding, I always say." To my mother he added, "You know your daughter can't resist the kind of bait I'm offering."

My mother smiled a wistful smile. "He may know you better than you think, Cassie." Then she leaned to whisper, forgetting we had a guest. "Don't put your fingers on your lips, dear. It'll give you pimples. That's why Margaret's skin is so clear."

"That and the luxury of being a child," I said. Then to Josiah I said, a mocking to my voice, "We can talk again next week." I didn't take my fingers from my face.

The adventure of it appealed: a private car, the enthralling West, the promise of San Francisco. I wouldn't be leaving much behind here. Depending on how well financed my father had left us, there might be no school. Perhaps I'd have to watch the counters in Papa's mercantile more than on an occasional day, if there was even a store to work in. My hands and time might well be occupied with labor, not with reaching for what I thought I wanted. I looked at my palms, softened with glycerin, and imagined them in a tub of suds keeping Papa's counters clean. Papa'd always talked about the virtue of planning ahead. Somehow, he just hadn't.

Josiah's offer promised thrills and novelty, as far from boredom as I cared to be. My need to act, to plunge in and consider the consequences later, maybe that was what turned the tide. I'd read what Aristotle had written about self-discipline, that it was man's—and probably a woman's—hardest-won victory. Yearning, after all, tests discipline and leaves wisdom wanting in one's youth.

Josiah and I spoke the following week, and the next. Discovering my birthday occurred in February, he bought an amethyst from Africa he gave me over dinner. We spoke of books he liked, of European authors, American too. "I like Sir Arthur Conan Doyle, myself," he said. "All those mysterious details." I said that I'd read Huxley's work on agnosticism, and he sat back and cocked his head, hand on his chin. "Deeper thinker than I thought," he said.

"The West can tolerate it, I suspect, if you can."

I gauged his tolerance for delicious pleasure, my bent toward luxury and extravagant mood. He didn't fail me, was systematic in his responses, and appeared to wear well the indulgent tones I'd need.

Josiah sent fruit for us to eat while Margaret, Mama, and I trimmed the Christmas tree in the parlor.

"He's found an attraction in you," Mama said, "though I hadn't expected it. Maybe that jaw line." She looked me over as though I was a market melon instead of her oldest daughter. "Or your apple-cheeked skin. Don't know where you got that from. Must have been your father's side."

Mama reached down as though to touch me then changed her mind. Her eyes began to swim. The movement of her hand brought with it the aching scent of rose water.

"My people are all so fair skinned," she said. "Like Margaret."

"Like Margaret," Annabelle said. The bird pecked at a seed, holding it with one foot while the other gripped the perch.

My mother pushed my sister's hair back from her temple with her fingertips, and the two smiled at each other.

Margaret said later it was always just in my mind, my belief that I carried seeds of parental disappointment inside myself, but I could see it, did see it, in the little movements that marked my status as lower than my sister's in my mother's mind.

My eyes rested on a corner of faded wallpaper no longer attached to its glue.

Mama left the room to twist more pine garland, leaving Margaret and me behind. I watched my sister make sure each candle sat perfectly level before picking out another, checking its wick then placing it in the fan-like holder.

She reminded me of an English setter: regal in carriage, lean, with no tendency to girth, a working dog shrouded with devotion and duty. My younger sister and I shared the same hazel eyes that dropped slightly at the corners, similar waves in our dark hair, and the same slender frames (at the time), though my mother often said Margaret was not so well built "for having children" as I was with my greater hip curve.

"The Lady Margaret" I called her, not because of her looks but for her virtues. Like noblewomen of old, she had many, and they were as solid and unshakable as the rocks of an ocean reef.

Not that she imposed them on me. No, it was the very fact that she was so natural in her goodness, without knowing it, that gave her nobility. Her serenity, her sureness about life, her absolute answer to every question, even the difficult ones about doing what was right, came easily to her, I think, and caused the envy.

"He's a nice man," Margaret said. "Reminds me of a teacher the way he carries details in his head." She squinted up at me from the needlework she'd picked up now that the tree was trimmed. She was working on one of the beatitudes.

"He does seem to have a generous side," I said.

Margaret turned the needlepoint over to examine the side no one would ever see, picked at a thread there, making it perfect. She turned it back before speaking, giving me her full attention.

"I know a dozen girls who'd take his offer," she said, "but I'm glad you aren't going to. Looking to marry just because you can wouldn't be right without some care in it."

I stared through the warbles of the handblown window glass onto the busy Corning street. The bare oak tree between the neighboring townhouse shimmered in the December frost. Pine trees towered in the distance.

"I try to think what Papa would have wanted," she said. "I like trying to please him."

Her words stung like a hot poker to the skin.

"And wouldn't it be too dreadful to live with someone you didn't love," she continued, "in some strange and foreign place? On the ocean." Her voice had a wispiness to it.

"You'd all be there with me," I said, lifting my bustle so I could sit on one of Mama's needlework chair cushions. I adjusted the snood at my neck, looked about for the latest issue of *Ladies' Home Journal* I'd left somewhere, hoping to distract myself from my father's death still hovering around us like fresh smoke.

"And he's promised to give us almost anything I ask for. Think of the possibilities!"

"Oh, Cassie," Margaret said and shook her head. "There's so much more to life than the drama that draws you."

"How could you possibly know?"

She scowled at me, then rethreaded her needle and spread the needlepoint over her skirt. She smoothed the wrinkles and stuck the pin into the cloth with the sharp point visible.

The day after Christmas my mother took a firmer stand and said I shouldn't marry the man. Perhaps she did not wish to live with the responsibility of forcing a decision on another. Maybe she did not want to wear the weight on her shoulders of a marriage gone sour as four-day milk, if that should happen. Or perhaps she knew that blame travels too easily along another's trail, and she wanted no straight path to her door if things proved rough later.

"Not that his lineage isn't proper," she said, turning her back to the coal stove in the corner. "But he's a man who'll want submission and a settled house. He likes the fluff of interest now, but when he goes to work, well, it won't be like this, Cass. Marriage is a calling, if you love someone. Servitude if you don't." She rubbed her hands behind her for warmth. "Suspect he's dazzled by you and not thinking well. Thinks you're tameable. You can do that to a man, Cassie."

Josiah was the grandson of a prominent and well-loved New Hampshire governor, a respected engineer who had helped create the city of Corning's water system, a man who knew his mind, that's how I saw Josiah Stearns. I suspected his brain rarely got addled.

"He had no little fortitude to come forward when he did," I told my mother on New Year's Eve when I'd finally decided. "It'll be an escapade, something new and interesting to do, traveling west and walking there on the arm of a prominent man."

"You never walk, you stride," Mama said, shaking her head.

"We'll all stride. I've nothing to lose and the promise of a party. What more in life is there?"

Margaret started to speak but a look my mother gave her bought her silence.

"I think I'll move the wedding date up, too, just to see how he handles dissension."

He was older than I was by ten years, wiser and more experienced, and had proven himself generous. But it was his willingness to take us all—wife, mother-in-law, and a younger sister—that sweetened the sourdough started with my father's death. And when I thought of my marriage that way, as an act of rescue for my family, perhaps even at my own expense, a warmth filled me and took away the awful ache of blame that had draped around my shoulders the day my father died.

Aside from a new date, nothing I initially bargained for, however, became mine.

No lavish wedding ceremony. "Too soon after the funeral," Mama said.

No expensive reception. "Too much planning needed for such an event. We'll be leaving soon. You took too long deciding," Josiah chided with a sting of truth.

No lace-and-satin gown to grace my frame, exposing bare shoulders through a gossamer stole. "Much too unseemly," Margaret and Mama concurred when they saw the pattern for the dress I'd planned on.

Josiah's parents arrived from New Hampshire by private car on one of the more than sixteen rail lines his grandfather had interests in. A distant dowager, his mother looked down at me through pince-nez glasses. I heard her say to my new husband's grandmother, "Quite a beauty. Josiah will have his hands full." I wondered if she was pleased her son had chosen to take his young wife so quickly to the wilds of Washington and away from society's long nose of caution.

And so I married him, Josiah Stearns, on January 10, 1890, within a month of my father's funeral. It was a small service in the January cold, with just our families attending. The starkness of the vows and the solemn Episcopal service at the university chapel scrubbed away forever the distant dream I'd harbored of a lavish event frothy with lace and sparkling wine shared with someone who had swept me off my feet.

I wondered what my new mother-in-law thought of the ring Josiah placed on my finger. He said it was an heirloom, and it surely sparkled like old wealth.

My mother didn't seem the least distressed that in the end I'd decided to defy her.

After the service, I thought we'd planned to take the private car to New York City, but Josiah instead arranged a hotel room in town. I found the decision tasteless, and it marked the first time we fought.

"We'll be going upstate the day after we would have returned from New York, all of us. Seems ridiculous to make the trip then go around again. Listen, now, Cassandra. We'll have a supper and celebrate right here."

"I think not!" I said. "Not have the memory of a fine hotel with flowers and music and being served by waiters I don't know? A night to remember and cherish? I thought we'd surely stay someplace finer than right here! Even Williamsport would do."

"Nothing wrong with Corning's accommodations," he said then added, though I doubt he intended it as a threat, "But if you object, you can always go home tonight. I could too. Give me more time with my parents."

I never asked him how he explained his presence at his parents' side; he never asked me what Margaret and Mama thought. They wouldn't have said. My look as I crawled into my childhood bed without a husband on my wedding night singed their lips into silence.

On the appointed day in January, Josiah's cab arrived to take us to the train. The house looked sad stripped of its furniture and fringe. Mama walked through each room as though memorizing what had happened there, what part of her she left behind. She held Margaret's hand in one of hers and patted her eyes with her hanky.

We'd already sent Annabelle to live with Annie, and I'd taken slips of plants and a cutting from the same tree rose we'd planted on Papa's grave. All the details were drawn into a tight little valise.

"Want to make a last walk-through, too, before you begin your adventurous new life?" Josiah asked. He had a way of smiling sometimes that used just half his mouth, and he did that now. It made me think *halfhearted*.

"No sense hovering in an empty house or dwelling on unpleasant things. I am taking a cactus and some other cuttings with me, though," I said, holding the small cutting in a leather bag filled with New York dirt. "I'll fill the rest of empty up out West."

"With my guidance," Josiah said.

I should have admitted right then it was all a mistake. With the image of Annabelle, caged, still fresh in my mind, I should have stopped it before we went further. But I was never good at redemption, always destined to continue a road once I'd begun it.

CHAPTER 3

FOREIGN TRAVEL

❊

Margaret, my mother, Josiah, and I rode by coach as far as New York City and there boarded a private car to take us to the West. Mama had wrapped our household belongings in round-top trunks tied up with her tears. Except for hats and dresses and shoes needed for the journey, our things were shipped and would follow us, eventually bringing with them the scents and smells of a New York life now gone.

I didn't think the leaving touched me. Only Annie's clinging good-bye moved me to tears and created a surprise that the lack of my presence could so affect another.

"This is quite the entourage," I said later, running my fingers over the smooth wood panels of our railroad car. Dark-skinned porters opened curtains and settled tapestry valises on the floor while my mother and sister poked their heads into the small rooms beyond the living space. My tapered nails sank into the stuffed chairs and striped divan. "Newlyweds who bring in-laws with them on their wedding trip. Fascinating."

"They won't be sleeping with us at least," Josiah said.

"Are you so sure I will?" I said.

He looked over the top of his glasses. "Now listen," he said. "That's past.

Over and done. Time to move on."

"Maybe I'll be of the new thinkers and remain celibate."

Mama entered the room hearing only my words, and she snorted.

"Mrs. Woodhull says we bring entire generations with us when we share a husband's bed."

"Woodhull?" he said. "Isn't she that woman who champions those crazy things like women's rights and spiritualism?"

"And unencumbered love," I said.

"You don't let your daughter dabble in that sort of thing, do you, Mrs. Hendrick?"

"I've no control over her. Never have."

"You aren't one of those, are you?"

I shrugged my shoulders. I wasn't, really. It was just something I'd read. But I heard a wariness in his words and thought some future influence nested there.

Following dinner of salmon and fresh greens served in our private car, we retired to spend our first night together as this new family constellation.

My mother and sister retired to Pullman berths, one over the other but just a mahogany panel from our own square bed. The wood between the rooms was dark and shiny enough to reflect my dog-collar necklace before I removed the velvet strip for the night. I sat wide-eyed, clasped hands resting on the nightdress that covered me neck to toe, and stared at my husband. And while my husband may have thought the argument of our wedding night "past and over," I did not.

My mother coughed just inches from my head. I heard her say something muffled to Margaret. Josiah smoothed a crease of his starched nightshirt between his fingers and cleared his throat.

"I've decided to wait until we're in a proper bed in a proper room before I confirm my marriage vows," I said.

"Now, listen," he began.

"No, you listen," I said, grabbing the pillow and wrapping my arms around it. "The decision's made. You can remain here or take the divan, whichever you prefer." I punched the pillow to make my point.

He started to protest. I saw his mouth open then close abruptly. He swiped his pillow, stuffed it and a thin blanket under his arm, and padded toward the door. "I may need Sherlock Holmes to solve this marriage mystery for me," he said, his hand on the brass latch. "But I leave it to you to decide when you wish to become Mrs. Stearns." With that he opened the door and quietly closed it behind him.

By the third day, I had talked myself into a tingle of excitement, less for my marital state than for the journey. We were, after all, chugging across the country in luxury on a palace car of the Central Pacific Railroad heading for the City of Angels and then on to San Francisco. Later, we'd board a C. E. Wood or Northwest Lumber Company ship heading north to Hoquiam, Washington, and our new home. The train stopped at various stations nestled beside the tracks in cities I had only read about and now had smells and sounds and sights to mark them in my memory. Those without means to travel on a private car or who chose not to purchase dining-car meals took their food there, at each little station.

"Let's us eat at one, once," I suggested, and Josiah took my elbow to help me disembark. We consumed our beefsteak, fried, and potatoes the same, our meal served by men the color of henna. The food, served hot, tasted both strange and stimulating, and I made up exotic stories I later shared with fellow travelers on the train about the food and fashion presented.

Each afternoon "train boys" brought to our car a paper, which Josiah devoured. They also sold sweets, canned beans and bacon, and dime books I found I could lose myself in with less effort than gossiping with a friend I didn't have. I rather liked not having hot irons and laundry to occupy my hands and someone else to fix the meals, though I noticed that inactivity seemed to gather fluid at my ankles, making them stretch against my high-buttoned shoes.

"You'll miss the scenery," Margaret told me, putting her hand over the page to gain my attention. "And you're chewing your nails again!"

"It looks the same," I said, curling my fingers in. I glanced out the draped windows. Landscapes didn't feed me as they did Margaret. Excitement did and extravagant people and the fantasies of the stories I scribbled on my pages. "I wonder if it will always be so brown and barren?" I said.

"See how the colors change on the grasses and sage and the snow on the rocks? Don't you wonder what made those markings that look like stairs or what the creatures out there live on?"

"An ancient sea," Josiah said, looking up from his *Times*. "Little creatures pressed into the rocks. Called fossils. Once beneath water." He adjusted his glasses. "And no, it isn't always brown. In the spring, the prairie's covered with flowers and the grasses are as green as forest moss. Quite lovely, in fact," he said and returned to his paper.

"Told you," Margaret said. She stuck her tongue out at me. She chattered Josiah from his paper, then proceeded to discuss the terrain and Josiah's strange wealth of knowledge about a variety of subjects never before mentioned within my hearing. He sounded much like that teacher Margaret imagined when he talked with her, spouting facts and figures. Margaret appeared fascinated, her eyes rapt with interest, a Greek sponge, regardless of the subject.

I buried myself in Haggard's adventurous novel *King Solomon's Mine* then tiring, wrote in my diary until I realized I had nothing to write. No new insight or adventure to tell. I laid the book down and snapped the lock, then wandered about the main train, watching passengers. I often swished my skirts—unescorted—to the other cars while my mother, Margaret, and Josiah napped.

So many people traveled west, so many faces filled the wooden seats with hardiness and hope. An old Indian sat near the far door opening, a blanket wrapped around him against the cold. I wondered how he saw his world changing, riding through it faster than an exhaled breath. Children dressed in dark tones of blues and blacks and browns and smelling of two-day-old cabbage and wood smoke played jacks in the narrow aisle. Some stared then smiled as I stepped over them; others scowled and scratched at their dirt-smudged ears until I squatted on the floor beside them and signaled that I'd like to take a turn. Their eyes grew wide with my lack of skill and my willingness to sprawl myself to catch a stone.

I imagined them heading for the mines of Oregon to work as "rope boys" on the coal cars I'd heard Josiah mention. Or as children dressed as flowers shining from a stage serving as background for a San Francisco star. Their mothers in their triangular *babushkas* tied beneath their chins were royalty escaping from cruel viscounts, their fathers with calloused hands just secret agents for Pinkerton's Detective Agency, all on the trail of finding romance and adventure in the West.

Their journeys I fantasized as purposeful and expansive, something my decision to come west still lacked. All we shared in common were the tracks that clattered beneath us and the splash of ground seen between them when we pulled the chains in our convenience rooms. I stood for a time, holding on to the back of one of the empty seats, watching the world go by. We'd be in Cheyenne soon. I felt the weight of the mountains on my chest, causing my breath to come shorter. My head buzzed. I thought I should find something to eat, something starchy or sweet to feed my incessant gnawing.

"Give a double eagle for them." Josiah spoke, coming up behind me as I watched out the window. "Your thoughts," he said when I turned to him.

"A twenty-dollar gold piece? You'd pay too much."

His voice had startled me. He did not touch me, though a husband could have without raising the eyebrows of even the oldest matron in the car. All were occupied with cracking nuts or lying with their mouths open as they caught a snooze or brushing crumbs from their husbands' stained vests. Several huddled with their children near the wood stove at the far side, rubbing their hands into the crisp morning. Smoke watered my eyes as it always did.

"Let me be the judge of that," he said, catching himself from stumbling at the rocking of the car.

His voice blended with the steady rhythm of the train surging along the tracks. We'd rarely had a moment alone except to share our silent, nighttime berth. I had no objection to the shape our marriage took. San Francisco seemed soon enough to submit my will to his. Meanwhile, it taught him discipline, I thought. Besides, I didn't know what kinds of conversations I should have with a husband, or how they might differ from a man who shared my bed.

The presence of Margaret and my mother had proven a welcome diversion on this journey, and I noticed, now, their absence.

"Perhaps we should go back," I said.

"Not yet. I've offered a gold piece for your thoughts."

"And I've said it was a poor investment. You'll never be rich enough to waste your money on me if you use it up on musing women," I said.

"Let me be the judge of that," Josiah said and reached to touch the wetness forming at the corner of my eyes.

"The smoke," I said, not wanting him to place emotion where it wasn't.

"Your fingers, placed there on your mouth, is the sign for 'eat' among most native people. Did you know that?" He reached for my fingers and brushed them from their usual place, cupped at my lips.

"How fascinating," I said. He held my fingers in his.

"I'm waiting," he said.

"Decisions," I said then. "About what matters in a life, what's its purpose."

"That's a surprise," he said, stepping back from me, his half-smile easing onto his face. "You're far too beautiful to addle your mind with such thoughts."

"Too young to think but not too young to marry?" I said. "Makes you the husband of a dull, dependent child."

"You're no child, Cassandra. And no one would dare to call you dull." He cleared his throat. "I know this hasn't been easy. And I do want this to be a good decision for you."

"It isn't you," I said.

He laughed. "If not me, who?"

"I meant, it isn't about you," I said. "Nothing you can settle in my mind."

"A woman of your beauty need not use her mind at all to get what she wants."

I stepped back from him in irritation.

He held his palms as though warding off a blow. "Not my intent to insult a lady."

"Margaret's the lady," I said and turned from him.

"Your little sister admires you greatly."

"She doesn't think of me as a lady."

"Perhaps she thinks more highly of you than you do yourself."

I shrugged my shoulders and turned away. "It's her nature to be kind. She is to everyone."

"You throw it away," he said. "I wouldn't have guessed it of you." When I didn't answer, he continued. "Someone so lovely and gifted should be comfortable with compliments by now, not shrug them off as so much engine smoke."

"I'm aware of my rather round features. My hair has too many waves, and I'm short. Obviously, I like to eat, juicy, soft, and sweetened foods. Even my fingers speak it without my knowing." I jabbed at my lips. "I place that against words like *lovely* and what my own eyes can see in others, and I don't think of it as shrugging off anything. I simply think you are in error, sir, in your assessment."

He grabbed my shoulders then, holding me so I was forced to look at him.

"You really don't know, do you?" he said, wonder in his voice. His eyes moved over me, taking me all in like a man preparing to feast from a ladened table. "You can't see it." With one hand he reached as though to lift my chin. "You entice people, Cassandra, like a fragrant bloom attracts a bird. Like crackling heat before a thunderstorm. All promise and anticipation without being sure."

Beyond him I saw an old grandmother open one eye, watching us.

My husband touched my chin with his smooth fingers, ran his hand along my cheekbone, thumbed some moisture from my eyes. He pulled me closer to him. "Don't you see how others look at you?" he whispered. "The way you dazzle them?"

The grandmother's eyes were both open now, and she had nudged her sleeping husband.

"I'm a fortunate man to be married to someone like you. You're stunning." His words came low, from his throat. "Absolutely. I can't believe you don't know it."

The couple's eyes were staring now, and I wanted to do something shocking, perhaps kiss my husband in this public place or slap his face, tickle him, something to warrant their attention. I wiggled my eyebrows at them, and they grinned.

But the stroke of Josiah's fingers on my face felt almost painful, and I returned my eyes to him. I saw a hunger there, some deep appeal. My fingers made their way to his face, stroked the gentle dip between his nose and his lip. The touch seemed to burn against my fingertip.

"I'm going back," I said and pulled away before he had a chance to change my mind.

"I traveled here once on Thomas Cook's excursion train," Josiah said later that evening while we waited for a meal at the dining car. Across from me he chewed on a celery stalk, the leaves still sporting spots of water where the chefs had rinsed it. The afternoon sun sent a spear of light against the gilt-edged wall panel making Josiah's blond hair almost white. From the salt spoon, Mama had spilled salt for dipping, and she picked up a smidgeon of it she tossed now over her left shoulder. Margaret sat beside me in a grown-up suit with yellow buttons against burgundy cloth. Her olive skin looked like ivory cream.

"I was just a boy, and we were with a group of English tourists, my parents and I," Josiah continued. He brushed at his left ear. "It was one of the first times people traveled just for fun. My grandmother scoffed at such a waste." He smiled. "She would have gasped at Webb's train. Used four cars for a dozen passengers served by maids and nurses and cooks and porters. One whole car just a nursery. They had Pinkerton guards along too."

"That was when you learned about rocks and things?" Margaret asked. She swung her legs beneath the table until my mother frowned.

"And engineering," Josiah said. "Man named Condon traveled back with us from Oregon Territory once to the Smithsonian. He had rocks he said were dug from mountains much like those." He nodded toward ridges we passed by in the distance. "'Palaces of nature,' Byron calls them. Washington has them too!"

Margaret had asked me questions about our new home, and I thought she'd ask Josiah now, but she was quiet. I kept my questions to myself and instead spoke with fellow travelers, inviting several to join us later for dessert.

We ate well of sugar-cured hams and champagne sauce, salmon, and raspberry tea. Josiah didn't seem to mind the gatherings of people I attracted nor the additional expense brought with them. He spoke with confidence to strangers and nodded his head as they talked. For me, people were challenges to see how much I could learn of them then entertain them, without exposing too much of me.

Mama glowed with all the activity and splendor. The dark lines around her mouth didn't sink as deep. I knew she thanked Josiah often for his charity. For a moment, I thought of all her changes and the loss of my father. I wondered if she cried at night.

That was the night Josiah changed his mind.

Mama retired after the meal that included spirits. A banker and his wife traveling to Los Angeles, a doctor and his sister, and an "adventurer" with a well-waxed mustache had joined us for the evening, people I had struck up conversations with about a book they held or a ring worn or the feather in a hat. Even the cactus I took for walks in other cars invited conversation. People liked to talk about themselves, I found. Sometimes I waited with masked patience until they'd finish with a story because everything they said brought forward something I was sure they'd want to hear from me.

This time, I'd invited the five to join us in our private car for dessert after dinner.

"You're too young," Mama said when I raised my glass for wine.

"I'm a wife," I said. I swallowed. "Ought to have some privileges."

"On special occasions," she said to our visitors. "Otherwise rum'll be a person's death."

"First trip across the country?" the banker asked. "That's special," he said when I'd nodded yes.

"Helps a body sleep," his companion noted, lifting her glass.

"I've no trouble there," I said. "I fall asleep anywhere, nod off before you can say scat."

"The sign of a clear conscience," the banker said, and we laughed, even my mother. Our guests soon finished their baked Alaskas, and after conversations and coffee they left.

"I'll be in later, Mama," Margaret said as our mother rose to retire. She nodded agreement, patted Margaret on the shoulder, and closed the berth door just as Josiah left the car. He returned followed by a porter carrying a bottle of French champagne.

"Only fifteen cents extra for delivery," Josiah said, smiling. He told the porter how to hold the bottle with a towel so the cork popped without a sound and then sent the man off, pouring three glasses before offering up his toast.

"To my wife," he said, his fingers like a violinist's holding the bulb. He handed it to me. His eyes sparkled through smudged lenses.

"Cassandra. Named for the mythological woman who warns of doom," he said, lifting the second glass.

"And is disregarded," I added. "And, my name is Cassie, not Cassandra."

"I didn't disregard your wishes for wine," he teased. "And Cassandra's a beautiful name. Lends dignity."

Only my father had used that name for me, and not in tandem with dignity.

"Her prognostications were ignored, yes," he continued, "but not her person. Cassandra's words were discounted but never her."

"Joe. I think I'll call you Joe," I said. "Josiah sounds so stuffy."

"Maybe I am," he said.

"You need a name that fits the adventurer in you," I said. "A western man with honesty attached to it. Like Joe."

"Honesty matters to you, then?" Joe asked, still holding the champagne glass out before him.

"It does."

"Yet you aren't truthful with yourself."

"I've never known Cassie to lie," Margaret said.

"To herself."

"To you, Joe," I said, toasting him.

"You must know you have much to offer," Joe said. He talked to me in a tone as though Margaret had left the room. His eyes never left mine.

"You're describing Margaret," I said. "Not me."

Margaret's eyebrows came together as she pinched her forehead toward me. I wondered if she would taste the wine Joe had just handed her.

"I look forward to our marriage," he continued picking up the third glass. He lifted a blond eyebrow. "May it be harmonious, long, and fertile."

He raised the thin stem like a tulip to sunlight. He sipped and swallowed, his Adam's apple bobbing like a tickled nose in his neck.

I decided to ask then why he'd married me.

He coughed into the champagne. "Listen," he said, "marriage is an engineering feat, nothing more. Survey the terrain, design a path through the rocks. Take water through troughs to reach the destination, and there you have it."

"I pledged thee my 'trough'?" I said.

He laughed openly now. "Yes, and I fell in it."

I took a sip of the wine, my first ever.

"I planned to marry," Josiah continued though he turned to speak to Margaret, "when I got to Washington State. A businessman is expected to entertain, and as secretary to the power and light company, I thought a local girl might fit in well. But then I met your sister." He lifted his glass to me, drank. "And she is a fire that draws deep and burns long whether she knows it or not. How does Ambrose Bierce say it in that story he wrote? 'Beauty: the power by which a woman charms a lover and terrifies a husband.'"

He emptied his glass. "Though it's reversed for us. You've charmed your husband and hopefully would terrify any lover."

Margaret said, "The Bible says, 'Beauty is a fading flower.'"

Josiah watched me. "Listen, your father died and there was an unplanned path through a rock. Even though it happened quickly, I felt we wanted the same things."

I wanted excitement and intrigue, plunging toward passion and fullness of life. I wanted laughter and music and dancing and food and gay times. Those qualities did not appear to ride easily on Joe Stearns's shoulders.

"It's quite economic in nature, marriage," he continued. "But if you must know, I flipped a coin for you." He winked at Margaret. "Bunch of lumber people heard I was looking for a wife and told me of one or two potentials. Your name came up, but several said you were too high strung for such as me." He laughed. "Said I wouldn't be so lucky to pursue you, but I won the toss. They gave me three months to succeed. They paid off our wedding night. But I did spend most of the night with my parents," he added in his defense.

"How fascinating, Joe," I said at last, emphasizing his name. We had both stepped over the word *fertile*.

I watched the amber bubbles drift upward toward the lip, swallowed again and waited for the burning in my throat to stop.

"With no evidence of doom to even notice or announce alarms about," I said, much more confident than I felt, "who needs a Cassandra?"

"I do," he said.

I lifted the champagne to my lips. This time the effervescence tickled my nose, creating a giggle. I sipped again and thought I heard Margaret gasp. I took a larger swallow.

The sound of wheels on tracks filled the room, and I drank the rest of the amber lost in the rhythm of railroads and wine.

"A man succeeds by his cunning and skill. When a woman succeeds, it's just luck. Here we've gotten things reversed."

I stood, buoyed by the warmth in my stomach, unnerved by my husband's quizzical staring as he refilled my glass.

With my movements, the forest-green silk of my dress sounded like a gentle rain swishing over my taffeta crinolines, settling in a whisper around my legs when I stopped. I put the cool tulip to my face, my temple, and then my lips again, dizzy from my swirling dance. The wetness and cold caught my breath, and I exhaled long then put the crystal to my lips and emptied it.

Margaret glared while I tasted the possibilities of newfound freedom nestled within this foreign place called "marriage."

It took but a moment more for the sensation of the wine to move within me like a deep, melodious song. The liquid eased into the back of my throat, smoothed by the fragrance and the taste of cool air, turning warm as it soothed through my body like a long-awaited adulation. I wasn't sure if it was the drink or the sway of the train or some growing realization that caused my heart to beat up in my head.

Margaret set her glass down untouched. "I'm to bed," she said, her voice coming to me through a fog. She lifted the edges of her skirt, arms straight and tight to her side. She stood and turned. "You might consider the same, Cassie. You get so easily tired."

"Not a wink's need for sleep tonight," I said, motioning with my glass toward Josiah. My husband hesitated then moved forward to refill it. I finished the liquid and saw the bottom of my glass. I set the crystal next to Margaret's untouched one, and lifted hers.

"Cassie..." she began.

"You scoot off to bed," I said, motioning with my free hand. My wedding ring glistened in the gas lamps, sending sparkles between us. "We married people have things to discuss. Or cuss," I said and laughed, my voice foreign to my own ears. Giggles and pluck played billiards in my head.

Margaret's knuckles turned white against the burgundy skirt they gripped. "Papa and Mama've never done such!" she said. Her lower lip slipped out in a pout.

"They didn't?" I said. "Why, you and I are here as proof they did!"

"The cussing," she corrected, her cheeks burning. I heard a shake in her voice. "They never spoke ill words to each other."

"Never know what married folks do in their privacy," I said, running my fingers over the smooth wood of the writing desk I walked beside. I swirled around the room with new vigor. My thoughts lifted with my boldness.

"It's not a subject for children," I said. "But I'll let you know about some marriage 'cuss-doms' in the morning." My lips felt fuzzy when I ran my tongue over them; I continued to stare at her.

Margaret turned, stepped through the narrow door, and clicked it shut. I knew hot tears of embarrassment worked their way down her fine-boned cheeks at that moment. I wondered if my mother would come to her rescue or why I'd said those things. I had no reason to make Margaret upset, and yet I couldn't stop myself from speaking.

"It's the champagne," Joe said, reaching to take the glass. "Listen. Perhaps you've had enough." His eyes looked beyond me as though waiting for my mother to stick her head out and protest.

"Oh, I didn't marry a father," I said, slipping away from him, crystal in hand. "And you can't be telling a 'lovely young thing' what she can and can't be doing. She's just surveyin' the terrain, like a good little wife."

"Don't twist my words," he said, one blond eyebrow lifting. "It was as genuine a compliment as my warning. You'll have a headache in the morning as it is, Cassie."

I was swirling again, feeling stronger and bolder, not worrying about the morning. I smiled at him, waved the empty glass as I danced by, and this time Josiah—Joe—reached out for me, pulled me into his chest, then held me at arm's length. His fingers burned along my bare arms.

The glass dropped empty to the Persian carpet and did not break.

"First champagne can be deadly," he said, his words thick. "Especially at this altitude." His breath smelled sweet and warm against my ear. "I should have told you."

"You're so much older and wiser," I whispered. My head buzzed. I became limp in his arms, dropped my head back, and offered him my neck.

Irritation as from an impatient parent pierced his voice as he shook me upright. "That's enough, Cassandra."

"That's enough, Cassandra," I said, Annabelle-like.

I looked Joe in the eye then, fuzzy though he was, and saw confusion face me. Joe acted unsure. His eyes strayed again to Mother's door.

No one would be rescued, I told myself, and threw my arms around my husband's neck and kissed him then for the very first time.

Fumbling followed, fingers probed against petticoats and starch, our breathing mixed with kisses as our bodies lumbered toward the bed. Weight pressed, pulses pounded into sharp sensations that pierced the honey haze brought by wine and inexperience, made me aware of agitated pain. The thirsting startled into foreign, then pulled away and left me hungry and unsatisfied in a frenzied sort of way.

What did I know about marriage, about the expectations of a lifetime? What I knew about that foreign state most women visited whether they wished it or not was what any eighteen-year-old would have sorted out: Husbands were taciturn, wrapped their lips around clay-lined pipes rather than words; wives appeared weak, yet only the wealthiest had knuckles smaller than their fingertips. Children arrived, consumed energy and time, were raised, and good ones responded to their parents wishes. Young women were given up to marriage, young men received them, and then it started once again.

Couples seemed to make contact by bumping into one another rather than by touching.

I tried to imagine a marriage where people behaved hardily and with vigor, weaving passionate spirits with constructive deeds, two people made more than who they might have been alone, one without the other. I could think of no one. None among my distant aunts or uncles, none among my school chums' parents. The closest I could recall was the butcher and his wife, who shouted back and forth, making each other and their customers laugh as they wrapped fresh chops for matrons of the neighborhood. Children scampered around their feet, ran quick errands, and had the bright look of someone fed more than beefsteaks at the family table. I'd last experienced them the day my father collapsed. I liked being sent on errands there, but until that moment, beside a sleeping husband as we rocked across the country in a palace car at dawn, I had not wondered why.

Joe faced the wall, already into deep sleep. I tried to follow. Real and dream wove themselves together, wrapped up in a cloak of loss.

Joe—as he became for me—had taken his breakfast in the dining car when I awoke. I expected he was now in the smoking car chewing on his own clay-stemmed pipe. No words had passed between us in the morning, nor looks either, to my relief. I feared that if his eyes once held mine, he'd see the discomfort I felt, know he'd been proven correct: I did have a headache and a stomach as flimsy as a french-flowing mantua. I wore both well into the morning, too miserable to worry about what my mother thought, or even Margaret.

"Your face is as puffed as an adder's," my mother said when I entered the drawing room of our car. Late-morning sunlight filtered through the windows. "Whatever did you do last evening? Don't rub at your eyes, dear. Must be something in this western air that doesn't agree with you," she concluded, lifting her teacup from its saucer.

She'd taken to this palace-car living, lounging on the divan as though she'd always had others to wait on her, fix her meals, brush out her dresses. Her face glowed in her growing state of rest, and I was as pleased for her as my envy would allow.

"Something she drank, I'd guess," Margaret said with an uncharacteristic bite to her words. She stood in the convenience room across from the bedrooms, her narrow shoulders just visible in the doorframe, her feet bare.

"They bring in spring water," my mother said. "And yours is the tender tummy, dear. Cassie has the stamina of a horse."

"Were you and Papa happy?" I asked.

That stopped my mother's cup midway to her mouth.

"Such a question!" she said.

"Of course they were," Margaret said. She popped her head back out from the mirror, stepped out, and drifted across the carpet to the stove keeping the curling iron hot. "Papa brought you little gifts and things. Isn't that so?"

"He always stepped outside to smoke," my mother said. She pushed herself from her chair, took the curling iron from Margaret's hand, and began making sausage curls for her younger daughter. "Married forty years. Twenty-one before you came, Cass."

"But did you look forward to things together? Work toward something? Did he make you laugh?"

"Marriage is not a laughing matter. It's what must be done, and your father and I did it as well as any, considering. Like Josiah, your father had eleven years on me."

"But you were taller," Margaret added.

"The important thing is that we made a bargain and kept it. 'Til death do us part."

"So love wasn't in it?" I asked.

"It was indeed," she said.

She finished Margaret's hair, pulling the thick curls into a cluster at the back of her head and tying it with ribbon the color of blue bachelor's-buttons. She assessed it, her head moving this way and that. Her slippers poked out beneath her day gown she smoothed across her knees as she sat. Margaret eased across the thick carpet toward the window, chin up and still, as though carrying ten books on her head.

"Love, dear, is a journey, not something you can count on being the same over the years, between husband and wife, especially. So much happens. Good days and bad."

"Like traveling?" Margaret asked. She refreshed Mama's ginger-scented tea.

"Somewhat," Mama said. "Most of marriage is tending, doing what has to be done. Not very glorious at all. Like a garden. Keeping weeds pulled before they get so big you lose heart and just let the thing go. Sometimes it doesn't even feel like you're progressing, but you keep at it because you know it's what's needed and you have hope there'll be blooms and fruits some day."

"What about love?" I asked.

"Oh, love," she said. "Well, love's what makes things bloom." Mama had one tiny mole on the base of her neck, and she stroked it with two fingers. "The love that really matters, of course, arrives with children. You'll understand that when you have your own."

She seemed lost in memory, her eyes drifted shut. I thought she might have fallen asleep.

"We waited long years for you, Cassie. Twenty-one. Twenty-four for Margaret. That kind of tending can never be discounted. And once accomplished, God honors the gardeners as much as the flowers."

Mama opened her eyes and looked at me straight. "This is something I'm hopeful you'll remember. The whole purpose of an honorable marriage, Cassie, is to raise up children to be the best they can be. No amount of self-sacrifice is too much to ask. None. It's the only kind of garden that makes a difference. Especially for a woman. Everything else is distraction."

CHAPTER 4

HUNGRY

❀

San Francisco could have kept me forever, the shops seducing, granting permission to swaddle myself in mauve and mint delivered straight to our suite at the Palace Hotel. My mother and sister and I slipped ready-made dresses over our silk-taffeta petticoats worn over princess slips. We giggled before the gilded mirrors trying on hats with veils and exotic feathers, holding muffs and white leather shoes, a velvet cape of deep purple to cover the leg-of-mutton sleeves or an open-necked opera gown. Satin and linen and whalebone spilled over the striped divans, making the room look luscious and feminine.

Or maybe it was the day or two of walking up the steep streets for the vista views of the bay, pausing beneath scrub oaks to inhale the moist air that captured me.

"Wait up!" Mama gasped. "These hills are a trouble on my knees."

I turned, seeing the top of her and my sister's hats making their way up behind me, dark dots and feathers fanning the scene of Pacific beyond. "What I let you talk me into," Mama said when she caught up to me.

"I'm puffing more than *you* are," Margaret said. She gasped as I did at the vast view over housetops to the harbor below. The bay hosted a dozen sailboats drifting like paper cuttings on a placid pond.

"Not sure it's seemly to be walking like common folks," Mama said. "Are you all right?"

"We'll take a cab back," Margaret answered.

We hailed a carriage for our return. I loved the coolness and the greenery about the estates we rode by. Some days we'd sit in an open cab. Once our driver took us to a distant point with tall iron gates and fences surrounding rolling lawns of lush grass.

"It be a private hospital," the driver said, his voice lowered as though the patients inside might hear.

"Tuberculin?" Mama asked. She fanned herself, and the sweeping peacock feather and felt fruit on her hat swayed with her hand.

"No, for those what's got demons or clowns living in their minds. Won't never recover."

"Ever recover," my mother corrected.

"It's an asylum?" Margaret asked. She peered over Mama to examine the manicured lawns more closely.

"Imagine being caged forever," I said.

"Looks restful," Margaret said and sat back.

"But to have someone tell you what to do each day, when you could eat or sleep or what to think about, when you could leave." I shivered.

"Not unlike a mother must, at times," Mama sighed. She smiled and revealed her one dark tooth before putting the fan to her face.

"Shrubbery looks exotic," I said. "Look at those black hollyhocks. And what's that cluster of blooms by the gate?" I craned my neck to look back as we passed.

"At least they've a pleasant view," Margaret sighed, always finding the cheese in a thing and never its holes.

Maybe San Francisco captured me because I breathed more deeply in that city. The air lifted me, unlike the cold winds that blew across Cheyenne and rose dirty snow-like dust near Salt Lake. Or perhaps it was a slow deciding in that city that I had chosen wisely, secured a marriage to a stranger who so far had lavished all of us with gifts and allowed our independence. I envisioned a life free of care, even without suffering and with excitement for myself.

We spent four weeks beside that bay, but it was far too short. Someday I'd come back, for that city patented self-indulgence, an invention I recognized. In the morning we lounged and ate at our leisure. We dressed, then with parasols flared we walked. I had never experienced such bustle and bust, such a cacophony of language and voices, street clangs and steam. We found museums and concerts, plays of Ibsen's and readings of Yeats. Mama feigned tiredness, Margaret, too, but I badgered them into discussion groups where women spoke as stridently as men of world affairs, arguing the circumstances of the suicide of Archduke Rudolf, the Austrian crown prince, or the effects of Marx on Germany's Social Democrats. People didn't mind bumping into each other on the street as they rushed to assay offices or investment houses. New wealth invigorated even the street beggars who all wore shoes, even though the sidewalks weren't cold. Fresh dyes in the dress shops set my eyes to watering; strange smells of hanging meats and fowl in the marketplaces had the same effect on my mouth. Even alone, I spoke to strangers standing beside me at the fruit stands or places where hot food was sold on sticks. I loved how they laughed with me, the men, how they tipped their hats with smiles as our hands reached for melons or a colorful kite hanging from a shopkeeper's door.

Mama told me once at a confectionery shop to stop flirting, but my husband corrected her. "She can't help it," I heard Joe say, a certain pride in his voice. "It's just who she is."

My husband's occupation escaped me. I had no idea, really, what he did or how he did it, but he attended a variety of meetings while in San Francisco. He left early and arrived back late, tired and not the least bit interested in my day except to raise his eyebrows at the stack of boxes lining the hotel suite's waxed tables.

"Not much available in Hokium," my mother said, moving the cactus to a site nearer the window.

"There comes a limit," Joe said. Tobacco stained his teeth, and his smile had a yellow cast to it. He smelled of smoke-filled rooms. "And the pronunciation is now 'Hoquiam,' like a quill. Or so Emerson tells me. Called it that since 1882."

"A wife needs to be presentable," I said.

"Margaret needed school things," my mother said.

Joe stared through his finger-smudged glasses, and for the first time I felt my mother walked beside me in this marriage. It seemed sad that it should be as though the two of us walked in step against my husband.

Our hotel rose near the water, and in the morning I spied ships like museum paintings outlined by lacy curtains set on calm seas. Wisps of fog danced with the wind replaced by birds that swooped in and out of the scene. Small finches fluttered before the many-paned window then flew on. This kind of luxury wrapped itself around me like the Siberian fox fur coat Joe bought me and said I'd need once we reached our new home. The nap of the fur shone like jewels caught in the gaslight of our suite. I buried my face in its softness and inhaled the scent of clean snow.

San Francisco also fed intellectual pursuits when Joe introduced us to the wife of one of the Washington lumber barons staying at our same hotel. I doubt he expected it to lead to what happened.

Beatrice Smith invited us to a lecture given by Dr. Anna Howard Shaw, a woman who had chosen to leave her life as a privileged student of divinity to work with poor women of the Boston slums. A tall, shepherd-faced woman, her outrage at the lives of these women had led her to lecturing and to the National American Woman Suffrage Association.

Mama would have nothing to do with it, though Dr. Shaw was both a medical person and had a theological degree.

"She lectures for the WCTU," I told her, but even that association's plan to reduce drink had no effect on Mama, or Joe, for that matter. Joe's approval came because Mrs. Smith had extended the invitation.

"Never hurts to associate with success," he'd said, though at the last minute he was detained by business and we heard Dr. Shaw without him.

Even this well-traveled woman who was our escort had caution. "Don't allow yourselves to become mixed up with the National Suffragettes," Beatrice warned as we rode in her hired carriage to the lecture hall. "They've crazy ideas about marriage and divorce and controlling births and such. I heard that Mrs. Catt speak once. Growing up in Wisconsin certainly didn't keep her ideas stuck in the north woods. Believe me, some of her ideas should have died there for lack of sunlight." She shook her head, swaying her double chin. "What matters is the vote, pure and simple. That's what'll change the status of you girls and poor women and better the rest of the country, too, believe me. Keep the immigrants where they belong as well."

She patted Margaret's gloved hand.

I would have preferred to be just two married women afforded an evening out and wouldn't have given what was said by Dr. Shaw more than passing interest if I had been allowed such a privilege. But with Margaret along, I knew there'd be questions. And I'd end up later defending something I wasn't sure I even cared about just to challenge Margaret's sure and perfect view of things.

Margaret was more taken with the lecture than I was, at least her discussions later revealed some agitation with the philosophy expressed. I heard the words about the right of women to choose what they wished in life, to choose careers besides marriage. But the vote wasn't needed for that. Individual action was needed. Personal boldness. Pursuing pleasure needed no laws.

Two other California events proved even more memorable.

The first was the theater on my birthday evening, February 27. We had dined at the Metropolitan Restaurant next door, then made our way with our wide skirts along the plank walk, pushed through the gilded double doors and into the astounding room that beyond the curtains Joe said slanted toward a stage. The lobby like a well-furnished parlor sported life-size images made from photographs of important persons who had performed there. One that caught my fancy was of a regal-looking Indian woman of about my height.

"Princess Sarah Winnemucca," the brass label beneath her picture read.

"One of the last of her tribe," Joe said, noticing my interest. "War wiped out most of them. Just didn't adapt to necessary changes." He flicked something imaginary from his left ear. "Wrote a book and raised money for her Indian schools. Tried to get some land back. Futile effort. Probably where your plume came from," he said, nodding toward my hat. "Poachers."

"She's beautiful," I said, noticing her clear dark eyes that stared without apology into the photographer's lens.

"Suppose so," Joe said, though I could tell he'd never considered the possibility before. "Clear image." I made a mental note to find the book he said she'd written.

An orchestra warmed up, and the four of us settled into seats in a side balcony. Along with the tickets, Joe had purchased a set of jeweled lorgnettes that not only brought the singers closer but proved useful, later, for spying birds along the shore from our hotel window. Margaret used them to gaze even across the lobby, expressing delight with what I could see with my own eyes.

The performance itself was sung in German, of which I knew not a word. Joe translated some of it, but it didn't matter. For those two hours, I belonged to another time and place, transported there by songs and music and the actions of men who sang their way across the stage to gather up a woman in their arms and sweep her from her dreaded life to deliver her to joy. I was absorbed, as much a part of what was happening on that stage as if I'd been moving between the curtains myself.

"It's like your life," Margaret whispered, leaning over to me.

"Not a whit," I said, not turning to her. I wondered how she could even make the comparison. These women had been swept along, followed their hearts. I had only my head engaged.

The final event of note was a night spent at "The Queen of American Water Places," the Hotel del Monte, a luxurious castle-like building at the southern end of Monterey Bay.

We arrived through a vista of trees and cacti, oaks and flowers nestled around parcels of thick grass that made the hotel appear to be set in the midst of a park. Ladies with ankles showing and gentlemen in wide straw hats played croquet on different courts of lawn despite the cool weather. Men in gartered shirt sleeves wielded bows and arrows to the gloved applause of their ladies. Bins of fine sand had been brought in to form a beach for children. The play area was surrounded by walkways lined with tulips and crocus and yellow daffodils in full bloom.

"I'd live here forever," I said, taking a picture in my mind of the elegance and intrigue, of how someday I'd find a way to live surrounded by this kind of splendor.

"Cost a fortune," Joe answered, putting out his hand to assist me from the carriage.

"It's so green," I said. "Will Hoquiam be?"

"Not with grass," he said. "Place is still being settled. Lots of trees and stumps, though. Shipyards and mills."

Inside, the ladies' billiard saloon intrigued me most, and Joe and I almost had words over my wish to play one more game making us late for dinner. Something about the smooth slip of the cue through my fingers and the feel of the rich finish of wood as I leaned into the Brunswick and Baeke table gave me the sweetest thrill. The smell of polished wood filled the room. Joe said I exhibited some natural skill, but I could tell he disliked my wishing to display it. I thought him stuffy for moving me out, his fingers on my elbow guiding me past brass spittoons.

"It does keep your hands from your mouth," he said as he placed the cue in the round rack and escorted me into dinner.

We followed the waiter into the dining area, and I asked Joe to seat me where I could see the wide range of people. Instead, he pulled the chair where I'd face him and the wall. I asked for lamb chops seared and garnished with mint sauce. Joe gave the order for roast beef without gravy. When the waiter poured wine, he ignored my request, instead taking direction from Joe's almost imperceptible shake of his head. Each subject I spoke of resulted in some minute correction by my husband so that by the time I asked the waiter for dessert, I found myself working instead on steam.

"Not yet," Joe said. "We'll have coffee first. Be a good girl now and just wait."

I stood, my napkin dropping to the floor. "I've had enough," I said. "No dessert for me."

"Sit down, Cassandra," Joe said. "You'll want to hear this I'm sure."

Mama and Margaret exchanged looks. I sat. Joe ordered tansy mulled wine. Then over the chocolate mousse everyone tasted, he made his announcement.

"It's time we discussed what I expect when we reach Hoquiam."

For a brief moment I remembered Dr. Shaw's inspiring lecture about the importance of women obtaining the vote in order to control their lives.

"This is the first project entirely under my direction," Joe said. "Once in Hoquiam, I'll leave early. Spend most days at the sites or the office letting others know how much steam production they can expect for the day. The North Shore Electric Company is just starting out. It could mean a great deal for our future." He wiped his face with his napkin, and I noticed a thin blond fuzz appearing above his lip. I had thought it milk at first, but could see now he nurtured a mustache.

"It is not sound for women to come to my office," he continued. "Should you have need of me during the day, you will send a messenger. A secretary will be available. He can reach me wherever I am. I will expect you to run the affairs of the house I've secured. Later, I'll build our own home, but the town is newly incorporated and little is available."

He looked at my mother, not at me.

"I'll expect my noon meal ready precisely at twelve-fifteen and my supper at seven sharp. I will breakfast at my office so as not to disturb your morning routines."

"I'm sure the cook could prepare something for you," my mother offered. She cleared her throat once, then again.

"No sense in having a cook with three women in the house," Joe said. His smile slid across his face like a glacier.

"That would be an outrageous display of wealth, unlike this hotel and meager dinner," I said. "Your grandmother would have approved."

He raised an eyebrow at me. "Appearances are everything. You'll understand that someday, Cassandra," he looked over his lenses. "You'll be expected to behave accordingly."

"I'm not a child."

"No, you're not. Neither are you independently wealthy, though I've indulged you on this trip. When we arrive in Hoquiam, things'll be different. I'm a public servant of a kind, needing to show proper respect for finance. We will live accordingly, a wife in her proper place."

His tone of voice and the lift of his nose were more telling than his words.

"When necessary, we will have associates in," he continued. "You will be expected to plan these events to demonstrate frugality. People resist investment in a company associated with extravagance. At the same time, the evening must be memorable."

"That should be easy," Margaret said. "Cassie knows a *hundred* ways to have fun."

"The remainder of the time is yours to be spent as you wish, with my approval."

"Cassie wants to continue music lessons," Margaret offered. "Speak for yourself, Margaret," I said, but she didn't.

"Whatever isn't squandered in the household budget can be spent with some personal discretion," he said.

I could feel a burning in my stomach, not unlike the eating of a too-rich mousse on top of beefsteak and soup. A kind of slow seethe stopped just below my heart. What had we agreed to when we accepted this man's "generosity" and "stability"? What kind of future did he lay out for three women in a Washington wilderness?

There was nothing impetuous and romantic about his marrying me, I could see that now. "This is just a transaction for you, isn't it?" I said. "An economic exchange with the added benefit of someone you call 'lovely' reliably waiting on your porch."

"Sound familiar, my wife?"

The realization took blood pounding to my head.

"As. Your. Wife," I said, "I have certain expectations of my own."

Joe's napkin paused as he dabbed at his mouth.

"I thought you might," he said, then grinned that halfway of his. His smile made me feel like a four-year-old first challenging her parent's thinking. He signaled the waiter for hot coffee. He leaned back while the waiter filled his cup. "Let's hear them then."

I'd spoken without thinking and wasn't sure what I wanted, but surely nothing that would barricade autonomy and adventure, my wish to plunge fully into life.

"My own allowance, to begin with," I said. "It would be unseemly for the wife of someone in your position to have to request money as though she were just a common laborer being paid for piecework. I'll expect it monthly and not seek your permission to use it."

I stirred my coffee with silver that felt cool and smooth. A string quartet played Mozart's Third Concerto in G minor beyond us, able to lift their music above the din of voices and the sounds of spoons against Spode. The coffee smelled rich and dark, and I concentrated on the steam rising from the narrow cups to calm the shallow breathing that threatened to make me sound girlishly weak.

"If I want to buy clothing or property, I will. If music lessons appeal to me, I'll hire a tutor. If I wish to purchase a horse, I shall, or give money away to an orphans' fund or the Boston slums. That, too, will be my choice."

"Oh, I doubt you'll have property in your name, despite how autonomous you wish to be." He spoke over the top of his lenses. "Independence is for the men of this world. Women find their hopes filled in family relations."

I met his steady gaze then and was surprised when he dropped his eyes first. "You'll keep an accounting," he said, patting his pocket as though look-ing for his watch fob, and I realized he had accepted my first demand. I wished I'd thought it through.

"And I'll be allowed two trips from the area a year," I said, improvising. "Back here, to San Francisco, if I want. Or to Portland, Seattle, New York. Maybe even Russia."

I saw my mother's eyebrows lift at that suggestion.

"You'd need companions, dear," she said.

"Perhaps," I said.

"Until the children come," Joe said. "One trip."

"Cassie wouldn't want to travel with small children," Margaret agreed. Her hazel eyes were wide with wonder. Dark tendrils of hair splayed from her temples. She looked lovely and so young. "Would you, Cassie?"

"I might," I said. I laid the spoon down and sipped.

Joe cleared his throat. "And in return, I might have more of my own to prescribe for my wife."

"As a husband should," my mother noted.

"A wife may have more too," I said. "Especially a wife who plans to hone her business sense to the fine point of her husband's."

I rather liked the look of surprise that greeted my eyes as we ended the round of that marital spar.

Hoquiam, in the Quinault language of the Indian people who lived there long before us, meant "hungry for wood," though how anyone could be hungry for it in the midst of so much was beyond me.

Hoquiam, the town, nestled in the shadow of dense and towering mam-moths, a virtual feast of forest and thicket that failed to announce at first an oppressive sense of darkness and weight and limited horizons.

We'd seen nothing but this kind of wild and timbered land since our ship's captain pointed out to us the mouth of the Columbia River as we sailed by it the day before. Little else before that. Firs and hemlock, spruce trees and lacy cedars hid any open vistas and stifled the growth of aspiring shrubs and ferns and seedlings struggling in their shadows.

I was grateful for the wide, deep harbor known as Grays that we sailed

into, across the bar and by sand spits promising openness and escape to endless sea. We shared the ship with jowly businessmen returning from the City,
as San Francisco was known, along with lean-faced laborers scanning the
shoreline for lumbermills and the shipyards that consumed their days.

I'd seen Mrs. Smith—Beatrice she insisted we call her—the lumber
baron's wife in her dark caped dresses and small box hat, just a few times.
Margaret and I strode around a deck that on a return trip would bear lumber to the City. Noticing that my ankles did not swell if I walked each day, I
left Mama to nurse a fluttering stomach in one of the twelve cabins squeezed
into the heart of the ship.

Neither Margaret nor I suffered from seasickness despite mother's
description of Margaret's weak stomach, and so we would chat amiably with
those of like minds who caught the sea air. Sails cracked and snapped as we
walked.

We had talked about Dr. Shaw's work among poor women in Boston
and about Wyoming's precedent-setting statehood giving women the vote.
But I felt lectured to by Beatrice, dragged not lured by her intense blue eyes
and thin lips pursed into resolution. "You must simply put your divine high
spirit to work on behalf of women's suffrage, Cassie," Beatrice persisted.

"My divine high spirit plans to be engaged in better things," I said
though I wondered what I would be hungry for in Hoquiam, and if there I'd
be filled up.

Joe pointed out some of the people he'd met in San Francisco: Harry
Hermans who wore a high top hat and a financier's sharp gaze; George
Emerson, who, it was said, bought up Pacific coastal lumbermills for a San
Francisco tycoon named Simpson, then paired up with him to make a for-
tune.

"Emerson's even been to Williamsport, P. A., looking for mills," Joe said.

"That's where Burr and I were married," Mama said. "A lovely coinci-
dence."

They were all barons set to harvest God's bounty.

And bounty there was, if one saw it that way. Birds of a dozen varieties
dipped and swooped over our ship and dotted a sky as gray as a goose's belly.
A deer or two appeared like stars in twilight beneath trees that blackened the
hillsides as far as the eye could see. Stumps as tall as the oaks we'd left in
Corning dotted the inland shore like altar boys before a forest throne. Smoke

drifted up from many of them, signs of slow burns making room for the houses of wood built to replace their space, and I wondered to myself if our home would have stumps poking up through wet vines and ferns to frame the view.

"That's what the Spanish and English and Americans have argued over," Joe said, nodding with his chin to the landscape. I supposed he spoke of the trees, though I wondered if it might not have been to have the choice to leave.

I shivered, my wool cape sodden and my bones chilled in the few short minutes we had stood on the rain-slickened deck. Wind whipped at the sails, cracked them like sheets on a line. Water seeped into the seams of my high-button shoes.

Easing inland, I could make out individual trees as they speared upward from a dense undergrowth that reached in most places to the sea. The massive trunks and slender needle-lined branches caught the steady rain and sealed the moisture in their needles and leaves. Lighter shades of green within the forest lent iridescence. Inside the harbor, the wind lay down.

"Quite majestic, isn't it?" Joe breathed at my side. His eyes scanned the shoreline and beyond where the timber rose green and black beneath ridges of snow-dusted trees in the distance. Blood-red vine maple, western larch not yet yellow, pale green and new growth and an occasional shrub sprinkling amber were the only colors to break the dark.

"No sense to tuck your neck, Miss," one of the mates told me as he walked by. "Rain'll come to ye just as fast with your shoulders hunched as not, and ye'll have a headache to boot."

I suppose my face showed surprise both at his familiarity in speaking to an unknown woman and at his words of advice. I relaxed my shoulders instead of hunching them against the weather, my eyes focused outward instead of at my feet. And I was no wetter for the effort.

"That's probably why my neck aches." I rubbed at it with my gloved hand.

"And a pretty one it is, Miss, wet or no," he said and grinned, and I grinned back.

I wondered if Joe would intervene, but he did not. I thought then that while Joe spoke of rigid rules and required decorum, this strange dark hungry land might be bolder, more indulgent, allow pushing at the limits of what was accepted or permitted.

Soft mists drifted at the shore blending with the warming fires outside long plank lodges pointed toward the bay.

"Indians," the mate said. "Friendly, though."

The scent of burning wood rose up to greet me and I sneezed. Beyond, on either side of a south sloping river lay the settlement of Hoquiam.

Our ship eased past the village distinguished by long, narrow boats—Chinooks, Joe said they called them—set back from the water. Piles of clam shells rose like blisters on the white sand. A few muscular men of darker skin worked on dugout canoes in the steady drizzle while shorebirds hopped among them. Neither rose up as we moved toward the river.

"Mercy, so small," I heard my mother gasp as we stepped into the boat to take us to the dock. I didn't know if she referred to our craft or the town, but both deserved the breathless prayer she uttered as she pulled her cape tighter around her shoulders.

The city may have been just incorporated, but it appeared as no town in my experience. Batches of homes backed like wary cats against the timber, rubbing themselves beneath branches and trees. And while the population was said to be several hundred souls, each grouping appeared to exist by itself, separated by clusters of greenery: ferns and firs and stumps and mud and needle-covered ground.

As we moved closer, I could see how the tree trunks stopped all sunlight and space in the dense undergrowth, but closer to the river, lushness stood out. Thin lines of paths, like snakes, made their way along the timber near the river that bore the same name as the town. The paths did not enter the trees, at least that I could see.

And everywhere, just beyond Hoquiam's limits, towered the canopy of timber shooting one and two hundred feet into the gray sky. I felt a kind of panic rise into my throat and swallowed to keep it from entering the world as a scream against the bigness of it, the darkness, the weighted quiet.

"We can find open spaces," Margaret said, her gloved hand rested on mine.

It bothered me she knew I'd have to.

A man who introduced himself as Willard Stems, Joe's secretary, met us at the dock.

"Careful of the wet, now," he directed, rain dripping off his hat. His voice

was raspy, and he reminded me of an undernourished ferret with his dart-
ing eyes and wiry frame and quick movements. I pushed at him as he placed
his hands at my waist to assist me, my one arm wrapped around the potted
cactus. "That step can be tricky, miss," he said.

"Missus," my mother corrected.

"I'm quite capable," I said. I glanced at Joe hoping to witness his protest.
None came as he was assisting Margaret, and I wondered what my husband
could be thinking of to allow this strange creature to touch me, even in assistance.

The house did nothing to ease the growing anxiety I felt at our arrival.
It was a two-story, narrow home without whitewash set off by a cluster of
wild shrubs and stumps. Windows on either side of the windowless door
made it appear to have long, cramped eyes sadly staring out at the wooden
walk. Puddles of water stood everywhere catching the constant drizzle, and
we jumped over one to start up the steps to the narrow porch. Needles
floated in the dirty water.

"It'll look better in the morning," Margaret said coming to stand beside
me. "Or when the rain stops." She slipped her hand inside mine. Her palm
was small and warm for a moment, and I held it, feeling a rare protective-
ness. She was here because I was and not of her choosing at all.

Mr. Stems and Joe carried our cloth bags from the carriage, stepping
over thick, black worms that raised slick heads.

"Slugs," Stems said, grinning at my discomfort. Margaret bent to pick
one up.

"They're smooth," she said. "Look." She held it up to my face. I shivered
again.

A key was produced and the door opened to a narrow hallway with a
carpeted staircase rising up through it and doors to rooms on either side.
Warmth from the living-room fireplace drifted out from the door to the left.
A bare table stood in the foyer, and on it I placed the cactus and pulled at
the fingertips of my gloves.

Beside the plant, my mother set her wrist purse and the hat she pulled
from her head, shaking rain from it like a wet dog all over the wooden floor.

"How often does it rain like this?" she asked.

"Maybe three times a year," Stems answered her, opening doors to a parlor and a kitchen.

"Really?" Margaret asked, hopeful.

"Winter, spring, and fall, with rarely a shower through July and August." Stems's smile was met with blank stares. "You get used to it. Eighty some inches most years. Mainly in November and December. We'll be into the dry season soon. Your garden will surprise you. And the flowers. Anything grows here if the sun hits it."

"What the slugs don't get, I imagine," I said, starting up the stairs.

An armoire sat at the top of the steps. Four bedrooms, two on either side of the stair rails, stood with open doors. Only two rooms had beds.

"I'll furnish the other rooms when the ship arrives," Joe said coming up behind me with one of the bags. "Looks like this is the largest." He entered the room over the living room. "Put things here. Air it out a bit. Smells rather moist, don't you think? I'll be back for dinner, Cassie." He kissed the top of my head then turned to leave. "I'm sure Stems has put things in the cool shed out back."

Moist air? Of course it was moist. What did he expect inside a rain forest? Wet wool is what it smelled like to me. And wet wood. And wet slugs. Whatever else there was in Hoquiam I would wager it was wet.

"This is it then?" I asked, the tone of my voice stopping him as he started through the door. He stuck his head back in.

"Don't be troublesome now, Cassandra," Joe warned. "We can discuss your concerns later."

Through the upstairs window I watched the men leave in the carriage, the horse making its way past smoking stumps and scattered lumps of slashed branches apparently waiting to be burned. An ache of envy slithered across my soul, a touch of dread that what was here would not sustain me. The shipmate's grin came to me. He had bouyed my day.

My mother's voice rose from below, and I heard Margaret's light laughter lift up the stairs. Whatever could they find to be joyous about, I wondered and listened but couldn't make out their words.

I looked out at the thickness of trees in the direction Joe and Stems had driven. I felt as dense as the timber, as shrouded in mist. I wondered if this Hoquiam could have been named by someone seeking, though others might say he had abundance to spare. Tears pressed behind my nose. I shook them back and began to unpack.

CHAPTER 5

PACIFIC PRESSURES

❖

Vapors lengthened the season in Hoquiam. The rain became an expectation as familiar as breath. The downpour didn't happen every day, but when it did, it came in torrents, sheets of water impossible to see through. Wind drove rain into every weak place, every shingle, every unsealed window or doorjamb. And when it didn't rain, fingers of mist folded themselves around the trees, rising and disappearing with the heat of each day. It spoke a language of its own, this weather and land, talking through the trees and mist and skies as gray as old pewter, promising a time when the polish of the sun would make it shine.

The Power and Light Company consumed my husband. Sometimes whole days passed without my seeing him and I was fast asleep before I felt weight on his side of the bed. If I slept, he didn't waken me. Instead, he'd lift the book from my hands and lay it on the round bedside table, evidence he had been there despite the empty bedroom in the morning.

I took on the task of making our moss-covered house into a home wishing I had Clarence Cook's book, *The House Beautiful, Domestic Interior Decorating*, to guide me. Hoquiam had no library, Joe hadn't consented to a day trip to Portland yet, and my books had still not arrived. I was forced to call upon my imagination and what I remembered.

I discovered a certain talent I had to bring colors and fabrics and papers into a bouquet of design. Wallpaper of roses arrived on the steamer *Alliance* making its way from Portland to Hoquiam every Thursday by 7:00 P.M. Bold roses soon appeared, pasted over the boards of our bedroom. I turned matching material into drapes to cover the windows instead of the shutters. Red tassels Mama said must have come from some disreputable house hung on either side of the casings. I made papier-mâché roses I painted in contrasting pink to spill over chipped water pitchers I found on the back shelves of Johanson's Furniture and Undertaking Establishment.

I made so many trips to the mercantile looking for odds and ends that Mr. Johanson began setting aside objects he would otherwise have thrown away. I gave old shoes new bottoms, painted them then filled them with dirt and replanted cactus starts that now flourished in each room of the house.

The moments in Johanson's shop had an added benefit: the charge of lightness that came with talking and chatting with others, smiling and batting my eyes. Mr. Johanson's pink cheeks burned brighter when I entered his store. He scurried to wait on me, bringing from beneath the commerce-smooth counter treasures he'd set aside with me in mind. Once I noticed his wife grimace as we talked and made sure after that to chat with her, ask about her aching hip or her grandchild's progress. Soon, she too made her way to assist me, finding pleasure in waiting on someone who listened as well as lightened her day.

When the project of house decorating neared completion, it was summer and I hungered for something more. I badgered Joe until he delivered a fine thoroughbred I'd located for my use and didn't make me pay for it from the household funds.

"You're so small," Joe said when the horse circled on the lunge line. "He must be sixteen hands."

"He's gentle enough," I said. "Gelded last year."

"Listen, Cassandra. Don't attempt jumps with him," he warned.

"Wouldn't think of it, Josiah. As long as he has spirit, size won't matter."

Joe laughed. "Says something of yourself as well."

Sun speared often across the timbered hillsides like the promise of a friend, hopeful and encouraging, the way it could appear through fluffy clouds hovering over the bay. Those days Shiloh and I rode the trails beside the water, away from the smoke and stench of people, seeking the sandy, wet-scented beaches where we raced the waves of the incoming tide. I felt at one with the horse, powerful, controlling such muscle and surge despite my tiny frame perched atop the English flat saddle, reins held in both hands, parallel and low. Wind raced through my hair I let hang down my back like a child's, and we did jump, but low jumps, over driftwood and small streams cutting their way to the sea.

He was a good choice, the gelding, and for the hour I rode each day, I never thought of hunger. But when fall and winter came round again, my husband forbid me to ride saying the trails were too icy or slickened by mud. I considered defying him, but putting the horse at risk was not my way. Instead, I relegated myself to the stable to inhale the scent like no other— that of hay and warm horse—and brushed Shiloh's winter hair smooth.

Then I considered school.

Margaret made her way each day beneath the trees, along the paths to the clearing where the school sat nestled beneath tall firs. I'd watched the bobbing umbrella she carried disappear into the dark trees amazed at how they consumed her, as though she might never have been.

The Lady Margaret's adjustment had been complete within days of our move to Hoquiam. I envied her ease of adjustment.

"Inclination," she told me, squinting up from her journal writing when I mentioned her apparent peace. "It's changing how you *see* things instead of waiting for things to change. That's what the headmaster says."

I saw things differently, all right: she had routine, friends, play-party invitations, and school; I had a distant marriage.

"They've few books," Margaret said, "but the slates are good and the *benches* are as smooth as slugs. And the stove warms things in a twinkle. It's too bad you can't come," she added, a tease in her eyes. "Won't be long and I could be teaching."

"Wouldn't be seemly a'tall," Mama answered for me.

"My teaching?" Margaret asked, surprised.

"Of course not, sweetheart. That would be fine. It's the invitation to Cassie that's troublesome."

It was a discussion I'd already had with my mother and Joe, one I'd lost. I saw nothing odd about wanting to join Margaret in school, but both informed me that what lessons I might need to learn I could discover at home or where other married women did, in the Women of Woodcraft Club or volunteering at the recently built hospital. Neither appealed to me, both so consumed with the elderly and ill.

So I waited until Joe left one morning and Mama slept late and then like a loyal dog I followed Margaret to school. It was the most glorious day!

Margaret joined in the complicity. She told the headmaster she was bringing her "little sister" to school, and when I arrived he seemed taken aback. I wore my hair long like Margaret's, held back with a burgundy ribbon.

"I thought 'little' meant younger, Miss Hendrick," he said. "I'm young in spirit," I assured him, "and I am littler than Margaret. At least shorter."

I proceeded to entertain his students, bringing giggles then peals of laughter with a kind but accurate replication of community people they would know: Mr. Johanson's laugh accompanied by the holding of his belly as if he'd split like a melon if he dropped his arms; Mrs. Gunner's waddle and prattle as she sold eggs and milk at the corner, and three or four more. I even mimicked Robert Hunt, a suspicious sort of man who crouched and darted down the streets acting mad at times as he challenged even honest men, accusing them of cheating while they made change at the store. Nothing unkind, just enough to invite recognition and make the children feel all wise and smart at the correctness of their guesses.

"That'll do, Miss Hendrick," the headmaster had said, brushing tears of delight from his face. "We must get back to our lessons."

As we left that day, the headmaster held my hand in both of his and said he hoped I would put my mind to work as well as my high spirit. The look he gave me left no doubt he had enjoyed his day.

But when I attempted to attend the second time a week or so later, the headmaster met me at the door. Margaret stepped on inside, chin tucked into her chest.

"I had no idea you were Mrs. Stearns," he said, his words as icy as an east wind. "You should have told me. Your vim should go to worthy things instead of putting headmasters at risk."

I stood as exposed as a pumpkin after the patch's first frost. My cheeks felt hot with shame. He'd closed the door and left me standing, my shoes still soaking from the puddles I'd sloshed through.

Home became my cave after that. I made sure my mother knew it, and

I reminded Joe through notes if necessary that I'd been dutiful as a dog.

Envy comes to mind as a way to name the mist that settled on my shoulders in that hungry place. Envy, that Margaret had something to look forward to each day. Envy, that the moist air from dense skies buoyed her, didn't pull her down. Her face looked constantly washed, so soft and clear. It was as though her hunger was being satisfied in this Hoquiam while mine gnawed at my ribs.

Even envy of my mother appeared one morning as I observed her reading a book and dozing whenever the mood hit her. After years of watching her father and brothers leave for work at the mines and sending her own husband off to the hardware business while she diapered and directed two girls three years apart, she was now able to direct the cook Joe had relented and allowed us to hire. Something good had arrived for her on the same journey that had taken my father.

But it was my envy of Joe and his ability to set his days—and mine—that worked on me like a needle against a thimbleless finger. Even the bulbs and plants, crocus and tulips, irises and gladioli, their fragile skins flaking off on my fingers like ash against snow, were not sufficient to fill me up.

Our trunks had arrived, and I'd removed bulbs from them, brushing off thin grains of dirt, all that remained of New York. They'd appeared just as I'd placed them, wrapped in brown butcher's paper and tied with a string.

Seeing them made my heart ache not for New York but for my father. I remembered him standing behind me one day while I knelt in our door garden back home. "Promise of spring, are bulbs," he'd said. "Signs of faithfulness, that's what you're plantin' in ready soil. Believe I like the burying best, though, worryin' the soil a bit then waitin'. Break up that clod there, Cassie." He pointed with his walking stick. "Like checkin' to see if they've risked their noses out the ground. Always anticipatin'."

"I like the flowers and the fragrance," I'd said.

"Nay," he'd corrected, "the hopin's worth twice the happenin'."

The bulbs were barely buried beneath the ground beside the house before another torrent of rain fell. I wondered if the irises would rot as the ground seemed to in places, become spongy with water seeping up everywhere through sand.

The rose tree I'd planted had done well though it grew spindly as a newborn colt, not straight and true like rose trees of New York. As I walked or rode Shiloh about the town, I noted a few flower gardens and the sweep of door gardens that thrived the best. Admiring the blooms, I often left with cuttings of a Persian or copper-gold rose or seeds from columbine along with garden tips to thwart the slugs. "A pie tin of stale beer lures them," an old Hoquiam resident told me. "They drown in the ale."

Snow fell once or twice that winter and the next. I watched children sledding down a tree-dragged trail and exchanged hot cider for the use of a sled.

"No wonder you tire," Mama said, "playing like a child."

The white cedars were drifted with a light dusting in December bringing Christmas and a view out the window that rivaled the original Currier and Ives print Joe hung against the iris-flowered parlor wall. Farther upriver, snow was said to stay forming into drifts, but in Hoquiam it felt like winter tropics. Most of the holiday season shone green instead of New York's familiar white.

Walking proved difficult with the mud. Yet every day I was not allowed to ride Shiloh, I made myself ease into the forest and, breathing slowly, stepped like a cautious heron moving between water and soil. Beneath the huge trees, I entered a dark, wet vastness, allowing the silence to console my shoulders like a cape until the weight of it felt oppressive and shortened my breath. I inhaled, all of my senses engaged. I'd walk as deep as my fears of the closed-in spaces allowed, swallowed by tree trunks wider than streets.

I suppose the weighted stillness, anticipating more, felt something like my life. But there I stood, umbrella at my side, staring upward to the tiny opening of sky the Douglas firs afforded, forcing myself to rule some unknown dread until I could bear it no longer. Then I'd swirl around, drawing mist and sounds of birds and quiet inside me, inhaling the scent of matted needles so strong that I could taste them. The rush of bark and greenery and sunlight filtered swirled around me until I raced out of the woods, gasping, grateful for the tracks to mark my trail, refusing to imagine what might happen if I went too deep inside the timber or stayed too long there and became lost in its dark depths.

"Why do you go if it bothers you?" Margaret asked when I told her once of the short breath I experienced in the trees as I swirled. "It's *telling* you to stop, your breath is."

"Because I love the feel of it, the total magnetism of it. So consuming I forget how bored I am each day, how full of ennui. Besides, there's nothing in the trees that should scare me, and it bothers me that I am a bit."

"There's *plenty* to be wary of," Margaret said as she gathered up her school slate. "I never leave the paths. One wrong turn and poof," she snapped her fingers, "you might never come out."

"I'd look for the sun," I said.

"It doesn't shine there," Margaret said in her teaching voice. "That's why nothing grows low on the ground except where there've been fires, or they've cleared timber. Your breath is warning you of real danger. Don't ignore it just because you can."

"There's an exhilaration," I persisted, walking partway with her. "Wondering if I'll faint before I stop spinning or turn to leave, or if the lightheadedness will whisk me in another direction altogether, maybe in deeper than I'd planned. Maybe someplace where I might not even find my breath or where it'll require all my will to get me out." I swallowed, the feeling coming back. "When I decide I can't take it any longer, when the fear mixed with anticipation becomes a heat up to my cheeks, then I start back out. It's as though I'm in a competition, Margaret, racing myself, seeking something. Pushing to reach the edge before my breath gives out."

I could see by my sister's eyes that what I said astonished her.

"I don't know how to explain it," I said, turning away from the intensity of her gaze.

"Sounds like something *bewitching*."

"That's it!" I said.

"Oh, Cassie," Margaret whispered. She hugged her arms to her breast. "That's so dangerous, putting yourself in peril just for the thrill."

Beatrice dropped by to chat, her words leading always into suffrage.

"Your Joe's a likely one," she offered one day, leaning toward me as though we might be overheard. We were quite alone. "You'll see. He'll hold some public office as sure as there're slugs on the steps. And if you do what's right, when he does, we'll have a foot stuck squarely in the door for women's rights, slug or no."

"He'd slam that door," I said.

"Needs training, Cassie," she said, patting my hand in that familiar way she had. "About responsibility to his fellowman. Or woman, in this case."

"He's a surveyor, Beatrice, an engineer." I pulled my hand from beneath hers and stood, straightened the summer scene I'd hung behind the horse-hair divan. "He's interested in rocks and little notes in books and how water builds up steam, not votes. He doesn't think it right that women should vote. Seems to think men will lose their independence if we do."

"Times are changing, though. He has that resolute look of a man willing to go the distance for something. He may as well feel strongly about his wife getting the vote as anything."

"Wouldn't it be nice," I said, "to feel such passion?"

"At least come to the meetings, Cassie. We're an entertaining group."

"Maybe," I said, but imagined instead forming a ladies' billiard hall in the spring and the wincing such an idea would place upon my husband's face.

I did go to one of Beatrice's meetings, looking for any acceptable diversion. I met Ida Soule, the daughter of another lumberman and we walked home together.

"Traveling, that's my ticket," Ida said. "I want to step into every country in the world. Wouldn't that be just dandy?"

"Don't see how suffrage'll help with that," I said.

"It'll prepare people to see women in different places. Let them know we can live outside the shadow of a father or a brother or a husband."

"Too late for me," I said. I kicked at a pine cone that skittered across the boardwalk. "I've already been cooled by that shadow."

My life changed on February 27, 1892, and not just because I reached the age of twenty-one.

"Somewhat of an irregular rhythm," Dr. Campbell said, "for someone so young."

His exam complete, he pulled his head out from under my petticoat. Examinations were so awkward. The doctor was the son of the founder and first postmaster of Hoquiam. His father's two-story house still stood across from Emerson's Northwest Mill. Following medical school in the East, young Dr. Campbell had returned to Hoquiam to begin his practice.

I sank into the chair, tired from standing while he probed and poked.

Dr. Campbell combed his mussed hair with his fingers and removed the stethoscope from his ears and sat. Indian beadwork covered the string that held the instrument adding a note of color and cheerfulness to his otherwise drab vest. A rusty spot marked his white cuff.

"Still, you should have no difficulty. You're young. Good, wide birth canal. But a little caution is warranted about that heart," he said as though to himself.

"Could my activity make a difference?"

"Mental outlook," he continued, tapping his finger to his temple, "that's what'll matter. Did you plan this baby?" He pushed both hands on his wide thighs and stood.

"There's a choice in that?" I said.

"Oh, quite," he said, pouring water into the porcelain bowl. "Quinault and Chehalis both have ways. Greeks and Romans did as well. I just assumed, with your age and access and your conversations with Beatrice and Ida, well, that you'd read Mrs. Blatch's works on voluntary motherhood."

It annoyed me that he knew of my friends and contacts when I knew none of his. "I'm unfamiliar with the idea," I said.

"Never hurts to be aware of new thinking. Where would we doctors be without it?"

"I didn't think motherhood was something a woman could control," I said and smoothed my skirt at the front, adjusted the bustle as I sat. "I'm not at all sure how I feel about children, but I didn't think they could be, well, just ordered up. Or out."

"Oh, quite," he said looking up at me in the mirror over the washbowl. He had fluffy white eyebrows that raised and lowered as he talked. A bald spot on the top of his head I'd seen as he'd begun to examine me was no longer visible.

"Having one will be all right," I said. "They're loving enough."

He reached for the towel and wiped each finger. They were short, stubby appendages and he pushed at the cuticles as he talked, facing me now. "It doesn't always work that way."

"Whatever I put my mind to, I can have," I said and wondered about the petulance in my voice.

"Babies are people," Dr. Campbell said, one eyebrow raised. "Make their own choices about what they'll give or how much. Yours has let you have months without sickness, am I right?"

I nodded. I'd been aware that my skin had taken on a sheen I attributed to the moisture of this rain forest we lived in. And my body had become more rounded, but I did enjoy Mama's bread and I hadn't ridden or walked much. But I'd not been ill a minute.

"It'll be a way to fill my days," I said, "since I'm to live in tree shadows my whole life."

"Excuse me?" he said, folding the towel and hanging it on the towel rack on the back of the cabinet.

"To powder it and dress it and hold it. What could be more rewarding?"

"Quite," he said. "We'll hope for the best, then. I'd say August."

Something told me not to lift my glass of wine in celebration on my birthday dinner, and the cigar smoke usually made me sneeze so asking Joe to remove himself to the outside porch when he first arrived home came as no surprise.

There was no gathering for my birthday despite the occasion. "Wouldn't do," Joe had said to my suggestion.

"The Christmas party was well received," I reminded him.

"It was. Too soon to suggest another. Don't want to appear extravagant. Besides," he added, brushing at his moustache, "Willard needs time to recover from that Virginia Reel you forced him into trying. Poor man was exhausted by that high stepping."

"He's such a slug," I said, working on the tiny buttons pulling now as they marched down the front of my dress.

"He's a responsible man, Cassandra, not prone to foolishness. You look radiant tonight, by the way."

It was 6:45 P.M. by the hall clock, and it surprised me now, his being home before 7:00. He'd brought foxgloves, too, and lunaria to soften his earlier refusal of an occasion, I imagined. The translucent spheres of the money plant looked silky in the light. I wondered how he'd secured them in the midst of a February freeze.

"They're like words, you know, Cassie," he said. He fidgeted with the ribbon around the bouquet.

"No sweet williams, I see." He looked puzzled. "'One may smile but be a villain still.' That's a sweet william."

A look of annoyance crossed his face.

We stood in the upper bedroom furnished now with a maple dresser and bed, a round table holding my diary and fringe over lamplight, and a rag rug to seal warmth rising from the living room below.

"Twenty-one agrees with you," Joe said.

He attempted to kiss me before handing me the flowers, but I anticipated it and turned, reaching for combs to secure my hair that felt thicker in this Washington weather. I bent low, as though to adjust my shoe, well away from his reach. He waited for me to stand then kissed me on the forehead, kindness in his touch. I leaned into it and let the moment linger before accepting the flowers from his hands.

Why I avoided him at times, I did not know. Even in the bed we shared I felt far away, as though he lay with someone else, not me. Rarely did I allow myself a kind of playful smile or flirting with my husband, a flutter to my eyes and tongue. The promised matrimonial bliss had not burst forth. Joe acted ill at ease when I stopped my mind from wondering and imagining, when I did experience pleasure in our time together. I didn't tell him, always dreading the flush of shame I knew would follow such an admission in the morning. We didn't speak of it, just let the disappointment seethe beneath the surface.

It must have been on one of those occasions that the child now growing beneath my heart had been conceived.

Joe had taken to wiping his glasses with his linen handkerchief when he had something to say, and the movement now reminded me of Dr. Campbell's toweling his fingers earlier in the day. I thought of announcing my husband's new status as a future father, but I wanted to keep the joy to myself, develop this relationship as I chose, feel his presence beneath my breast before any others knew of it.

"I've another present for you," Joe said putting his handkerchief back into his breast pocket. He took a moment to align it with the stitched top. "Would you like it now or later?"

"Depends," I said.

"Can't you just answer 'now or later,' Cassandra?"

"Now or later, Cassandra," I said.

"Here it is then." He yanked the package from beneath the bed and shoved it into my hand.

I could see by the size of the box that it would be nothing dainty. Perhaps a store-bought dress or fur piece. I didn't want to envision anything, didn't want to get hopeful, and yet I did. The image of elegance, something to wear around my neck, flashed to my mind. Maybe gold earrings or a cameo brooch. Joe was always saying my eyes were the color of pure amber, and I thought maybe he had secured some of the ancient resin, might have had a setting made. But so far he had kept to his pecuniary ways and had repeated little of the extravagance of San Francisco.

"It will add to the parlor," he said as I unwrapped the paper. A red velvet-covered photo book stared back.

"Those old photographs you had shipped will be ruined if they're not cared for properly. I had Grandmother send this from New York."

Disappointment must have filled my face.

"Not a gift to push your nose up at," he said. "Cost a fair bit to have it shipped too." He sounded angry, but I sensed something else.

I shrugged my shoulders.

"That's so unbecoming, Cassie," he said. He jerked the album from my hands, set it aside. "Christmas is just past. You were well remembered then. It's a quite practical gift we'll have need of with the baby coming."

I wasn't sure I heard him, but my heart had and my eyes reflected it.

"Dr. Campbell told me." Joe looked down his straight, pale nose at me. "It's his duty, Cassandra. I am the father and have a right to know. You should have told me straightaway. I imagine you've told your sister and mother?"

"No one," I whispered. "Just settling on the idea myself."

"Listen. You'll have to do what others tell you now. Without argue. It will be a new experience for you, Cassie. Set you on a woman's path. You've someone besides yourself to think of now."

I knew then that anger born in loss is nursed by loneliness and fed by empty dreams. I had no intention of putting this child at jeopardy, no wish to do anything but what my body would allow and what my dreams and hopes for it would warrant. For Joe to assume that this could only happen if I did as he said, be nothing but a doll others handled, was like being slapped with his hide glove into some cruel duel. A flush of feeling reeled into me, took away my breath.

"It's seven," Joe said, unaware of my ire. He opened the door, his tapping foot demanding that I walk through. "No tricks, Cassie. Time to begin your routine for the baby. Let's not be late for dinner."

TO WILL
A THING

❁

The sun shown often in March, flashing through the trees, unveiling the polishing needed on the windowpanes, sparkling against moisture left by fog clinging to exquisite spider webs. The paths beside the cedars that wove to the rivers and spotty lakes dried up enough to walk on. I took the occasion to go alone. I carried on conversations with the infant growing deep within me.

"Should we sail a bit? It's calm enough." Or, "Did you hear that rumble next to your head? Those kippered salmon stay for hours!"

I spoke of blooms and plantings as I saw them. I read out loud passages from the classics, and on Sundays, I concentrated on organ music drifting over the pews at the Methodist Church. This baby gave me someone to divide my moments with and the sense of always owning independence yet never feeling alone. I had never been so aware of myself, my movement, my breathing and skin. Each day promised novelty, and indulging in spiced pickles or frozen creams meant giving not just to myself but to others.

Joe had no idea I instructed my child. At night as my husband slept, one arm across my chest, I'd think thoughts of kindness for this child I carried, imagine his tiny fingers someday squeezing mine in recognition of our bond. I saw him as both strong and generous, a man who loved living and who would one day love a wife. I shared none of these musings with Joe who insisted that I stay inside, eat bland foods, leave Shiloh stabled, take no risks whatsoever.

"I may as well be dead," I said, slamming doors that brought the cook or my mother running to see what might have fallen from the plate shelf in the dining room when Joe made some correction to my plans.

I tried another strategy: I told Joe what he wished to hear. "I'll lie down. I'll take naps each day. Yes, rice cereal and wheat bread only, and I'll have Cook order more milk delivered."

If he'd presented these directions as concerns for me I might have followed them despite the discipline demanded. But he delivered them as edicts, requiring opposition. For him, I was a nest, an incubator like the kind city hospitals used for infants too anxious to face the world. So I told him what he wished, just to keep him quiet, then made my way outside to do exactly as I planned, exactly what I knew would fill me up.

The time spent in walking made me stronger. Or perhaps the increasing sunshine and longer days lightened my spirit. Or maybe it was my choice to stay on the paths and never enter the dark and arcing timber that could lure me into fast breathing and risk.

My hair grew thick and silky, my stomach steady. The whalebone corset that held my shape even when it stood on the floor was relegated to the closet. I felt better than I ever had, and I discounted Dr. Campbell's warning against my walking (to avoid tiring) or taking in fresh air (to avoid the croup), against socializing (to avoid cigar smoke or the coughs of others). I was to stay calm and quiet, avoid laughter that might strain my heart, and refrain from riding (which could damage the child). His orders bordered on ridiculous, and I suspected Joe told him what to say.

I continued to see the good doctor, despite his violation of my privacy that first time. Joe would hear of nothing less. But I held something back.

Dr. Campbell responded "Quite" to my assertions that all went well. I knew he and Joe spoke. I had plans of my own for this infant. And they were quite good plans at that.

I made my way to meet her on an afternoon when my mother napped, Margaret took a music lesson, and Joe left to tromp the watershed area that provided the power of his system. She was a Quinault, a woman well known for her gifts with labor and birth.

I'd secured her name from Beatrice.

"Oh, good idea, Cassie!" she said. We walked as though racing, back from a suffragette gathering I'd begun attending for the outing it provided. Our cheeks were rosy from the spring wind and the high level of excitement generated where women have found a common bond. A cab followed behind us and would drive me down the last street so Joe need never know how much I walked.

"Women are revered among the Quinault, you know," Beatrice said. "They have land wealth and hand it down to their children while their men bring in whales and salmon and such and make those beautiful carvings. You've seen them. Of birds and animals, on their houses and those adorable boats. But it's the women who decide things, plan the potlatches and give-aways and feasts. Their winters are full of partying," she said and sighed. She gathered the fox fur of her collar around her face. It muffled what she said next but she repeated it. "We could learn something from their arrange-ments, let me tell you."

"I'm interested in a midwife's skills," I told her, "not her social life."

Beatrice pouted then added, "She's quite good, though a bit unorthodox. But you can't argue with success. One of the skidder's wives had a trouble-some pregnancy some years back, and the baby decided to arrive in a snowstorm. A breech birth, it was. The woman bled and they couldn't get her to Dr. Campbell but sent for him while another boy ran to the village.

"Mary, the Quinault, came. She knew, somehow, that the breech position was worried by the cord wrapped around the baby's neck. She talked the woman into a deep sleep, if you can imagine being able to do that! Then she oiled her hands with eulachon oil." Beatrice held her gloved fingers together as though holding the tail of a fish. "From those little smelt, hanging over the baskets that collect the oil. They trade it. Used to be considered like gold." She wrinkled her nose. "Anyway, Mary reached inside. They say she pushed the baby back up, dislodged the cord and twisted the infant so his head was even right. Then she talked the woman awake, told her to push and *phsst!* Out he came."

"The mother lived?" I could see my breath in the cold night air.

She nodded. "Don't know what Mary did to stop the bleeding, but she did.

They named the boy Robert. He's that Hunt fellow you see about town. Oh, hear me tell! I shouldn't be speaking about problems with you still carrying!"

Images of a difficult birth were not what inspired me to seek out Mary, however. It was wanting to rule what happened inside of me that made me seek experience, though the picture of an almost-strangled child grown into a lunatic man carried incentive for caution too.

A good midwife worked well for having the baby on my terms. I would deliver during the day, when no one was home except the cook and me. I had willed the arrangements, planned them in my thoughts. I believed I could make it so, was seeing the world with clear eyes. When the pains began, I would suggest Mama take a nap if she was home and send the cook for Beatrice who would gather up the Quinault woman. I had such plans!

If I liked the Indian woman, I'd share my secret with her. I'd know when I met her.

I had gone alone.

Faces of several children gazed down at me from the narrow walkways set above steps as straight as a ladder. Standing straight and still like dock pilings, they'd been watching me approach along the beach. I'd stepped over clamshells and pebbles, hiking my skirts up to slide over driftwood logs tossed there by high tides. Behind the village, the shoreline firs speared into the sky and looked like charcoal etchings drawn against gray. With the back of my hand, I wiped my eyes of the wood smoke hovering in a windless bay.

Closer, I wove myself between slender dugouts secured to steps leading to the cedar lodges set well above the shore. The bay's water lapped against the sand. A dog barked somewhere behind the lodges.

In front of me, eyes looking down, gathered the children, and they stood so solemn I was almost afraid to speak.

"I'm looking for the woman, Mary," I said to no response. "She takes care of babies." From my stomach I made an exaggerated mound into the air with my hand. One child giggled at that and pointed behind her. I couldn't see what she directed me toward as I stood too low on the beach, so I scraped my smooth soles on the steps to leave behind the mud and began to climb the ladder.

The children moved back as my eyes lifted over the edge. I saw then the sign the child pointed to, printed in English on the side of a cedar house. "Cheap," it read.

It wasn't what I had in mind, but I decided the English word would better lead me to Mary than would these somber children, and so I went inside. One or two of them followed me in. The others scampered into timber.

The air proved smoky from the fires, and a series of quick sneezes announced my arrival.

"Blackberry tea will do you some good," an old woman said, her voice rising at the word *you*. "Want some?"

She stood behind a counter formed from a single split log, her arms slender, her elbows tight against her bulb-shaped frame. Her skin was the color of copper and looked as smooth.

"Is that what's so cheap?" I asked, dabbing at my nose with my lace hanky I then slipped up my sleeve.

"Ya," she said. "Lots of cheap things for sale here. Make you a deal on those." She nodded with her chin to the group of men lounging beside a table dwarfed by the cavernous room.

They moaned in mock woundedness.

"I'd rather take my chances on the tea," I said and laid my bag on a counter as smooth as a piano key.

"Good decision," the woman said and laughed. She turned her back to arrange the tea, and I saw that she wore her black hair in a smooth twist wrapped with a tawny strip of deerskin around her head.

I lifted my bustle over the stump stool and sidled up to the rounded side of the log counter that still bore smooth remnants of bark. My legs dangled without touching the floor.

Behind the bar, boxes stacked and leaned beside tins of food with faded labels. The building must have served as part of a trading post at one time which explained the "cheap" sign. As my eyes cleared, I noticed dogs snoozing, too, and a few more men playing cards. Most were round-faced and short. They all stared, waiting for me to make my request again, I suspected.

"Mary is not here now." The old woman motioned with her chin to one of the children who disappeared outside. "She comes back later. You can wait?"

I said I could and did, finding the experience fascinating. A couple of the men sat at crude tables carving and smoking their pipes. Elk hides and heads lined the walls along with baskets and oars, an old faded print of a seascape, and a hodgepodge of saws and nets, fishing rods and wedges. The walls wore a mixture of native world and white.

"This would make a good place for billiards," I told the woman as I looked around.

She laughed. "Who wants to sit around and watch the big behinds of old men leaning over tables? Young men, maybe," she said and laughed again, a big deep rumble that rose up from her round belly. She served my tea in a china cup. "But all of them are taken or at sea."

"What about the winter?"

"Ya, ya," she said sounding like a good German. "They're around then, but we sit and tell stories and fix harpoons and nets and weave baskets. Wouldn't be no place for that with a billiard table."

"Not even for a women's billiard room?" I asked.

She cocked her head at me and squinted into my face. "Haven't heard of that kind. You got some strange ideas."

She spoke with familiar in her voice, and I liked it and asked her name. "Melody," she said and laughed again as though she knew well its meaning.

"That doesn't sound Siwash," I said, using a term Joe said meant all Indian people. The laughter stopped along with her jolly goodwill.

"That word is not spoken here," she said.

I would have defended myself for my ignorance, but the door opened and a woman no taller than me and twice as round entered followed by the child I'd seen at the steps. The round woman walked straight up to me, her print dress a straight line from shoulder to the floor, her hair a thin twist woven with colored cloth. She did not smile, and I worried that she had heard my unintentional insult. Instead she stopped in front of me and spoke.

"You have a baby coming."

It was not a question and she did not seem embarrassed about mentioning my condition in front of the others.

"Yes, summer. August."

She startled me then by lifting my fingers cupped at my mouth. She shoved my dress sleeve up with one hand, knocking the lace hanky onto the floor. Her fingers rested now on the inside of my wrist, warm fingers cradling me in gentle strength. Mary lowered her head to my chest and held me on the stump, her ear to my heart. The center part of her dark hair was straight as a fir tree. She listened a long time.

"Did she fall asleep?" I asked Melody with a lightness I didn't feel. "Maybe she's too old."

"Hush!" Mary said but did not raise her head.

I began to fidget and wonder when this interview had become hers to give instead of mine.

Mary raised her head. Her eyes were dark and shiny like pebbles in a stream. I thought they carried clarity.

"You must eat no more red meat nor even look at it," she said, "or risk your baby."

"That's ridiculous," I said pulling my hand from hers. "Superstition. The kind of thing my mother might tell me."

I was surprised that Beatrice would have spoken so highly of someone so primitive in her thinking. I started to gather up my wrist purse, disappointed.

Melody reached for my arm. "You wait," she said. "Mary is good for you."

"You do not do well," Mary said staring into my eyes.

"I've never been stronger," I defended. "I need someone who will agree to come when sent for, if they're good enough, and can help deliver a baby." I snipped out my words. "I expect no trouble whatsoever, and it will be in the morning."

"You got some strange ideas," Melody said again. "No baby comes like that, not even to a white woman who plans everything."

"Mary's good enough," Mary said. Her voice sounded like gravel pushed by water. "But sorrow, for your infant, is written in your heart-sounds so you must be careful."

"Dr. Campbell told you that, didn't he!" I said.

"No one tells me nothin', but you."

"Just say yes or no, then." I slipped off the stump to find myself eye to eye. Her gaze went through me, as though peering to my soul.

This encounter felt lost to my planning, lost to my rules, and I made a feeble effort to regain command. "Can you deliver my baby? Will you come when I call or not?"

"I would come," she said. "But you will not call."

The unsettling I felt as I headed for the plank door came not from concern about my health nor even from questions about Mary's ability. No, it was my fear of Joe and Dr. Campbell. That they had the ability to touch me even in this village, become part of a plan I'd just formed myself, proved terrifying to a woman wanting to chart her days. Even when I did not know who I might take into my confidence, they had reached here, touched Mary, before I even arrived. They must have spoken with her. How else could she know?

"I'll call when I need you," I said, "if you're as skilled as they say."

"She's good," Melody said. The others nodded agreement, mumbling, and I realized everyone there assumed they belonged to this conversation as though we were all gathered about a family table.

"Just give me directions so I know where to send for you when the time comes. I don't want to have someone running about trying to find you. And keep Wednesdays open."

Melody laughed. "You come back. Maybe I get a billiard table for you," she shouted as I pushed through the door to the outside and sneezed.

But Mary's part became irrelevant when Joe announced a few days later that he would hire a live-in nurse to be with me until the baby came.

My mother thought it wonderfully generous. Margaret cooed with the devotion such charity showed. But I knew what lay behind it: Joe's wish to control all of me, make sure he knew what would happen every moment, keep me quiet and thirsting, controlling even what happened inside.

"I have the name of a nurse," I told him when I realized he would not be talked out of a guard.

"Not some loon-brain Beatrice has put you on to? Not necessary for you to worry your pretty head about this, Cassie. William has contacts. We'll take care of it."

"Where were you born?" I asked Joe later that evening.

Margaret looked up from her book, like a cat alert to danger.

"All Stearnses have been born at Grandmother's," he said. He folded *The Washingtonian* and pressed the paper's creases perfectly with his fingers. Then he picked up his pipe.

"In New York?"

He nodded, tapped the pipe bowl in the ashtray, and wiped the tobacco on the tray's edge with his finger.

"I suppose that's an important tradition."

"Same four-poster bed my grandfather arrived in. Shipped from London." He sucked on the pipestem and appeared lost in thought until he caught the look on my face.

"Now listen. Dr. Campbell's a fine man, quite skilled with difficult pregnancies. Don't fancy any wild ideas, Cassandra."

"Does seem a bit wild here. Wouldn't I do better back East, with all those fine hospitals? And for a Stearns to be born where they always have been?"

I picked up the stereopticon as though interested. My hand shook a bit and I laid the viewer down. My fingers drifted to my face.

Joe stared but did not answer. I took it as a good sign.

I asked Dr. Campbell about it the next day in my effort to create an ally.

"No," he said. "Trip wouldn't be good for you."

"But it's early enough. And on board ship or even on the train all I'd do is lie around. We'll be there in but a few days, really." I flashed my eyes at him. "I'm young. Taken good care of myself, just as you and Joe told me to do. You don't really see any signs of trouble, do you?"

"Irregular rhythm concerns me. Some clouding sounds."

"But can't that happen with any pregnant woman? Of course our bodies sound differently. There's another being inside scraping their shoes on the mat."

He laughed then said, "Quite."

"You don't have to say my going back would be a wise idea, though eastern hospitals do have some advantages, like those incubators. Just don't tell Joe that my going would be bad. That's all I ask."

He looked at me, maybe for the first time seeing me not as J. O. Stearns's wife but as a young woman awaiting her first child.

"I won't risk the baby. I won't."

"You'd never forgive yourself if you did," he said. "And neither would Joe." His fingers moved up and down along the beadwork of his stethoscope. "All right, I won't say it will harm you, but that's quite as far as I'll go."

"Listen to me!" The force of Joe's words made me take a step back. "I forbid it!" We prepared for bed that evening.

"Sh-h-h. It's all arranged," I said. "I'm going east to stay with your grandmother and have my baby where all Stearnses have their babies."

"What if your condition worsens while you're en route? No, I won't have it." His wide forehead was grimaced in frustration. He pulled coins and pencils from his pocket and knuckled them into the handkerchief drawers.

"It's not a 'condition,'" I said, turning my back to him to fluff the pillows. "I'm pregnant, not ill." My heart pounded telling me how much I wanted what I'd said I'd do.

"Dr. Campbell's worried about your chest sounds." He spoke with parental disgust in his voice, as though tired of always having to instruct me.

"Dr. Campbell knows the hospital has wonderful advantages and the trip will relax me." I turned to watch him.

"Grandmother's too old to look after you," he said.

"I'll take a nurse. Isn't that what you wanted?"

He shook his head and I could see my firmness had rattled him. That and perhaps his own uncertainty about the medical care promised in Hoquiam.

"Out of the question."

"The way to prevent this, Joe, is to lock me up." I swung my arm to take in the room. "Which you won't be able to do. Imagine the strain that would place on the heart you're so worried about. And what would people say if they heard that the secretary of the utility has jailed his young wife?"

"You're being a child."

I felt the heat rush to my cheeks. "As you still treat me."

"If you behaved more as an adult, I'd take great pleasure in treating you as one. Your self-centeredness gets in the way." His mouth was a rigid line, his mustache thin and sharp as a knife slice.

"I'm selfish? What about you?"

"This is nothing to squabble about, Cassandra." Joe was pacing now, hands clasped behind his back. "You simply will not return east, and that's the end of it." His voice was steady and low. "I can't believe you'd risk your own child."

"I will not risk my child," I said, my voice raised. I knew Margaret would hear me; Mama too.

I felt as if I leaned over a fire of hot coals.

"I've some work to do in the shop," he said and walked to the door.

"I promise to take care of myself. I'll do what Dr. Campbell asks and the other doctors when I reach New York. But I'm doing this. Please, Joe, don't make it worse."

He continued to hesitate at the door.

"Must I have your approval even for what happens inside of me? Is your contempt for me so great you think I'd injure our son?"

Joe's face wore a mixture of scowl and pain. He shook his head slightly.

"He'll be healthier if I'm happy."

"You wear me down, Cassie."

"And we'll come back in the fall, baby and me." I could be generous now, tasting victory. "The next generation of Stearnses born in New York will come back ready to settle forever in Washington State."

He shook his head, but I saw resignation in his face.

In the end, it was my appeal to tradition that won him I believe, that and my assurance of good health. I never spoke a word about the breathlessness I sometimes felt as I walked and now, as I packed. I never let on to anyone how tired I felt or how unsettled I'd become by Mary's ear resting on my chest and the things it told her. Perhaps I did not wish to acknowledge those alarms even to myself.

And I did set out for New York in April, but I did not go alone. Why Joe and my mother felt an inexperienced eighteen-year-old was capable of caring for her older sister was beyond my comprehension. I didn't need caring for, I could manage on my own.

But somewhere in the days that followed, my body made my mind up for me, and I accepted their demands, too tired and too uncertain to resist it.

My stomach had been acting like a sea invaded every time I ate. A burning my mother called "heartburn" latched itself beneath my breast so that food that did act tasty at first bite soon burned and I had to wait between swallows to make sure each stayed down. Red meat set my stomach to flutter. And my legs ached behind the knees so that I woke crying the night before we were set to leave.

Joe rubbed my legs with his smooth hands. He didn't speak, and I fell back to sleep amazed both by the relief his hands brought me and by my husband's willingness to give it free of a rebuke.

I determined to negotiate with Margaret as soon as we boarded the ship in April, discussing with her the conditions of the trip. I was quite sure my sister would honor reason and conviction.

"You've *promised* you'd be careful," Margaret said, "but you know how you *are*. Sometimes—"

"I'll be careful. But I want to do this my way. It's my baby, my body, my adventure."

"You take such *risks*, Cassie. I worry over your choices. I'm not sure you think things through. Remember that time when—"

"Think what you want, just don't interfere."

She was quiet as we packed the trunks. "All right. But if I think you're doing something you ought not to, I have the right to speak of it at least, without your fussing at my mention of it. Agreed?"

"Sounds reasonable," I said.

"And you'll give my suggestions serious thought?"

"If you don't offer too many and none erode fun."

We boarded the train in Los Angeles with our truce intact, and so the trip back became a time I felt as though my child belonged to me. I made all the decisions for us, about what to eat, who I would let join us in the dining car, what time we would sleep. At Margaret's mention of it, I agreed to keep my voice quiet when I spoke with her and resisted all my usual efforts to argue. As the scenery passed by, I forced myself, as Margaret suggested, to see it in my mind as vast and varied instead of limited and brown. When Margaret gave me more information about a subject than what I wanted, I simply smiled at her as facts tripped from her tongue. Only good thoughts entered my head, only ideas worthy of the loftiness of a child. I even read the Scriptures, something I'd set aside some months ago, and this time tried to understand them. (It was that decision, I believe, that let Margaret truly trust me.)

I did wonder once or twice about my mother, what her pregnancies had been like; and what kind of mother would have agreed to let us go away without her, what would have kept her from saying she would travel with us, too, instead of deciding to continue to manage her daughter's husband's home? I stopped those thoughts and others that condemned me for my passivity in allowing Margaret to come along and intrude.

The child was a "he," I felt sure of it. I wondered if others could sense that it was a boy I carried. Strong and purposeful movements led me to that conclusion. He liked strong tastes, to be cool at night. He carried a will of his own. I couldn't imagine a girl-child kicking my ribs with such force to make me gasp. I had thought a girl would be pleasant, would be more understood by me, my having preceded her with emotion and wish. But my own mother's experience as a girl before me had not allowed her to raise me with more wisdom than my father's. So I decided a boy would be easier to be with. It was a restful thought, this carrying and planning for a boy.

He responded to my control, my boy did. He moved or settled depending on my conversations and my mood. I continued to read out loud to him, to the occasional consternation of those sharing the car. My baby would quiet as I eased my comforter around me. I felt him rock into his pool of water and just float as though both our thoughts were carried on soft breezes across the bay. By day, he swirled within me, resisted the corset that bound us tight for the trip; at night, he floated upward, a stretch of thin skin and pale chemise all that separated our beating hearts.

I took him with me everywhere the porters on the train allowed us. Of course, I did not show much yet, still had a waist to speak of, just looked like a fuller woman. I noticed one or two men smile deep at me in the dining car. On one occasion, a traveler even had a red alpine rose sent to our table, and we were asked if we would mind his company at dinner. Margaret gave me her arched eyebrow but did not argue with my decision to let a businessman, a father of three, he told us, share a meal and laughter. I was disappointed that he knew nothing of the flower he'd given me, had just bought it for a pittance for its intense red beauty from an old crone at a recent stop.

Once a man expressed curiosity about the two of us traveling as we were, without companion. Sometimes Margaret would clarify with, "this is my sister, Missus J. O. Stearns," as though the name should mean something to them. Or perhaps it was her way to say that I was married and thus independent enough to travel on my own, but also already taken.

She was a tall woman, Joe's grandmother, with hair the color of cotton puffs and a scalp as pink as fresh shrimp. She had a poodle's quick movements and intelligence, a guard dog's ready scent for danger. Her household staff adored her, a sign of both her fairness and a care that cut across class.

She'd been ready for our arrival, telegrams and letters having preceded our journey, and acted as though our presence was a gift rather than an intrusion. Her maids held kind and willing hands.

At first, I found I did not need much help. The Stearnses' estate was large and promised interesting places to which I could walk and keep myself quite active. I made calls on one or two of my old school chums, had a joyous reunion with Annie. With an old beau and his sister, we drove out for an afternoon.

Margaret busied herself with the Stearnses' library tucked away on the third floor. She kept up her journal and wrote long letters back to Mama and Joe when she wasn't chatting with Joe's grandmother or the household help. In all, it was a quiet time, the lull just before water boils.

"You're just carrying high, dear," Grandmother Stearns said one morning in June.

"What does that mean, Granny?" Margaret asked.

Margaret straightened the woman's lacy collar that draped over her narrow shoulders as she stood behind her. We sat in the living room with the east sun and a view of reflecting pools and flowers through the french doors. Margaret walked in front then, so she could both see and hear Granny's answer.

"It's a girl," Mrs. Stearns added without argument.

"You can really tell that?" Margaret asked. "Just by looking?" She squatted in front of her to reach a harmonica she handed to the elder Mrs. Stearns, the instrument a contradiction in this dowager's hand. Margaret had taken to Joe's mother as though she were her blood grandmother.

"Oh, my yes," the woman said. "Been wrong only once these many years."

"Wrong this time," I said.

"Cassie's so lucky to have you, in case anything goes poorly."

"Why should that matter?" I asked. "About how high the baby is?"

I crossed my arms on the shelf of my body as I lay on the daybed. Through the narrow door-windows I watched gardeners clipping fragrant roses, snipping at box hedges, bracing up gladioli, and cutting hydrangeas with blooms as large as babies' heads. A sweltering heat hovered above the brick walkway, rising like heat waves above a cookstove.

"Something about the way they fit themselves inside," Mrs. Stearns said. "High ones are usually smaller, too, so they slip right out." She breathed into the harmonica and ran down the scale holding the last note in celebration.

"'Quite right' about that," I said in perfect imitation of Dr. Campbell. Margaret laughed and started tapping her slipper to Mrs. Stearns's tunes.

Friends returned invitations through the month, and Annie and I often laughed and chattered long into the night.

"I think you should rest more, Cass," Margaret warned one evening before Annie arrived. "You're looking tired."

"Oh misery," I said. "It's the only fun I have. Surely my boy loves a good time!"

And even the Lady Margaret joined in the mirth that evening as my stories of the West brought tears of laughter to Annie's eyes.

"Is it as wonderful as Congressman Roosevelt made it sound?" she asked. "With vast open spaces and men who tame the elements?"

"Not our West," I told her. "It's dense and timbered with streams and seeps that make everything dark and wet. I suppose those woods are being harnessed. But they're not like our trees, Annie. They're huge and soaring. They keep a person confined inside. The ocean has the expansiveness you're looking for, not the land. Maybe you should come with us when we go back, see for yourself."

"Truly?" she said. She ran her fingers through her red hair. "You're such a star, Cass, such a star for me to attach myself to."

But by mid-June, my star had fallen, and I found I needed help with my swollen ankles, puffed eyes, and labored breathing. And by the Fourth of July, the very reasons I had given Joe for our being here—spoken just to get my way—had now come to pass.

Something was very wrong, even though I rested, even though I willed myself to find no alarm in anything, ate with care and mostly read and slept. Still, my heart raced and my head pounded and my faced puffed up like a dumpling. The elder Mrs. Stearns rushed me by carriage to the hospital where the doctor said I must remain unless I promised to go home and stay in bed.

I agreed.

But on July 11, in the middle of the hot spell no one could recall as worse or lasting longer in Corning's history, I would have given up all future joy for an infant who slipped out easily.

It had begun the day before with a weeping of my body, a slow seeping I did not recognize as signaling the beginning of my separation from this infant or the arrival of great pain.

Granny and Margaret were both out. I felt better than I had in days. I dressed and took a short walk around the garden speaking with the groundskeeper. It was when I bent to pick a rose the wetness came, not enough to worry over as I'd been aware of something like it two or three days before. But the gardener stopped midsentence, took my elbow, and turned me toward the house, his calloused fingers firm against my sleeve.

"Looking pale, Missus," he said and rapped alarm against the estate's front door. I knew something was wrong or he never would have approached that entrance.

And while the wetness persisted throughout the day, even while I rested, I found it annoying, not a sign. When Margaret and Mrs. Stearns returned they found me sound asleep.

Even in the night, when my stomach cramped, I thought it due to indigestion. But in the morning, I curled myself around my bulging stomach. Short gasps punctuated my breathing; sweat beaded on my forehead. "Margaret," I gasped, "call Granny."

"Still no water?" the woman asked. "The bag hasn't broken?"

"None to speak of." I panted, words rushed out in between gasps of pain. "It's just the sausage I ate," I said. "He doesn't like pork, I guess," and held myself against a wave of ache.

"*She* doesn't," Margaret corrected.

A spasm of pain shot against my chest.

"Best we get the doctor," Granny said and swirled from the room to do just that.

They hovered about me in the gaslight. The doctor palpated and pressed despite the gasps of choked pain his touch induced.

"And you've had no gush of water?" he said standing back to run his hand across the back of his neck.

"I'm leaking like a glass eye," I panted.

"How long?"

"Three, maybe four days." I felt myself begin to cry with the effort of talking and warding off torture, holding my stomach, seeing his eyes search for answers.

"And you've stayed resting?"

I hesitated. Margaret gasped.

"It was nothing. Just a walk. In the garden."

"Oh, Cass," she said, "how *could* you?" Then she bit her lip.

"Time we took her," the doctor said. "Like some help at hand what with that heart. Anesthesia could be ticklish."

My body offered nothing that promised anything so lovely as a tickle.

After hours of thrusts of pain that ran one into the other like a sea of knives sliced through me, they did risk the ether. I sank back, my head spinning from one end of the bed I laid on to the other, descending deep and fast until I was no different than the fluid my baby wallowed in. Then like a freshet flooding through a timbered ridge, I rushed and rushed until I disappeared inside the deepest, darkest pit.

CHAPTER 7

VOYAGE

Faces hovered over me accented by worried eyes that did nothing to stop the suffering raging through my frame.

"Cassie!" Margaret said, her face pinched over me. "Can you see me? Are you all right?"

I tried to respond, tell them something, but I drifted.

"She's all right, isn't she?" Margaret spoke to Granny. The older woman sniffled, and then I disappeared again as though drowning under sharp petals flaked off smooth rock.

Sounds intruded, an occasional smell but mostly when I awoke, pain stayed. How many days had passed this way I neither knew nor cared to. One day I felt the need to hurry back. I willed myself to speak.

"Baby?" I said.

Granny started from the chair she dozed in.

"Baby's fine, dear. Just fine! Margaret! Your sister's back!" She lifted my head to sip from the china cup. "Oh, thank you, thank you" she said, and patted my hand, the lace at the base of her sleeves tickling my temple.

"Baby was as white and chalky as a snail," she said, "but she wailed good with a slap, like they all do."

If that was true, that my baby'd arrived, I couldn't understand why my body still ached with stabbing pain, my heart pounding, wrapping me in anguish.

"I've had him then?"

"Your baby's a *girl*," Margaret said rushing in and leaning close to me. "With the softest blond fuzz for hair. Like goose down."

"I hurt so," I said, my mouth so dry.

"Course you do. It's the stitches," Granny said, patting my hand. "We'll open the windows now, get you fresh air. You'll be better in a day or two."

But they didn't understand. The pain was in my chest as well, too high for stitches, and all through my breast and ribs and well into my abdomen and stomach. Even in my legs.

"Don't you want to see her?" Margaret asked.

"Her?"

"She was born on the twelfth. She's beautiful. What *will* you name her? Lucy? From your middle name? Maybe Ann, after Mama?"

Name her? This girl-child who'd arrived on a train of betrayal and pain? I didn't have the strength, perhaps not even the care.

"You do it," I told Margaret. "You pick a name." I sank back into my dark swirling world of distance and deep pain.

July 31, 1892

Dear Joe,

Hopefully you have received the wire sent some days past to announce the arrival on 12 July of your first daughter, Isabelle. She is a child of some substance with Stearns hair, blue eyes, and strong will. (She bears no resemblance to me in these areas!) Her arrival came attached to distress, and the physician was obliged to take her from me by cesarean section, an event I would not advise for the weak or fainthearted, both of which I apparently am.

Suffering I've come to believe is a part of life though your grandmother has been most kind in assailing it by bringing Marjorie here, a stout Ojibwa woman who nurses Isabelle. Margaret, too, has been a gift. I have been pleased for her presence. While it pains me to admit this, you were right to have her join me. She writes this letter as I have been too weak of late, but I trust she is not putting words into it other than my own.

Are you still announcing steam delays? Have you harnessed more water? Where is the nearest trough, or do you remember that conversation? The weather has been beastly hot.

Our return is not yet determined. The delivering physician advises waiting until I have regained some strength, a directive I feel compelled to follow as I have no reserves with which to argue (you may be pleased to know!) though doing anything a medical man recommends bears some forbearance on my part. I find them somewhat barbaric in their tactics.

Please greet our mother and share with her the news of her new status.

With fondness I remain,
Cassie H. Stearns

My child had seven days of loving from my sister before I even heard her name. I nourished her before then, they told me, though it was a gray memory.

The nurses extracted milk from my breasts with a pump, as though I were a cow with those new milk contraptions. They commented each time at how uncooperative my body was, how "selfish," giving so little milk to my needy child.

They said it as in humor, but it brought no joy to the ache I settled into. And while I was grateful to have some small pressure taken from my body, I was mortified by the process that treated me like carrion, resentful of the intrusion and reminder that others ruled my flesh.

So when I first felt the tiny warm form against my breast, first brushed my hand across the down of her head, kissed the fingertips no larger than a tear, I felt ambivalence, too: strength from her yet so inadequate for the task.

"You'll take to it, Cass," Margaret said. She lifted the now wailing child from my chest after another disastrous attempt to nurse. "Nurses say it's a natural thing. Some take more time than others." Margaret had not a hair out of place, all piled on top her head in twists held tight by abalone combs.

I did yearn to see the baby's tiny mouth gain strength from what I had to give, just as she had for months inside me without effort. But she was not what I expected, and my body did not belong to me now, but to some strange and distant seventh sense I did not recognize. Her delivery had taken all power and will and left me just enough to raise my head to see her in the wicker basket set beside my bed. It was as if the very sap that made my blood run had clogged somewhere beneath my heart.

When my milk dried and they no longer brought her to me for pathetic attempts at nurturing, the same vacillating fog consumed me. My child had made such effort to slip her lips on me, a skin touch to her cheek resulting in the root and nibble of hoped for success. I wanted her to have success. It was my first and best intention for her.

But I was grateful to be forced no longer to watch her work herself into a frenzy, grasping for unanswered response at my breast.

Mrs. Stearns secured the wet nurse. The woman brought her own new-born, and she fed both her boy and Isabelle.

She was an Ojibwa woman, from the lakes region farther west. Marjorie, she said her name was, and her baby's father had been the gardener whose hands had helped me from the box hedges just days before the birth.

She stood tall and healthy after her delivery handled at home. Her words had a whistling sound and her speech was reminiscent of the maids of southern travelers I'd encountered on the train. She soothed me, made me believe I had done what I could for my child and needed now to swim through the malaise back to health.

"We all different," she assured me. She had a baby at each breast and rocked against the thick carpet in my upstairs room. I could see her well, propped as I was on white linen pillows braced beneath a mahogany-held canopy. "Mustn't worry yourself none 'bout that. You soon be well and your ba-bee drinking kid's milk. You can feed her sure, then, like a mother should."

But as the weeks wore on and my strength waned like a melody played against a December wind, it was Margaret who began holding and feeding the baby she had named, Margaret who blew on her belly to bring about giggles, who talked to her, showed her the world, Margaret who listened to her soul.

With insufficient vigor to even wander about the house, I allowed myself to appreciate Margaret's effort. Instead of being envious or angry, I took to daydreaming and imagined myself whole again, wondering where my life would take me now, just twenty-one and having survived the tribulations of a difficult delivery. Maybe in the arms of Joe dancing to a stringed quartet. Not Joe, not dancing. Joe preferred his tinkering with gadgets and cameras and miniature trains.

I dreamed of riding when I was well, maybe with Joe. Not Joe, who didn't like horses nor have the time. Maybe with Belle. Yes, we'd take pony rides together, find a thing of joy to share.

Thoughts of Hoquiam brought back the house, how I'd arrange a room for Belle. Perhaps I'd refurnish all the rooms, something to look forward to, something to consume me once we came back home.

After recovering from the restriction my body placed on me, I even imagined Joe greeting us at the dock, sweeping me into his chest, holding me close and my responding, grateful for his presence and his patience. He would reach for Isabelle only after he had secured me in his arms. Then he'd hold us both, the strength of his grip releasing the bow beneath my chin and setting the ribbon to the wind—my hat, too, but for the pearl pin from Mother to hold it secure. He'd hold me alone, then swirl me, be the genesis of longed-for passion, and I'd feel the thrill of love through touch and sweet-tasting kisses of my husband. Margaret looked up from her book at my sigh.

September 12, 1892

My Dearest Cassie,

Grandmother writes that you have been too ill to dictate or pen of late. I have suggested she take you to New York City to University Hospitals to see if they can find a cure there. You are well advised to take advantage of their medical understandings. Please be obedient in this. You should also be drinking spring water and not tiring yourself.

Thank Margaret, please, for sending the baby's hair snip. It truly is like dandelion down. Margaret's words of encouragement are appreciated. She is a fine sister to us. I am pleased our daughter sleeps almost through the night and tolerates goat's milk well. It is a sign of her good sense, a requirement for a Stearns child.

My work continues with some new angles. I have brokered some sections, and we will reap the benefit. The plants have not done well without your touch. I threw the cacti out myself as they became so scraggly and never bloomed.

Your mother is in good health. She has taken up an interest in clocks. If you come upon one that chimes, you might pick it up to please her.

I have begun working evenings in my machine shop on a model steam engine complete with all the tiny parts.

You should plan to return by Christmas. I have booked passage for a December arrival and will look forward to greeting you then.

Your husband,
Josiah O. Stearns

I would like to say that I remembered the first months of my child's life in great detail, the way mothers do, by writing down their first smiles, first choice to move, first signs of independence. But I do not. This gap of memory did not make me love her less; in fact, I loved her all the more for becoming a person on her own, so early separate from myself.

And she needed to be separate. No child should be attached to a sinking mother, one wearing out just to breathe, which is how the spring months found me despite my efforts to the contrary, my mind filled with fantasies I thought would make me well. Hours ran into days that ran into weeks that all seemed the same except for the changes I could see in Belle. She became my clock marking the passage of time.

"I want you to just snap out of this, this *doldrums* you've put yourself into," Margaret told me as she walked back and forth, Belle asleep on her shoulder. "You've a wonderful child. A good life waiting you. Marjorie says lots of women have post-baby blues but they *recover*, they come out of it. The doctors say the infection is gone by now."

"You don't understand," I said and turned my face into the pillow. How could she? I didn't understand myself.

We did not return to Hoquiam for Christmas. Instead, I began taking small walks around the grounds. I imagined a time when I'd feel strong again, to plan a party or two, orchestrate a glittering evening of laughter and good friends. Not that I had many friends, I acknowledged, though I had a fair share of acquaintances in Corning. It took patience, compassion, and some wisdom to develop lasting friendships, something my mother would have said I didn't have much "a'tall of." But I could gather people to me for conversation and merriment. I was good at gathering. In New York, people gathered to coo at Belle and watch her make bubbles between hiding her face in Margaret's blouse. Belle was the attraction, even for Annie, I suspected when she came to call and cuddled Belle in her arms.

"You have a beautiful daughter," Annie said. She had stopped by to attend church with Granny, Margaret, and Belle.

"It'll be her curse," I said.

"Oh la! Your life hasn't been so terrible," Annie said. "You—"

"I'll be glad when you feel up to church," Margaret interrupted. She pulled white stockings onto Belle's chubby legs. "An Easter message could lift you."

"We're filled by different things, Margaret," I said and wondered to myself what could fill me up.

"The music then. They're singing Handel's *Messiah*. You always enjoy hearing the trumpets." She stuffed Belle's little arms into her spring dress, tied the satin ribbon around her middle. A flat-brimmed straw hat completed the ensemble.

"Nice to see you're exposing my daughter to music," I said.

Margaret smoothed Belle's dress that fluffed over her arm giving Belle an opportunity to pull on her aunt's earring. I winced for my sister, but she gently replaced the earring with her finger that Belle now gripped and gummed.

"Doesn't that hurt?" I asked.

"It's nothing," Margaret said. "Natural thing while she's teething. You're not the only one in pain, Cass. Those who love you and see you disappearing and don't know how to help, we hurt, too, wanting to make it better. I'd like nothing more than to see you up and partying if that's what it takes, though I wish being with your daughter was enough."

Belle reached out to touch the dampness at Margaret's eyes, a gesture that turned Margaret to the door Annie held open. When I said nothing to stop them, those who loved me best, left.

I had a telegram sent to Joe just after Easter, and when my daughter was ten months old, Joe traveled back to take us home. I imagined him sweeping into the room with a flowing cape, brushing his blond hair back behind his ears while rushing to lift me to him. His mustache would be thick and full, his shoulders filled out and firm. He would smell of Cuban cigars and leave a fleck of tobacco on my tongue when he kissed me.

Instead, he eased through the door and wore a shocked look.

He found me lounging on a wicker chaise in an upstairs bedroom, a thin shadow of what I'd been, with skin as pasty and pale as unbaked bread. His blue-green eyes held wary warmth, as though uncertain if the woman who sat before him could really be his once vivacious wife.

He paused. Robins chirped against the summer midday. Bees swarmed about the lilacs blooming just outside my view.

When he knelt beside me, smelling of cologne, he lowered his head to my chest. His blond hair exposed a thinning patch at the back.

"Grandmother said you were improving," he whispered. "I had no idea you were so down. I, that is…" He cleared his throat and looked at me.

"It's all right," I said, for once generous and forgiving.

"I thought you were being dramatic in what you had Margaret write. I…"

Fatigue still had its way with me, but I had enough energy to move my fingers through his hair, then to stroke his cheek. The mustache had disappeared and he had distinctive lines around his eyes and even at his ears. He looked older than I'd remembered. "They said it was a virus. Miserable thing affected my heart."

"I should have come sooner," he said.

"Nothing to do for it." I shrugged my shoulders.

"Don't, Cassie," he said, looking at me. "You must not minimize things, especially important things. It makes it worse."

"Have you seen Belle?" I said, hoping he hadn't gone to the nursery first.

"I have." His voice became lighter. "She's quite active. And beautiful, like her mother."

"Really? Acts a bit shy to me. Like her mother, too, I suppose."

"That, you could minimize," he said, "though I'll be glad to have you both back just the way you are."

Something arrived with his words that comforted me, and for the first time, though it was not the romance of my dreams, I was pleased to have him with me, ready to gain strength from what he offered and if all went well, to fill me up. It was not the sufficiency I thirsted for, but it promised to drive boredom off and thus held merit.

A kind of hesitation followed. I sensed Joe wished to say something more. I wanted him to say something more. I almost spoke to him of what mattered, of what I thought I could give and what I believed I needed to survive, the passion and the pleasure.

That I found no words to bridge the awkwardness marked the trail I'd later take.

Joe remained silent, still a man who wore his feelings held to his chest as though they were a hand of cards instead of pathways through one's breast.

I believed he wished to have us back, and more, that I'd be pleased to be there. The thought felt warm wrapped around me, and I sank for the moment into the comfort of his arms. I could settle for what he offered. I could control the fire within that made me want to spread my arms and swirl into the riptide of my life. I would recover fully and make this gift of joy my husband offered last forever, wrapped up in family reunion.

We waved our good-byes to the wet nurse and Grandmother while the porters loaded our trunks of little clothes and shoes and photographs of our time in New York. Margaret lingered with hugs to Marjorie and her boy, to Granny and the maids and cooks. Annie's trunks too. Several had been sent on ahead. Her face was flushed with the excitement of heading west.

Joe held his daughter on his lap, urging her to wave at "Nana," blowing her a kiss she copied with her tiny palm. I waved too, adjusted the lap robe around my legs.

Perhaps, I decided, this was all that life would give me, what I was meant to have: a kind though distant husband, a daughter, healthy and calm, family and friends who prayed for me when I couldn't for myself. What more dared I hope for inside a body where longing still licked my neck?

Belle, or Izzy as Joe called her, grew tall, her peanut-shaped body soon becoming angular set on sturdy legs that took her everywhere over rolling grass and shifting sand. She walked and talked and amazed me from the distance set between us. She loved the parrot, who'd made the trip under Annie's care. Her presence along with Annie's gave Joe a household full of skirts and powder that he didn't seem to mind at all.

Annie fit in perfect as a pickle at a picnic. In the evenings, after she left Mathews Shipyard where she worked as a receptionist, she'd play with Belle and later tell me stories of commerce and trade. Margaret taught school now, reading voraciously, getting books shipped in from places south. Mama moved from clocks to make tussy-mussy, clutching flowers to doilies she never gave away.

Joe indulged my need for change in how we furnished every room, a different theme for every season. He permitted my invitations to new and different people who sat like colorful birds bobbing their heads along the docks as they lined the long mahogany dining table. We had Chinese cooks now, maids and waiters, too, to help.

Hoquiam at last boasted a theater where I declaimed at times, memorizing long poems I laid on the music stand to cue me as I practiced. A local baseball team took our time, something that interested Joe and Belle more than me.

Joe's business ventures expanded, and he now rubbed shoulders with men such as San Francisco's Asa Simpson, who owned ships and mills and a coal mine near Renton. Joe petitioned Lodge #64 and was elected soon after.

Parties and gala gatherings became a part of my days. We spoke of New Zealand's giving its women the vote, of troubles in the eastern banks. We set up music nights and once or twice took a ship to Portland to see performances such as Verdi's opera of tragic love, *Aida*. Joe went along for appearances, but he preferred his tinkering and the spoiling of his Izzy. Even at home, his routine included disappearing to his workshop as soon as his child was put to bed.

If any had asked him, he would have said his life was full, I'm quite sure he would have. And others would have said we lived a charmed life. Belle had the usual childhood bumps and scrapes that skipped beside necessary learning, but she proved healthy and full of vigor. I was pleased for that. The one or two occasions when she'd had an upset stomach or ran a fever and mewed soft sounds of misery, I found myself alarmed then shamed at my lack of compassion.

"It isn't that bad," I'd said. "Cook'll find a cracker for you, you'll feel better. Margaret?" I'd finish and find my sister to offer comfort from her seemingly endless well.

I'd attempt to distract Belle when she proved moody, the way Margaret could, but it didn't soothe as I'd hoped. More than once I wondered what I lacked when I watched Margaret slip in and simply hold my daughter, rocking gently, providing just what she needed.

"How I wish you'd allow yourself to give a little more to Belle," Margaret told me one day. She'd come upon me staring through the window at the sea.

"I'm not aware I don't," I lied. "I have generous bones. I give my share to charities."

"Joe does," she said. "And that's not what I mean."

I faced her and felt my jaws tighten by the serious look on her face.

"You're always seeking after thrills, it seems to me, looking toward the next event or party or applause. Even these decorative changes." Her hand spanned the room where new drapes with fringed valances had just been hung. "They're just distractions. Loving Belle could be so enriching if you'd let it. All this, it's so short-lived. Next month you'll want another change, something else, when right here in front of you stand a child and a husband who need love now. It's like you're waiting for something. Maybe you don't think you deserve what most women would be delighted with, I don't know—"

"Why, you're envious!" I said.

"I am not!" She lifted her arms and face toward something in the ceiling with a gesture that said "frustration." She shook her head and her words were calm when she spoke again. "You miss it, Cassie. Which is my point. You miss much because you don't love. I—"

"I love as I can, Margaret," I said. "I love as I can."

Joe acquired for us a larger home in 1896, the year our Belle turned four. We overlooked the harbor now, and I imagined I would always live there, inhaling the ocean air that brought good health with it, listening to my mother's clocks and Margaret and Belle's soft chatter. Belle loved her pony, her riding lessons, her music, and her books. She was observant and unassuming and little trouble, it seemed to me.

Beatrice and others frequented our doors. Once, in the spring, I took a walking tour with friends along the shoreline to Mary and Melody's village. Joe claimed work as usual, so our gathering ripped at wind-dried salmon without him. Belle and Beatrice and others watched brown-skinned men race each other and the ocean in their hand-carved canoes, breezes playing with our hair. Melody teased me about my billiard table when she saw me, a subject that always came up when I made my way to her "cheap" establishment. I noticed when we stepped inside to warm our ears and stomachs with her cider that my lace hanky dropped so long ago was now nailed upon the door.

I rarely thought about Mary's warning of distress for my infant. I believed she had it wrong. It was *my* life's survival that had been in question, my closeness to death her warning meant. Belle's happiness had never been threatened.

My mother grew larger with her ease. She traveled with Margaret and me and Belle to distant ports, twice a year, just as I had bargained for that day in San Francisco. Both she and I took up painting, an instructor coming in to also tutor Belle. A piano appeared as a Christmas gift one year. A red satin ribbon stretched across the baby grand, promising good times, like a red collar on a black Labrador retriever. I redid one of the parlors as a music room while Joe developed a series of pulleys and chains to lift the baby grand to the ceiling. It hung there, out of our way, unless Belle wished to practice or I chanced to play. "Won't take so much room at the ceiling," he said staring up at his handiwork. "Never liked a cluttered place." It was why we didn't have dogs.

Life went on in as much of a routine as I had ever known. Margaret had a wide variety of suitors but found something each one lacked, or perhaps she set her standards higher than she should have. She enjoyed teaching, acting as a tutor to the children of the mill owners preferring private schooling, a "common role" for her my mother said, nose in the air. I think the children added to her colds and asthma episodes, but Margaret found pleasure in it, stepping over mother's indignation.

Annie, too, waited, content to live in the West. Her work as a receptionist was a challenge she found exhilarating, she said, and a way to meet others. She spent her only day off with work at the church.

We had no other children, Joe and I. Didn't even try.

I didn't say I couldn't have them nor even that I shouldn't. I said the university doctors spoke to me of risk, and Joe accepted that condition. The subject came up only once after that. My mother and Margaret stood with Joe and me beneath a sun awning watching Belle ride her little pony across the rolling lawn that sloped to the bay. It was a glorious summer day that shone bright against Belle's blond hair bouncing against her black riding jacket. The water rippled in a breeze, a perfect robin's-egg blue. White sails of the three-masted schooner *J. M. Weatherwax* sailed in the harbor beyond.

"Would be nice if she had a sister or brother to join her," my mother said. She cooled herself with an oriental fan.

"Perhaps a cousin instead," Joe said, his voice carrying a teasing sound.

"That would do too," my mother said. "If our Margaret ever marries."

"All in good time, Mother," Margaret answered. "I'm waiting for the *perfect* man."

"You're already twenty-two," Mother said. "And you do much better with children than your sister. Unfortunate she's only had one for you to raise." Her wrist moved the fan vigorously enough I felt the breeze of it on my own hot face.

I suppose I should have been distressed at what my mother said, and I was, some. But truthfully, while I adored Belle, I did not begrudge my sister's efforts to teach and nurture her, be a special person in her life. I was not the best of mothers and more than one child would have made it so much more difficult to hide, so much more agonizing to admit.

Days when clocks broke the silence of a house, when I felt a longing for something more that I did not understand and felt I might just burst from the weight and stillness of my life, those days, I'd take walks into the forest. I packed a basket with me now, of chocolates that melted into creams, of breads and apple butters, provisions I thought would fill me, but they failed. Even so I savored every crumb, my finger lingering on my lip to relish each tiny bit. Still hungry, I'd then swirl myself to feel the wind against me, smell the rotting leaves and needles soft beneath my feet. Tchaikovsky's *Pathétique* played inside my head, a symphony so deep with unrequited passion, when I'd heard it played in Portland, I had wept. I pushed the edge those days, seeking passion, seeking satisfaction.

Joe built the big house in 1898. Mourant and Romans designed it and just letting the contract made the paper. The three-story colonial-Queen Anne rose on the corner of K and Tenth Streets with all the floors and finishing done in Washington hemlock. A reception room the size of our first home's living room greeted guests. He'd planned a parlor, a library with electric lights, a dining room and kitchen and three bedrooms. Joe even built himself a workroom and on the second story, two rooms were set aside for photograph development, a new hobby he'd taken up in earnest.

He had lessened his frugality. A new home, the furnishings, supporting family and a friend, my mother's whims, my wish for frills, none of it raised his blond eyebrows, not once. He no longer functioned as just the "chief secretary." He'd become a businessman having invested wisely in this wild Washington land. With Dr. Campbell, he even owned beach property where they hoped to build a hotel.

In fact, several from back East had invested in Hoquiam by 1896. More lived in the town, a few others from San Francisco and the Soules from Chicago. Joe'd invested in the lumber industry and bought timberland of his own. He had not only designed the water system but had seen potential there, and with three others now owned the North Shore Light Company and acquired the six thousand acres necessary to secure their investment.

The land they purchased gave up clear streams racing beneath canopies of trees, streams that could be diverted and for a price, poured into cisterns to be troughed and then pumped out into tin tubs and copper sinks. The streams, dammed, gave up steam power Joe's company sold.

They found rich resource in the timber and in adjoining cleared lands they bought, surveyed, and platted with plans to sell to those easterners seeking a tepid climate of lush green and sea.

"And when the railroads come," Joe said, "we'll be able to log those farther areas for a fraction of the cost. Get it all the way to the coast, right through Hoquiam," making his point tapping his finger in the air.

He'd begun talking a bit more with me about his business, though it seemed in fits and starts, so I was never quite sure of the details. John Soule and he spoke often, and I tried to overhear. They spoke of Asa Simpson and his son L. J., who had come up from San Francisco and was said to have his father's business skills. The Simpsons owned the Diamond S sailing and steam vessels, North-Western Lumber Company and Simpson Lumber Company, too, as well as numerous California and Oregon investments, and this L. J. was the apparent heir.

"If you'd talk with me more about it, I'd understand better," I said.

We were being driven to a reception at the mill manager's, and the horse faltered and paused as much as it moved.

"Can't you control him?" Joe raised his voice to the driver and then to me mumbled something about doing things yourself if you wanted them done right. He'd been terse during our dressing to leave, like steam bubbling beneath the surface of a boiling pot.

"I think it might be green broke," I said. "I don't recall seeing that animal to harness before."

"You'd remember?" he said.

"I do know horses."

"Sometimes your forgetfulness annoys me," he said, looking out the narrow window. "It's why I don't bother to explain much."

I did forget little things, much to my own annoyance, like where I put things or why I'd entered a room. But I kept detailed lists of anything Joe told me to do so he wasn't inconvenienced by the occasional lapses in my mind. Tiredness, that's what I attributed it all to, that and tasks that lacked prime purpose.

"Despite what your suffragettes would have you believe," Joe continued, "women do not have a head for business."

Such comments always made me wonder what he thought *was* in women's natures, a musing that would be followed by a sense of guilt over my mothering of Belle.

"About this event tonight," I said, stepping over what could have taken us into deeper water. "Are you going to be talking about your shingle company?"

"Don't mention *that*, please. Tonight's a courtesy, just a reception."

"I'm well aware of social amenities," I said. "It's one thing I'm competent at."

Joe seemed distracted, then said in a lighter voice, "Emerson'll have his hands full running the mill with Daddy's son hovering about."

We approached the estate of George Emerson, a man who managed the

North-Western Lumber Company for the Simpsons, and stopped where a cluster of men had gathered.

"Been relegated to Hoquiam, hoping he'll stay out of trouble, I guess," I heard a man say as Joe helped me from the buggy.

"Got kicked out of school in California and lost a dime or two of daddy's money, not that Asa couldn't afford it. And a ship or two in Europe. That must have bitten a bit."

"The Captain always did know how to spice up an affair," the other man said, and his laughter turned into a cough.

"But who would've thought his son would be the one having it?" the other said, and they laughed as they tapped out their pipes on the bottom of their boots.

"Word is," a potbellied man said leaning forward in a whisper, "that he and a friend of his brought back more than pineapples. Shipload of native girls from the Sandwich Islands, grass skirts and all, they say. Rose such a ruckus partying, the sheriff arrested the lot."

"First time that old jail was ever full at once," said another. "Can't believe his money didn't buy him out of that."

"Maybe he didn't want it to."

All the men laughed as they walked back inside behind us.

The first time I saw the subject of their laughter, his tall back was to me, and he leaned into a conversation and the very flushed face of a friend. I heard her tinkling laugh as he spoke to her, the daughter of a mill owner. The women standing on either side of her laughed, too, their presence nourished by this tall man's apt attention. He spoke again, a deep voice. They fluttered their fans. I watched him place his tanned hand on Frances Soule's bare shoulders, almost ached with the touch as he slid his arm across her back, to her belted waist, cutting her from the crowd like a good horse moves out a calf. He nodded to those left standing while guiding Frances as though she were the only woman in the world, not just in the room.

"Smooth," Joe said, "I'll give him that."

I was surprised he'd noticed.

We moved about the room ourselves, my husband and I, circling, chatting. Someone mentioned the signing by Russia and China of the Manchurian Convention and that the novelist Harriet Beecher Stowe had died. We women flashed fans to our faces, against our bare shoulders and the August heat. The men gathered into clusters, and the women to others. I knew most of them. Beatrice spoke of her favorite topic; Margaret had arrived with her latest escort. Annie was absent, the affair reserved for those of slightly higher station.

Chandeliers sent sprays of light across perfumed coiffures. I enjoyed the laughter and exchange of smiles and conversations, the way people leaned into my whispering stories, laughed when I wanted. "Let me tell you what Belle said about her hobbyhorse," I told a gathering sipping wine. "'He'd be in better shape if he hadn't wintered underneath a pile of leaves.'"

"We'd all do well to watch where we winter," a deep voice behind me said to gentle laughter, and I knew without looking it was the voice of Louis Simpson.

I turned. Something passed between us.

We exchanged a recognition nod as I moved on behind my fan, aware that my heart pounded faster and my face flushed more than from wine. Our paths did not cross again until dinner was announced and we were ushered to the dining room set for fifty. But I had been aware of him and could have told anyone who might ask where he stood or sat. There was something about his presence, something alluring and quite foreign, almost compelling, that kept him like an afterimage in my mind.

He was taller than most of the men, Joe included. He wore a tanned and rested look. But what made him stand out was how people eased aside for him, like sailboats that let a grand yacht pass by, content to admire and remain in the ripple of its wake. Not out of fear or intimidation did they move but because Louis Simpson charmed them into wanting to step aside.

At dinner, Louis sat to the right of his father's co-owner and manager, George Emerson. Unlike the other men in the room, he wore a pale blue silk cravat at his throat that brought out the threads of his pearl linen suit. His shoes were white leather. Ruffles appeared at sleeve cuffs as he stood to offer up a toast when all our glasses had been filled with fine wine.

"To Emerson," Louis said, lifting his glass, "to whom my father has given the task of taming me."

Polite laughter followed.

"George will need all your good wishes in his efforts and the stamina of a prize bull to do it." More laughter, then Louis added: "Or was that what I was hoping he'd toast to me?"

Men guffawed at that, women blushed.

Each of us raised our glasses to Emerson, then lowered our eyes to the rim. I liked how this man had put the rumors into the open so easily, subtracted some of gossip's negative power while adding to his own. It was what I was thinking when his eyes met mine, far down the table, and I held his gaze as I sipped.

The intensity of your look found its way deep inside of me. An almost painful gaze, ripping at my soul as though nothing secretive could ever lay between us. I looked away first, began speaking about nothing with the gentleman seated on my left, tracing my collarbone with my finger as we talked. A warm flush lapped at my throat. My eye caught Margaret's quizzical gaze from across the table. I was aware of everything and nothing, only you. And although I couldn't see you, I knew you still stared, far down the table, your eyes searing through me. My heart beat in danger, knowing before my mind what lay ahead.

CHAPTER 8

DECEPTIONS

❀

I did not speak to Louis Simpson that evening nor see him for some days, though he invaded my mind without ceasing. When I least expected it, the memory of his dark eyes set deep, watched me over glass. His gaze had been so brief, a second, maybe two or three, but in it I had memorized the thickness of his eyebrows, their lift in recognition; the straight line of his nose above full lips, raised at the corners that slid into an easy, consuming smile. On his firm chin he'd allowed to grow a black, pointed beard, Russian style.

"Don't day-sleep, Mommy," Belle said, pulling on the sleeves of my dress. "Finish the story." We sat in her room surrounded by Beatrix Potter's books with exquisite colored drawings of gardens and rabbits.

"I'm sorry. Don't know where my mind went," I said, not knowing it would be the first of many lies to myself, to her, and then to others.

My eyes turned again to the page. My daughter curled into the crook of my arm, leaning against my breast, and I shook myself of his image, willed him away as I read.

It was possible in the beginning.

I suppose those for whom first love comes late in life can speak to this, of wondering where that rush of fervor comes from, the giddiness of youth washed in, of wishing for the ache of recognition and of touch, yet fearful should it happen. A nervous blotching covered my neck in places. Night dreams threatened days.

I listened for any talk of him, scraps of news Joe might bring home, and told myself it was idle curiosity, just something to break the monotony of my days, bring color to the paintings I no longer toiled over. Never mind the quickening of my heartbeat with the mention of his name, never mind the images I formed with a whispered comment about the entire floor his apartment consumed, the lavish way he'd furnished it with paintings and tasseled pillows; the late-night visitors said to pass through its doors.

Margaret raised her eyebrow when I volunteered to do the marketing one day, watched me warily.

"Why the sudden interest?" she said.

"Just being helpful."

I used the errand as an excuse to glance at customers with broad shoulders and baritone chuckles. I'd turn, anticipating, then feeling such a schoolgirl loss when I discovered neither were his. Daydreams of him filled my hours, about who did his marketing, what kind of foods he'd choose, what made him laugh, whether the Hawaiian girls were gone, how he spent his time. At night, to fall asleep, I drank an extra glass of wine and remembered each detail of our encounter from a distance down a table. I awoke, awash with shame and hunger.

Harmless, I told myself, an innocent voyage without action washing into wish. I'd never act on it, not with such a public man, not with a scoundrel such as he painted himself to be. Besides, I wouldn't have to make that choice. He didn't know I even lived.

Still a restlessness gnawed at me as it had when we'd first moved to Hoquiam. I craved immersion into senses, food, and frenzy. Joe's little ways I'd come to live with irritated, the humming while he tinkered, his patronizing answers. Both my mother and sister seemed provincial, at fault for their contentment. I did not need this now, this agitated distraction of my days.

I took to riding more, faster and with fury. The trees beckoned again when I walked. I returned breathless but still yearning, empty even though I'd had my fill.

So when I opened my eyes following an all-consuming swirl on a summer's day beneath a canopy of cedars, I gasped. There stood Louie Simpson.

I thought at first that I had wished his presence so intensely that I had caused him to appear. My heart pounded. I reached my hand out then jerked it back when he spoke.

"I've come here every day," he said, "hoping I'd catch you." I unbalanced myself stepping back. A large fir tree behind me kept me upright. The bark felt rough and firm and real against my back. The scent of moist earth and dying needles lifted up with the brush of my shoe. The trees cooled us, shadowed the afternoon.

"How did you know...?"

"Saw you one day, in that wine-colored dress." He nodded to the one I wore. "Thought it was a pileated woodpecker fluttering about." He smiled. "Heading out of town on a timber cruise. Saw you from a distance. Wanted to get closer."

His eyes were warm syrup. I could almost taste the sweetness on his lips.

"Afraid you might not be real, that I had just willed you into being the other night when we shared that glass of wine."

His presence was the vortex of a storm. It stung my skin, pierced my depths as it depleted my breath. Though my feet stuck in the needle-covered earth, my world began spinning. I leaned against a tree that stood solid and firm; I willed it to extend its strength to me.

"I need to go," I whispered.

"Don't be coy, Cassie." His voice caressed. "This is no child's play we're into."

He reached for me. Stirring and alarm swirled together.

That he could have entered my thoughts so completely and then materialized before my eyes to continue a conversation begun only in my head was both unnerving and sublime. How had he done it? What kind of power did he wield? He walked too close, too soon, my fantasy at risk of being real.

I swallowed and lifted my eyes to his. "I have a family," I said.

"I know." He didn't drop his eyes. "I know everything about you, how you spend your days, what you think of, what you wish for, where your tears fall, the way your hair smells in the morning." His eyes washed over my face. "The smoothness of your skin, what fills you up, what leaves you empty, everything about you. You're what I've been searching for my whole life, the other side of who I am."

He touched my hand then, and the collision of our skin caused an ache so foreign, so deep inside of me, that I whimpered.

"But what about—"

"Sh-h-h," he said, interrupting with his fingertips to my lips. "We're not there yet. When we know what we're about, there'll be room enough to wrap that in and all you need to know of me."

I knew that pain would follow this someday. I knew that I would hurt and others, too, but I discarded conscience, suspended it for sensation.

Louie folded my hand in his and kissed my palm. A fire burst inside me, consumed my breath, threatened death, but I did not die. Instead, I touched his face, and thus began the voyage of decision that would take me to the edge of breathless and to choices—oh the choices—that would change how I existed.

What you tell yourself is that you can have it all, that you deserve it, that life is short and so you must hold tight to what brings fleeting pleasure. You tell yourself that you can handle anything as long as love is in it. You may even say out loud that God must understand. How else could one explain such qualities of heaven being stored within? You don't allow yourself to look into the future far; you don't permit the thoughts of what might happen if others see the fire in your eyes. You refuse to ponder past commitments but look to now, this moment, and convince yourself that it will always be enough.

So it was for me, this consummation of a yearning.

Margaret knew something was amiss within days of my encounter.

"Are you working on a *fever?*"

"Just the temperature changing," I said. I'd been brushing Shiloh and carried the scent of horse sweat into the house.

"Your heart's susceptible, Cass. Need to take a shawl with you when you're out. One's always folded on the hat chair and I've got one—"

"I'm plenty warm."

"Plenty warm," Annabelle repeated and cackled.

Margaret stared at me. "Are you *sleeping* well? Thought I heard you up in the night. Whatever happened to that clear conscience of yours?" She laughed but stopped when I didn't.

Thoughts of Louie Simpson consumed my every waking moment, imagining where he was, reliving every word and touch. I felt ravished by a force beyond control. Blemishes appeared on my neck and stayed. I began nipping at the edges of my nails.

Then we arranged to be together, just to stand beside each other at a gathering, a quick touch as we stood with a crowd at the ball game. I would recall the scent of his cologne, the way he stood as I approached, casual, one knee bent as though he could relax in any situation, his head forward, listening before I said a word. He dressed in ivory colors and never showed a smudge even though he spent his days near shipyards and coal mines and sometimes crawling through dense undergrowth beneath trees.

That he traveled away often failed to cool my imaginings. That his mother and brother visited and stayed with him did not prevent our growing risks. We scheduled times to talk in the timber. That the paper covered every theater event he might speak at or party he gave, commented on the Diamond S uniforms he purchased for our local baseball team, even noted when he was sickened with "La Grippe" or that he was a public figure, none of it stopped our sliding toward each other.

Belle passed her fifth birthday with my thoughts of when he'd next return. While she blew on her candles, I anticipated the smoothness of his hair between my fingers falling in gentle waves on either side of a center part. When she ran her fingers through the sugared frosting I recalled the softness of his breath on my cheek when he kissed me in greeting—as he did every woman at every gathering—though he lingered longer with me. And when she opened her father's present to her, I barely noticed, wished for a gift from Louie in my hand, so quickly did betrayal become ingrained.

In 1898 when Louie built his own building within sight of Joe's, I imagined him leaving for work in the early-morning fog or rehearsing for one of his character sketches performed at the theater. I wondered if he'd imitate that unfortunate Mr. Hunt who I could mimic for the children, a man who sulked and shifted his eyes and thought every man lusted after his wife. Delusional thinking, though she was a pretty thing. The closeness of Louie's living, just scant steps from my own home, added intrigue. I pushed aside the memory of my father and his "hopin' being worth twice the happenin'."

The swirl and chase were all consuming.

What charm Louis saw in me was a mystery. He said it was my rich embrace of life, my vibrancy. I didn't share with him the fitful sleep I had now nor the dark thoughts that woke me even when strong wine had sent me first to sleep.

"It's there, though," Louis said as we danced at a party he threw at Heerman's hall. Joe had declined the outing but sent me off with his good wishes. "In your amber eyes," Louis said, "and the way that smile lights up your face like a firecracker in July. You take on challenges. I've seen you with Beatrice and some of the others. You can argue either side. I love listening to you talk about the Spaniards and their war. Interested in rights rather than responsibilities, like a lawyer in your mind. I could watch you all day long and never tire."

For some strange reason, I believed him, and believed I could be more than what I'd been as long as I knew he was there behind me.

He had dreams too. Bettering his family's fortune, being the first to do things, experiencing everything there was. He wanted to make a name for himself by doing something good for people, leaving a legacy behind him, for a family he didn't have yet, too busy having fun. "As Alyosha says in the *Brothers Karamazov,* 'one must love life more than the meaning of it,'" he jested.

"I'm not familiar with that work," I said.

"Russian. Philosophical and brooding." We glided across the floor, our eyes held tight. "A friend from Moscow read me the sections. Translated it. Sent to learn shipbuilding, actually."

"'Eat, drink and be merry,' then," I said, "'for tomorrow you may—'"

"No room for the morbid," he said and eased me toward the cooling wine.

I told myself we were just friends, that at last I had found someone with whom I felt content. We met to talk, after all, amazed that our interests ran so well together. Music, the arts, the love of travel, of sights to cleanse the eyes and soul. He introduced me to the thoughts of exotic men such as Nietzsche and of Tolstoy. At discussions with a dozen others he could orate easily on life, weaving meaning from the arts and ancient thinkers into wars and current events.

We even shared a similarity in how we viewed the land. He loved the look of a well-manicured estate, had been to Hotel del Monte and marveled as I had over the lawns and fountains, the rich foliage and flowers. "It's tended lawns that separate civilized from savage," he noted.

"I like roses best," he told me once, stopping to talk as I worked out in my garden at a time he knew I'd be there. "Showy flowers, too, like hydrangeas and peonies. People will walk a distance to see those. Heard once of this pastor who planted an entire acre of flowers near Oregon's gold-fields. People walked a day to see the blooms and take cuttings and dry blossoms for keepsakes."

He knew the language of the flowers and said the columbine spoke the loudest to his heart. I knew the columbine's meaning: "I will not give you up."

He read poems to me as we sat against a fir tree in the denseness of the forest, and he could speak as one who'd been there at the Roman baths of Caracalla, walked beside the Dnepr River rushing through the lush Ukraine. "We did the European tour twice," he told me, "and Dad's sent me a dozen places. Mother loves museums and galleries. I love the vibrancy of Russia best, so alluring yet illusive and distinct. Like you," he offered, then kissed me with a passion my heart had never known.

I did not consider my time with Louis a betrayal to Joe, a man who found little interest in my ideas, would never have wanted to waste his hours in poetry or philosophical argument the way Louis and I did. No, I told myself there was no harm in this liaison, this tryst between friends.

In fact, Joe received more attention from me because of it. Louie filled me up, I had reserves now, and I made sure I gave Joe all my consideration when he sat across from me at dinner. The questions I asked about his day and business were genuine and well thought out. He couldn't wonder about my thoughts when he was absent, wouldn't imagine that while he answered, my thoughts were of another and not him. Joe acted pleased. Why, my rela-tionship with Louis was a gift to him!

Such are the deceptions that keep a grip on guilt.

Even Belle benefited, I decided. She was with me once when we encoun-tered Louie on the street. He suggested we have tea together, something acceptable with a child present. He ordered Earl Grey for us and an ice cream for Belle, and it was a lovely outing. I was giddy with the public-ness of it, the delight at having an innocent encounter with a handsome man of some reputation, sitting in the midst of others at surrounding tables. It was something I could tell of later, even to my husband. Louie's conversation with my child was full of interest and sweet joy. They liked each other. I imagined us a family.

Only later, when Belle asked why I laughed so funny when I was with "that man" and didn't notice until she told me that she had spilled her cream, only then did I begin to wonder at my deception. Only then did I ponder how long we could go on, my Louis-Louie and I.

Occasionally I wondered if someone might see through us. Would we let the familiarity of our liaison slip at the dinners and receptions? Could this anticipated thrill that took us closer to the edge be something I could still step back from? Would I? Could I live without the frantic, the fullness of the thrill that Louie being in my life had brought?

Being with him became a satisfying inspiration; time without him took my breath away.

We met then, full and passionate, in his apartment. We took the irreversible step. I said it was no different than loving in my mind, but even that deceived. For he had filled me, as I had never been. I did not know that such sufficiency could end and leave me with an even deeper hunger.

My weight dropped after that. I slept through wild, vibrant dreams, often waking in the night fearful my heart was having an attack, cold sweat beading on the space below my nose. I could calm the pounding by bringing his voice to memory, focusing on the gaze of his eyes, his smile of invitation, the sensations of skin to skin, my belief I had control.

A dinner evening I prepared for Hoquiam's lumber and finance people daringly included Louis Simpson on the list. I found watching him move within the confines of my home as stimulating as a stolen kiss. And later, I could imagine his presence there beneath the seascape painting or pretend the drift of his cologne still hovered near the Boston high chest.

We exchanged gifts at Christmas time. Neither of us had given the other any hint of it. We planned to meet at the Quinault village on the pretense of buying kippered salmon for the season. We would exchange holiday wishes there.

I sat at a plank table at Melody's establishment. I had come here looking for Mary a few weeks earlier, wanting to ask about my chances to have children. I hadn't found her and took it as a sign that I was not supposed to worry.

While I waited, I worried.

Once Louie had not come at all to an appointed place, and I had stayed longer in the denseness of the forest than I ever had before, my mind a weather vane pushed by frantic winds. Fear then anger pushed aside by guilt and grief bubbled up from an oozing sense of loss so deep I thought I would sink away forever. Abandoned. That was how I felt making my way back home without having seen him, not knowing why he hadn't come. I'd wept into my pillow, and Joe had reached for me and held me, and I could not feel the shame of it, my husband offering comfort in my betrayal.

A letter had arrived a day later. In it, Louie confessed his wish to end things, for my sake, of how he feared for me. "I am not promising a future, not a marriage," he'd written, "nor have I ever wished to hurt you. Should our liaison be revealed, it could destroy you. I could not live if that should happen." He had ended the note with his wish that I forgive him for not appearing and his hope that we could meet again someday, as friends. I'd heard later that he had joined the Soules on a trip to the Sound.

His distance devastated me. But the following week, resolute, I returned to our assigned place and time and laid the lap robe over needles and leaned my head against the fir tree, closed my eyes and waited. A woodpecker drummed to mark its territory. Wind sighed through the cedars, a sound so soothing, so subdued that I could sleep. No worry touched me. He was the other side of who I was. I knew he would come again and so he had, both of us quite sure now we could not breathe without the other.

So while I waited at Melody's that Christmas of 1898, I didn't worry that he wouldn't arrive, only that something bad might happen to him on his way. Perhaps some accident with his horse on the icy roads. Maybe a mud slide causing him to turn back, a creek rise to overflow. I suppose I worried that some evil would befall him perhaps as punishment for what we chose to do, some suffering appear that his Russian novelists said belonged to life as much as breath did.

Melody brought out blackberry tea. The steam from it burned my nose and I sat back, sniffing, stifling a sneeze.

"You alone?" she said. I nodded. "Pretty strange. You always with others, like bees to honey. You wait for your man, ya?" I felt my stomach clutch and then relax when I realized she spoke of Joe. "You finally get him away to come with you? Bring your girl too?" Her eyes scanned the smoky room, looking for my family.

"Just waiting for a friend," I said.

She looked at me, tipped her head and grunted. "Flushed up for a friend," she said.

Her comment made me nervous, that even this woman who saw me rarely should notice a difference in my person when I anticipated seeing Louie.

"Who's that?" I said, wrapping my gloved hands around the tea mug. I nodded toward a man with a rounder, darker face than most of the others. He sat slumped over in a deep sleep, but I could tell he was tall.

"Oh, he's a lost one," she said. "One of those Oregon Indians who let alcohol make decisions. Goes by Standing Tall, but he stands low since he left his woman and kids behind. Comes here winters. I give him a place to sleep sometimes, behind the stove when he takes the cure and gives up whiskey."

"How sad," I said and meant it. "Wouldn't his wife forgive him?" I asked swirling my tea in its cup.

"Don't matter what she does. He don't know how to do it for himself. He has some strange ideas, like someone else I know."

"Why doesn't he just go back, once he's sober?"

"Can't never go back," she said.

"Sure he could. You can do anything you set your mind to."

She stared at me until I dropped my eyes.

The door opening rescued me from self-reflection. Louie strode in like colorful leaves rising through wind. He stomped his feet of the slushy snow, pushed the door closed with his heel, and began unbuttoning his fur coat all the while scanning the room until he found me. His smile opened then, added to the pink of his cheeks as he headed toward me, pulling his gloves off as he walked, running his fingers through his dark hair.

Melody watched a moment then headed back toward her split-log bar. I heard her say loud enough for Louie to hear too: "Beware of that friend. His coat is fox but he has the look of a wolf."

"Not a lone wolf," Louie said to her, "now that I'm here with a pretty one like you." He held his arms out to Melody as though he would wrap her in a bear hug.

"Don't need no bear or wolf or fox," she said as she slipped beneath his arms. She shook her head as he gave her a look of mock sadness. "Got a dog to keep me warm," she said.

"The more I see of men the more I like dogs. I've heard that somewhere before," Louie said as he sat down at my table to the music of Melody's laugh.

"Not from me," I said, "though as a philosophy, it has merit."

He recoiled, wounded. "You women," he said and reached for my hand.

"You love us," I said. Some men just warmed to women, liked their company and the way they engaged, the scent of them as they whirled through a room inviting softness and chatter. Louie was one of them.

He started to protest but stopped, nodded then said low enough for no one but me to hear. "I've brought one woman a gift. Can I give it to you here, or do I have to let you find it buried under the roots of cedar at the fork in the road?"

"You first," I said and handed him my own gift box and glowed in his look of surprise. His strong fingers lifted the cover. Against blue velvet sat the diamond pin I'd selected for him, saved money from the household account to purchase. He would wear it at his throat, against a cravat of silk.

"It's handsome," he said, holding it in his fingertips. "Much too fine and totally undeserved, but I will treasure it, always. Here's yours," he said, his wide hand presenting me with a small, exquisite box.

Inside was a pheasant pin forged of gold. Coral and amethyst and onyx formed the tail. Set into the bird's breast were a dozen tiny diamonds.

"I don't know how you'll explain it," he said, a sadness in his eyes, "or ever be able to wear it. But the sparkle and splendor and the bird in flight, it was exactly you."

I pinned it on my dress, catching the clasp in one of the tiny pleats that marched across the bodice so that it took me longer than I wanted.

"Do you think you should?" he asked.

"I'll take it off before I step inside the house. But I wouldn't keep this in its box today for anything."

He reached to help me, then stopped himself, looked around to see if any had seen him make such an intimate offer to a female friend.

He slouched in his chair, gazing at it and then me. "I hate this lurking, this never being able to be totally together. We've got to find a way, Cassie," he said, his fingers laced into his dark hair. "Before I go insane."

I had no solutions to offer and surprised myself by assuring him that our relationship could go on forever just the way it was. I imagined spending the rest of my days with him. I skipped over the painful parts, the paths marked by boulders that could only be rolled onto others as we attempted to push them aside.

Mr. Hunt became the excuse for the leaving, but he was not the reason. Louie said the man had threatened him, something about Louie being interested in Hunt's wife.

"Of course that's lunacy," he told me. "I've no interest in her. She does favor your coloring though, dark hair and perfect skin."

I leaned against him in a closed cab. It was evening, May 1899. "And I thought you had eyes only for me."

"Might be good for me to leave, at least sell the apartment so I don't look quite so permanent. Let the dust die down."

"Have you a buyer?"

"Stine's interested. Could be gone by June. Let Hunt's fears relax."

My family believed I was at a Woodcraft meeting. Beatrice didn't expect me there as she'd received a note from me saying I was home ill. She would be horrified at my being with Louie. She was a suffragette but as most were, she was fiercely loyal to marriage, condemned any act or person that threatened the sanctity of it.

Louie and I sat at the end of a dark street, far from a gaslight that might shed light on the longing in our faces or the agony in our eyes. His mother and younger brother, Harry, visited so his apartment was not a place for comfort or talk.

"I'll go with you," I said, wondering at my boldness when I heard myself say it.

He pulled me closer to him. "What if Joe won't give you a divorce?"

Now that the word had been spoken, it seemed too formidable, too irreversible to consider.

"Maybe we could just meet in San Francisco," I said.

He was silent a long time. "No. People expect it of me. But you, Cassie, you'll bear the brunt of any scandal. The best way I know to protect you is for me to leave, before we're discovered. Shouldn't see each other, not ever again." He sat forward. It was no manipulation, no idle threat. He put his head in his hands and leaned, elbows on his knees. Torment thickened his voice. "Stop this, before we can't turn back."

Of course it's what we should have done. Of course it's what I should have encouraged, but I didn't.

A panic clutched at me instead, as though someone had taken away my air. I swallowed, caught my breath, thought of crazy things to counter the fear that losing him created. I felt my chest tightening. Being without him was more terrifying than not knowing how Joe would react, not knowing if I could live with the label "divorced." It was as though I'd die if I didn't have Louis's touch to look forward to, wither away if I never saw him again. My mind stirred in a fog, a tightness I waded through wondering how I'd live if Louie Simpson left my life.

"And you mustn't leave Belle," he said.

Even as he said it I wondered if she might be happier without me. She was close to Joe and Margaret and Annie.

"I love children, Cassie. I'd like a dozen. Hurting an innocent one might be more than even I can live with."

"Don't you want to be with me?" I asked, panic rising into my throat.

He groaned and pulled me to him. "You don't understand, Cass. You just don't understand. I'm not worth this grief to you and others. Things you don't know of me, who I am, what I've done…"

"Sh-h-h," I said putting my fingers to his lips.

The horse shook his head, the sound of the harness breaking the quiet. A dog barked in the distance.

"I love you Louis-Louie," I whispered into the night and reached for his hand, caressed a callus on his finger.

"And I you, Cassie-Casey."

He kissed the top of my head. Silence settled on us.

"I've never said that to anyone before," I said. "Not to Joe or Margaret or my mother. Even Belle. I'm not sure why I'm so selfish about it."

He kissed the soft space on my temple, close to my eyes. "Means all the more because it's said so seldom. Never passed by my lips either, despite my reputation. Except for my family, of course. But you'd have to look long and far to find someone who loves you more than I do, Cassie."

"Margaret says I should love more," I said.

"This isn't what she'd have in mind."

"Whatever I do will either tear the heartstrings with the stretching or I'll be left back here alone, trying to sew up my life. And my loss, if you go." I took a long pause sensing how much strength such stretching would take. "I never was very good with needles and thread. I prefer ripping out over the self-discipline of repair."

He sucked in a sob. "We've hurt people," he whispered. "And will more."

"Isn't that the meaning of adultery?"

He leaned back. I felt more than saw his eyes blinking back wetness. "Only evil could make a man deny the pain that waits him on a horse named stolen pleasure."

As it happened, Margaret inadvertently set the sparks on fire that rearranged my future. She hadn't intended it of course. She would never have done anything to foster turmoil.

We sat in the dining room, light from the east filtering through the trees sending spikes of glitter across the stained glass that marked the window tops. Margaret wound the yarn I held between my hands, my arms bent at the elbows, palms facing each other. I resisted the urge to scratch at my wrists. The rough, yellow yarn swooped low onto my brown linen dress that stretched across my knees tucked beneath me.

"That Simpson man is making quite a name for himself," she said. Her square little feet peeked beneath her dress, free of shoes.

"Oh?"

"Some ideas he has about that watershed property your husband owns. Guess he's branching out from his father's shipyards. Willard Stems was telling me. He's quite the lady's man, too, isn't he?" She had the sweetest little-girl's voice even though she was almost twenty-five. The high pitch and softness made even menacing thoughts sound innocent and light.

"I don't know what you find promising about that detestable little man," I told her.

"Willard has his faults. All men do. But he makes me laugh. He enjoys the company of children."

"Hmm," I said.

"I don't think he fancies a one of them."

"Who?" I said.

"Young Simpson. He's always smiling and chatting, like he appreciates their company. Just puts the men a bit on edge to see their women flutter back so."

"Maybe they've reason to worry," I said. "George Hunt thinks so."

"Not from what I've seen. All talk and no action, I'd say." She scratched at one foot with the other. "That one's likely to never settle down. Besides, a man like that would be less boisterous around a woman he loved, not more so. That kind of man always is."

"You don't think he has one serious girl?"

She thought for a bit, wrapping the yellow yarn into a ball.

"If becoming mellow is the criterion," she said, laughter on her face, "then you'd be the likely candidate for his advances." She emphasized each syllable of *candidate*. "Like all men, he acts a little tongue-tied around you."

"Tongue-tied," the parrot said.

"Oh hush, Annabelle." Margaret gazed up at me through the glasses Joe had bought for her following an appointment with a specialist in San Francisco. She squinted less now, and I could see that her eyes had a merriment to them as well as wisdom.

"We old matrons can still slow them down, is that what you're saying?" I said.

"You slow Louis Simpson down, at least," she said and smiled.

My heart rate rose, wondering if she knew what she was saying, might even be baiting me. But she was guileless, manipulation as foreign as a failure in her experience.

I watched her, wrapping and twisting the yarn, her eyes on her fingers. Suddenly she stopped. She let the ball of yarn drop lifeless into her lap. The Lady Margaret stared at me, her eyes larger through the round metal lenses. They held both surprise and piercing pain.

"Oh, Cassie," she whispered. "You haven't done anything so foolish as..."

I looked away.

"But it's so wrong!"

"Love isn't!"

"Love? You call it love? Marriage is an honorable thing, Cass. If you break your vows, why, terrible things can happen." A tirade followed, about the mistake I was making, just living for the moment without thought for tomorrow.

"You mustn't let it go *any* further. Use that strong will you have to tell him no. Pray for strength," she said, her voice pleading with me, "to resist him."

"It isn't only him asking."

"Oh, Cassie. Disaster always follows—"

"I don't really need your advice," I said.

"And what kind of sister would I be if I didn't try to stop the terrible pain that lies ahead for you? And for those you say you love?"

"I'm glad you know," I said. "At least I have someone to talk with about this. It's been awful—"

"No!" she said and held up her hand. "I don't want to hear any of the sordid details. It's wrong, Cassie. Any way you put your hand to it, you'll get burned. And others'll get singed, too, if not wear scars for life."

"Why should I have to give up the one great love of my life to remain in a marriage that is more convenience than anything, has been these ten years," I said. "For you and Mama more than me." A wounded look crossed her face. "Tell me why? Isn't life supposed to be full and rich and wonderful? Abundant? Why should I be passed by?"

"There's Belle, for one thing," she said. "She doesn't deserve this from her mother."

"Can you promise me that if I stay with Joe she'll have a good life? Will that earn me some noble place in paradise? Is that what it's all about?"

She shook her head. Tears formed in her eyes.

"I don't know," she whispered. "It doesn't seem fair, but things aren't always. I just know there are rights and wrongs, Cassie, and we pay a terrible price when we step over the one to embrace the other."

"I'm the dramatic one," I said, pasting on a smile.

"This is no game," she said, her words hissing. Her chest heaved with her effort at breath. I thought she might have one of her attacks, but she calmed herself. "I'll pray that you'll come to your senses. Not be so foolish. It's all I can do."

She wrapped yarn with a vengeance then, the wool strands pulling tighter against my wrists.

"Fools seldom respond to wisdom," I said. "We need pain not prayers to change us. And we make our own heaven or hell. God couldn't care less about prayers for me."

I was sorry I'd said it as I watched her wipe her cheek with the back of her hand, adjust her glasses to reduce a slight fog.

"That's not true," she said, her voice tiny, wheezy, and thin. "It's simply not true."

I told Louie the next day that Margaret knew. The news propelled him into action.

"I'm leaving on the next Simpson ship," he said. "I'm promising nothing, Cass, but if you want to come with me, you can."

CHAPTER 9

DEPARTURES

❀

Belle sat across the breakfast table just before I rose to let Louie in. She spread a butter lump all around her pancake, in deliberate wheels, circling, until all the butter melted and each inch of pancake lay smothered.

"Please pass the jam, Mommy," she said, looking up at me through Joe's blue-green eyes. Dimples marked her cheeks. "Didn't I do good, Mommy?" she asked sitting back. She smiled with pride when I nodded.

With precision, she plopped a spoonful of strawberry jam in the center and began spreading again, slowly, as though she had all the time in the world to make circles of red, circles and circles, inside to out.

She looked up and smiled at me as Louie and I paused in the doorway before heading to Joe's den. Her eyes formed a question mark of confusion that settled on Louie's face. His eyes reflected misery as he turned from her to me.

At first Joe must have thought Louie was there to talk of timber or of shipping. A look of disbelief overtook my husband when I failed to leave and began talking to him about Louie, that I was leaving with him and wanted a divorce. Disbelief and then a smirk. He said nothing for a moment, and then I saw the rage rise in his eyes.

"Get out," he said to Louie standing beside me, and I felt a burning knot form in my stomach. My heart pounded as though threatened. Joe's words ignored me, seething like pressed steam. "Go, you, you, defiler. You wife-chaser. You steal from me my most precious possession and then dare to stand before me? You..." A muscle in his jaw twitched.

"I am not a possession," I said, too late wishing Louie had not come.

Joe's eyes bored into mine. "Didn't I take good care of you? Haven't I given you everything you wanted? This house?" He spread his arm to take in the luxury of the room. "Security? Your family? What more could I have done?"

His voice carried pleading with it.

I had no answer for him. It was not his fault.

"What has he told you?" he said. "That he'll marry you? The man's a playboy." He spit the words out. "Listen to me. All those parties and that apartment, built right across the street." For a moment his eyes betrayed an image formed in his head. "Right under my nose, Cassie!" He shook as though to rid himself of it. "He's dozens of women—"

"That's not true," I said. "He loves me. And I can take care of myself. I may never marry again. I certainly don't need marriage."

"Maybe you don't need a divorce either then," Joe said.

My heart caught a beat. "I'm leaving either way."

Joe grunted, pushed his hands as though dismissing me. "This won't get you what you want," he said. "You'll face the pain of this someday, of always reaching, heedless of others. And no one will be there then to make it better."

"I will," Louie said.

"I don't need either of you," I told them, irritated by the direction of the discussion though I didn't know why. "I can manage by myself."

"If our marriage is to work, we will have to make changes," Joe said, then he began to bargain. "First, there will be no more indulgences. Second, I'll spend more time with you. I can see that's been a problem. Third—"

"It's too late, Joe," I said reaching to touch his sleeve. He shook off my hand as though I'd touched him with a hot poker and it was at that moment I think he truly knew.

"I've made this decision of my own free will. It doesn't matter whether I sail with Louie Simpson or not. All that's left here is to work out the details of my leaving. That I am is already decided."

He stared at me then, and I could not deny the anguish in his eyes. Perhaps if Louie had not been there, I might have relented, allowed myself to stay, to try again. Perhaps I could, in time, have convinced myself that living a lie was better than leaving this good man.

But Louie was there with the promise of his devotion, the hope of intrigue and intenseness.

"It's Belle we need to talk about," I said as Louie stepped closer to me, put his arm around my shoulder lending firmness to my words. "About her coming with us."

"No! No!" Joe's hand slammed against the oak desk with a force so powerful I stepped backward. He'd never raised his voice before, I realized, as the ink bottle vibrated to silence.

Joe glared at me through his smudged glasses a moment more, and then the torment turned to something else. I could see it shift in him from the twitch at his jaw to the thin line of his clenched lips.

"I've dealt long enough with your impulsiveness." His voice could cut glass. "Time you faced the consequences of your rash acts, your...your obsession to pleasure." He turned his back. "Belle does not belong with the likes of you."

"Please, Joe. She can't be left behind."

He looked out across the green lawn toward the forest that had concealed my secret for so long.

"You've made your choice. Now I've made mine."

"She's just a child, she needs her mother," Louie said.

"You just want things your way, Cassandra, full of hedonistic pleasure," Joe said. "It's something you might have considered before you deceived her into believing she was first in your life."

"She is!"

"Leave," he said then and never looked back.

That evening in the bedroom, my mother clucked her tongue at me and my craziness, which she said made "no sense a'tall."

"You'll be sorry soon enough and be lucky to have Joe take you back." She wailed then, a wrenching kind of cry. "Think of the scandal!" She fluttered her hanky as though the evening were hot.

"I'm not coming back," I said, throwing corsets and high-button shoes into my trunks. Louie had left to pack his things, our deciding taking on a frenzy of activity. "We're going to live in the City. Belle and Louie and I."

"What'll I tell people? Poor Belle! What terrible shame!"

"She won't have to deal with the shame. No one will know."

Big teardrops formed at my mother's eyes and dribbled unblotted down her cheeks. She watched me grabbing things from my drawers, rushing into Belle's room and back with more things. "Can't believe you'll leave before you're divorced. At least wait until you're properly married. Think of what that'll do for your child!"

I stared at her. "I'm doing what's best for her by taking care of myself."

My mother snorted. "Too many of those meetings, you ask me."

"I didn't, but you're wrong. Beatrice'll be the first to condemn me. She so believes in marriage."

I slept in Belle's room, and though she wore a question on her face, she enjoyed my being there, the way I made a game of it.

We headed to the dock before dawn the next morning. I didn't know what power Joe might enlist to encumber our way, but it would be greater, I imagined, the longer we waited to leave.

"Don't hurt me, Mommy," Belle whined, and I apologized for squeezing her arm getting her into the carriage.

"Just hurry," I whispered.

"Where are we going?" she whispered back. Her eyes darted for signs that others might join us. It was early morning and the fog hung conspiratorially, covering the cobblestones of the drive.

"On a ship," I said to her and smoothed her dress over her knees while giving the order to head to the wharf.

"Papa's coming?" she asked, twisting back. "And Auntie Margaret? And Nana?"

I let silence answer, my heart pounding and pushing through the May morning to the clop-clop of the horse.

We arrived before Louie. The driver unloaded the luggage, helped Belle and me step down, then I sent him away while we waited in the mist. The day promised to be clear and bright above the rising morning fog.

A momentary disquiet seized me, that perhaps the plan to leave with him was more than Louie planned. Maybe I'd pushed too far too fast, perhaps he'd left, maybe wouldn't even meet us. My eyes searched the murky morning for signs of him. Would I leave without him? How would I survive?

Would I go back? A steamship whistle breathed into the mist. My head planned ways to help my heart avoid feeling.

I heard a carriage moving at good speed. I swallowed hard afraid to recognize relief.

Louie jumped out, then turned to help someone else disembark.

It was Margaret.

"I came to get you. Margaret was up…"

As soon as she stepped from the carriage steps, she flew to me. Her arms held me so strong and firm I felt almost crushed.

"Auntie's going with us!" Belle sang out.

Louie stood by, his hands resting gently on Belle's shoulders.

"You can't take her with you, Cassie. It's wrong. You know it is," Margaret said.

I was startled by her plea. "Most natural thing in the world for a child to go with her mother," I said, recovering though I sounded preachy even to myself.

"*Mother* is more than a word," she said. She pulled back and twisted a handkerchief while she spoke. It was something I'd never seen her do before. "It's a state of the heart. A commitment. Not just for the moment but for always. One you never made, Cassie, not ever."

"Margaret…" Louie said.

"It's true!" she snapped at him, then back to me, calmer. "You can't ask a child to live in your sin. Don't compound your guilt, Cassie, just because you can."

I had no time to weigh her words now, no time to let them sink in too deep.

"We're leaving," I said and pulled Belle from Louie's fingers, moving her before me up the gangplank.

Just that quickly Margaret's voice changed to contrition.

"I shouldn't have said those things. I'm sorry. She's your child, I have no say, I'm sorry." She twisted her hanky, then stood straight and almost calm. "I'm just so worried about you both."

"We'll be fine," I said. I straightened my hat, stood back. The pearl hatpin Mother had given me at Belle's birth held it tight to my head. "Tell Annie I'm sorry I didn't say good-bye." My voice became scratchy. I didn't like the feelings that churned.

Margaret squeezed me again. We held each other for a moment longer, then releasing me she said to Louie, "You take good care of them."

"Best I can," he said.

I stood as tall as I could, still shorter than she, took one last look beyond her, avoiding her, staring instead at the wharf and the town appearing now through the lifting mist. I was leaving. I started up the gangplank, Belle's hand in mine.

My daughter's hand felt wet and she hesitated, putting my bravery at risk. I turned to see what held Belle back and looked into Margaret's eyes.

At that moment, I envied her as I never had before. Not her beauty and grace, not the gentleness of her spirit, but her strength to take the right steps, give to others in the right way, seek forgiveness, even change her mind.

I was not good at redemption, at turning back. That was Margaret's hallmark, something foreign to me.

Looking at her, I knew what I had to do.

"Take Belle with you," I said, almost shoving my daughter toward her.

I saw Louie flinch, his fingers tense on Belle's thin shoulders as Margaret rushed up the gangplank to take my daughter.

"Are you sure?" she said, bending, opening her arms to her niece.

"Auntie Margaret is going to look after you for a while. Along with Papa. Until Mama finds a place to stay and you can come to live, all right?"

"No!" Belle said throwing her arms around my legs. "I wanna go with you."

"You need to stay with Margaret." I pried her arms loose. "It'll be better. Let go now, Isabelle. Be a good girl."

She hesitated, then tore her arms from me and twisted. She ran, hitting Louie mid-thigh as she passed. She lashed at him with her little gloved fingers, like a cat pulled from a dog not knowing her rescuer offered protection.

"It's not his fault, Belle," I said. "Go with Margaret now."

My child sent me a look of unblemished poison as she stepped away. I thought I would break like old glass shattered at her feet. She held her head high, her back to me as Margaret caught up to her and wrapped her in her arms.

"Go," Louie said to me then. "I'll be right with you." He touched my arm giving me just enough pressure to continue up the gangplank while his long legs took him quickly back to the carriage. He reached inside. He and Margaret exchanged some words, but I couldn't make them out. He bent to Belle, said something, but she turned to Margaret's skirts and sobbed.

I forced myself to face forward, not to hear the crying of my daughter, instead to think of trees and blue seas and the happiness I hoped to find.

Louie caught up to me and spoke in a tone of comfort mixed with regret. He handed me a cluster of white and yellow columbine he'd gone back to retrieve. *I will not give you up*, the flowers said.

I wished I was the kind of mother who could have left the blooms with Belle.

We boarded the *J. M. Weatherwax* and headed south to San Francisco. An assault of emotion washed over me. Louie held me against his chest, stroked my face for hours, while I shook and shivered as though all warmth had vanished from my soul.

"It'll be all right, Cassie," he said. "This is the complicated part. Like William Bryant said. 'Life's a harsh nurse who roughly rocks her foster children into strength.'"

"What about her real children," I said.

"We'll be stronger, Case. You'll see."

Did I hear hesitation in his voice? Some small seasoning of indecision? Had he really wished for this? Had I? I pinched my eyes tight, cupped my fingers to my lips. I couldn't understand why getting what I wanted didn't take the sting from leaving what I'd had.

Louie could do nothing for the wrenching cries that woke me in the night, a cold sweat shivering me beneath the coverlet. Always the same dream, of Belle reaching out to me sobbing while I ignored her. In my dream, Louie lifted me onto a prancing stallion, all my will lost in handling the animal, keeping myself from falling off. I could hear my child crying, sobbing my name, but I could not get the horse under my control. I could not turn Belle's way so I could pick her up, maybe take her with me. Instead, I rode off, alone, without Louie or my daughter, under the influence of something else.

I'd become aware that I held the reins so tightly that the leather cut my hands. They bled in my dream. Then I'd wake, breathing hard and fast, frightened even more in my waking that it was the injury to my hands that jarred me from my nightmare and not the horror of having abandoned my child.

I wanted this divorce. I could live with the consequences in my awake time. My suffering simply meant I was alive. My nightmares told me something else.

Louie secured a series of rooms for us at the Palace Hotel. We would remain there until the divorce and, I assumed, our subsequent marriage was final. What would happen after that we didn't discuss.

The San Francisco social life was open to me. I had that to consume. Louie introduced me to it as much to take my mind from leaving Belle as anything. I wanted him to reassure me, to allay any fears I might have had that Joe might be right about this Simpson son. He did his best to indulge me, himself as well. In between he visited his family's estate, the "lair of the clan" I called it, and stayed busy with his father's work.

In evenings unscheduled, a kind of tension drove us, the way the wind pushes at sails. We couldn't go forward without the pressure but neither could we rest along the way.

He located a music instructor who came to our rooms and worked with me at the piano. I expressed interest in the flute and a silver one arrived the following day, the felt beneath the keys fresh and plump stopping the air into clear and perfect notes. Louie brought books for me that I stacked beside the round divan and asked a Russian friend to read to me, translating a deep evocative novel. I wondered if Louie had some hidden message by sharing a book about an adulterous affair by a character named Anna Karenina. Louie located a book in English by Sarah Winnemucca that I'd once mentioned would be fun to have. I paged through it during hours I found myself alone, memorizing sections I might declaim if I ever had the interest. In the evenings, we went to concerts and operas, and I lost myself in the agonies of lovers and unrequited love and forced behind me nagging daytime questions of why my rush to pleasure with all the freedom we had longed for hovered around me more like torment than carefree independence.

The weather was perfect, opportunities immense, but malaise kept me from them. A certain mystery attached itself to the bows that marched down the side seams of my cape. In the cloakrooms at receptions Louis took me to, I overheard people wonder out loud about me, where I came from, curious of my Simpson connection. I was a woman with no past, but it did not intrigue me now. Even our liason without the threat of exposure lost its lustre.

The Washingtonian arrived from Hoquiam presses and included nothing of me now, as though I no longer lived. No one sent letters asking me back, no one gave room for any change of my heart. Except for the notice that a "C. W. Stine had moved into the former home of Louis Simpson" nothing more of Louie appeared either. We were wiped off of Hoquiam's face like the last lick of cream about to go sour. At least until the shooting.

We had gone for dinner with friends of L. J., as people in the City called Louie. We had fine wine I consumed too much of but felt certain would help me sleep. We'd laughed and shared stories and talked almost until dawn in a Market Street restaurant while the headwaiter accepted tips to let us stay after closing time.

Our companions, the Prescotts, were fine people, associates of Louie's work at one of his father's mills, and for the first time since arriving I felt hopeful, allowed myself to enjoy an evening of conversation and companionship.

It was still dark when the Prescotts invited us to their apartment, and we stepped out into the street to be greeted by the sounds of a delivery wagon plodding toward us full of clanking bottles of milk. We laughed, waiting for its passage from dark into dawn. I started to step into the street and would have waved to the drayman almost asleep in his seat, but I stumbled instead. Louie bent to catch me. As he did we heard the *boom* then *thunk*. The drayman grunted an "Oh!" of surprise. We both looked up to watch him slump forward.

Louis grabbed the handrail to pull himself up to the man when the second *boom* crashed glass behind us. The horse startled, jerking the wagon and Louis. Mrs. Prescott cried out but I couldn't understand her, wasn't sure where she even stood. Smoke drifted over the horse screaming in terror, the wagon jerking back and forth while Louie grabbed at the horse's bit. The sickening smell of powder mixed with blood met my nose.

Louie caught the harness with one hand, talking to the horse while looking beyond. My heart pounded into my head.

A third boom, another crash behind us.

"Where's he shooting from?" I yelled, understanding now, the effort taking all of my breath.

Louie crouched, pushed me until my knees tore at tiny rocks on cobblestone and my face scraped against the street.

"You all right?" Prescott shouted from behind the wagon. I could see his legs crouched over his wife, both in the shadow of the building.

"All right!" Louie yelled back.

The headwaiter ran out to the street but retreated when Louie hissed, "Get back!"

"There! Behind that carriage," I said, poking my head up enough to see a dark form slip between buildings across the street. A police whistle shrilled its way into our ears already ringing from the closeness of the shots. Two officers galloped past us, clattering on well-shod horses. A third pulled up short and helped to steady the drayman's horse, then climbed onto the seat to check the man.

It happened in a heartbeat, like a phantom, as though part of a shadowy dream. The police questioned us at the station smelling of smoke and old sweat, well into daylight, but we had no knowledge, nothing to tell them of motive for the crime. Until they brought the man in who had done the shooting.

The drayman, dead now, was George Elliot. That's what the paper said. And the murder had been committed by one Robert Hunt, late of Hoquiam and now of San Francisco's city jail. The *Washingtonian* reported it thusly, the last entry it carried about Louis Simpson for some years to come.

> The drayman, Geo. Elliot, leaves a wife and four children. From the account given in the *Examiner*, Hunt was in search of young Simpson, against whom he had a grievance, but stories are conflicting. The shooting was entirely unprovoked. Mr. Hunt was believed to be crazy by everybody, but he was let go, because he appeared harmless.

I tried to remember Robert Hunt at the baseball game in Hoquiam or at one of the declamations. Had he come with his wife or was it after Mary Hunt had left him? Had Louie been too attentive to her at some event? Or was it enough that she and I shared a likeness, and here Louie and I were now, off together in this city, enough to make a crazy man get jealous?

"Unprovoked," the paper said. I shook myself. Who else would hurt from the choices of our lives? I didn't want to think of it. I drank more fine wine, hoping to forget.

After the shooting incident, something changed. Louie would return with a brooding look to his face, distant and solemn. At least that's when I thought it began. I assumed he carried Elliot's widow and four children with him, too, though I knew he'd sent them money, helped out as he should. In my own hand I sent them a letter, included money for support, but what more to do baffled me. I'd remind Louie that he had done all he could. "Unprovoked," I said. "It wasn't your fault."

On bad days, he couldn't be comforted. Instead, he'd lament what a horrible man he was to have taken me from all I knew, from my child and my family.

"You're my family," I said. "I tilled this soil myself and have to accept whatever grows."

Sometimes I couldn't bring him from his anguish, and I wondered then if more than Elliot's death grieved him, if some other trigger shot him to the core.

Into the abyss of knowing came doubts and questions. Perhaps his family objected to our relationship. Perhaps my infidelity was more than his Protestant parents could bear.

Alone, I found glasses of wine kept me from thinking, helped me avoid the view of small hands reining in a pony or blond hair bouncing on a slender child's back.

I began writing long letters to Margaret, letters of description of my new life, the fun and flourish of it all. "Fiction" I called it, inspired by the journals I filled with the thoughts that frightened me. I asked of Belle, that my good wishes be expressed.

Margaret wrote back short, newsy letters of little consequence, though I could hear her precise pronunciation and her emphasis of certain words. And she said that Joe objected to my letters being read to Belle and so that part would stop now, another ending I was forced to face.

I suspected Joe monitored her words to me, too, so I examined them like an archeologist looking for clues, of how they'd explained my absence, how they'd gone on without me.

Apparently quite well, I decided, reading the latest issue of the paper. Joe'd missed not a beat of the metronome in my leaving. He branched out, began constructing apartment buildings on the lot next to our first house.

Absent information about Belle, I told myself that she, too, did well. She had Annie, Margaret, and Joe. She'd do fine, maybe even better with me gone. She'd learn of independence and searching for uniqueness; she'd someday see a mother who'd been strong in reaching for what she wanted.

Then I'd pour another glass of wine.

Louie decided I should meet his family.

A gathering of finches is what it was, in a lavish, abundant garden, rich with interest, color, and a euphony of sound.

His mother, the former Sophie Smith, daughter of a lumberman from Racine, Wisconsin, was every inch a refined and cultured woman. She was some years younger than her husband, who was forty-nine when they married. I'd seen her once or twice in Hoquiam when she and Edgar or sometimes her youngest son, Harry, visited Louie. Her arrival always made the paper, but I had not met her, ever, and I had some anxiety about the gathering. She treated me like fine china.

Louie's father was another story. The great Asa Simpson, lumberman, shipbuilder, fleet owner, industrialist all, was said to be worth twelve million dollars if he was worth a dime. "Moneybags," Louie called him, laughing, "like Kalita, the Duke of Moscow who collected taxes for the Khan and convinced the Russian Orthodox Church's leading Ecclesiastic to move there too. He changed destiny. Dad's like that."

A smallish man of my height, he had a quick glint to his eyes and blunt boldness to his words. He had authorized the expenditures for the lawyers, so he knew that part of my life, but he made no criticism of it, at least not while I could hear. Instead, he acted as though my presence were a foregone conclusion of a story his son was still writing.

"Got yourself a spirited one this time, Louie. Pass the crab, Mother," Asa said and pointed with his fork to a platter the shape of a huge fish that held six crabs in the center of the table.

The Tiffany chandelier sent sparkles over the main course and across the backs of the tall Queen Anne chairs. Wooden frames of silver spoons marked by cities—Milan, Paris, Dresden—lined the dark walls, souvenirs, I supposed, of their European tours. A Loetz vase with a sterling silver overlay held roses as a table piece.

"Looks like your rescue's worth the effort, though," Asa Simpson said. His bushy eyebrows raised once or twice toward his son.

"You always did have an eye for a beautiful woman, Dad," Louie said. Sophie took it as a compliment of her. At least she smiled. She held a silver pliers in her hand and cracked the red crustacean's crust.

"Beauty isn't what it's all about, now is it, Cassie?" Sophie said. Her words wore a veil of charm. She smiled, but I felt coolness not warmth.

I wondered what Louie might have told them about my life in Hoquiam, what they'd gathered for themselves. Their smiles to me appeared genuine. The comradeship among them in my presence was comfortable, not forced.

"No, no, Nan," Sophie said, and I noticed one of the two sheepdogs lower its head and step back off the rug. The other sprawled on the hardwood floor, his head resting on paws as close to the edge of the Persian carpet as allowed.

"Lots to consider," Asa continued, though I didn't know about what.

"Edgar, please don't draw into the flesh so," Sophie said to her second son seated next to Louie. I guessed him to be about eighteen. "It peeves my ears and is unbecoming to your good breeding."

"My brother, Louie, died trying to bring a woman and her child to shore. Louie's named for that brother," Asa continued as though his wife had not spoken about her son's sucking at flesh.

"Daddy's had ships wrecked off the Oregon coast," Edith said. "Uncle Louie was a passenger on a Simpson ship that ran aground." She was a pretty girl, younger than Edgar, who shared her father's intense gaze and mother's slender frame. She wore a ruby ring the size of an ink blotter. "They named a reef for us."

"That they did."

"Did they all die?" I asked still back on the uncle.

"Everyone who was with him," came a soft, almost reverent boy's voice.

"Tell the rest, Harry," Edgar said. "Don't make it all sound like a funeral." Edgar dipped his fingers in the bowl set near his glass for that purpose, patted his mouth of the butter with quick, flashy movement.

"But it was," Harry said, "for Mrs. McDonald and her baby and Uncle."

"You forget the adventure in it!" Edgar said, kicking him under the table. Then to me, "Dad's schooner *Quadratus* ran aground crossing the Coos Bay bar. They thought to bring the woman and her child in by putting out in a lifeboat. Turns out, those that stayed onboard were the ones to make it. Ship came ashore at Charleston Beach while the lifeboat overturned."

"Sometimes caution is the right thing," Harry said.

"The mill machinery they recovered became Dad's first venture in lumbering," Edgar said. "Got it before there were South Slough pirates."

"Pirates?" I said.

"Would have beat old Smith if the ship hadn't sunk," Asa said. "As it was, we were the second mill there on the north bend of the river 'stead of the first. Foul bar."

"Just people collecting salvage," Harry said, "not really pirates at all. Some of the loveliest apple trees in Empire City are salvaged trees. Doctor Tower's lot in Empire has two or three with good yields. And Collver's been shipping apples since the seventies, though I doubt he collected the trees as salvage."

"He made the right choice," Sophie said. The lace around her bodice was antique white and it set off the luster of her olive skin. She could have been Spanish or of the Ukraine. "He hoped to save them and that is what matters. He understood his responsibility and acted accordingly."

I thought I saw Louie's head sink deeper into his greens with her words.

"To him who has been given much, much is expected," Harry said.

"Pretty," Mrs. Simpson said, "though I can't say I miss it all that much."

She'd moved on to another subject, though no one but me seemed to have any difficulty following this family's journey of thought. "A little too primitive for my bones."

"Now don't go scaring Cassie off," Louie said, patting my hand beside his at the table. "It's to be our home and I don't want her to have any ill-conceived notions."

What was to be our home? A salvaged mill? Where pirates operated? Who said anything about my leaving the City?

"However did L. J. talk you into Oregon?" Edith asked me.

"I didn't know he had," I said.

"Oh, brother," Edgar said, looking up with a twinkle to his eye. "You're in hot water now!"

Louie laughed and raised my hand to his lips. He gave me a look with such imploring I smiled, though I didn't feel placated.

"Big brother's a charmer," Edgar said and touched his knuckles to the back of his brother's hand, causing Louie to drop my palm so he could meet his brother's knuckles back. The words "childhood ritual" came to mind.

"Boys," Sophie said, holding the silver pliers in midair. "Please. Your dinners."

"If you don't mind my asking, do you like the coastal climate, Cassie?" Harry asked. His voice was youngish, hadn't changed yet, though I guessed him to be sixteen. He had lusciously long eyelashes.

I tried to answer with confidence, but the discussion about Oregon troubled me. Louie had made no mention of having decided something so major. Perhaps he'd planned it as a surprise, though everyone else appeared to know.

"I've never visited Oregon," I said.

"We were under the impression you were from that wild place," Sophie said. She dipped her hands, wiped them on the linen, then lifted two sugar lumps from the cracker jar into her tea. She rang a small bell at her side, and the serving maid dressed in impeccable white entered through a side door so shiny the wood reflected the woman's image.

"Hoquiam," Asa said. "That's what I told you."

"Hmm," she said. "I'm surprised we never met there. The only Hendrick I encountered was named Margaret."

"That's my sis—"

"Well, that's a coastal community, anyway," Edith said. She leaned back, waiting for the maid to lift her plate.

I guessed Edith to be a few years older than Harry. They all had Louie's pale cashew skin and sensuous eyes, though Harry's eyes were deeper set, had a pondering quality to them while Edgar's were ripe with whimsy.

"She'll love it," Louie said. "It's the kind of place that grabs at you, Cassie, all that tangle of vine maple and fir, the spruce and red alder. And myrtlewood. One of Dad's ships has myrtlewood in the captain's quarters.

Positively glows! And the water! Rivers and sloughs. Ships come in, from all over, taking coal out of Marshfield and shingles and boxes. Can grow anything. Half the eggs and butter in San Francisco come from Coos Bay. Well, almost," he said when his mother raised an eyebrow at his exaggeration. "You can live off the clams and the land. Those wild strawberries. I remember that first time you took us there, Dad. Huckleberries and salals so plump and dark one mouthful was enough to satisfy you."

"Until the next bite," Edgar said. "Sort of like a good woman."

The two younger boys howled at that. Mrs. Simpson gave them a stare over her tiny glasses, but it was obvious she adored these children sitting before her. She wore diamond teardrop earrings and a thin diamond necklace that glittered when she shook her head ever so slightly, attempting to control her children. Edith, too, wore diamonds on her ears, and she grinned as she reached across the table and touched her knuckles to her brothers'.

"Now children," Asa said and cleared his throat, a sign the children took to mean to quiet down.

"Just as soon as we set shore," Louie said turning to me, "I'll take you berry picking, out to the lighthouse." He kissed the knuckles of my hand. "And into the firs. Something to behold. Oh, we three'll have a great time in Oregon."

My heart skipped a beat.

"Three?" Edith asked for me. "Do you have children, Cassie?"

"No, no," Louie said, "no children joining us just yet. No, it's my family we'll be adding with, right Harry? Ol' Harry here's coming with us." He dropped my hand to reach across the table and touch knuckles with the youngest Simpson.

RIPTIDE

❁

The argument we had later back at the hotel was the first of many and had a quality to it like the tides beneath deep surf. In my family, dissatisfaction was expressed by removal or withdrawal, by heavy sighs and lifted eyebrows, nothing spoken, loud or banging. Silence marked the presence of the peril. I was a misfit among it, finding great release in insults and shouts, pan slamming and spit.

Louie came from a tradition of three boys and a vibrant, outspoken father. It wasn't that Louie liked to argue. I think he often said things just to placate me, a kind of comfort-fan, soothing with what he thought I wished to hear, wanting so to please another, dealing with consequences later when he hoped he could charm away discomfort.

It was what he tried first following dinner, the charming.

"Thought you'd be pleased to have another about," he said. "Ol' Harry's a good fellow. And he loves pretty women." He reached for me. "You'll have him eating from the palm of your hand in no time. Just like me. He won't be in our way."

"I wasn't invited on this journey and I don't like being told how it's to end."

He looked chastened. "Should have said something. Only wanted to surprise you. Do better next time. Forgive me?"

"You still don't understand, do you?" I said. He was holding me now, our arms wrapped around each other's waists. "I don't like surprises that change my life. I like the reins."

"Loosen up a little, Case. I'm not fencing you in. Not asking you to marry me, challenge that suffragette heart of yours." He wiggled us together.

"But you want me to leave with you for this Coos Bay and what, just be with you?"

"Can we talk about this later, when we're both rested for the fight?" He smiled and gave me his Labrador look.

"You've invited another person to live with us in a place you've never even mentioned. You've assumed I'll just trot up there with you. You've no right."

"No right?" I felt his hands tense around my waist. "No, I suppose I don't."

"Not even if you were my husband, which you aren't, and may not be if this is how it's to be."

"Cassie," he said and lifted my chin with his wide hand. "Don't let's argue. It pulls us apart."

I pulled back. "I'll argue if I have to."

He threw his hands up and stepped back. I could see from the look on his face that he accommodated to a point and then in an instant could explode.

"Live where and with whom you want," he said. "Be right and unhappy. See if I care." He poured himself a snifter of brandy and tossed his head back taking it in one swallow.

"That's another thing," I said. "When did you decide we would live in Oregon?"

"Suppose that's a problem for the little lady too," he said pouring another dark swirl into his glass. This one he held with a death grip, the liquid shaking like crosscurrent tides.

Now my face was hot and I could feel myself stifling a scream. "Equals don't treat each other this way," I said, "deciding without talking."

"You did," he said.

"I did not! I came here where you worked, and that's been fine with me.

I haven't said anything to push you." I stomped around the room, punching pillows, straightening books into neat little piles, circling while I shouted at him back over my shoulder. "What's in Oregon that entitles you to take us there? What made you decide we should go to some remote shore? Not even a mention of it! Do I mean so little to you? Are my views of such little weight?" I forced back the tears I could feel behind my nose. "What are you running from? Another husband after your hide?"

"You decided," he said, "left me out of it and ignored my will." His voice seethed with anger.

"What are you talking about?"

"About Belle."

"Belle?"

He set the snifter onto the marble tabletop so hard I was sure both would break, but they didn't.

"She's *my* daughter," I said. "I'm amazed you'd think to have some say in it."

"She's a part of you, Cassie. I have some interest in her too."

"Joe wouldn't have let her stay," I said. "It's ridiculous to assume so." I punched a pillow on the divan, feeling it in my stomach.

"We'll never know, will we, since you sent her back."

There was a sternness in his jaw, and he was shouting now. "Come if you want! Or not. It's of no matter to me. In the future, maybe we'll confer about such matters. For now, not!"

"If we have a future," I said and jerked open the door to the hotel's empty hall.

"Don't threaten, Cassie," he warned.

"One thing you'll soon learn about me if you haven't already is I don't threaten. I act."

I held the door steady waiting for him to stomp through my resolve. He stood like a statue for a moment and then spoke, calm and deliberate, offering an out I'd almost gone too far to take.

"Truth is, Cass, that's where Dad wants me now, at the mill on Coos Bay. Where my work is. That's why I'm going. Harry too. Would like you with me, but it's your call."

I closed the door. At least he wasn't shouting.

"I know you told Joe you didn't need to marry. Maybe you didn't mean it, and right now we couldn't, not with your status and all and… But we can't live there as Louis Simpson and Cassie Stearns."

"Hendrick," I corrected.

"It wouldn't work in that country, with my representing Dad. Wouldn't be right for you either, for folks to think you and I were just living together. In sin." He choked on the word. I searched for another for it but he pressed on. "I thought Harry would lend, oh, respectability, show folks Dad approved and all."

"What are you asking?" I said. The evening felt like a riptide, debris swirling in different directions. The wine interfered with what I needed to grasp, but it was coming to me the way a bad dream lingers even after one's awake. I felt my chest tighten, the sign of forced choice.

He fidgeted. "Don't know how to say this." He took a deep breath. "Just want you to come with me. To Oregon. Don't want to be separated." His fingers brushed from his eyes to his chin as though he could wipe away strain. "I'm as obsessed with you as you are with me." His words slurred a bit.

"And that means…"

"I want you with me, in Oregon. As Mrs. Louis Simpson, even though you aren't."

A kind of darkness fell as I made the decision to live the lie. Something about the way his eyes pleaded, the way he reached for me, the way my breath weakened when I thought he might have walked out that door. They all told me I could not let him go without me.

"Wouldn't ask you to do this, Casey, I wouldn't. If there was any other way. It's just… I know we could wait until the divorce is final, but I want you there. And then there's—" He made a turn. "I'll never forget you for this, Cassie, if you come. Truth is, don't know if I can do all that Dad wants up there without you. Big decision, his trusting me in this. With you by my side, there's nothing I can't accomplish."

Didn't I want adventure and intrigue? Didn't I act to have fullness? What would I gain by staying? What would I lose if he left? I let myself be swirled into the vortex of the future.

In the days following our fight and my decision, Louie couldn't have been more attentive. Diamond earrings were delivered the next morning followed by flowers and a note that read: "Let us never end an argument with a threatened exit."

Naturally, we told people we were having a quiet, private ceremony, a calm event, deceptively so, not unlike the ocean on a still day that lies placid, covering the twists and turmoil of the deeps below. Such was now the nature of our lives.

Everything on the surface appeared tranquil, as though by some unwritten rule we'd not discuss the things that might put waves into the lull. No mention of Belle or Joe, no mention of Oregon, not even Harry. We would speak of what was present until after our apparent honeymoon, when I would move from being a divorcée in everyone else's eyes to a very married lady.

At least that's the charade we told people, anyone who asked. But we would have a honeymoon if not the wedding. To do less would create more questions in his circle since no one would be invited to a ceremony.

"Won't your parents wonder?" I asked. "Your brothers will be disappointed not to be included in a wedding." We stood in my Palace rooms, half-packed trunks spilled over with dresses and books around us.

"Have to say something to your sister," he said, avoiding my question.

"I've written. Told her we were getting married and might be moving. She knew that couldn't be. Her letter back singed my fingers. *Horrified, scandalous*, words like that. She fears for my soul, she says. She thinks we should live apart." He rubbed my back as I talked. "Assuming you'd still want me as your wife after such a separation."

He stopped rubbing. "Why would you wonder about that?" He flipped his watchcase open and closed it with his thumbnail.

"I may like this marriage well enough to want to make it legal when I can," I said, "give up my *independent* state." I laughed and remembered later that Louie hadn't.

Fine champagne flowed at the reception we planned in lieu of a real wedding. While the guests were gracious and congratulatory—mostly friends of Louie's parents—I found small solace in the gathering. The laughter and the chatter didn't feed me as it might have. Something lingered, some pall, like the lull said to come with hurricanes halfway through their force. And it came from more than learning that the Simpson mill town we'd be living in was dry as a desert drifter's throat.

We "honeymooned" at the Hotel del Monte, but it was not the sweet event I had imagined. Oh, there were moments I convinced myself that I had every right to be here, that some vows spoken before a minister or judge bore little weight. It was the tiredness of change that must have made me sad.

"I'll play ladies' billiards tomorrow until I've calluses on my hands," I said. We listened to a harpist while we dined.

"Not if I have anything to say about it," Louie said and laughed. "I want to take you up Mount Tamapalis, to the academy where I went to school. Walk in the gardens if you'd like."

"I guess I didn't realize we shared that interest. Though I prefer potted plants. Easier to control and contain."

"Only half the reason my young hands look as weathered as barn boards." He turned his palms over and back. "Like to wiggle my feet in that beach sand too."

"Me too," I said and leaned across the table to kiss him, hopeful for the moment.

Later that evening, Louie shaved off the Vandyke beard, or at least he allowed me to. Without it, I could see the fullness of his mouth and trace with my finger his strong, angular jaw. I rinsed the shaving brush and sloshed the razor through the now tepid water in the hotel's porcelain bowl.

Louie wiped my hands with the Turkish towel, then kissed the pads of each of my fingers, individually. He looked at my hands. "How old are you, Casey?"

The question was so far from anything I thought might be on his mind that I was dumbfounded.

"I'm twenty-one," he said, "Twenty-two on the first. Just so you know." He crushed the towel into a ball and lobbed it into the corner wicker basket.

"I wouldn't have guessed." I swallowed. "Only twenty-two come September? Maybe it was your hands that misled me."

"Experience is the key," he said looking at his short fingers and wide palm. "To business," he added to my raised eyebrow. "So, tell me. How old are you?"

I fidgeted free of his reach for me. "Does it really matter?"

"Not a whit," he said.

He leaned back on the bed. A string quartet played on the lawn below our hotel window, the music drifting up like the aroma of a gourmet meal. Pink and purple hydrangeas spilled over their white pitcher adorning the dresser. A wreath of baby's-breath and lavender and tiny dried bud roses hung on the wall over bed and mixed with the scent of the fresh-cut flowers.

"Just something I've never thought to ask you before. Curious, now we'll be together in Coos country. Start our own family some day."

His words caused a grimace to wash across my face. He caught it in the mirror.

"Are you all right?" he asked. He sat up and pulled me to him this time.

"It's the talk about children," I said.

He sat quiet. "Someday then," he said.

"I suppose we shouldn't have any secrets," I said, my voice tight. "So I'll tell you. I'm twenty-eight. Twenty-nine next February twenty-seventh."

He cocked his head the way a poodle does when considering. "Happens I love older women."

I pulled myself from him, began tidying the wash basin, folding the towel with a perfect crease.

"Even if she can't have children?" I kept my back to him.

"We've had this conversation before. You can. Just don't know about me." When I didn't laugh he said, "You're serious."

"I might not be able to have another. After Belle's delivery, there were complications of a sort, to my heart. It was never clear, exactly. My recovery took a toll. I should have told you, but I was afraid if you—"

"Must've been hard for you." He pulled me into the wrap of his arms. "Wish I could have been there."

I never loved him more than at that moment, for caring about how I felt rather than sharing his own disappointment in what my message must have meant.

Did I believe what I told him, that I couldn't have children? Or was it something made up in my mind, something meant to protect me, to give safe harbor to fear? Who knew what berth the thought was tied to.

The music from the lawn concert drifted up and filled the empty spaces now claiming my mind until Louie spoke again, this time with a certainty I never questioned.

"I'd like children," he said, "a dozen if we can have them. But you should know this and never forget it: Nothing will ever stop me from loving you, Casey, nothing, no one, no thing, no how, not ever. No matter what strangeness the future may bring into our lives nor what vagaries from the past, you can count on this one thing: Until death do us part, you will always be first for as long as we live. Forever. No matter what else should happen."

I had no reason to doubt him.

There was also no doubt in my mind that Louie loved his family. Not more than me, perhaps, but almost. They were like a litter of puppies together, biting at each other's heels, rolling over and onto themselves turning every small or large thing into play. Competition like a fragrance hung over them in their conversations, their ideas, in the way they baited each other with ideas and teasing. They argued about politics, business and economics, religion, philosophy, Rhode Island red chickens, and the maturing of trees. Yet I sensed that if any were in trouble, needed total attention or rescue, that the litter would be there for him or her with every resource, every fiber that love and devotion, even deception, allowed.

That Louie should choose to spend time with me when such a family would serve him so completely added to my awe about this man I'd consented to live with.

"You're a Simpson now," Louie said as we rode back from the hotel behind a matched team. Their tails twitched against flies.

"Which means?"

"Innovation," he said. "Ideas and the power to get them through. Means generosity too." He was thoughtful. "Being the best at something, or at least giving something worthwhile your best, your all. I'm not sure what that is for me yet, but I have a feeling about Oregon. Make a fresh, clean start there. Show Dad I can do it."

"Did he come out on the Trail?" I asked trying to imagine how this small, wiry man had managed to accumulate such wealth.

Louie shook his head. "Landed on the Oregon coast just twenty years after the first white man recorded there. Beached in style, too, on board one of his ships. Already made and lost a million by then and gained it back. Took one look at those stands of timber and knew it was a perfect place to build an empire. The mining and coal, that's all come later. Oregon's still the chance of a lifetime. And I know. Dad's given me a few already that I've blown." He looked sheepish. "Used to gamble some. Lost a ship once or twice."

"Apparently I'm not the only one who kept a secret," I said.

He looked away, out the round window. "Dad's banker friend had to bail me out once too. Dad's trusting me in this and I won't disappoint him."

Asa Simpson did trust his son, but he also liked insurance. Not on his ships, of course. He never insured his ships or cargo, giving fate her due. But when it came to his sons, that was something else. Which was, I think, the real reason Harry came to join our life in Oregon as soon as it began.

"Harry likes it," Louie said, "or at least he did when we were younger. But I'm pretty sure Dad had planned to send him to keep me accountable. He knows I'd never do anything to put Harry at risk. Doesn't matter that I have you to keep me on the straight and narrow now." He grinned. "Ol' Harry'll be a good friend to you. You'll see."

I had hoped we could have privacy in the transition of this lie, with just the two of us, my Louie and me.

We stood aboard the Simpson schooner *Repeat*, a four-masted vessel, 148 feet long, that had been in service four years when we boarded her in September 1899 along with a load of hardwood, oak and walnut, some other passengers returning from the City, and bags of hoped-for mail.

"Built in Dad's shipyard at the bend of the Coos Bay," Harry told me. "We've a shipyard in Grays Harbor too. 'Spose you know about that one. Our *Western Shore*'s set records for passing under the Golden Gate and reaching Astoria in less than two days. Took eighteen hundred tons of wheat from there to Queenstown, Ireland, too, in barely a hundred days back in '75."

We stepped over the coils of rope as thick as a man's forearm and listened to the steady swoosh of the Port Orford cedar against the showering waters of the Pacific. The snap of the sails punctuated the groan of the riggings. Sea gulls trailed after us as though we led them, but they sought the fish our moving through the water stirred.

"Not that you need to worry your pretty little head about such details," Louie said and smiled.

"I've no problem with details. But you should know now, Mr. Simpson, that this Mrs. Simpson intends to learn quite a lot about shipping. Among other things." It was the first time I had referred to myself in this fashion in the presence of others.

"Sorry!" He held his hand up as though warding off a blow. "Didn't know you were interested," he said and clicked his heels together followed by a bow.

"Joe never let me care. He said I was too addled and forgetful."

"Happens if your head is full of things not worth remembering," Harry said.

"Well put, Ol' Harry," his brother said. "Fine with me to have the newest manager of the Simpson interests in Oregon be supported by a beautiful woman with good—"

"If I'm not interrupting," Harry said, "I wonder if we could talk about what I'll be doing at the mill site."

"You," Louie said without hesitation, "will be in school, at the Marshfield Academy."

"But the other times, I mean."

"What did you have in mind, Harry?" I wondered if his inclination ran to timber cruising or perhaps to surveying land. Harry surprised me.

"If it wouldn't be too much trouble," he said, "perhaps work with a local doctor?"

"Noble idea!" his brother said, patting him on the back. Harry stumbled a bit with the force of his brother's goodwill.

"Every family should have a doctor, isn't that right Case? O'Harry here'll be ours."

"I suppose doctors have their place," I said, "though I don't think much of what they do. Guesswork mostly."

"Best guesses we have," Harry said.

"I knew a Quinault woman, untrained as a physician, who I think knew as much." As I said it, Mary's pronouncement of putting my child in distress rushed into my thoughts. I shivered.

"Cold?" Louie asked. He didn't wait for an answer, wrapped his big arm around me and pulled me closer.

"What's that sound?" I said becoming aware of a kind of deep barking lifting up from the sea.

"Simpson Reef," Harry said pointing to the array of rocks jutting out of the waves.

"Sea lions," Louie said. "Look at them. Fat, lazy things." He pointed to rocks south of the river mouth that we were passing. The lions lay like brown slugs halfway up the slanted, striated peak of sandstone a few hundred feet from the shore. They barked into the sunshine.

"The males are easily killed," Harry said. "The Indians hunt them for the oil and meat. Males stand and defend, and the females rush into the water to save themselves. And their young."

"Eat hundreds of salmon and steelhead, and I can't see a single thing they add," Louie said.

"We don't always see the whole picture," Harry said as we sailed on by.

"Sounds profound, Ol' Harry," Louie said, then, "Cape Gregory Lighthouse!" He pointed to a high point on the starboard side. "That's where we'll picnic before the week is out." His voice held the excitement of a schoolboy being let out for the summer. He took in a deep breath. "I want you to so love this place, Cassie," he said, squeezing my shoulder. "It's where I always want to be. Even before I knew whether you would share it with me I loved it. Your being here just makes it as close to heaven as I'll ever come."

"There's the *Encore!*" Harry shouted, as excited yet as I'd seen him. He pointed to the steam tug making its way across the bar toward us.

"One more time," Louie said, "one more time across that bar." Our eyes turned together to the north jetty of rocks that marked the Coos Bay mouth.

The tugboat disappeared in the swells, then eased its way beside the schooner and deposited a pilot to assist in our crossing over the bar.

Something like a held breath began then as the tug eased into its place at the bow, connected now to our ship as it began the passage between two giant forces: the pull of the ocean coming to shore and the rush of the bay water, west. Transition, from one great force to another, that's what this was, what I was facing too. I wasn't where I'd been nor where I'd be but somewhere in between, like the river bar, and it was roughest here, could bring the ship aground or pull us through. But we wouldn't want to stop, not here, not now. We had to keep going.

The tug ensured more than any other way that the ship would arrive. Margaret had her Guide, even Louie seemed led by the lay of this land, the future it promised. Harry had the dream of career. For the moment, I could name only Louie to guide me. Louie pulled me to him like a lighthouse beacon. Louie immersed me, filled my senses, gave me purpose. Only Louie made me glad to be alive. I had the vaguest sense it would not be enough.

Swells that took us deep into the surf splashed against the hull and forced a thin layer of spray over us.

"We can go inside," Harry said.

"Want to?" Louie asked.

"I like it here," I told them both, and I could see that Louie was pleased, Harry a little worried.

"Why don't you go, Harry?" I said. "Make sure everything's ready for our departure."

He nodded and disappeared, his hunched shoulders so unlike his taller brother's.

The steam engine of the tug labored under the weight of its pull. The ship resisted the turn into the opening that appeared where the Coos Bay wrestled with the sea. In the distance I could see other ships anchored, waiting for the tide to turn. A ship towed a boom of logs upriver like a contained flotsam of sticks. Some smaller vessels sat anchored closer to the timbered shores.

"It's busy," I said.

Louie nodded, his eyes off in the distance. "Those ships have come out of Marshfield, farther up the bay, past our docks. Passenger steamer makes the trip four times a day."

A swell pushed against our ship.

"Are you nervous?" I asked, the bar causing my stomach to churn up its dinner. I took a deep breath, swallowed.

"About the crossing? No, not ever. The *Encore*'s a worthy craft. Pant like a dog," he directed and let his tongue hang out over quick breaths. "Cuts down on the nausea. Try it."

I felt silly but panted, and either it worked or crossing over the bar into smoother waters settled my stomach.

"Just thinking about what lies ahead for us, how things work out sometimes," Louie said as though in the middle of a conversation with me. "John's dying came as a shock to Dad, even though he'd never admit it. John Kruse. He managed Dad's shipyards. That's really why I'm here. John's son took over and he needs my help. The opportunity couldn't have come at a better time." He looked at me, then away. "Well, maybe at a better time."

We moved up the river, and I could feel Louie's excitement as he pointed out features of the landscape and intricacies of the narrow bay that looked more like a river. "There's the mouth of the South Slough," he said, and I saw the edges of a mud flat being swallowed by the incoming tide. "All tidal, here," he said. "Mailboats, butter and milk deliveries, log booms, all arrive or not, based on the tide. Look there," he said pointing to the tops of a cluster of houses. "Empire City's the oldest county seat, since '53."

"I didn't realize people had been here so long," I said.

"We're intruders, all right. Stole the land, no, 'requisitioned' it from the Miluks and Hanis." He thought again. "No. We stole it."

Sand dunes one hundred feet high appeared in the distance as bald heads with tufts of sea grass and scrubby trees growing as hair.

We rounded a spit of land jutting out like a pointing finger. The bay made a sweeping bend from the ocean, not unlike the flow of a question mark. At the base, it opened into a wide and calming expanse of seawater. "Don't know how I feel about living at the bottom of a question mark," I said.

"Apt description though that makes Marshfield at the period of the question mark." He pointed toward wharfs down the bay. "Our bend still has room to grow with twice the beauty, I'd say."

White clouds swept with a stiff broom hovered above the timbered shores allowing sky as blue as Belle's eyes to arc over the bay toward the sea. Smoke spouted from shipyards and lumber mills farther south and to our immediate left. Gulls and terns and tiny finches, black and yellow and dull red, flitted about as the tug disconnected itself, no longer necessary to our destination.

On our right, in neat and orderly fashion, stood a dozen small houses painted white, a dock and shipyards, a mill belching out smoke and a company store. It could have been a painting on a postcard from Maine. Above it all sat a shingled house with a cupola that might have adorned a summer cottage overlooking Lake Erie back in New York.

"There's home!" Louie said, his head nodding to the shingled house.

Two, maybe three stories, it was a modest building with a view of the bay. Wide steps made their way from the porch through a cultured garden the details of which were hidden behind box hedges except for the fruit trees and a sidewall of purple climbing wisteria. A length of smaller steps reminding me of those at the Quinault village marched down the sharp bank from the house to the dock.

Off to the side was a zigzag of boardwalk of yellow, freshly milled lumber making its way with handrails up the side of the bank to the house. I could smell the fresh lumber above the tidewater. It reminded me of Hoquiam.

"Steps can be hard on a person's heart," Louie said in explanation, and I marveled again at his thoughtfulness turned into action. "Ordered in the walkway so as not to put undue pressure on yours. Looks like they've done a fine job."

Our ship eased next to the dock, and I felt the familiar thud and wrench of lumber against lumber as it lined up against the pilings. The view of the gardens and house one hundred feet above us disappeared as we closed into the wharf. A dozen or more men rushed about the riggings, continuing to lower the sails, throwing ropes and securing the vessel. I bent my knees to balance as I'd found worked best. And when we were secure, with sea gulls dipping and swooping and the sound of steam escaping from the lumber-yard nearby, I took my Louie's hand.

My heart fluttered a bit, in excitement I imagined. I looked at him, with his handsome face, tightly trimmed sideburns, a decided cleft in his chin. He smiled back, then held my fingers in a comforting curl inside his palm. Maybe I could find my fill here, with him, in this place. It wasn't what I'd planned exactly, nor what I'd hoped for. But I had crossed the bar and here I stood. I placed my leather shoes on the dock and took my first steps onto Oregon's wild shore and into my unplatted future.

IMPRESSIONS

✿

Seeing the Oregon coastline near the bar, spying the jagged rocks tumbled like a child's toys against a forest of hills so thick it was almost black, I'd say the word to describe my first impression of Oregon was *formidable*. I found it an awesome unyielding land of green twisted vines, sunset-red woodpeckers, and wild blossoms blooming above sand dunes and spilling beside deep sloughs.

First impressions matter, that's what my father always said. Of course, he meant it as a way for me to always look the finest, be on my best behavior to influence the impression others walked away with. "No recoverin' the bad effects of a first impression," he said more than once.

Oregon gave no bad impressions.

Sea lions' barking, an occasional seal too, those were the sounds I remember. That and the pounding of surf near Simpson's Reef, the plunge of water sometimes rising a hundred feet in the air and splashing to treetops. It was immense and intense and promised the novelty and intrigue that I thought I needed to fill me, make me whole. That it was also an uncontrollable land did not occur to me until much later.

My first thought about the house overlooking the bay was its invitation to abundance.

"You'll be the lady of the manor," Louie said. "Dad gave it to us. A wedding present." He swallowed and I saw a flush work up the back of his neck.

"Of sorts," I said.

It was smaller than the home I'd left, but the setting was spectacular with a view of water and timbered hills. The smell of sawdust from the mill drifted over latticework separating the house from the place where Louie would work.

Two Chinese cooks met us at the plank steps, offering friendliness with their eyes mixed with wariness from what they held in their arms: four silver-white poodles, freshly bathed.

"What do we have here?" I asked.

"Meet Lung Lem," he said, "and his cousin Ming Ho. You've a dozen cousins, right, Lem?"

"Good have you back," the man said through a smile that turned his eyes to two ink lines across his face. "Where Master Harry?"

"He'll be about shortly."

Both men bowed then, their thin braids falling forward against their blue shirts. Louie bowed back before introducing me.

"They hold four dogs without names who wait for the mistress of the manor to place the nomenclature on their noble heads," Louie announced next in his orator's voice.

"How ever did you get them here without my knowing?" It didn't matter, the pleasure of their presence was complete. "Have we ever spoken of dogs?"

"Always describing people by their breed," Louie said. He mimicked me: "'She's thin as a greyhound,' or 'He's loyal as a bird dog,' 'Dainty as a poodle.' Thought you should have some of your own to inspire you."

"They're wonderful," I said, and squatted down. "Joe never wanted dogs about with their shedding and such." I looked up to see if my mention of Joe had offended Louie, but he didn't appear to have noticed.

I clapped my hands and the Chinese men watched their charges squiggle and leap from their arms to race across the goat-cropped lawn to reach me. The puppies stood on their back legs, one on top of the other, falling over each other to lap at my face, pushing up under my chin, shrill yap-yaps gaining frequency and pitch. One had a weepy eye that made the soft curls around it appear pink. It stayed back, a little more reserved than its brothers.

"Reminds me of your family," I said and laughed.

"Never."

"You're right. These dogs are more orderly than that!"

"Wonder how you'd describe me," Louie said, his eyes twinkling.

"Oh, no poodle, that's for sure," I said, my index finger tapping on my lip while I thought. "You're a large, alert, very intelligent happy-as-a-tramp Labrador retriever. Big and bouncing. Love to run and hunt and sweep things off the table with a flourish. Plunges into things."

He looked wounded again, then decided what I'd said was complimentary or accurate and laughed. The poodles pushed at me, already wanting my attention on them instead of Louie. When I fell backward they pounced, pulling at the feathers and flowers that lined my box hat, brushing my skirts up high enough to show my pantaloons and expose bare ankles above my high-top shoes.

"Ah, the lady shows a little leg," Louie said as he attempted to pull me from the melee. He fell himself, and the dogs piled on him, too, his sleeve cuff popping loose as they pulled at him and barked in pleasure. He lay sprawled across me, my stomach heaving, my eyes to the sky.

"I've never understood why a society that lets a man gaze at a woman's neckline is horrified by the sight of her ankles," he said. "Of which the latter you are currently exposing."

I chuckled against him, pushing.

"It's good to hear you laugh," Louie said as he sat, "even at my expense."

"Yours!" I said pushing at my skirts. "Look at me. I've scared the cooks away!"

Lem had stepped back inside and pulled on Ming Ho's wide sleeve to bring him in too. They stared at us through one of the many-paned windows from the living room. Through the shrubs, I noticed legs, then people standing on their front porches, craning their necks to look our way.

"Like a true Simpson," he said and made one mad effort to push away the poodles, pull me up to stand. "Create a ruckus the minute you step foot in town."

"At your instigation, sir," I said.

"You've been well trained, then," he said and swirled me about holding me tight to his chest. "Now to name the dogs. The classics? Plato, Cicero,

Aristotle, or Russian like Igor or Andrei?"

"Their personalities should name them."

I looked at the mass of warmth at my feet. "The largest one should be Beebee, short for Big Boy, and the one who's barking most, over there, we'll call her Beatrice." Louie laughed and nodded, encouraging me to go on. "All right. The Lady Margaret, for the daintiest one, and the little one, standing back, with the little pink on her face, how about Rhodie."

"For Rhodedendron?" he said, sounding surprised. "How did you know I had one planted for you? Over there, on the north side." He pointed to a waxy-leafed plant next to the house. "In the spring it'll bear white."

"Yes. BeeBee and Beatrice, Rhodie and Margaret," I finished pointing to each dog in turn.

A whistle blew from the mill next door, startling us both.

Louie laughed. "Announces when to get up, lunch, and when to go home. Dad didn't want anyone to wonder. You'll get used to it."

The waning afternoon cast long shadows from the fir trees on the west side of the house, and I felt a breeze I hadn't been aware of.

"Happens this time of day," Louie said. "You've got goose bumps." He took his jacket off and laid it around my shoulders. "There's so much I want to tell you about this country, Cass, so you'll love it the way I do."

"I'm already beginning that romance," I said.

We stood hand in hand then, moved the dogs back with our toes, and Louie brushed the grass from my skirt, untied the bow of my hat askew on my head and held it like a wooden pail by the wine-colored ribbons. Tree roses grew within my view that made me think of Papa. Chrysanthemums clustered near the stairs, and Louie broke the stems of several yellow ones, placing them inside my hat he still carried by the streamers. He looked to put a blossom in his lapel, remembered I wore his jacket and slipped the bloom behind my ear. He handed me the spray of flowers. His fingers pulled at the wisps of hair barely touching my cheeks, then with both hands he lifted my French roll with the tips of his fingers, his thumbs at my temples. I felt a tingling along my scalp.

"I feel like I'm in a dream," he said, his voice thick. "To have you here, so beautiful, so alive. I don't deserve this, I..."

"Don't," I said. "No self-scolding, please. I don't want to think. I want to feel."

He let me go. "Well, then, I hope you feel the excitement of this place. With you here I feel like I'll do something grand."

"I've never thought of myself as inspiration," I said.

"Our own frontier. Just like Dad had, but different."

As he spoke his arm swept before him to take in the arc of the view. I reached up to remove the cuff hanging from his sleeve and followed his arm to the wash of the bay and beyond, sights I'd wake to for the next years of my life.

Perhaps I'd be forgiven for what I'd chosen, a man over my child, passion over pragmatics, guilt rather than responsibility.

I could have stood there at Louie's side forever, inhaling what was, seeking inspiration, that act of breathing in. Just the two of us and a puddle of poodles at our feet, gazing into our future. Without the lie of our lives, it might have been perfect.

Louie motioned some of the workers still craning their necks to come over then, and introductions went around. He knew everyone, especially the children who tumbled about with the dogs. People were kind and polite, a little in awe, I thought, of this man with his wide-open arms. They stayed a moment, then the men tipped their hats, and the women smiled as they backed away before the awkwardness of what to talk about had room to intervene.

Harry said then, "If it wouldn't be too much trouble, could you please tell me which room you'll want to be mine?"

"Take your usual," Louie said. He did not startle at Harry's presence as I did. "No sense in rearranging things."

Harry nodded and moved up the porch steps past us. He disappeared into the living room, past the cooks, and out of sight. We followed him inside.

Even with the dogs rushing around at our feet, I could feel Sophie's presence in the house the moment I entered. Warm woods and flowered paper, a mandolin music box stamped with British importers Houghton and Gunn, striped divans, and silver sets marked her style with elegance and grace. But there were signs of Asa, too, nautical signs. A barometer set into shiny New England maple, a world map with tiny pins marking the countries the Simpson ships had sailed to. Old gray oars hung from the sloped ceiling over the bay window the way rifles hung in some woodsmen's homes. The coatracks were small anchors, or replicas, bearing heavy slickers and hats. The Boston high chest had compass inlays of light and dark wood.

"Some room for rearrangement," I said already planning change.

"Really? I've always liked it the way it is," Louie said, "but you go right ahead and change things."

Louie led me upstairs and showed me the room he and Edgar had shared as boys, where Edith stayed, and Harry's door.

"We'll let Ol' Harry have that one," he said nodding to the room that faced west. "He likes sunsets. Our room faces east. I always like the dawns."

We passed by the cooks' quarters reached by a narrow, winding staircase that led up from the kitchen.

Our room would be on the second floor as well, two down from Harry's, with a dormer facing the bay, overlooking part of the doorgarden and the docks. The cast-iron tub with claws feet—big enough for two—that took over the alcove off the bedroom caught my eye first. It was deep and someone had embroidered "Double Berth" on a pillow covering meant as a headrest for slumbering bathers. A commode with a pull chain pointed to the most modern of conveniences.

A canopy bed with a homesteader quilt gave the otherwise all-white space its only color. The smell of lavender soap from the alcove was fragrant enough to penetrate the room.

"Mother thought you might like to decorate our room yourself," he said, "so she had their things taken out. She didn't stay here much. Dad was always busy. She came mostly for us boys, I think, because we loved it so. She and Edith really belong to the City."

Above us, accessed by a ladder at the end of the hall, rose the cupola I'd seen from the outside.

"Can see for miles up here," Louie said, talking as he climbed. He pushed up against a trapdoor of sorts and a graying light mixed with a musty smell poured down. He reached for my hand and steadied me from above as I came up behind him.

"Watch the ships round the point before they dock. You'll be able to order the cooks and have a hot meal for me when I've been away," he said. The sky was dusky already, the day later than I'd thought.

"What makes you think I won't be with you?" I said.

"Might at that. Hadn't thought of it. I will now, believe me, I will."

A telescope pointed toward the heavens. There was a single chair and table and one narrow cot clustered into the little room of windows. Three windows with wooden shutters faced the bay. Another window opened toward the mill and a tiny one faced the millworker's hill; still another toward the sea.

"Good place to write," he said. "All quiet. Sometimes I'd come up here, when mother wasn't in residence, and compose." He straddled the chair and leaned against the window sill, chin resting on his hands.

I opened one of the windows, letting cool air into the closed-in smell. I could hear frogs croak, the cry of an egret drifting across the sky. Beyond the immediate horizon of riggings and rope rose dark hills of firs and cedars not unlike the land I'd known in Hoquiam, land that was "hungry for wood."

"A house on the bay," I said with a sigh.

"Someday I'd like a place that overlooks the ocean too," Louie said. "Bay's peaceful and calm and changes with the tide and the temperature, but it's nothing like the ocean. Nothing's as exhilarating as a winter storm crashing and spraying against the rocks or as peaceful as watching the permanence of a sunset over wave after wave. Even on a moonless night the white of the crest reaches out to a man. Nothing's as unchanging yet constantly unpredictable."

A spire of smoke drifted up through the lace of trees into a clear and darkening sky. A flicker of orange flame smaller than a seashell appeared across the bay. It was like a painting almost, so pristine and uninterrupted.

"Hanis," Louie said, somehow knowing that I wondered about the smoke. "And to the south it'll be Miluk."

"Indians?"

"What's left of them. Coos people. Peaceable as can be. Just out getting salal berries or looking for the last of the black huckleberries," he said. "Little family units, mostly. The rest were rounded up a few years after Dad first came here. Never knew why, really, except for their land. They didn't do any harm. I guess farther south the Rogues did. Wiped out most of them resisting the removal. Some hid in the underbrush. Others were hidden by settlers who didn't think it made sense either. Only way for them to stay legal or try to keep their allotments was for them to marry a white man. Or woman, though it went to the women, mostly, to secure the family line. Some of Dad's captains took Indian wives." He hesitated as though to share more, then said, "Other prominent men, too, in the old days."

The words he spoke took on a distant tone, as though they held something more beneath the surface.

"So much for the peacefulness," I said.

"Little is what it seems on the surface."

"Like us."

Into the pause he stood. "How can you doubt?" he said and kissed me. I would have stayed in his arms forever, then, imagining our perfect world-of-the-moment would never change, was as certain and long-lasting as the thick and solid timber seen through the pale scarf of smoke.

"I've hired a maid for you," Louie said. "A Coos woman." His voice had that strange and distant quality to it, something I couldn't name.

"Will she live here too?" I asked.

He shook his head. "Has a family she tends to. Thought you'd like some help during the days. And some female company."

"Maybe I could find my own maid."

Silence filled the room.

"Done it again, haven't I?" he said. "Trying to be helpful and messed it up."

I shrugged my shoulders. "You're new to this, but your arena of good-will is still pretty wide. Gives you room for mistakes and forgiveness."

"A man like me needs a good wide berth for both."

Harry developed a routine. He was a night person. I'd hear him downstairs, the chairs scraping at odd hours, the light from his lamp casting ghostly shadows on the night fog that hovered over the bay outside the window. He stayed in his room most of the morning, reading, I assumed, until I knocked on his door one morning because of a strange smell.

"I dissect them," he said of the bird carcasses stretched against oilcloth on the table. Tools of taxidermy—knives, cotton padding, arsenic, and needles—lined up beside it. "Anatomy," he said. "Botany interests me too." He appeared invigorated and rested.

"This air agrees with you," I said wrinkling my nose. "Tea?"

"It's actually a little too damp for me," Harry said and coughed. "But Dr.

Glisan said once there is not a more healthy spot on the globe than along this bay."

"Tells you what those medical men know," I said. "Tea'll do you good. I'll take some with you. Downstairs, out of this scent."

"Dr. Horsfall uses teas," he continued following me down the stairs. "And other plants too. Did you like Lottie, then?"

"She's fine."

Lottie, my Coos Indian maid, had playful dimples set into cheeks the color of wet sand and front teeth with a space wide enough to spit blackberry seeds through. She had brought a buggy and taken me out through the trees behind the mill a brief way along the Old Wagon Road, explaining the names of flora and fauna as we rode. She told me about the mines, one named Libby, as we made our way to the wharves at Marshfield, the largest city on the bay. I had wished it was Louie showing me the sights, not Lottie, that I could have stolen moments with him in a carriage instead of a proper outing with one's maid.

It had been pleasant enough, though I felt that I was being examined as well as entertained. And I must have seemed wistful.

"*Think* about it," she'd said.

"What?"

"You aren't here. I see it in the way you watch the horse's ears twitch like they'll fly off if you look away. You miss the birds."

"I haven't."

"My mother carries a deep basket for clams," Lottie said. She flicked the reins on the mare's behind, and we continued on the road. "Has a small bottom and a wide top, so others see when it fills up and help her empty it before it weighs too much."

"How nice."

"She says I notice first, always offer help before others."

I stared at her. She gazed straight ahead, the reins loose in her sun-browned hands, the breeze not touching the tight twist of thick hair that rolled around her head.

"If I need help for any burdens, I have my husband to share them with," I said.

"Hmnn."

"I don't know that I need a maid," I told Harry later over blackberry tea.

"I can dress myself. And Lem and his cousin do all of the cooking and laundry and tend to the gardens too, it appears. Just leave me room for puttering."

"May be wrong, but I think my brother meant her as a companion for you," Harry said. "I'll be in school by December."

"I expect to have *him* as my companion."

"He'll be busy, and Lottie knows everything about this place. She can take you to the dunes and teach you about the rivers and the ocean and where best to clam and fish. She's quite strong. She's rowed out to rescue people in storms and once—"

"You know quite a lot about Lottie," I said.

"We practically grew up with her. She was always a part of us. She and Ellen. Not so much when our mother came. She took care of things then. But when Mother couldn't join us, Ellen—that's Lottie's mother—paddled us across South Slough, took us to the bays, helped dig clams, told us to roll up our pants higher so we wouldn't get wet. She laughs a lot, like Lottie. Her sister married Jake Evans who has the pack string out near the lighthouse."

He bit into a piece of bread Lem had smothered with thick, white butter. I wondered if he had any idea of the relationship he'd just suggested.

"I think I'll work at making my own friends," I said.

"If you don't mind my saying so, unless a person has lots of family around, they can't have too many friends. Especially ones like Lottie."

The encounter created a kind of wariness with Harry, a circling like two discordant cats centered around Louie. If I had raised a child into Harry's years, I might have recognized it as that challenging time between childhood and independence. But I saw it for what it appeared to be, a competition. And it soon became clear that *my* wishes, not Harry's, were the ones that startled Louie. He and Harry often made explicit plans, had something else arranged well before I knew. They acted surprised when I said I felt left out.

"So sorry," Louie would say, "I thought you and Harry had talked about his not visiting in the City next week," or "Didn't we talk about the horse?" The latter from Louie after I expressed surprise about his brother's plans to ride out with us on a Saturday the South Slough way to talk to a farmer about buying a mare.

"I thought I was getting the animal," I said.

"Are. But Harry knows horseflesh, and I thought he ought to pass his judgment before we put money down. Thought you'd want that. Besides, it's always more fun with a crowd!" He touched my nose with his and grinned. "You know that yourself."

"If it's to be my horse, I don't see why Harry needs to be involved. And I don't want you thinking for me without checking."

My voice held the petulance of a spoiled child, but I had a novelty planned for the day: a pleasant buggy ride out the Old Wagon Road, a check on the horse, and dinner at the Empire Hotel. All with my apparent husband, the two of us, alone.

"If it's a problem, I can certainly stay home," Harry offered.

"No problem," Louie said. His voice and arms invited his brother in. "Casey here'll be glad you came when you render your opinion, won't you Case?"

"It'll be fine," I said. "Just check with me next time, darling. I don't like surprises."

"Absolutely!" Louie said.

The horse turned out to be a gentle dapple gray. A quarter horse they called her, bred for speed for short distances who didn't need any of Harry's insight as far as I could tell. I had plenty of my own.

"Steeldust" the rancher said her coloring was.

Harry rode her first, making sure she didn't suffer from any jags like swamp fever or that she wasn't "goose hipped" or a "star gazer." "Her tongue's fine," he said holding her mouth gently with his hands. Her stride was good, not goose hipped.

Louie kept a steady chatter with the farmer, but it was Harry who conferred with him about some discrepancy in the horse's age, and so Louie managed to lower the asking price by several dollars.

"I'd like to ride her," I said, and they all looked surprised.

"Don't have a sidesaddle, ma'am," the farmer said, "less'n you brought one."

"Not necessary," I said striding past him. I set my foot to the stirrup and brought my leg and skirt over in the western style of the men. I adjusted my corset and pulled my skirt against my legs, then took the reins.

Harry raised his eyebrow, but I could see that Louie was delighted by my boldness as he tipped his hat to me and grinned. The farmer frowned.

"Give her her head, Cassie," he said. "See what she'll do."

We rode along a trail beside the backwater. A wispy fog hovered over the long grasses cut by fingers of water. The mare was surefooted, and I liked the feel of her even though it had been almost a year since I'd ridden and then with a flat English saddle, not this odd western one.

The horse may have sensed how green I was, for I felt her stop and lower her head just before she lifted her hindquarters in a twisted kind of buck.

"Hang on, Case!" I heard Louie shout, and I did, kicking the horse and pulling her head up, surprised at how much better my balance was riding without a sidesaddle. "Don't let her get you down!"

The mare tried it once or twice more as we moved out along the trail. I eyed the marshy area between us and the slough vowing to avoid it. She seemed to accept my authority. When I pressed my knees she broke into a lope, and the move beneath me felt as gentle as a back-porch swing.

"Good girl," I said and leaned forward to pat her shoulder. "We'll get this down yet."

"Horse'll be the little wife's then?" the farmer asked as I walked her back toward them and Louie helped me dismount.

"The horse will belong to this *woman*, yes," I corrected.

He raised his eyebrows. "Meant no offense, ma'am. Didn't know being called a wife was a trouble. Must be one of those Democrats," he mumbled, "never satisfied."

Edgar arrived later in the month and brought with him a surprise—my sister, Margaret.

"I sent you a letter," Margaret said. "It was forwarded by the hotel to the Simpson estate."

Her tight French braids pulled her eyes back making them almond shaped behind her glasses. The sea air brought pink to her high cheekbones etched on that exquisite face.

"Brought the letter myself," Edgar said. "Course, I could have put it in the mail pouch and then told you I'd had this dream, that a beautiful woman was coming to see you and then, here she'd be!"

"Edgar has a reputation for practical joking," Harry said in explanation to my sister.

"But how did you know the letter said Margaret would be coming, hmmm?" Louie teased.

"She came to the house," Edgar said, "but you'd already left for Coos Bay. I'd never read someone else's mail."

"Unless you could do it without getting caught," Louie said and lifted his knuckles for a knock.

"You malign my reputation, brother," Edgar said.

"That doesn't take much. Remember that time—"

"Quiet, you two," I said. "Let's get Margaret settled."

I took her arm in mine, and we walked slowly up the zigzag boardwalk leaving the boys behind to bring her bags and what other luxuries Edgar might have stocked in from California. The dogs barked with the visitors and knotted themselves in and out of our feet. Margaret raised one of her finely arched eyebrows when I introduced her to the Lady Margaret with four legs.

"At least she's the elegant one," Margaret said and laughed.

"How did you talk Joe into letting you come?" I asked her when we were alone.

"He isn't *my* husband." She licked her lips. "And I had an eye appointment in San Francisco. Mama didn't want to make the trip. She said the seas in November can be rough. I didn't *know* you'd come here, Cassie, and no one from home knows I'm here."

"Oh," I said.

"I just felt I *had* to see you, to know that Louis was treating you well, and to urge you— Which I *see* he is. This is a lovely setting." She looked around. "Do you like Oregon?"

"It's weaseling its way into my blood." The walk up from the dock cut my breath. "Wait until you see the garden. Louie's father laid out the yard. Some of the box hedges are already twenty years old."

We walked to the top, entered the gate, and dipped our heads below the low-hanging Chinese maple. "He has ship captains bring back trees and tubers from around the world," I said, "anything exotic or unusual, to see if it will grow here."

Behind us, Louie and Edgar handed Margaret's bags to Ming Ho. Louie called to Harry, waved at me, then signaled by pointing to his pocket watch that they'd all be back later. His leaving made me uneasy.

The afternoon being unseasonably warm, Margaret and I sat on the porch after she'd removed her hat and gloves and slipped off her high-button shoes. The dogs at last lay in a heap in the last rays of sunshine on the lawn. Rhodie found comfort sprawled over Margaret's toes.

I gave the order for Lem to bring cookies and tea, tapped my fingers on the wicker arm. Into the silence of waiting I finally said, "How's Belle, then?"

Margaret cleared her throat. "Wretched."

"No need to be so gentle."

"I'm sorry. I don't mean to be hurtful, it's just that she misses you terribly. You're her mother, after all. The rest of us are just, well, paper cutouts for her."

"Not so little as that," I said. "I'm sure she's happy in familiar surroundings."

"You perjure yourself, Cass. And now Joe has, too, telling Belle you're on a trip. I thought it a mistake. The truth is *always* better, I think, but it was what her father decided. Do you miss her?"

"I'm not a block of stone. But there's nothing I can do. It's done."

"Not true, Cass. You could have her now, if you lived alone until the divorce was final at least. She's so miserable I know Joe'd let you have her. Or you could come home. You could—"

"I am home," I said, holding my hand to stop her.

She sighed. "When you let this inside of you, when you finally face the choices you've made, Cass, I fear for you, for your heart." Her reference to my health threw me off balance. "We're all concerned."

"Afraid an angry God will come to punish me?" I smiled.

"He comes to love, Cass. Forgiveness comes out of love and recognizing our errors and His desire to transform us, make us full and whole. That's what I fear you're missing in life. The fullness that comes from removing the wall between you and God."

"I'll be fine," I said. "Let's talk about something else."

Margaret sighed. "They've no idea you're here with Louis. Mama was horrified enough that you left Hoquiam and were in the same city together. We thought, with Joe not contesting the divorce that, well, you'd be setting a marriage date."

"Would Belle want to see me sometime?"

"She'd see you now, Cassie. She's not the one keeping the distance."

"Joe is resolute if nothing else. I'm sure he wouldn't let her come."

"It's always been easier for you to find others to blame rather than yourself." The dog moved from her feet, found refuge beneath a hydrangea.

"I'd see her, bring her right now if Joe'd let me."

"How convenient for you that you can't marry yet. Ensures the distance, doesn't it? Do people here know of your status?"

"You've gotten more biting, sister," I said.

She shook her head. "It wasn't what I planned to say, why I came to see you. I just wanted to *know* that you were well and to tell you that I thought Joe would relent once you and Louie marry."

The scent of cinnamon tea wafted over us.

Margaret set her cup on the wicker table and took my cup from me. She pulled her chair in front of me so our knees touched, then placed my hands in hers, studying our fingers. "I have wondered so often if there was anything I could have said that would have made a difference in how you decided. Maybe if I'd prayed *harder* for you or been a better person. Maybe taken better care of you. Especially when we were back in New York, when Belle was born."

"That's long past."

"I actually *liked* being there though, looking after Belle. I liked picking out clothes for her and holding her tiny hands and teaching her to talk. I loved Granny, and sometimes I know I acted as though Belle belonged to me, that you were Belle's aunt and not me. I shouldn't have." Her glasses slipped on her nose and she pushed at them with her fingertips. "I wondered if maybe, well, that I might have *done* something that kept you from becoming attached to Belle, by my being so close. Something made it easier then for you to leave her, to fall out of love with Joe."

She didn't look at me, just ran her index finger in circles around the back of my hand. Her nails were silver white and narrow, as perfect as petals. "I'd feel just *dreadful* if I had. I'd want your forgiveness, Cassie, if you could give it."

Something in her tone caught me unawares, and I heard myself speaking words I hadn't arranged.

"Sometimes I wonder if I'm capable of deep feelings, or sustaining them, for a child or anyone. When I get what I think I want, I just seem to want more. It's like a terrible gnawing at my insides. I feed it and feed it and just feel a great yawning of empty." I pulled my hand from hers and stood, uneasy at my disclosure. "But nothing you did had anything to do with my leaving her or Joe. Knowing she has you there makes me less of a monster in my eyes, I suppose. Don't think I could have left her with a stranger."

"But that's part of what I mean. Maybe I was *too* close to her."

My silence considered the idea.

"Can you forgive me?" she asked.

"That's silly, Margaret. If you'd done something, but you haven't. Not everything that happens to someone else is a result of what you did or didn't do. You're powerful, but not *that* powerful." I said it as though teasing.

"But I loved taking care of her. And you were sick, and I may have taken advantage. Or insisted Granny ask Joe to come for us. So he could have made you care for Belle."

"You were eighteen," I said.

"Just say it," she said in her soft voice, "if you wouldn't mind. Just say you forgive me."

I fidgeted. Talks of guilt or confessions, redemption or forgiveness churned in a tight corner of my mind.

"Please, Cassie."

"You're forgiven then." I shrugged my shoulders, not sure why her insistence annoyed me.

She took my hand and looked up at me from her chair. "Thank you."

"I don't remember anything about mortals being able to forgive."

"It's what makes room for love," Margaret said, "when we've offered up forgiveness and the other has accepted. Both have more room that way." She took in a deep breath as though she'd rid herself of a great weight. "Is there anyone *you* want to ask for forgiveness? It would ease your spirit, Cassie. Maybe let you find that happiness you want."

I searched her face for manipulation, some orchestration of what had just transpired between us, some hidden meaning. But her eyes held only openness and a loving invitation.

"I'm feeling a little chilled," I said, pulling my hands from hers to rub myself from the cold. "Think we should head inside."

The sparkle washed from her eyes. She nodded and in that moment looked older than I remembered.

"It's my impression," she said, "that no matter how carefully one chooses, Cassie, there is *always* a price to pay for getting what we want."

CHAPTER 12

PLANTING SEEDS

❋

I am an icicle hung before a candle. I am inside, glowing gold and warm but cold and melting, drop by drop. I watch myself become liquid and fall, form into something dark and sharp beneath myself like crystals blackened in a fire. Cold and hot at once and screaming, I fall into something curdling and fixed.

"Wake up." Lottie shook me.

"What?" My heart pounded; my tongue was thick and dry. I looked around. The gaslight flickered against an empty wineglass. Light spilled over the room. I tried to gauge the time. "Is Louie back?" I said.

"Long time ago. You sleep through them, into morning. Bad dreaming?"

"Very," I said before I had a chance to think about who I confided in. "I felt consumed by something black and hot and cold and sharp all at the same time." I shivered. "Someplace evil."

Tears pressed behind my nose and eyes and something made it difficult to breathe.

"So much sadness," I said. My voice broke. I feared crying in front of her.

"Think about it," Lottie said, and she stroked my head the way a mother soothes a wounded child. "If you let others help, it will not be a place to live forever."

"Where aren't you going to live forever?" Margaret said. She stood in a traveling dress of wine with tiny flowers that made her face look almost translucent in the morning light. "Surely you're not talking about here? Look at that sunrise." She stared at the bay, an act that gave me a chance to swipe at my eyes and clear my throat. "Spectacular, all the gold and light."

"Perfect day for the lighthouse trip, if you ask me," Harry said entering the living room from the kitchen. He wore dark knickers and socks and red suspenders over his collarless shirt.

"When was that planned?"

"While you slept," Margaret said. "Did you know you snore, dear sister?"

"I do not!"

"You do," she insisted.

"Lottie's been packing baskets of cold ham and chicken and cranberry dishes from McFarlin's bog," Harry said. "Edgar brought fresh fruit. We're all set except for you."

"Did you bring your dried berries, Lottie?" Louie asked. He filled the stairway and ducked his head to enter the living room. He stretched and yawned at the same time. He wore wheat—light shirt, pants, and even white leather shoes.

"Four," she said.

"Good. We'll eat one now," Edgar said striding in from the outside. "Horses are ready but no sense making our stomachs wait for Lottie's treats. A Simpson should never have to wait for what he wants."

"Come along there, woman," Louie said pulling me from the chair. "You looked so comfortable last night I didn't have the heart to wake you. But you'll be the last one ready if you don't move on."

"As expected," Margaret said and rustled my hair as she passed by.

"How did I lose a whole evening?" I said to Lottie who remained in the room. "I hardly remember anything after charades."

"Think about it," she said and followed me up the stairs.

Two carriages were harnessed for the six of us, and along the way we were joined by some of the Flannagan clan who Lottie told me had hidden an Indian woman named Libby in their flour barrel rather than permit her to be removed from the coast. Louie had also invited a young farmer named Gus Anders living at the Winchester arm of South Slough. With Jake Evans, he waited for us to cross over at the sandy beaches of Charleston.

I still felt in a fog from the terror of the dream. I wondered about what had gone on around me while I slept, oblivious. The word *muddled* came to mind as we headed out the Old Wagon Road, a trail that proved muddy but not deep enough to stop us. It wound its way west then south across the Pony Creek, crossing through trees and rambling foliage and hints of sand dunes in the distance. We rode by Bastendorf Beach and watched sandpipers race the waves. The lone poodle brought along barked at dogs we drove by.

Edgar happily explained to Margaret about the crossings. "Movement is downstream, toward the ocean, happens in scows and river boats and canoes rather than carriage roads. Rivers need less tending."

Dairymen and potato growers and chicken farmers brought their wares downriver with high tide going out, and if they were lucky, sold all the milk and eggs and potatoes they had and returned with the incoming tide sometime the same day. "Might shoot a duck or two or a little blacktail or elk," Louie said, "and have their trip home lit by moonlight."

"Or be stranded for hours if fog rolls in. If he's ever late, sister," Edgar said to me, "don't blame some woman, just blame the fog." He and Louie laughed at that.

We arrived midmorning at the crossing site and loaded our things into the canoes that Lottie had ordered up for us. She rowed the cedar dugout I rode in, and it was on this trip that I met her mother, Ellen, and watched her easy banter with Louie. On this trip, I lost my hat and the pearl pin Mother had given me. And on this trip, Louie let escape that he had not forgotten his very real wish for a child of his own.

I responded with the breathless need I had for passionate engagement, to feel and rush and so avoid discomfort. I'd stood up in Lottie's canoe on the choppy waters of South Slough.

"What a crazy thing to do!" Louie said, though his eyes sparkled with excitement when I reached the shore that day. He stepped into the water to grab me and swing me from the craft.

Lottie speared the canoe onto the sand, and Edgar and Margaret and Harry rushed to greet me. Rhodie had ridden in a basket in Louie's craft, and the dog bounded out now, leaving small footprints in the sand. Gus, the farmer, clapped his hands and brought him back.

"Egads!" Edgar said. "Some kind of thrill seeker you've harnessed!"

"A little too thrilling, if you ask me," Harry said joining us. He had a worried look on his face.

"No one did," I snipped at him. "It was thrilling, actually."

"Maybe a new event at the races," Ellen said with a hint of scorn to her voice.

"Don't do it again," Louie said still holding my hand. "At least not without a pole to hang on to. Way too risky."

"Are we ready for lunch?" I asked.

"Not until we reach the lighthouse," Harry said. "It's too perfect a place to eat."

"But these beaches are lovely," Margaret said gazing around. "And it's so warm. Feels like we're at the south of France."

"The lighthouse's vorth the vait, then?" asked Gus. He had a wide, sun-beaten face broken by an open smile, topped with sand-colored hair. A "Swedish Finn" they called him.

"Anything worth having is worth waiting on, isn't that right, brother?" Edgar said.

Louie actually blushed. "October sun can turn cool pretty quick," he said. "Not too many more chances to picnic at the Point before winter. Best we proceed as planned."

Jake Evans was waiting with his pack string of mules accustomed to carrying picnickers to the shallow ocean beaches or to the lighthouse where books could be exchanged with the keeper. We loaded ourselves and the food baskets and Rhodie back into hers. It was a short three-mile walk up and down the ravines, in and out of the dark timber. I noticed Gus Anders shared words with Margaret across the back of a mule, two in front of me, his hand holding his hat as he talked. I heard her almost schoolgirl laughter at something Gus said and noticed his eyes stayed on her face despite the sun's beating against his as it broke through the thickness of trees.

The greenery on either side of the trail was as thick as a Christmas tree. "Are you sure there's an ocean through there?" I asked.

"Should be seeing it soon," Louie said.

"How *ever* do you keep this growth under control at the house?" Margaret asked as our animals closed the gap on their lead ropes and came up behind her.

"Brute force and awkwardness at my place," Gus answered, and my sister laughed. I noticed he had wide hands.

"Hoquiam must have been covered with this kind of tangle in the beginning," Margaret said.

"A whole community immigrated from Finland to this area. Did you know that, Cassie?" Margaret asked sharing some detail she'd learned from Gus.

"Part of Sveden for so long," Gus said, "ve carry both histories on our backs. Plenty heavy with one, I tell you."

"Czar added to that history, too, if I remember. With that Swede defeat," Louie chided him.

"Ya, that one ve don't talk about so much!"

The pack string wove its way over a rise and beneath trees looking like a brown thread sewing a skirt of green. A mule stopped and pulled on its lead rope, and Gus gently tugged it along over the matted leaves covering the ground. Then through the trees appeared a blue different than that of the rivers or the sloughs.

"Ocean!" Harry shouted. He looked like a satisfied cat with his announcement.

"Drats!" Louie said. He walked back beside the string to knock knuckles with Harry. I watched Edgar do the same.

Before us, the lighthouse stood, alone on an island of land about one hundred feet from the mainland. The separate caretaker's house stood closer. The wind picked up and brought with it an uneasy feeling.

Jake Evans and Ellen helped unload mules while Margaret and Louie and I walked toward the edge separating us from the lighthouse that soared more than a hundred feet into the sky above the water. The wind we hadn't felt in the ravines whipped at our skirts and forced me to pull strands of my loose hair from across my face.

"You're sure this is better than those beaches for eating?" I said.

"Trust me," Louie said.

We stopped at a series of pulleys and cables and a small basket tram that Louie and Edgar now began pulling back from the lighthouse. We would be cabled across the cut of open space of ocean separating the lighthouse from the land we stood on.

"Here's a peril we've prepared for you," Edgar said. He licked at his mouth like a cat about to snare a mouse.

"It can't be as bad as that. There are people already over there," I said, but the feeling of the dream swept over me.

"Last year Tom Wymann lost his leg when a cable broke. Joe Younker and Tom's girl and a guest they were taking over all crashed onto those rocks," Harry said.

Margaret and I looked over the side. Breakers crashed up against the boulders maybe sixty feet beneath the tram. The spray of water made the rocks look like dark crystal.

Harry and a Flannagan man crossed over first in the basket without incident. Margaret volunteered us next.

"I'm a little afraid of heights," Margaret said, "so let's get this over with." A patch of pink appeared on her cheekbones or perhaps her face had lost some color.

"We'll be fine," I said.

Margaret gripped the basket with both hands. I felt my heart begin to pound as the men helped us inside the basket.

We jerked across the opening, the sun hot against our faces. The heavy cable groaned on the pulley. Beneath us, the ocean waves strained upward, splashing against the spit of land that held the lighthouse, sending cold spray toward the bottom of the tram. The crash of the water against the rocks drowned out light conversation, and I had the foreboding sense that I had been in this place before. Cracks in the stone scribed the rocks all the way to the ocean.

"Hang tight!" Louie yelled. The cable jerked, and we started to swing.

"I don't like this," I said, gripping the sides.

"Danger! Danger!" Edgar shouted. His voice was frantic and high pitched. He was jumping up and down, looking pained, then pointing behind us where neither Margaret nor I could see without some effort to twist in the narrow space. I just wanted to be very still, but he kept pointing. My hair caught on the cable as I twisted.

"What is it?" Margaret gasped. "Are we going to crash?"

"Couldn't be," I said, skilled at denying disaster.

Edgar's face had the look of someone about to witness a terrible calamity as he pulled on his cheeks with his hands. The cable began to shake, and I saw Edgar's hand grip it. The movement and Margaret's startled cry caused my heart to skip. I tried to see what Edgar pointed to toward the lighthouse and the ocean, tried to catch my balance in the basket.

"Prepare for the end!" Edgar shouted. "Prepare for the end!"

"Cassie!" Margaret gasped, stretching to see, her wispy voice strained and close to tears. "Are we going to die?"

My heart pounded. "I can't get turned around." The basket lurched and swung in the wind with my efforts to twist.

Finally seeing where Edgar pointed, I let out a gasp of anger and relief. "May all your stallions be shy breeders!" I shouted at Edgar who stood holding himself with laughter.

"What is it?" Margaret asked.

"A bad joke. Some 'end' to prepare for. Just the lighthouse operator reaching for us."

I could see Louie smiling, but to his credit he didn't seem to share in Edgar's mirth.

We lurched to a stop and the keeper shook his head. "That Edgar reads too much Poe," he said. When Edgar's basket arrived I hissed at him, repeating my insult.

"Ouch!" he said as though I'd struck him. "Can't you take a kidding?"

"Margaret was terrified. You've no right to upset people just for your pleasure."

"Look who calls the ocean wet," he sneered.

His words added to my own slapped me, and for the first time, deep inside my stomach, I felt what it must have been like for Belle and Margaret and even my mother, to have me leave with no thought to what might happen, whether Joe would look after them or tell them to leave. Had they felt hung over a chasm, wondering if they'd crash on sharp rocks?

"You may wish someday that you'd been kinder to us, Edgar," I said. He bowed low. His dark hair cut close against his neck invited pinching, which I did. His yelp gave me some small satisfaction.

Louie carried Rhodie's basket, and he clucked at us as he approached. "Now children," he said. Rhodie barked as we stepped onto short, wind-blown grass and reddish lichen clinging near the ocean's edge. In the distance a series of jagged scallops marked the rugged coastline. I watched, mesmerized by the waves while pulling my loose hair from my eyes.

Rhodie freed herself and sniffed at everyone's shoes. Wary of the high cliff, I looked for the leather leash to attach to her collar. "Drats!" I said. "I've forgotten her tether. I hate forgetting like that."

"It's quite a female thing," Harry said. He chewed an unlit cigar as he walked toward us. "I've been reading Freud's work on hysteria, and he comments on that feature of the weaker sex."

"In the German text?" I snapped.

"Actually, yes. But I'm sure it would say the same in English."

I left him standing while I borrowed Margaret's straw hat and removed the ribbons, one to serve as Rhodie's leash, the other to tie up my hair. "Does your Dr. Freud comment on the female creativity?" I asked.

Jake Evans and Ellen were the last to cross over, and they broke out baskets of bread and still-cool butter wrapped in leather. Edgar unloaded dark bottles of ale he passed around to the men. Only Gus and Jake waved their hands in refusal.

Appetite makes a good sauce. I hadn't realized how hungry I'd become. We sat on old quilts and devoured foods that tasted better in sunshine.

"Tell us some stories, Ellen," Louie urged.

Ellen dropped her eyes and smiled before offering a grandmother creation story, of how the world came to be from the ocean and how two sojourners had split a basket to form land and that the fir trees had grown from eagle feathers they'd placed in the sand along the shore.

We passed the dried fruit, ate some of Lottie's pie. The topics turned to politics and prices, and we women had our say right with the men. Rhodie pestered to be freed from her leash.

"Go take her," Margaret said. "I'll pick up here."

"I help too," Gus offered to the oohs and ohs of Edgar.

"Ignore them," I told Gus and swopped Rhodie into my arms.

But the dog, like me, wished to walk. I pulled her back from the edge and kept the ribbon tied to my wrist. Louie signaled me to wait up, and I watched him stride with long legs across the grass. The wind blew his coat out behind him.

"How'd you like it, your first Pacific picnic?" He took off his coat, and his beige suspenders formed a V across his thin-striped shirt. His famous silk shirts had been hung in the armoire for special occasions. He chewed on a chicken leg.

Beyond us, the ocean foam rose and expanded like gentle breaths against the rocks below. Sea lions shot through the roll of waves like brown cigars. I reached up and wiped some of the chicken from Louie's chin. He smelled of fresh ale mixed with cranberry and fowl.

"It's beautiful," I said, turning back to the sea. "Would be nice to have a place with this vista without a worry over the dogs. Maybe a cove somewhere." I pointed to a pearly piece of sand just south.

"Sunset Bay," he said. "Good place for development."

I stood in front of him, my feet at the rocky edge. He gave the remains of the bone a toss to the sea, and a gull swooped down but missed it. Louie licked his fingers then wrapped his large arms around me forming a cove of us as though we stood there alone. It humbled me, the vastness of it, made me wistful in a mournful sort of way.

"All that force," I said. "Endless and eternal."

"Men have become believers over it, all right, considering how it got there, why it keeps on coming day after day. The sea and the stars. All of that."

It was the first time any question of theology had come up between us.

"And are you?" I asked.

"A believer in God? There've been times, yes, and times, no," he said. "Inside the great cathedrals I feel a sense of power, but every day, in this world, I don't know. Suppose that's why Dostoevsky intrigues me like he does even if I can't translate the Russian well. It's that struggle between good and evil and God and individual choice and what code one should live by. All that fascinates me."

"From your thinking head, not your feeling one?"

"Suppose so. Not sure we can ever hope to understand why we're here or where we came from. I think we have to choose for ourselves a course and follow it with conviction until we die."

"That seems so hopeless," I said.

He shrugged his shoulders.

"Although it does take one from the realm of sin, that kind of thinking, and thoughts of being burned in hell for having acted," I said. His arms tensed around me, but I did not feel secure. "It has some merit, your way to discount sin. Especially for someone sucked within it."

The wind blew icily across us, though the sun still burned hot.

"Wonder if there's any pie left," I said pulling myself from him. "I'm ravenous with hunger."

Margaret left on the ship north with no plan to return.

Louie began a kind of routine that surprised me with its predictability and what I thought as tedium. Up early to lift barbells on the bay porch, his chest muscles straining with the weights. Wearing a towel around his neck, short-sleeved shirt with a row of close buttons and knickers, he'd take hot coffee from Lem's hands, then walk through the garden with the dogs romping around his feet. I'd hear them all bounding up the stairs to our room where their plunge to my bed was a sign that I should rise, the Lady Margaret finding my toes to lick until I did.

Louie'd bathe then, dress, and between bites of fresh grapefruit—peeling several pieces he fed to me—he talked about his day ahead. Then down the steps to the shipyards and the mill where he met with foremen for reports and exchanged directives his father had sent to him on a just-arrived ship. He'd be home for dinner at noon straight up, and sometimes nap, then off to work and back for supper around seven. He'd spend the evening visiting colleagues with mills from Marshfield and businessmen and investors. He spoke happily of work and the men who implemented his and his father's goals, and I listened with a listless air of envy from my chair surrounded by my books.

It surprised me how little Louie expected of me. He acted content to simply find me at home to kiss my rosemary-scented hair as he walked by to tease Lem. He'd look over my shoulder as I read and hum agreement when I informed him I'd be buying some new frock or Victrola, a Gibson-girl corset or more rats to heighten my hair. I kept up my journal, and with Lottie and alone, I made trips to the lighthouse exchanging books.

Louie paid scant attention to the accounts of my days, but he acted most pleased when I had done the least. Sometimes he behaved as though the very drive that kept him moving was foreign to my soul. Even riding proved an effort with the horse stabled some distance from our home.

"I'd suggest you take the bicycle," Louie said, "but I keep remembering what that doctor said, about your need for rest and living easy. Wouldn't want to risk a future Simpson." He smiled.

"I doubt my resting has a thing to do with it," I said and didn't tell him later that I'd taken the bicycle and ridden hard, my thighs and knees ached still from the effort of forcing the wind against my skin, the wheel between my knees.

I took to wearing the practical knee-length bloomers permitted on the contraption around the house as well. But bicycling, even with the dogs racing by my side, brought little pleasure, perhaps because no one else rode along the road ruts with me, perhaps because the joyful sensations were so short lived.

The last Christmas of the 1800s came. We wove dried beets and cranberries on string and packed little stockings for the workers' children. Louie knew all the children's names, and his face beamed almost as brightly as theirs. We passed into the new century with friends and Edgar's arrival and imported French champagne. At the party we argued and shouted about the Philippines demanding independence. Later Louie invoked icons of intellectuals and ethics when we spoke of purposefulness and life.

Harry trotted off to Cooper College to study medicine as planned, and I found I missed him. Lottie brought her family to visit—a husband who worked in the cranberry bogs and a boy and girl still in school. Benjamin Jr. had large ears low on his head and his sister, Rachel, though only six, was both gorgeous and plump.

The man acting as my husband conferred with his father, who arrived from the City throwing everyone's schedule into a dither for days and leaving each of us gasping for breath as he left.

And nothing came of Gus Anders's interest in Margaret, though I pawed at the possibility. "Oh, not for me," Margaret wrote, "but he and Annie would be perfect together." She must have passed along his name as the two struck up a correspondence, at least Gus mentioned that once when he came for dinner.

Gus and Louie'd talk for hours about farming, an appeal that surprised me. It was such a solitary activity, hardly engaging of a man like Louie.

"Like the idea of getting my hands in the soil," Louie said when I suggested my concern. He motioned with his hands to direct one of Lem's cousins trimming the box hedges on the south side of the house.

"It's 'the idea of it' that fits you, more than *doing* it," I told him. "Besides, you like the sunrises, the beginnings of things but never the endings."

"Never thought of it like that."

"Lots of people like the satisfaction of a finished project, not just starting dozens, seeing things through to the end. Margaret, for one. She's always sewing things up."

Louie signaled his approval, and the blue-clad Asian moved on his knees to another section of green.

"You never were good with a needle, if I remember." He patted my hand he took now in his.

"No, I like the excitement of the beginnings, too, the thrill of the uncertainty of it all, the conquest, not knowing how it'll end. Once I know, I tend to lose interest. It's why I always plant things in small pots, I suppose."

"Like the beginnings of a romance," he offered.

"Beginnings of anything."

"Does our life bore you, Cassie?" he asked. His fingers tensed over mine.

"Does it you?"

I thought he hesitated a smidgeon too long before he suggested I was being silly.

I suppose I was bored, or maybe lonely, though I did not call it that, couldn't then. Acknowledging such a feeling would have tarnished my view of independence and my belief in self-control. No, I said that I lacked pursuit and hoped Louie might say something to pique my interest. When I sighed that I was tired, Lottie offered native teas and potions she said would help. Once she even suggested that perhaps my tiredness came from having too much to sort each day.

"People who capture things become weighed down, like stones wearing in the sea," she said. "They feel lighter when they give things away. My people have feasts that always end in giving and they end up feeling better."

I noticed her wide front teeth rested on her lip when she finished with her insights. But she spoke on a day when I was feeling dull and disconnected and didn't want to hear of giveaways and weights.

"My head's a poor tipple you think?" I said, referring to one of Louie's pieces of mining equipment that accepted all sizes of coal, then sorted the ore into its proper places.

"May be," she said, making it two words.

I wondered if she knew the other meanings of a tipple, such as "one who drank alcoholic liquor intemperately."

"I think my tipple's fine," I said.

I sent her home, then stayed busy for the afternoon organizing by length and color the striped socks I wore for bicycling.

Perhaps Lottie was right. Perhaps I did need a giving away, something that might help me sleep nights, heal what I called a broken spirit. Activity didn't last long nor take away the malaise of my life. Louie, though attentive, did not spike the passion of his promise, perhaps like me needing danger to stir the thrill. Even dabbling in wine and drinking brought only brief reprise. Whatever wounds my choices sliced stayed otherwise quite wide.

More and more I imagined that any healing of a person belonged only to *their* efforts, what they could conjure up, not give away. The Eddy woman wrote of that in her "Sciences and Health," an article republished in my ladies' magazine. Healing of the body took vigor, starch, and force, but only God could do it. "We are all spiritual beings," she'd written, "our bodies useless." We needed to surrender to the spiritual to overcome the flesh. That's what the lady pastor of the Boston church said. I wondered about the orthodoxy of her views, but only later, after Harry and Louie treated me for an illness I did not believe I had.

It had happened quickly, or so they said. Harry'd come back from school, and Louie stood beside him. "Something's not right, Cassie," Louie'd said. "Look at yourself!"

"There's nothing wrong with me! I'm fine." I'd felt lightheaded for a few days, and my breathing had turned shallow. A cold spot formed in the center of my chest, acting like a melting ball of ice each time I took a breath. I felt a little tired, but it was nothing I couldn't convince my body to ignore. I attributed it to the heaviness of the air.

Louie shook his head at me as though I were a recalcitrant child refusing to obey its parent. He'd come home before the noon whistle, and now that I thought of it, he'd left later for the mill that morning. Or had he left at all? Perhaps he'd been working upstairs. I couldn't recall.

"How long has she been like this?" Harry asked. He already wore a doctor's analyzing look as he scanned my face.

"Won't rest. Moves around in a frenzy. Looked almost glassy-eyed this morning." He stared at me, reached with the back of his palm to stroke my forehead. "Skin has a sheen to it."

"Have you taken her to a doctor?" Harry sounded frantic, unbecoming to him, I thought. He looked rather fuzzy walking toward me.

"Refuses," Louie said from behind him, his voice whispery and faraway,

I suppose so I wouldn't hear them discussing me. "Can't reason with her."

"Pneumonia, maybe typhoid," Harry said. "She must be burning up inside. We've got to get her to a hospital."

"I don't think she'll go. She can be so stub—"

"Don't talk about me as though I'm one of the dogs!" I said. "I know how to take care of myself. I know my body. I'm fine. No one's taking me anywhere. If I'm ill, God'll heal me; if I'm not, then not."

The two stood shoulder to shoulder, and I was about to shout them back when the room turned into a buzzing in my ears and spun into a haze.

I don't like to speak much about what happened after. I remember only bits and pieces, of being on board a steamer, smells of seawater, sounds of rigging moving against wind, the roughness of the wool blanket wrapped around me, and the wet cloth Louie used to cool my skin. They said I shouted in the hospital, sent nurses scattering with my demands. I don't remember that. Only lights and caverns do I recall, followed by a time of weakness when I could not will myself to anything, anything at all. Lights flickered before my eyes. I shivered with heat while someone in the distance played my favorite Chopin piece.

Time traveled a lazy trail in the months that followed. Lottie stayed over often, when we returned home, caring for me and giving herself away.

Louie had sustained his father's business and strengthened it despite what the Eastern papers said was a slow recovery from banking scares and poor investments of the nineties. Old Town, where we lived, developed too. Louie enlarged John Kruse's building to school the children of the millworkers, and opened it up on Sundays for Dr. Strange to travel from Marshfield to offer Presbyterian services. I found the church's expansion annoyingly close, and didn't understand why.

With enthusiasm, Louie did his work. He responded to crises at the Simpson shipbuilding works or at the railroad spur line. If heavy runoffs tore out dams meant to capture logs, the rush and tumble of the timber could kill a man, and Louie had the task of offering condolences.

In expanding new markets, Louie traveled here and there to secure orders for the famous Port Orford cedar. Sometimes, I went with him. There are only so many times one can rearrange a living room or paint leaves and press them against fresh-painted walls. Music and the theater still interested me, but they lacked the stimulation they'd once offered. Few declamation events were scheduled so the work of memorizing poems while I pulled old blooms from the azaleas seemed a futile task. A certain rivalry existed between Marshfield and Old Town anyway, one that prohibited me from being totally accepted into Coos Bay society. At least that was what I attributed it to. I could imagine my ostracism if they'd known of my marital status. Besides, the poems or plays about good people wearing happy endings pricked a sadness in me, and after the performances, I found my sleep chafed with the rough wool of dreams.

Louie thrived with the challenge of his days. He'd even try his hand at things his workers could do best, such as wood chopping or tree topping at the annual logging days. He was in his glory at those events. I'd see Louie bend his head low to the men who worked the logs giving him full attention. He'd clamp a man's forearm when he shook his hand, always inviting him closer. At Fourth of July celebrations, he'd be asked to speak, and his voice reached even those standing in shade, farthest from the crowd. His words encouraged others in their efforts, made each person feel a part of all the progress along Coos Bay.

I was merely a box hedge circling the blooms in his garden.

Louie grew taller from the encounters, his chest fuller from the pleasure his presence painted on people's faces. He was a kind and generous man, and one I thought it might be fine to marry.

Legal papers arrived in 1901 noting the finality of my marriage to Josiah Stearns. I thought the divorce would at last signify both an ending and a new beginning, that perhaps now Louie and I could genuinely discuss our future together, something we rarely did. As a wife, I could make my way back to the happiness and passion that had once reigned my days, discard the guilt worn on my ever-rounding shoulders, find fullness for the hunger that gnawed beneath. It seemed an enticing plan, to be fully recovered in my health and to start afresh as Mrs. Simpson and try again for gain. But like so many other things I was discovering about myself, I wasn't skilled at foretelling the future.

CHAPTER 13

PROPOSALS

❋

I expected something different when I offered marriage to my Louie. Maybe my timing proved poor. Maybe I chose it because I participated in Annie and Gus's growing love affair, if only from a distance. Maybe it was learning that Margaret had found a beau named Fred Foster whom she planned to marry. It might even have been learning that my former husband and one Frances Soule, had nuptials planned for April, just one week after Margaret and her Fred. Any one of those events could have prompted choosing a crossing over that would take me closer to being Mrs. Louis Simpson.

Margaret did not invite me to her wedding. Oh, Belle would wear the loveliest dress and, with another nine-year-old, spread petals beneath a canopy of roses. Mother would give Margaret away, walk down the aisle beside her. And the reception would be held at Joe's home, my former home, in the massive living room with the piano anchored to the ceiling to make room for the celebrating guests. Margaret had written in her underlining hand that her husband-to-be did not want me present, a woman infused with scandal, living with a man who was not my husband.

"Just get married now that you *can*," she wrote. "Then I think Fred would relent and let you be here. It would be so *good* for Belle to see you.

You'll like Fanny, Joe's intended. She has the sweetest spirit."

I wasn't sure how I felt about my husband remarrying and his "Izzy" being raised by another woman. Everyone was entitled to happiness, I supposed. Hadn't that been the hallmark of my own journey, seeking pleasure, though in the recesses of my mind I'd held Joe out as someone I could escape to if things failed with Louie. A foolish thought, of course, one that denied that life was random and we humans self-destructive.

I broached the subject of marriage cautiously at first, noticing strange reactions. Something fluttered about, unspoken, the way layers of taffeta cause attention to things hidden beneath.

Looks passed between Lottie and Harry when I mentioned Margaret's marriage and my former husband's too. Edgar's visit later brought some raucous comment about nuptials, and Louie'd derided the state. Even Harry and his interest in the new psychology science unsettled me, about the way he spoke of things that made me think he looked inside of me and not without some judgment.

Perhaps my guilt propelled me, a growing agitation from my little lies, such as the one to the census man last year or when I'd trifle on about my "wedding" when those in our social circle reminisced of theirs. Perhaps the phrase "living in sin" could not be ignored by my "subconscious mind," that part of each of us that Harry said really ruled our actions, maybe even our souls.

"A person can't brush guilt from their shoulders like they can an Oregon mist," Harry'd said once when he spoke of Freud's new book. "Freud says that's what drives us as humans." He still poked pins in the wings of dead finches, stretching them for examination while he and Louie argued over ideas. "Tolstoy has merit, though," Harry said. "He thinks so many of us who have no need to work just to survive live an empty existence. Says we're selfish. He seems to think only Christian love can give a moral base."

"Ah," Louie said, "but he railed against the church and wrote that burning essay about the kingdom of God being inside of us."

"Spiritual conversion at the time of death, though. His latest works are about that, and if you ask me, that's the heart of existence, that conversion state. That's what will give meaning to life."

I could only listen to the discussions of their Russians and Germans, such works not yet translated to English. But I could take the words to heart and wonder.

Even Annie, when she wrote, expressed concern about my soul having violated something so holy as a commitment of the heart, though her arrival, unexpected, brought a joy I hadn't realized I'd missed: a familiar face, a friend from a carefree past.

"Oh, la!" she said as I hugged her on our dock, then held her at arm's length and hugged again. "Isn't this the wildest country, and you looking pale and puffy in it," she said.

"Don't hold back," I said, "just because we haven't seen each other for two years."

Annie blushed. "Nerves, flapping my tongue. I've come to finally meet Gus." She giggled in anticipation.

It was she who later turned the discussion to my marital vows. We had walked to see if tulips poked their noses from the winter.

"I never committed my heart to Joe," I said. "I did it for Mama and Margaret. To secure ourselves. I was so young. Louie has the distinction of being the one and only love of my life, so I don't think I failed my vows, not really."

Annie wore the long skirt and little bolero jacket of the working woman and still had a habit of blinking her eyes quickly before saying something she thought might bring on my temper. She did that now.

"Why not make it real, Cass? That's what I say. You might even have a double marriage with your sister if you pushed it a bit."

"Maybe I'll just suggest that," I said.

Why not? I thought, had been thinking for some weeks now.

Louie'd wanted a family. Perhaps now was the time to press marriage, sweeten it with family. I chose an afternoon when Annie and Gus rode out together in a carriage and Louie was rested following an afternoon nap.

He fidgeted with my mention of it, tapped his finger on the arm of the Boston rocker in the living room, and wouldn't hold my eye. Through the window, a rainbow threatened to break through the clouds over the bay behind his head. It had been a mild winter, and the grass was as green as the emerald of a peacock's feather. Yellow-and-white crocuses poked their noses from the earth with new promise.

"Why now?" he said. "Haven't I made you happy?"

"It isn't about being unhappy," I said. "Not the most important thing in my life, seeking happiness." I pulled nervously at the abalone combs holding my hair piled up on the back of my head, first with one hand then the other.

"Isn't it?" he said.

"This isn't. I'm just, well, with Margaret marrying, and Annie and Gus bound to, I just thought… Marriage doesn't really matter anyway to either of us, so, why not? We could visit Belle that way. Maybe even have her visit here. You said you wanted that."

"What happened to your independent woman?" he said smiling at me now. He turned on the charm, tried diverting me, making it a jest so he could take me somewhere I didn't plan to go. "Where'd you leave her? She looks quite good on Oregon soil, I'd say."

"She's right here," I said, pressing my fingers into my heart. "Urging her case for what she wants and thought her *husband* wanted too." He dropped his eyes with my look.

"Not a good time," he said.

His words cut like the Shrade knife he took now from his pocket. He opened it and with the blade he scraped mud from his work brogans, wiping the smudgy lump into his hand then looking about for someplace to put it. "Got some ideas for development I plan to press. Lots of pressure on right now, Dad's ideas and all."

My face flushed, and I could feel my heart pound as it pushed back the shame of rejection.

"We're not talking about a great deal of time," I said, forcing a lightness to my voice. "Just a judge, five minutes, and a signature."

"Why the change?" He scanned the room with his palm full of mud.

"Maybe my turning thirty this month. Maybe the weddings. I don't know. Does it matter?"

"Want to," he said, not looking at me. "Just can't say when things will let up enough."

He stood, dropped the mud into the wicker wastebasket, and wiped the knife blade on his woolen pants, pressing the mud in with his thumb like a farmer might. Then he stepped into the washroom.

He may have been gone but a moment or an hour while my mind raced and stumbled over our conversation. When he returned, his face was flushed and his eyes looked pinched. He knelt before me then and took my hands.

"I'd give you anything, you know that Cass. Even marriage."

"But?" I said holding back a sob gathering deep.

"I told you, long ago, I couldn't offer marriage. Wasn't… You said you didn't mind."

"That was before you asked me to pretend I did." I felt my own anger begin to rise riding on the back of fear and loss. "I've lived a lie for you, Louie Simpson, something I said I'd never do. I've stuffed terrible feelings deep, very deep, believing I could chuck them overboard once we were married."

A sound of anguish rose from him almost like a wail, climbed up and out.

"Isn't marriage what you wanted too?"

"Oh, Cass," he said, his eyes pooled with tears as he lifted his face to me. "So sorry, so very sorry. Just need you to stay with me as things are now. Please."

"Can you give me a time? Or some idea of what stands in the way? Is it me? Something I've done?" I felt cold and cut open.

His big head shook back and forth. "Me," he said, and I heard him repeat it, his words muffled then by sobs spoken into my skirt. "Just me, just me."

I pulled my hands from where he'd held them, left his head cradled in my lap and stroked his hair with my fingers. The sun set while we sat there. Lem began evening cooking noises in the kitchen. I heard the clatter of a carriage arriving back at the barn. A breeze came up, and the emerald grass turned gray.

"I need to go upstairs," I said feeling heavy and old and surprised at the burning inside of me contained by the chill on my skin.

What I needed was a friend, someone to console me in my anguish, someone I could give myself to with all my duped and dented torments and bad choices, someone who promised restfulness and peace, release from pain, who offered love despite my failings, my inability to change. A friend who would always keep my secret and feed me just the same.

Not Margaret. She was happy in her new marriage, wrote less often now, and didn't understand why I still chose to live my lie. Not Annie, either. She and Gus still corresponded, and she made trips south to see him, chaste visits, with Louie and me often as chaperons. I had no doubt they'd marry; wondered why they waited.

"All in good time," Annie'd said once brushing at my puffed cheeks with powder before dinner. Gus and Louie waited for us in the living room below, Gus having milked his cows and taken a steamer to our dock.

"You look so bloated," Annie'd continued. "Something's not right. Have you seen a doctor? Oh, that's right. Well, I suspect it would all go away if…" She collected her thoughts. "It's guilt, you know. That's what's straining you so."

"My heart's fine."

"Confession's what you need, Cass. Never know when our breath might be our last. Any of us. We may not have time to repent."

"No sense asking for forgiveness if you intend to keep transgressing," I said. "I remember that part."

"Wouldn't have to if you weren't so stubborn. What on earth do you gain by being this 'independent woman'?"

"What do *you* gain?"

"If you must know, some reserves. So Gus can buy one of those milking machines, and we can have an electrical generator for the house and not just his barn. I'm doing it for a reason that's worth waiting for."

"Oh," I said.

"Surely Louie wants to marry and have a family. Time's running short for you, you know." She skipped over my silence and spoke with a calm now. "Which is why we need God's love to renew us and make us whole. We just can't do it by ourselves."

"I'm long past saving, at least in the way you intend."

"Not ever!" she said and might have gone on but for the call from the men of their hunger.

I needed a friend not like Lottie, either, though she offered the safest port. Present and undemanding, she might have listened and offered solace, but in truth I did not believe I deserved the likes of Lottie for a friend. Not the likes of anyone.

I embraced French champagne instead.

Medicinal, I told myself, my submission to Harry's science. Taken at regular intervals just as a doctor might prescribe for someone prone to strokes. Hadn't my father died of one? Didn't I hear Harry say alcohol could keep the blood flowing freely in one's veins? Wasn't that just what my heart needed to forget the sting of rejection, the wounds I earned by hurting others? Something to help me achieve slippery sleep?

French champagne and fine wine. They could wash away my worries, let me pour confidence into crystal, share moments after breakfast, opportunities after lunch. Extra bottles stayed cool beneath loose hay in the barn. At the end of each day, I greeted Louie full of padded hope as well as amber in my hand. My golden friends warmed me.

In 1902, Louie purchased an entire town named Yarrow. Oh, it was a platted town already, with six buildings and a population of thirty, but it held great promise. Tom Symons had filed on it and imagined a townsite someday. But he'd done nothing with it. It was the very ground, flat and on the river and the bend south of us, that Louie could just see would someday become the largest port on the Pacific, closer to the bar and as promising as Marshfield's docks. And so he snapped it up for twenty-five thousand dollars and hired Carl Albrecht to burn scrub and begin to clear the ground.

I told myself that when Yarrow was complete, when Louie'd filled that need to do something grand, that then he'd be free to consider domestic commitments, free to marry me.

"It'll be the San Francisco of the North," Louie said. He curled against me in our feather bed.

"But you shouldn't have used capital to finance it," I said. "It reduces what's available for reinvestment in the mill and for maintaining the spur line. You should have sold something instead or extended your line of credit."

"Don't 'should' me, Cassie. A man never likes to be told what to do."

"Even if what he's doing is wrong?"

"Instead of folks rushing there for doctors or the opera, we'll have those here," Louie said. "With the finest hotels and restaurants, schools and churches, banks and milliners and apothecaries, hospitals, everything a man or woman would want."

"You left out saloons."

"That too, if they don't vote us dry."

"A willing man can always make his way to the floathouses at Charleston Beach," I said with some disgust.

"Men need their pleasures," Louie said. I decided he spoke of the beer and ale sold on the moored houseboats and not the favors rumored to be sold there with them.

"What will you call it? Simpsonville?" I said thinking of the logging town my ex-husband and Dr. Campbell had created in Washington and named "Stearnsville."

"North Bend," he said lying on his back, hands behind his head, his arms firm ropes of muscle. "This'll be Old Town," he said, tapping the head-board with his fingers. "What we build will all be new. Invigorating, starting something grand."

"You'll have to get them here, give them a reason, and the railroad," I said.

"You've put your finger on the key, Cass. Railroad'll connect us to the interior and expand shipping to the south and north, the orient and beyond. North Bend will be the biggest and best Oregon has to offer. 'It's the best deep-sea port north of San Francisco, L. J.!'" He mimicked his father's conversations with him. "'Got to promote it that way.'"

"Maybe you should prime the pump somehow. Perhaps give something away, as a promotion."

"Capital idea!" he said sitting straight up in bed. "Absolutely fine!"

I had done my homework as I could, reading and listening to the conversations of the men. It was not always easy with them stepping out back after a meal to smoke their cigars or clustering at gatherings in the park leaving women to tend to children, food, and each other. I didn't do it in public, but at our home, I smoked an occasional cigar and sometimes those slim cigarettes. Daring, perhaps, bringing a tickle of attention, but more an excuse to gather with the men and find stimulation from their discourse and learn what my husband planned by eavesdropping while he shared his news with others.

He continued imagining the future. "I'll advertise that a manufacturer who employs fifty or more will get prime river frontage, free. And a thousand feet for a public dock. How does that sound for priming?"

"You see the land and rivers as ideas, as seed for more, don't you?" I said. "Not just what they are to the average eye." He nodded at me with a pleased look. "The entrepreneur in you," I said.

"But always leaving some, for the next generation."

"'Feelings gone to seed,' Burroughs calls ideas."

"Mine are planted deep, Cassie. In this place, with the promise here. Everything we need is in this land. And if we do this right, we'll have a city that rivals San Francisco and does it by giving away more than it gets and leaves something good behind. It'll bring business and workers and families and children. They'll people the land like flowers in a garden, and this place will flourish. You just wait and see, Cass."

I wanted to bring up *our* flourishing. I wanted to talk about *our* family, to hear that kind of enthusiasm in his voice as he spoke about us. He had, at our beginning, and I ached to understand its leaving or what I could do to bring it back.

Louie was more attentive than usual after he declined my proposal. He brought back baubles and beads from his frequent business trips to San Francisco, Portland, and even Washington a time or two. Once or twice, upon his return I sensed a strange uneasiness between us, a space that I ignored like a corner of a garden where thin weeds sprout but seem too small to be troubled.

I did not bring the subject of marriage up again, but I still chose a course. I felt stripped existing as we did, and while a part of me believed that anguish meant I lived, another part still sought pleasure, happiness, and joy. And when I could not find it in the diversions of my days, I spent my time with golden friends and rode Ginger into timber.

I wondered what Annie waited for, maybe asking the question of her as much as myself. Four dogs puddled at my feet near the writing desk Louie had shipped for me from France. The walnut reeked of linseed oil freshly applied by Lem. I wrote to her: "You're already close to thirty. Louie says, 'Tell Red we'll buy what they need, as a wedding gift, tell them to do the deed.'"

"You know what they say," Annie wrote. "'The Irish and Dutch don't amount to much, but watch out for the great big Swede.' All in due time," she'd said, so much surer of herself than I remembered when she sat in our carriage with her flashing red hair watching me charm Josiah Stearns. "You can't rush my future, Cassie."

One never really knew another person until you read what they had written.

Finally, during the Christmas season of 1902, Annie arrived again, unannounced so I had no time to plan an elaborate party in her honor, no time to amuse myself planning menus and games. I think she let that happen with a purpose.

She brought with her a photograph of Belle and one of my mother, which she handed me first.

"She's becoming odd in her old age," Annie said looking over my shoulder at the image. "Collecting more and more things. Now it's tufts of hair from all of us and our combs and brushes. She puts them into little bottles which she labels, then with the maid sorts, over and over, adding to her supply. Gets the maid to help her. It's all so strange."

I could tell she spent much time still with Margaret, though Annie had taken an apartment in Hoquiam on her own. Both she and my sister had the habit of emphasis in their letters.

From her rounded trunk, Annie unpacked wrapped packages with lacy bows as she continued chattering. "Not to mention the tendinitis developing in the maid's hands." Her own hands were smooth as stones without wrinkles or rings.

"She's grown so much," I whispered.

"Your mother?" Annie asked then turned. "Oh, Belle."

I stared at the photograph of my daughter I held as tenderly as a new sprout, not commenting on the sadness in her eyes. "Lovely hair," I said instead. "It looks thick as cream. Is it still blond?"

"Your mother says she's as beautiful as you were at that age," Annie said setting aside her gifts.

"Mama said that?"

"She's already ten," Annie said.

"I know my daughter's age," I said more sharply than I intended. A look of pain crossed Annie's smooth skin, and I added with less force, "Thank you for the photograph."

Annie smiled. "Oh, la. Joe made it and used the developing chemicals himself. He knows I've brought it."

"He does?"

I petted Lady Margaret gently with my free hand. The dog had put on weight and lay now on the wide hassock, breathing hard, listening to our every word.

"I think the time may come, not just yet, but soon, when he will *relent* and let you see her," she said. "In the meantime, he's also consented to my bringing a photograph back of you that she might look at."

I felt ambivalent about her news and wasn't sure why.

"To what do you attribute his change of heart?" I asked stroking the dog's belly.

"He really is a kind man, Cassie."

"But why now?"

She hesitated then said looking straight at me, eyes blinking with a hummingbird's quickness. "Fanny's a lovely woman. She's sickly though. Asthma or something. And really, who can blame her? I'm sure she'd like some time without her husband's former family living underfoot. Your mother certainly has the money to move out. Always has had from what I heard, from those earlier investments, so it's not like she couldn't."

"Investments?"

"From the sale of your father's store, I suppose." She began unpacking again, lifting cotton unmentionables from tidy rows.

"I didn't think my father left much in trust," I said.

"Can't remember when I learned that. From Margaret or Fred, I suppose. My mother always said you Hendrick girls were left comfortably spoiled and wondered why you married so young." She caught a look on my face. "Why so surprised? Surely you knew."

We celebrated the holiday season with a large gathering as I sought ever greater distraction. Fireworks sprayed out over the Bay, and Edith, Louie's sister, had come from the City along with Edgar and his antics, of course. Several others joined us, including a few Simpson ship captains and their wives and the heads of his boatbuilding and mining operations. Dogs scampered about, quick-quick barks achieving pets and oohs and ahs over the red velvet ribbons tied around their necks. BeeBee followed Annie as she helped Ming Ho make last-minute rubbings on the silver set out for the guests. Annie rubbed the "Rogers" label of the gravy boat Mother had sent with her as my Christmas present. She wore a full white apron over her wine-colored bolero dress smudged now with dark tarnish.

At the evening meal, Lem and Lottie carried platters of just-caught bottom fish to the buffet. Greens and glittering candles and holly twined around the house bringing the freshest scent of the outdoors into every room.

I made sure that two crystal glasses marked each place setting. The Old Town area of the mill might be designated dry, but the Simpson house flowed wet with French champagne.

Later in the week we held the workers' Christmas party in the schoolhouse. Louie and Edgar collected the perfect tree and joined us women in the decorating. The oranges Louie had shipped in and the dozens of stockings stuffed with candy and nuts and a pretty doll or wooden truck caused an afternoon of squeals. More than once I saw a child riding Louie's shoulders and watched him bend to listen to a tot whose face was laced with chocolate. I felt a twinge of emptiness.

For New Year's, I arranged a smaller gathering even though I liked the bustle of the larger groupings best. I suppose I wasn't always sure how to be in smaller, exposing places and preferred the anonymity of crowds.

"You like to be the center of things," Louie had chided me once as I changed clothes before one of our more intimate gatherings of six or eight.

"And you don't?"

"I can always tell when you're nervous. You keep pawing through your wardrobe."

"You have your white uniform," I defended, "to stand out in a crowd. I just want to look my best too."

"You always do," he said. "I only wish you could forget yourself now and then and just accept that others find you fine."

Before the Twelfth-Day Dinner well into 1903, Annie made her announcement.

"I thought you'd be happy," Annie said. "I'll be able to see you whenever I want."

"Provided the tides are right," I said.

Something kept me from enjoying her news that at long last, she too would be living in Oregon, that I'd have a family of a sorts now to share with Louie.

"It isn't my being married that upsets you, is it?" Annie asked. "It's my getting married now, when you aren't, or without your help for arranging it."

She clapped her hands together as though an idea had just occurred to her. "Why not get married with us? Wouldn't it be fun?" The row of freckles across her nose had lightened in the dreary winter weather, and her skin had a creamy glow to it beneath the powder.

I frowned, glanced quickly from the dining room to where Edith lounged engrossed in a book.

"Don't they know?" Annie said lowering her voice.

I shook my head and led her out on the porch.

"Oh my!" she said continuing our conversation in the cold. "I just assumed that if we did, they did." She lifted my hands as though to warm them inside hers. "All the more reason then to make it legal in the sight of God and man."

"Not this year, I don't think," I said, looking past her.

She dropped my hands and pulled her stole closer around her shoulders. Her voice held sadness in it. "Folks back home would understand it all better if you would."

I shrugged my shoulders and lied. "I don't care much what they all think."

The smells of venison and elk roasts, simmered goose and duck mounded beside fresh pies and platters of chutney and apple relish drifted from the kitchen. Fresh greens, though slightly wilted, had arrived on a Simpson ship. All would be consumed at the Twelfth-Day Dinner. The discussion with Annie made me terribly hungry. I could almost taste Lem's sweet and vinegar dressing.

A thin layer of frost covered the grass where Louie and his brothers and Gus tossed a baseball, chased by white curls of dogs. Their breaths hung in the air like funnels of fog. Louie waved at me as I stood on the porch. I blew my nose and waved back, pulling my shawl tighter against the chill. Beatrice, the most alert of the four poodles, noticed me and ran barking toward the porch, her ears flipped backward in the breeze. Lady Margaret plodded behind. She'd be gone soon, I could see that.

"But I am pleased for you," I said to Annie. I held the door for the dogs to come inside. We stepped back in, and the blast of warmth fogged Annie's glasses.

"I didn't realize you and Gus had everything arranged."

"It'll be simple," she said, wiping at her glasses with her lace-edged hanky, setting the lenses to perch on her perfectly shaped nose.

"I didn't even get to shop with you. We'd have bought out San Francisco."

"I'm past that," she laughed.

Edith, a tall and slender beauty, raised her eyes from Conrad's *Lord Jim* she'd been reading, curled up on the divan. Beatrice jumped and nudged her under her arm. "I'll never outgrow shopping in San Francisco," Edith said scratching the dog's ears.

"Your brother may make you eat your words someday," I said. "He has such hopes for his North Bend. You'll want to leave that California land and come to Oregon for bracelets and hats."

Edith smiled, a dreamy look crossed her face. "I can't imagine a place that would draw like the City. But if anyone can do it, Louie can. Isn't that so, Beatrice?" She took the dog's head in her hands and massaged it.

I was quiet for a time and Annie, always perceptive, knew it served a purpose.

"There's something else on your mind," she said.

I looked at Edith then decided I could talk about this subject within my sister-in-law's hearing.

"Just thinking about Belle, how she'll miss you."

"Why, she's got Margaret, and now Fanny." Annie had her back turned, folding her woolen stole to lay across the chair.

"And she has Joe and your mother. And I'm not all that far away. We just won't all be in Washington together. It may even help her realize that people can leave and still love you. That you're not abandoned just because they aren't beside you every day."

"Did she feel that way when I left?" I asked. I wasn't sure I wanted to know the answer.

"I don't know what she felt," Annie said. "She's kept those feelings to herself, mostly. What I'd call a very private little person. But I've talked with her about how much she's loved by everyone. And about choices. What we have *control* over and what we *don't*. She hasn't shown a tendency to get caught up in blame and accusation and that's good. I think those are wasteful things, they only keep us from our goals. Of course we have to have direction."

No blame entered Annie's words, but I still felt the shame of them.

Annie squeezed my shoulders in a hug. "Oh, Cass. I just wish so much more for you, I do."

It was strange with Annie. I found her judgments quick and annoying at times. And yet with her I could also feel remorse. *Remorse.* It was what Lytton said was "the echo of a lost virtue" in his dark novel of Pompeii, and I felt as though I'd lost something deep that Annie's words now echoed.

"Do you think Belle and Mama will come down?" I said. "Maybe Margaret and her new husband?"

"No. They won't. The seas can be so hard this time of year and Joe's given no sign he'd even allow it. He can be quite peculiar, can't he? Did you know he won't step foot in Aberdeen now because he thinks the city paid the railroad to stop there instead of coming on to Hoquiam? Economics is what it was. Fanny says they have quite a lengthy trip to leave Hoquiam and avoid Aberdeen, except by ship. People can be so stubborn. Gus and I talked about getting married there," Annie rattled on. "But this is where—"

A burst of hungry men stomped through the French doors, scarves stripped from their throats. Cold air lingered on the wool of their Irish sweaters. Louie kissed me with a mouth he pretended was numb from cold.

"I neeb hep!" he said. "Hep!" He walked toward Annie, his hands pulled back up into his sleeve as though he'd lost them. He detoured toward me. "Hep me, woban!"

"Leaves more food for us," Harry said folding his neck scarf, "if you can't use your mouth."

"And we won't have to listen to him shouting at the fight later, either," Edgar said. "Hope it goes more than seven rounds this time." He pulled at his woolen gloves and crunched them into a clump.

I reached up into Louie's sleeves and touched his cold hands. He rubbed his cold cheek against mine.

His brothers tossed their scarves and gloves on the chairs. Gus hung his on the hook beside the mirror. Louie shouted, "Let's eat!" to Ming Ho and began pulling chairs out for the ladies while the Asian man bustled about to Lem's "Gory be!" shouts. "Sitdow, sitdow," he ordered, then served soup first accompanied by wide smiles.

"You're going to the fights?" I asked as Louie passed me fresh bread. "I saved a Christmas surprise for you."

"Fights're Twelfth Day tradition in Marshfield, isn't that so, Gus?" Louie said.

"Not one I've heard about," Gus said. "But I don't live here so long as you."

"Time you learned about this one," Louie said. "Eat hardy. The stoves might not be stuffed, and we'll need fuel to shout ourselves warm in Henderson's barn."

"Everyone carries a flask," Edgar explained to Gus as though he'd care, "we just need to bring mix."

The subject of the fights drifted away through dinner, and I didn't let myself think much on them. I felt wistful, wrestled with an unnamed longing.

Within minutes of the baked Alaska being served and consumed, Louie stood, the sign for Edgar and Harry to rise too. "To the fights!" Louie shouted as though we were all deaf.

He and Harry and Edgar pulled on Gus, who looked with apologetic eyes at Annie as he bundled up with the others and all were soon out the door.

"See you later, little women," Edgar said as he stepped into the night and pulled his stocking cap down over his ears.

"Have a lovely time," I sang out. The scent of wet cedar filled the air.

I smiled as Louie kissed my forehead. "You're taking this rather well," he said as I straightened his neck scarf.

"As a little woman should," I curtsied to the question on his face.

We women waved warmly as the men climbed into the carriage. But as soon as they were out of sight, I grabbed Annie's hand and pulled her up the stairs shouting to Edith as I moved.

"What?" Annie asked.

"Change into these cycling bloomers, girls," I said, tossing a pair of mine to both. "Be a little short on you, Edith, but I've plenty of warm socks. Grab sweaters by the door. I won't accept a protest, Annie, so just start dressing. We'll surprise the lads just so!"

"Oh, grand idea!" Edith said, all game as I knew she'd be with that Simpson blood coursing through her veins.

"We may be the tail of this kite," I said, "but tails often go higher."

"They fall just as fast and far, though," Annie said while she stuffed her feet into my stockings.

FROM A DISTANCE

❋

Edith and I pushed open the heavy double door of the stable. Ginger, my quarter horse and Louie's big gelding both nickered low.

"Not tonight," I told them and watched the looks of delight on Edith's— and wonder on Annie's—faces as I pulled loose hay from around two objects as drab and green as dried weeds.

"Help me," I directed. "We need to push them out."

"What on earth?" Edith asked as I turned the switch to get the motor going. "You're going to ride that thing?"

"We are," I said. "Annie, you'll be behind me. Edith, watch me kick to start, then do the same with yours. I've managed it just fine alone. We'll see if I can maneuver this Harley with a passenger."

They both stood drop-jawed, their breaths vaporized in the single head-light that now illuminated the night.

"Come on!" I said. "Took a cavalry of effort to get these things delivered without Louie's knowing. And if he doesn't want to wait around long enough to appreciate the presents he didn't yet get, then we'll appreciate them for him."

Annie's eyes turned horrified as I pushed my hair under the thin leather cap hanging on the bars. The moist air frizzed hers in tiny curls around her face. Her glasses steamed and she lowered them on her nose to look over the top.

"Do you think you should be out like this? Won't you get sick in the cold air? That fever you had last year could—"

"Just get on."

Edith grabbed a lantern and hung it on the bar that held the steering shaft. "Just in case," she said.

I swung my leg over.

"Is it safe?" Edith asked. She sniffed. The scent of leaking oil lingered in the air.

"The dealer said they all leak, some little thing they're working to replace. These are prototypes. Rarities! Perfectly harmless though. Ready?"

Annie's eyes blinked as rapidly as a caught rabbit's. I gripped the handlebars and kicked the starter. Edith did the same. A roar and grumble like tamed lions echoed against the mist. Annie held my waist firm from behind, and we headed off, scooting loose hay behind us as the engines growled into the night. The force pushed my arms left then right as I gained control.

We made our way laughing. Taking action felt wonderful. Over negotiated ruts, Annie squealed. Edith passed us, bent forward over the bars. She grinned as she sped by. The smell of gasoline vapors drifted around us.

"Practiced!" I yelled. "When Louie wasn't around!"

"Underestimated you, sister!" Edith yelled back and shouted then like a cowboy.

We made our way out the Old Wagon Road, the engine growl steady and true until we approached a steep portion of hill. My Harley coughed.

"What's wrong?" Annie yelled over to me. Her grip at my waist tightened. "Doesn't it go uphill?"

"Not without gas," I said.

We weren't far from our destination, and I let the Harley coast back down and off to the side where it coughed to a standstill. Edith turned around and putted to our side. A loud crack came from the exhaust pipe, and my machine went suddenly silent. Edith switched off her engine.

The night wrapped around us. "Guess they need petrol more often than I thought," I said. "We're not far from the barn, though."

We pushed the vehicles into the refuge of roadside vines.

"At least the lantern'll help us walk," Edith said.

"Sometimes the old ways of doing things are the best," Annie said. Her voice shook a bit.

The bicycle lantern swinging between us cast an arc of light that led us to the fights. As we approached the shed, we could hear bursts of shouts from inside the square building whose perimeter was lined with a dozen carriages and twice that many horses tethered to the posts.

No one heard us ease open the door.

It took some moments for my eyes to adjust to the smoke from the cigars and sheepherder stove stuffed into the corner. Men with fists full of bills sat on makeshift bleachers, shouting and yelling, then gathered more bills while sweaty men in buttoned unexpressibles and exposed chests punched at each other with bare fists. The sound of struck flesh made me wince as I scanned the crowd for Louie.

"See them?" I shouted at Annie and Edith.

Both were taller than I and could see what I couldn't. Edith's eyes were as big as biscuits, and I wondered if perhaps she might have been too impressionable for this adventure. My eyes followed what she saw, then, and they must have grown as large.

Louie sat near the front. The love of my life had a cigar dangling from his mouth, but it was the placement of his arm that caused my fume. It draped over the shoulder of a young, voluptuous woman.

Gus and Harry had already spotted us, standing near the door as they did, both observers more than participants. Gus rushed over to Annie and took her arm and Edith's, suggesting, "Ve all leaf now?"

"Take the girls and go," I said. "I've some business to attend to."

"Not me," Edith said, shaking Gus's arm off. "I'll see this one out."

She set her arms across her chest the way I'd seen Harry do when he didn't intend to budge.

"Least stand back by here," Gus said, and Edith let herself be taken from the main audience. She stood beside Gus and Annie and her little brother at the rear of a crowd smelling of malt liquor and sweet holiday sweat.

As I walked by, Harry's eyes held something strange, maybe pity, which annoyed me almost as much as Louie lounging near the front.

What was I do to? Leave? Watch helplessly? Flirt and flick my hair and eyes and join the fray? Embarrass him with the same humiliation his familiarity with the woman impressed on me? Just as quickly I wondered if I'd done something to drive him to this. Was this woman the reason he asked me to still live a lie? I expected his eyes to catch mine soon, or Edgar to poke him when he caught sight of me, but he didn't, and so I did what I thought would make the best of it.

Signaling Harry, I used his hand to step up the back of the bleachers behind Louie. Then one board at a time, made my way down each rickety step, moving out any man in my way with a smile and my "shh" signal. My eyes asked for their complicity. In that way I soon sat behind Louie.

When he turned left to gather up another drink with Edgar, both their heads buried in a basket at their feet, I tapped the shoulder of the woman he'd been leaning on. She turned with a glassy face to gaze at me. She wasn't much older than Edith.

"Honey," I whispered close to her ear, "that's my man your shoulder's a rest for. I'd appreciate your easing aside so I can take my place there."

Those who knew us or who weren't fully engaged by the fight before them watched for the one forming closer to their seats. Like spectators at an overturned landau, I could feel them waiting to see who'd come up through the hoods.

She had blue eyes, gluey with drink, but she came quickly to her senses. She giggled then, brought her fingers to her lips, nodded, and eased away.

I slipped down to take her place.

Louie didn't notice any change at all, even when I lifted his arm over my shoulder and snuggled up under him. He leaned to kiss the top of my head and shouted to the ring raising his ale with his left hand.

Across Louie's chest, though, I got a look at Edgar on the other side. When our eyes met, color drained from his face. His big eyes shouted *Danger!* but he was speechless, his words caught in his craw.

"What is it?" Louie shouted to him as Edgar, still dumbfounded, pressed against Louie's other arm. Edgar pointed to the woman who leaned against his brother's chest.

I would have given all the money in my possession to photograph Louie's face when he turned back and lifted my chin to see who'd taken the young woman's place.

It didn't happen there, not in the sight of all those people. No, there I made a game of it wanting to believe that was all it was, just a game, his arm around some girl attracted to his good looks or fame, he with no intention to do anything more than rest his arm on her slender shoulders while he shouted encouragement to the fighter he had bet on. I'd handled it well, I decided, allowed myself momentary pride in not plunging in, not hurting anyone else as I dealt with disappointment.

But I had time to wonder, too, riding back in the carriage, we three women on the laps of the men (all but Gus who had headed home to milk). I had time to wonder if perhaps there was another woman in Louie's life.

It was time to confront it, pull the weeds in that corner or let them choke the garden out. Of course, I should have waited until our heads were clear, I should have chosen better than I did.

"How dare you!" I said when the others had closed their doors to bed.

Louie's eyes were droopy, too, from smoke and ale. Even the brisk ride home in the carriage had not pepped them up. He wore that sheepish grin that marked his charm. It slid into a lazy, sensuous smile that at that moment infuriated me.

"How dare you openly behave as though what we have is…is nothing. For your convenience!"

"Innocent, Cass," he said holding his hands to ward off my blows. "Sure am. Don't know what you're thinking. Just a bunch of the boys gathered to—"

"Embarrass their wives," I snapped. "With no regard for their feelings. Thoughtless. Always letting others down. Me, especially." I turned my back on him.

"Didn't embarrass my wife," he said, and his voice had a staking to it, holding something up he stood beside.

"Because you don't have one," I said, swirling back at him. "And you don't want one. Just want to live like you did in Hoquiam with an apartment to rival the Sultan of the Sudan, looking at other men's wives, not just Joe's, but Hunt's, too, now that I think of it."

"Don't, Cass. Unprovoked, that was. The man saw something that wasn't there."

"A man's dead by your actions and a woman and children left to drift."

"As much your fault in those deaths as mine."

My breath sucked in as though I'd been struck. I heard an alder log snap in the fireplace.

"Is she married, too, that young girl on your arm?"

"Don't go farther than you can live with, woman," he warned.

"I've learned to live with my decisions!"

"We've all left something to drift, Cass. You left Belle and a good man, and I…" He stopped.

"Yes, what has the great Louie Simpson left unfinished that he cares to confess? That he lives in adultery and likes it? No responsibility, Daddy's money, no commitments, no obligations. Nothing real or lasting. No need to grow up. No children, no wife…" I searched for more insults.

I hoped the living room confined our words, where that night I expected Louie to lay his head. He dropped into the rocker, almost launching himself on the edge. His feet were planted solid so it didn't rock.

"All of it true except the last," he said.

I had to think of what insult I'd just hurled.

"Didn't embarrass my wife," Louie repeated, "because she doesn't even know what happened. Hasn't a smidgen of an idea."

"I know full well what you did in front of our friends. What kind of man are you?" I hissed.

"Married."

"Don't I wish!"

"No. You don't, Cass."

"Don't tell me what I wish or don't!" I glared, my hands on my hips, my eyes boring into him while his stayed locked to the floor.

"I have a wife," he said then. "She's the one without an iota of awareness of all this."

He lifted his face to look at me, eyes full of dread. Then he dropped his head low and held it with his hands. His fingers wormed through his dark hair.

"But we're not married," I said, not making sense of a thing.

"I am," he said, the words spoken without breath. I could barely hear him. "To a woman. In San Francisco."

His words exploded like a thunderstorm in New York. When he lifted his face this time, I saw horror reflected there.

"Wanted to tell you. Didn't want to hurt you. Or her." He ran his hand over his face as though wringing pain from it and failing. "Thought I'd been given a reprieve when you said you didn't need marriage and yet were willing to love me so, come here with me."

He stood then and took a step toward me, as though to hold me, but I stepped back toward the fireplace, as charred by his words as though I'd just stepped inside the flames.

"Wouldn't blame you if you left right now, but I don't want you to. Please, Cass." He took another step toward me. "Couldn't live without you, I don't think."

"Why aren't you with her?" I whispered.

"She's…in an asylum. She doesn't even know me, Cass. She's like a small child, her mind's all gone. Harry says she'll likely never recover. Frail little thing. Like a butterfly."

"Harry knows? Your family?" I shook my head and sank into the couch across the room from him. I was shaking. "Of course they know. They all know. They've been keeping the secret, like I was some…some child who couldn't know the truth! Or do they think I know?" I let that weigh on me. "What must they think of me?"

"Don't, Cass. Don't make it worse."

"It. Can't. Get. Worse." I knew then I needed to leave the confines of this room, this house, this lie a man could live with and never share, compounding the lie my own life had become.

I pushed past him, grabbing my coat and muffler.

"Where are you going? Please, Cass! Don't!"

I'd already slammed the door.

I saddled the startled horse, pulled the halter from Ginger's head, and slipped the bit into her moist mouth. She took it even though I failed to warm the steel; perhaps she sensed my urgency, my need to be away with her at once. It'd be dawn before long. I just wanted to ride, to feel the power of the horse, to feel something solid and real, something that was not a part of me but that I could control.

I heard the door from the house slam and took the stirrup at the same time. Louie jumped aside and shouted my name as we pushed past, and then we were into the darkness, swallowed by the trees as I gave Ginger her head.

Once out of sight I rode aimlessly, glad for the coldness of the air, glad for the distraction of the stiff saddle against my thighs, pleased by the stretch of the reins against my hands and the smell of sweat rising to my nose.

Ginger flicked her ears as we trotted then galloped then trotted to a walk. I talked loud enough to drown out the clop-clop of her feet, but not loud enough to drown out the words Louie had just carved into my heart.

By the time the sun came up we were on the Seven Devils Road, a twisting trail up and down, and then following a ridge with views of deep canyons. I'd somehow chosen it over the ocean. Something about the sea that day, its power and lure of the surf, frightened me, humbled me more deeply than I thought I could bear. We rode to higher ground beneath a pink morning.

On a grassy area I reined Ginger in and slipped the stirrup and jumped down. The ground was soft and a little slick and Ginger's feet sank into the green. She tore at the grass while I stepped through a row of salal berry bushes to peer over the edge into the valley below.

Elk fed in the deep green meadows making their way from the lip of alder and fir, placid dots on green laced with timber. A charming scene. From a distance, almost anything could look charming. *Charming*. The very word carried duplicity with it—softness teasing at guile; the confused voices of a gathering of finches.

I tried to form a picture of Louie's wife. Her size, her scent, the way she pushed her hair with her fingers, or touched her husband's hand. I wondered how they'd met, what had happened, what her rooms were like. And whether the garden of the asylum we'd once seen in San Francisco could have held her captive, fragile as a gardenia in a frost. How could I have missed it all these years?

Rage was a missing friend. I grappled only with betrayal and the rock of deep regret.

I suppose it was that and the silence of the morning that finally brought the tears, tears I hoped would heal. The sun rose. I prayed then, but it was a puny effort, one I felt unworthy to approach. It had been so long, I made my request from such a distance I didn't expect that God could hear.

Ginger nudged me in the back with her nose, then lowered her head beside me, offering the softness of her muzzle to my cheek. "Some things have no perfect answer, do they girl," I said.

As if she understood, she raised her head up and down, the silver bit the only sound shaking into sun.

I considered leaving him, choosing at the moment to start anew. But as I did, my heart pounded, my breath came short, and even my fingers tingled with the terror. Perspiration flushed through my skin so that I had to loosen my collar, gasping, afraid that I might die. A Bengal tiger in my vision at that moment couldn't have terrified me more.

It was not the swirling rush I brought on in the timber, not my moving to the edge and then stepping back, still well within my reins. No, it was a dreading, a deep foreboding that said if I left him then, went somewhere far away, that I would be so far from happiness, so far from what I wanted that I would surely die.

When I returned midafternoon, Louie stood waiting. I saw him from a distance, wearing his white pants, pacing in front of the stable. When he heard Ginger's familiar whinny, his whole frame straightened and tensed, like a deer waiting to be shot. Dogs pooled like sea foam at his feet.

"Been worried sick," he said, reaching for Ginger's bridle. "Out all morning. Girls took us to the Harleys, and I looked for you. Annie and Harry're all looking too."

I stepped off the horse and moved past him into the barn.

"Cass," Louie said, touching my arm. "I'm so sorry. Never meant to hurt you or even tell you."

"I'm here, Louie."

I didn't look at him, but I felt relief move from his fingers to my arm.

"I'll have to learn to live with who I am," I said, keeping my back to him. "I'm enslaved by you, Louis Simpson. Maybe to whatever it is about you that makes me believe I couldn't breathe on my own. Your promise. I don't know."

I moved away from him then, began uncinching the saddle. He stood with his hand on Ginger's neck.

"I do love you, Louie," I said, still not giving him my eyes. "More than I have ever loved another human being. I don't think love is meant to be this way, all twisted up with pain. I'd like to believe that I could leave. I should. It's a curse of weakness that I can't."

"I'll make it up to you," he said. His hands cupped over Ginger's mane. He stepped toward me. "I will, Cassie. I will."

I pulled the saddle and slid it onto its tree. The sweaty blanket I laid on top, and then began brushing Ginger out, concentrating on the scent of her flesh, the thickness of her winter hair.

"Just don't leave, Cass," Louie said standing behind me. "And if something happens, if she improves or the law changes to allow a divorce, I'll find a way to make it legal and we'll marry. I promise you, I'll…"

He reached for me then and I let myself sink into his arms.

I knew that I'd been offered redemption, a chance to turn around, and I had spurned it, truly chosen the rush and whirl of human weakness. I chose to stay with Louie Simpson, someone I loved for all his pain and foibles, someone I knew was the other side of myself.

Annie and Gus were married at the Swedish Lutheran Church in Marshfield, a church almost as old as the city. So devout were her communicants that they formed a congregation before even a city council.

Lottie and I rolled the lifting hair rats into Annie's with a special twist in the back from which Lottie draped a veil of fresh cosmos and baby's-breath. My friend wore a brown taffeta dress she had brought with her. It fit her tiny waist perfectly, and the sienna color had just enough red in it to contrast with Gus's dark suit and bring out the blush on his face. His shoes were polished to a sheen, and he couldn't stop brushing at his creased pants until Annie walked down the aisle on Louie's arm, her frizzy red hair a fire around her radiant face. Gus was all awe and grin.

I paid attention to the vows, I did, bit my lip to keep from crying and blinked back tears as much as Annie did.

Annie said nothing to me of what she'd overheard that night, but she must have written of it to Margaret because somehow my sister learned there was a Mrs. Simpson after all. At least she wrote of it to me and said she'd keep it from Mother and from Joe, but to consider now just getting out, coming back, and starting over.

Louie insisted on giving Gus and Annie a honeymoon trip to the Hotel del Monte, and they accepted some weeks after, though Gus had to arrange for someone to milk his cows the days they'd be gone.

"What do you know about it?" I asked Louie, both irritated and intrigued that he had volunteered us.

"I've read about milking. Gus's showed me. And I thought it would be good for us to get away for a few days. Besides, I have an interest in dairying."

It was a markable time in our lives, an opportunity to push strong feelings deep into double-turned soil, thinking they'd be buried there instead of gaining strength.

Through a steady gentle rain, we walked the cows down the muddy lane, pushing them with their twitching tails into the wooden stanchions with our words and willow sticks. They chewed their cuds as though set on their own timepiece that wouldn't be budged a minute faster.

I did try my hand at milking, wearing a wool bicycling outfit and a blouse with a nautical theme beneath a burly Irish sweater that came almost to my knees. I squatted on the little stool. Louie'd wrapped a white linen towel around my head and tied it at the back of my neck. It was the first time I'd let him touch me since the night I'd ridden Ginger and come back.

"Look like a painting by Monet," he said and pushed tendrils of hair beneath the linen pressed across my temples.

Pigs squealed in the background, waiting their share of the spoils. I sneezed from the dust of the dry hay the cows chewed on or perhaps the smell of manure and watched Louie's strong wide hands strip the milk from the cow next to me. I lacked the proper grip and rhythm. The Holsteins chewed to the rhythm of the milk hitting the side of the pail. I dipped my finger in and licked it, surprised by the warmth.

"I like the feel of this, Cass," Louie said into the side of the cow not at all disturbed that he'd have to milk all twelve himself by hand. "Jefferson said we should all have a pastoral connection to earth. Thought that'd make us humble and self-sufficient, from the humus of the soil."

"Is that why he was a slaveholder?" I said.

Louie grunted. "May not have been perfect, but who is? Gus has a couple of first-calf heifers we're to check on later too."

"As if we'd know what to do," I said.

"I would. Think I could handle it." He sounded confident.

"You're better at this than I thought," I said watching him squeeze and pull.

"Like the two of us here, away from the mill and the house. Some of the, ah, discomforting memories there." He hesitated. "Smell of the hay. Warm cows and cats arching their way around us. Inspiration for a poem."

I had to bend closer to hear him as he spoke, his head leaned into cowhide.

"Something good and clean about a farm, something that regenerates and doesn't take away the way the mill does or even a city."

"It's the 'idea of a thing' again," I said, a warning in my voice. "This is playing at farming so it's not the same as what it is for Gus. 'Playing at things' appears to be what we're good at."

"If you're going to stay…" he said, his head still into the cow's side, "can't keep torturing me or yourself with the bad in it. We deserve better, Cass. We're entitled to pleasure, that's all we did was reach for it."

"At someone else's expense? Guess that's been my pattern, hasn't it?" He remained silent. "I'll pretend she doesn't exist, push her out when she comes to mind, her and how wretched I feel. All of it, push to the sea."

"I think it's the only way," he said.

I knew of another but lacked the courage to do it.

"I'd like to find a place out farther, maybe on this branch or closer in," Louie said during the next evening's milking. He'd done the morning chores by himself, then fixed me a breakfast of pancakes and canned fruit. We'd spent the day keeping the fire going in Gus's stove, reading beneath the single light bulb hung from the ceiling and cooking biscuits and venison and thickening gravy. When it was time to milk again, I said I'd help.

"What happened to your ocean estate?" I asked over my shoulder as I lifted one of the filled buckets and headed toward the milk house.

"That too," he said coming up behind me with another. Milk spilled out onto my skirt. "I've a dozen ideas," Louie said, wiping off the milk with the cup of his hand. "Don't limit me to one." He laid the cloth over the bowl and poured the milk through it into the tulip-shaped separator top as I turned the handle. We watched the milk lose its foam and swirl, sucked into the center, separating cream from the milk. Cats mewed about outside the door, and the pigs squealed louder. A tabby switched its tail back and forth walking the narrow window ledge.

"Get a drying plant," he said. "Wouldn't have to throw all this good skim milk to the pigs nor haul cream so far to the dairies."

"Another plan you have?"

"Looking into it," he said, and he sounded serious.

"You best stick to timber and shipping. No money in milking."

Our "chores-ing" as Louie called the tasks, took several hours until the cows were fed and the cream cooled in cans at the spring inside the house built around it. The heifers were fine. I noticed that the milk spot on my clothes had turned stiff from the cold as we walked toward the house.

Gus had built his home on a hillside that sloped to Winchester Creek. A stilt-like structure secured the lower side. Blackberry bushes grew tall and somewhat contained behind a painted wooden fence lining the perimeter of the tidy yard. He'd planted a holly tree at the east corner that sported red berries for the season. Remains of a kitchen garden could be seen in the dark. Below, where one would have to walk to reach the dock, grew an orchard.

The moon was up by the time we walked beside each other, not touching our hands, making our way toward the house. Our breaths hung in the February air.

"Who'll take the milk route?" I said as we stepped up onto the porch stomping our feet of the mud and the cold. The Monarch stove warmed the kitchen. Louie told me who would arrive for the delivery as he put a pitcher of unskimmed milk into the icebox, commenting that an ice factory would be a gold mine in this country, too. His mind was a constant sorter of ideas and plans. I didn't care to think of building or finance. Instead, a spectacular view outside Gus Anders's window caught my eye. The moonlight glittered across the meandering waters of the Winchester that rose and fell with the tide. It was thin as tinsel in the moonlight.

There was a quietness here I could love.

Louie put his arm around me and pulled me to him. "You look beautiful as a milkmaid in the moonlight," he said and rubbed my nose with his. "Think I'll wait to light the lamp."

"You did the milking," I said. "And will again in but a short time."

"True, but you are clearly the maiden," he said.

"I believe the term should be matron."

"Sounds too old and stuffy, something you'll never be."

"I turn thirty-two this month. How do you feel about older women?"

Silence followed for a lifetime until he said, "Look, in the orchard. Black-tail."

I turned to where he pointed with his chin. A shadow reached into the trees and nibbled at leaves.

"Keep this area in mind when we want venison," he whispered.

Louis was elected mayor of his little North Bend that spring of 1903. And public dock space soon brought in new business interests as well. We invested in a woolen mill, and along with Peter Loggie and a Californian named Chauncey M. Byler and his wife, Laura, we created the Sash and Door Factory from what had once been the North Bend Manufacturing Company. It did quite well, too, turning out more than the broom handles coming out of one of Marshfield's manufacturing companies. Our North Bend had vitality, and those in Marshfield and Empire and other coastal places began to take note.

Louie thought his real coup came when he convinced Father Donnelly of Saint Monica's in Marshfield to build a hospital in North Bend. Louie donated land, of course, which rattled the city council of Marshfield. Harry was as delighted as though he'd donated the land himself, which, of course, he did in a way as what one Simpson brother did the others easily claimed some part of.

"I would have thought manufacturing a better investment," I told Louie while I tied his tie for the groundbreaking ceremonies.

"Assures the finest in medical facilities for North Bend," he said. "May be the smaller of the two towns but certainly the more progressive even if they do have the rail line south."

"More aggressive," I corrected, "like a pit bull that doesn't know when to quit."

"Don't be critical of me, Case," he said and lifted my chin with his fingers. "You know you love it when I'm winning." He looked into my eyes and cocked his head to one side. "It's the hospital, isn't it? You wouldn't mind so much if it were a theater or a school, but its being a medical service is what concerns you."

"It's the religious connection," I said. "Harry's Dr. Freud says religion is a 'universal obsessional neurosis.' Put that way, no one needs it."

"You'd listen to a man who thinks women the weaker sex? Tell Harry to read Pushkin's poetry to you. Wish we'd had it here with that typhoid pneumonia you had."

"Mercy Hospital," I said, ignoring him. "Sounds like something for sinners instead of sick people."

"What better combination? What medicine doesn't accomplish, God will."

"Somehow I don't think we're in any position to expect that," I said.

Louie next gave land away to churches, if they'd build, something else I thought strange and unsettling.

"Got to have things a family's interested in to bring settlement," he instructed. "Can't have all these single young men from the mines and the farms and the woods and mills lounging about with no reason to control their consumption or their tempers. Families'll do that. And they won't come without churches."

The Presbyterians did break ground with the help of Louie's donation of lumber, and later, I learned, some cash. The result was a new building in town and the schoolhouse freed up for dances and more theatrical shows.

Perhaps his biggest venture that year appeared later on the northeast corner of Sherman and Virginia Streets where Louie had built a two-story, one-hundred-by-one-hundred-foot building. I thought it a bit ostentatious. He even told people he'd soon be hiring architects to design an impressive hotel, noting that developers "needed a grand office space and restful places to sleep when they came speculating about how they'd invest in the future of North Bend."

Annie and Gus drifted into their own world along the Winchester arm of South Slough. Annie thrived there. I envied her farmhouse, her Holsteins, and husband.

Lottie and I made the trip to Annie's several times ourselves while Louie traveled south to the City.

"You look so peaked, Cassie. Need to find something to put your heart into," Annie said as she and Lottie and I picked blackberries later along the creek. Bees buzzed in the afternoon heat, and I itched with the sweat that spread like a stain over my skin beneath the long sleeves of my blouse. But I didn't feel tired now as I worked, and the day had eased my aches away.

"Berries aren't good enough?" I asked.

"Lottie, pour some sense into her."

"She listens to her own voice," Lottie said reaching into a hollow space of vines for plump berries hanging on a bush I'd already thought I'd picked clean.

"I keep busy," I said. "Laura and I are getting quite good at lawn bowling. Louie's hiring some new people, and I fully intend to welcome them when they arrive."

Annie groaned. "That isn't what I had in mind. There is so much more to life than frolic, Cassie."

"Cassie never lets her fun interfere with her pleasure," Lottie said to my surprise.

"I suppose," I said, "I could devote myself to the joys of drying berries or making Minute Pudding with sugar and milk."

"I'll soon have other things to occupy my time," Annie said.

I heard a lightness in her voice and craned my neck to look at her. Through the tangle of vines I saw that her face wore a Madonna peace. With a twinge of sadness, I realized she was pregnant.

Louie returned from that San Francisco trip and brought with him not just Jack London's latest novel, but a pearl necklace the likes of which I'd never seen. He acted almost shy as he gave the gift and oddly relieved when I accepted it. The pearls were exceptional, and he hadn't waited a moment after arriving to hand me the long box lined with velvet.

Each tiny globe hung like heavy kisses around my neck.

"For the most perfect woman of any in my world," he said sitting at my feet in our room. I admired the necklace in the glow of the electric lights he'd had installed. The hum of the light plant that operated the transparent bulbs filled in the sounds of empty spaces. I considered his words: "the most perfect woman of any."

A scent of perfume drifted to me from his clothes as he turned and walked away. I caught it in the distance.

It was not a scent of mine.

He had seen her. Or perhaps merely sat near a woman on the ship. His jacket at the theater coatroom had brushed a woman's cape or he'd found time to see his sister. Other thoughts lurked like unwanted weeds threatening to choke out new growth. I opened my mouth to express one or two, but couldn't. Wouldn't. Better to imagine than to know.

CHAPTER 15

SECOND CHANCES

❀

The few pieces of mahogany furniture Annie owned arrived by ship from Hoquiam and were unloaded at Charleston not far from the Coos Bay bar. Louie and I were to take the trunks and various furniture items by flat-bottomed scow down the Coos River then up the South Slough to the Winchester arm where Gus would meet us with a wagon. Later, Louie would get a little hunting in and had promised to let me shoot some ducks as well. I'd have all the dogs along to run and romp and gather up stickers in their fur. It would be an outing, a meaningless diversion, something I spent more and more of my time on.

But we had more than Annie's furniture to bring with us.

A large woman disembarked at the dock wearing a maroon cape and a hat that concealed a stuffed bird and most of her white hair as it swept around her head. In one hand she held a large white handkerchief she pinched over her nose. The other hand, gripped tightly, clasped a fragile-looking child I recognized as my own.

Another choice, another chance. How many are we given?

"Don't know if we'll be staying," my mother said, waving the hanky before her face. "Don't know a'tall. Came so Annie could see the girl since you haven't shown much interest."

Belle's blue eyes stared at me as she stood still as a heron, revealing nothing. The stand-up collar on her dark blue cape framed her pale, narrow face like a waning star in a morning sky. Beneath her arm she held an elaborate, detailed miniature steam engine almost as long as she.

"Papa's new wife is tired of us," she said after some time of scanning my face. Her voice was thin as spring ice. "Frances wants me to call her 'Mother,'" she continued.

"And what do you say to that?"

"I have a mother."

"You do at that," I said, and smiled.

"Regular international port you've got here," Mama said then. "Who'd have guessed it." She scanned the dock and the hustle and bustle of the mill next door. A large ship with an Arabic name printed in black eased on past heading to the wharf at Marshfield.

"Thought we should let Fanny have time without us," Mama continued. "Not that she hasn't been gracious these months. Going to buy my own apartment house. Been planning to. Did you get my letter?" When I shook my head she added, "No matter. Work just as well to stay with Annie as here, I'd guess."

"Louie wouldn't hear if it, and neither would I. We've plenty of room. Your arrival just surprised me."

"Takes a bit of doing to accomplish that, as I remember."

I stepped over her gibe and ushered them up the walkway. Mama gripped the handrails and nodded toward the stairs we hadn't taken. "You have someone in one of those chairs with wheels? They need this ramp?"

"Louie had it built for me. Because of my heart."

She grunted, and I wondered if she'd forgotten my illness.

Belle settled into the house as unobtrusive as my mother was demanding.

"I'd like the room with the bookshelves," Mama said opening the door to Harry's room and perusing the wall. "Smells antiseptic in here too."

"That's Louie's brother's," I said.

"He has family living here?" she asked, turning her sharp nose my direction. "Funny you'd have *his* family and not do what you need to have your own."

"He'll be leaving in a month or so again, for medical school."

"I'll have a chat with him about my lumbago," she said, "and this constant sneeze and sore throat. This room then," she said and pushed her way into the bedroom across the hall where Edith stayed when she came. "Get my things from the dock."

"Don't forget Annabelle," Belle reminded her.

"You've brought the parrot too?"

Belle and Rhodie slept in the cupola above us, and at night I'd hear the dog's nails click across the floor just before leaping onto the cot Belle chose to sleep on. Belle said she liked to watch the stars at night and have early light all around her. "I like the sunrise best," she said to Louie's accommodating grin.

We did take the mailboat up South Slough later with Mama brushing imaginary dirt from the seats. She barely restrained herself from wiping off startled fellow passengers with her endless supply of hankies while she made comments about this "wild place." Louie followed with Gus and several helpers in the scow.

Louie seemed delighted by Belle's presence, how her gentle curiosity balanced evenly against my mother's rush to judgments. In Belle, Louie found a comrade. He took her riding that late summer, buying her a western saddle with its high swell and cantel, wide stirrups set on a gentle horse. They rode to Sunset Beach near the lighthouse and kicked up wet sand at Charleston Beach.

Louie introduced her to the cupola's treasures, the views and constellations in the night, and showed her pencils and paper where she could write if she chose to. He took longer lunches, came home quicker and stayed later with Belle around, her blond curls resting still down her straight, narrow back. He didn't notice the glare she sometimes gave him when he spoke a little short with me.

Together, we took Belle fishing for steelhead trout on the coastal streams, and we gathered up little smelt in the night with me holding the lantern while they filled their buckets with fish serenaded by giggles. A duck shoot with the three of us sent me shivering from the damp slough. The next time, I sent the two of them out with Louie's new English setter, Ricky, while I curled up beside the fireplace at home, sneezing and drinking tansy tea pretending to listen to Mama's description of her aches.

On an outing to the ocean, I watched my daughter from a distance. I heard Belle squealing, tackled by the setter. Her dress flew into wind and twisted with the flying sand as the dog licked at her face. She rolled toward the water, the dog's paws grabbing at her like a bone until he stood over her, tail wagging. Belle laughed, arms over her face, her chest heaving, feet kicking. I ached with the love of it and all that I'd missed.

Without speaking, Louie carried two wooden chairs from the buggy and dropped them in a heap. He bounded down the dunes, sinking in to his knees with each leap, until he reached Belle and the dog and began running.

Harry strode by last, gentling my mother to a chair, then walking, nose down, toward the beach. He was almost nineteen but still had the baby-face look. On the beach he plucked rocks and shells he stuffed into his pockets. Belle ran to him and the two hovered over his treasures. Louie, barefoot now, caught up, pant legs rolled close to his knees, leaned into their interest, the three of them huddled and close.

"You could join them," Lottie said. She handed me a basket and spread out the blanket over the dune grasses. We stood out of the wind.

"Too old," I said. "Too late."

"You are what, twenty-five maybe?"

"That's a year I'd like to see again. Well beyond it now."

"No one guesses that," Lottie said.

Over Lem's fresh cinnamon rolls later, Louie listened to Belle's tentative voice as she told of her days at Hoquiam or how she and Harry had found a butterfly in a spider's web and had dried it on a piece of parchment. Louie gave his undivided attention to her, and I thought then that he was as kind a man as any in the world, that he could make a quiet child blossom like a late summer's rose.

The weekend before Harry left to return to Cooper College, the four of us played croquette on the goat-cropped lawn while Mama watched from the porch lounge, her legs wrapped in a wool blanket she spent hours pulling fuzz from. The game was spirited and fun, and for an instant I lamented Harry's leaving here for months despite his medical pronouncements. He'd lent a gentle tone when I felt agitated and did nothing to inspire what I called Louie's "adolescence." He encouraged my reduction of gin and gave spirited discussion over goodness and sin.

His leaving brought on the subject of Belle's staying.

"She's been a good influence on you, Cassie," Harry said. "You've changed some of your habits for the summer, you could add to that this fall."

"You're trying to make me a teetotaler," I said.

"It's possible." He concentrated on the slender sticks that crisscrossed each other in a pile on the dining-room table. Putting pressure on one tapered end, he lifted it free without disturbing the pile. "Your turn," he said.

"If you ask me," Harry pronounced as I examined my options for picking up sticks, "what you need is to find a direction, a purpose in life. Commit to something that can hold you. That's what you long for, what all of us long for. It's the human condition to find that passion that consumes us. Belle could be that for you. I think your not mothering her has had no small effect on you."

"You're being Dr. Freud again," I said, annoyed by his rightness. My accusation of his analyzing always stopped the conversation.

"Joe would never allow it," I told Louie when he suggested Belle stay too. I fluffed the pillows, aware of a tension knotting in my stomach but uncertain of its source. I didn't look at the eyes that could charm me.

"She's here now, isn't she? He permitted that."

"Staying is different. She needs to go back to school, to be with her friends."

"You could ask. Or have Annie. I like having her here," he said, removing his shoes as he sat at the edge of the bed.

"I never would have guessed."

"Don't you?"

"Mother's a bit of a trial."

"Even she seems to have mellowed. Think they both like it here well enough. They've accepted things."

"I told her we were married," I said, perhaps to watch him wince.

"Oh. I thought they knew the whole thing."

"I doubt they'd be here if they did. Besides, Mama's anxious to go home. She considers Hoquiam a more progressive place."

"Has electricity," he agreed. "But North Bend will, too, along with all the other amenities of a growing city." He pulled the suspenders from his shoulders and they hung there like unanswered questions. "Don't change the subject. Will you write to Josiah? See if he'll let her stay?"

"Everyone calls him Joe now. Sounds sort of sporty, doesn't it? And Belle says he's taken up hiking and climbing, with this Fanny."

"Don't be doing that, Cass, changing the subject."

"I'll write, I'll write," I said smoothing the embroidery at the top of the sheet, "for the little good it'll do."

And I did write, my simple request slipped into an envelope beside Annie's. But I didn't ask if she could stay the school year, only for a visit from her again each summer.

"She is to school in Minnesota at the Episcopal boarding center," Joe wrote back to Annie. "And must return to Hoquiam before the month is out to finish packing and making arrangements."

"He's sent a note to you too?" Annie said. "She's just so young to be sent away."

"Not right," Louie said. He swiped at a mosquito that had invaded the house.

"Suppose she'll have to be told," Annie said. "I may as well do it."

"No." I touched the note Joe had sent to me, my first contact with him in four years. "I'm to have the privilege of telling her."

"Telling me what?" Belle asked entering the discussion as quietly as a feather let loose from a pillow.

I found a gentle tone from the warning eyes of Annie and Louie.

"About an Episcopal school, in Minnesota," I said. "It's where your father says you're to spend the year."

"Is that what you asked him to do?" she said.

"Of course not. Why would you say that?"

She shrugged her shoulders. "Auntie Margaret said he'd still do anything for you."

She drifted out of the room as wilted as wisteria in winter.

"You see?" Louie said.

"The child's mistaken," I said. "Obviously." I waved the paper before his eyes.

"Think of the pleasure she'd bring," Louie said.

"A child wouldn't flourish with us, Louie. Not now, not with things the way they are." I didn't think I said it to punish him, it was spoken as truth, my truth at least. "It's better for her to be where her father says."

I found her in the cupola, writing in tiny cursive strokes in one of Louie's notebooks.

"I'm not very good at this," I said, crawling up into the small window room. It described both my climbing and my reaching out to my child.

I noticed everything from the bottom up as I climbed the ladder. Belle sat, her dark shoes tight together like two clenched lips. The ends of the bow that wound its way around the lower half of her skirt brushed her stockinged calves. The ruffles around her bodice made her look bigger over a very narrow chest held tight and straight. Her left hand lay motionless over the paper, the nails bitten to the quick. Her eyes offered no insight to her thoughts as she reached to smooth her French braids Lottie had twisted at her temples.

"Well," I said, sitting in a chair across from her. "What do you think about all this?"

Her eyes blinked once or twice staring at me before she answered. "Aunt Annie's wanted a baby of her own for a long time."

"I suppose she has at that."

"Children should be wanted."

"You were, if you're wondering. We had quite a time together, you and I, before you arrived."

"And after?"

My eyes moved around the small room, looking for someplace safe to settle.

"Granny may have told you. I suffered an illness after you were born. But your Aunt Margaret took good care of you. And your Granny Stearns. Your father, too, when he came back to get us. And Annie adores you."

She met my eyes, and I saw in them a pain I did not wish to witness.

"And in Hoquiam—I don't know if you remember but—you had a pony and we rode together. You rode your first horse when you were barely three. Maybe they'll have dressage at your school. What would you think of that?"

She had the gaze of a guard dog, I decided, eyes more prominent than chin, the full mouth more supreme than the perfect skin.

"Why did you leave me, Mommy?"

"I thought it was best for you." It was an answer I'd rehearsed from the day I'd gone. I wondered as I spoke if it was true. "We weren't sure where we would be. And my plans were so...unsettled."

"Are your plans settled now?"

How could I tell her I had no plans at all, just consumed and acquired and wondered why life seemed so empty. I heard a gull fly past the window. One of mother's clocks ticked beside Belle's bed. I considered my answer.

"Children get in the way," Belle said into the silence. Her words held no self-pity or deceit, though their insight cut me to my core.

"It isn't that," I said. "Your father will have chosen a good school for you, even if it is with a religious order." With my fingernail, I picked at a piece of food Louie had left behind during one of his writing sessions sprinkled with strong coffee and snacks.

Her face wore solemn well as she waited for me to go on. She could have been much older than eleven.

"Your father would never let you go to school here. There are no tutors to speak of."

"Louie could bring a tutor from the City."

"He doesn't have children of his own so he wouldn't understand how important a girl's education is, the opportunities for a good social experience."

She stared at me and said, "You don't need to worry about my staying."

She stood then and slipped past me, making her way down the ladder before I could even respond to the wetness I saw in her eyes as she passed. She made sure not to touch me.

I stayed in the cupola for a long time, staring out at the squall that moved from the ocean through the trees. The copper weather vane shaped like a rooster shifted with the winds and squeaked into the late afternoon.

What did it matter? I doubted Joe would change his mind, even if I begged. But why wouldn't I? What was it about her staying here that scared me? That I couldn't remain an interested mother? Maybe that I didn't deserve her forgiveness, didn't expect a new chance to complete what my mother said was the only reason for marriage, the raising of children, everything else mere distraction.

I glanced down at some of Belle's writings. She'd penned short sentences about birds she'd seen or flowers. Some small drawings graced the side of the lined page, and she'd written her name several times, each line darker than the next as though hard writing would secure an understanding of who she was and where she belonged.

Louie had left a few books on the table, too, and I slid them aside, reading their spines to see what he found of interest: *The Idiot* by Dostoyevsky, *Confession* by Tolstoy. One proved to be a photo album. I sat in the seat Belle had vacated to look at it.

The opening photograph and verse beneath it stunned me. Two photographs had been pieced together inside the front cover. On the left side of the composite photo, sitting in front of a fireplace, was the image of a child. The child's face had been smudged purposefully, or the child told to move during the making of the image so that he or she could not be recognized, a blur of shape and movement not unlike the childhood of our memories. The child seemed young, possibly four or five.

On the right was a picture of Louie sitting in his favorite chair, a book open on his lap. Behind him were symbols of his wealth: books, a painting, the model of a Simpson ship, a Tiffany lamp beside the chair. It was a recent image, when his face was full and handsome without a beard. His eyes held a faraway look but one that clearly gazed toward the image of the child. The two photographs had been rephotographed to be one image and must have taken time to arrange. I wondered who had photographed them and when.

Beneath the image he'd written a poem, the longing in the words an arrow to my heart.

He is rich in world's possession
Of lands and wealth's rich store
Yet childless, sits and reckons
That he is surely poor.

He sits there by his fire
And to him comes, there seems,
A vision of what he longs for,
The little child of his dreams.

My fingers lingered on the following page, but I closed the album before I turned it, not yet strong enough to see what other photos and poems and devastating feelings he had slipped inside. Had I believed that pain did not always follow pleasure seeking, or that some meaning waited for my life, I might have acted differently, given Louie and Belle what they both seemed to want. Perhaps found unshakable joy in my own life, as well.

Instead, I put Belle and Mama back on the ship north to Hoquiam. Only Annabelle stayed behind.

Early in 1904, Louie bought the Coos Bay Manufacturing Company and then built the box factory making use of local lumber. In discussion with Gus, the two formed the Coos Bay Condensary offering "Sunrise Milk" in little tins, a business that did quite well. In April, Annie had given birth to April, an adorable child the size of an eight-pound salmon. Gus acted as midwife. A spring freshet kept the streams high and full of fallen trees and wayward logs and thus too dangerous for any small-craft travel. Several days passed before word reached us and even more before I took the mailboat toward Winchester Creek to meet her.

"It was flawless, even for a thirty-two year old," she said. "Your warning wasn't true at all!"

What pain there'd been had washed away with the softness of her daughter's down and the strong grip of tiny fingers. Annie was up and doing laundry the next day.

"I can't imagine how you let her go," Annie said, "even if it is what Joe wanted. I'll never be able to put this one on a ship and send her off. Not ever."

"You do what you have to," I said.

"Don't kid yourself, Cass. You did what you wanted, that's what I say. Just as you always do. If you really wanted her with you, you'd have argued." April fussed with Annie's intensity.

Later in the year, Louie, his father, Edgar, a man named Falkenstein, and Peter Loggie pooled their resources to form the Bank of Oregon. Charlie Winsor joined the firm as an investor and chief cashier. Such transactions would have had little meaning for me except that Charlie Winsor brought his wife with him, and she became my truest friend.

She moved like a greyhound, well formed and lean. "Greyhounds have two speeds," I told her. "Thirty miles an hour and sleep." That was Kate Winsor, nothing flashy, exquisite as a strand of pearls. She'd somehow come to know herself and how to give to others without giving up who she was. She loved books, and her strong hands with tapered nails would hold even heavy tomes as she paced around their living room reading out loud her favorite sections. She was a suffragette and leaned toward temperance, too, and wordlessly raised her arched eyebrows when we served liquor at our home.

Kate and I spent hours conversing about the latest novel or biography, the poets too. Kate's other love was music. She played the organ and had the habit of removing her shoes to pump the pedals. She said she needed to feel the music everywhere, and leather came between her toes and the spirit of the tunes. Fortunately, the organ faced the Presbyterian congregation where she played, so few knew of her aberration, one that endeared her to me more as soon as she shared her secret.

"You've a wish to expose yourself," I said rubbing my hands over an imaginary fortuneteller's crystal ball.

She laughed. "You read too much Dr. Freud."

"Only his book on the psychopathology of everyday life. The rest is Ol' Harry's bad influence."

There were genuine bad influences in North Bend that gave us special interest. The growing number of brothels and saloons required home campaigns with husbands to make our point, since none of us could vote to clean them up or out.

"So you're willing to let them be at the floathouses at Charleston, just not within your view," Louie chided Kate when the four of us joined for dinner.

"They ought not be anywhere," she said.

"Which is your worst evil, the saloons or the houses of negotiable affections?"

"Which is the worse sin, drunkenness or adultery? They go together, you see," she said, "and you know it." I thought Louie might have blushed. Still, the room had warmed, and he'd just come back from stoking the fire.

"A growing city has lots of problems," he said. "Takes awhile before families bring in enough ropes to keep the young stallions corralled. Meanwhile, men need a place for pleasure. Play cards and wet their whistles. Only so many play-parties will satisfy a man."

"There's no arguing with her, L. J.," Charlie said leaning his broad back in his chair, sticking his thumb into his vest. He grinned, and a look of pride warmed his wide face. "She's a Presbyterian through and through. They're the ones who framed the Constitution and our government, so they do know how to wrangle. Might as well give in, at least tell her you voted her way."

Louie gave the sign of surrender, and we laughed and moved on to heavier conversations about the deaths of the Serbian monarchs the previous year and the Russian and Japanese War.

Belle did not visit us that following summer. This time I did write to Joe, but he said she'd elected not to come. I didn't tell Louie it was her decision so I had no one to help me hold my self-blame.

Annie announced she was expecting again, and Kate too. I'd thought Kate older and that another would be a strain what with her other child already nine. Kate confided that they'd been trying for years.

"Won't it be hard for you?" I said.

"Hard? Not how I'd describe mothering," she said. "Involving, exhausting in an invigorating way. But not 'hard,' like laundry is where all you can hope for is that it'll end and begin again. Charlie and I even looked into adoptions but something always got in the way. And then we came to North Bend to start fresh. And here we have it." She patted her stomach. She wore a flowered apron with the strings wrapped around her back and retied at the front.

"A baby around will mean fewer ladies' nights and little hiking for you," I said. We were in Kate's kitchen, her shoeless feet sliding quietly across new black and white linoleum to bring me tea, then swish back again for sugar. Finally, surveying the table and finding it acceptable, she sat.

"Yes, a baby will change things. But it doesn't have to be the dire prediction your voice makes it."

She squeezed a chunk of lemon into her tea and licked her fingers of the tartness.

"I can take her hiking with the Beautiful Club in a basket on my back. I did that with Joe. He saw both the ridges of Curry County and the sand dunes of the Pacific well before he turned one. Lottie says her people do it all the time. It'll be fine, you'll see. We can still plant flowers in the spring, just as we planned."

"You won't stay in, your last months?"

"Don't be a goose, Cassie! This is a new era. I've already ordered my dressmaker to make an expanding top and skirts with extra buttons so my clothes can grow with my girl."

"You're sure it'll be a girl?" I said.

"No matter. You see, this child is a gift we've long waited for. And like all gifts, you look to the heart of the Giver for direction, not so much to the size or shape or even the outward quality of the treasure. It's what the Giver intends you to have, that's what you pay attention to. That way you don't get caught up with fleeting things or find yourself envying something not intended for your life."

She took my hand in hers and held it, looking into my eyes. "We'll still do things together, you'll see. It will just take a little more effort than now. We'll have to plan things out. But we won't lose our friendship. It's just taking a new turn. Babies always bring change, but a hopeful kind."

I know I fidgeted on my chair. I pulled my hand from hers and reached for the tea. Lemon drifted in the air. My mouth felt dry. I noticed the sugar cookies were gone.

"No matter," I said, shrugging my shoulders. "I've been meaning to meet with some of Dr. Eddy's followers, and I know that's nothing that interests you. Now I will, without feeling badly about leaving you behind."

Kate stared at me. "I'm surprised, Cassie. I thought we were friends enough that my happiness wouldn't hurt you. You almost sound, well…angry."

"Envy is 'the tax which all distinction must pay,'" I said lightly, quoting Emerson. "Perhaps it's that." She raised an eyebrow in question. "No, not envy. I've just never been good with babies, that's all. And I've been interested in the Scientists' study of healing. I didn't think I'd do it this winter but no reason not to."

"I worry about you dabbling in such things, Cassie. Spiritualism and philosophy and psychology. You throw yourself into something without really thinking about it, it seems to me. And then it doesn't sustain you."

"It's just a study group. To learn about healing and mustering human potential. That's all."

"You're looking for something, Cassie, you are. I just don't believe you'll find it there."

I walked to the window and looked out. The Winsors had built in North Bend, on one of the high streets south of us, and their view took in the harbor and a valley of trees. I had lied to her, my best friend. A sprinkling of envy did live within me.

"I want you and Louie to be her godparents, or his," Kate said. She stood behind me, taller even though shoeless. "I want this child to know someone who makes people smile. To know a woman who is soft and strong, like you Cassie, who is beautiful on both the inside and the outside." She moved to stand in front of me, to look me full in the face. "But I also want my daughter to know a woman of purpose and passion, someone who has let herself be loved so has enough to give away."

She slipped her arm around my waist, and the press of her against me felt warm and reassuring. She stared out the window with me. "I want you to stand beside us, you and L. J., when we dedicate our child to a life that only God can really fill. Promise me you'll come, willing to answer the questions."

I nodded but didn't speak the words.

"Good. We'll be the first to use Louie's gift, you know," she said her fingers lifting a soft curl from my temple. "Such a splendid gift makes me wonder what guilt your husband's seeking penance for." She laughed then, in jest.

"What gift?" I said.

"Why, the sterling silver communal and baptismal set he just gave our little church."

CHAPTER 16

TILLING
SOIL

❀

Relationships are very like a garden. They must be tended often, weeds pulled while young and not ignored. Seeds must be watered and watched daily after planting, celebrating their push through cobbled soil. It cannot be the idea of a thing, the vision of oriental ponds and rose-covered arbors with little girls in white dresses dwarfed by hydrangeas. It must be the work of it, the place where fingernails are chipped and dirtied by the digging.

Along the rugged coastland of tangled vines and trees, tending a garden took discipline and effort. I do not remember when I allowed the weeds to overtake mine.

Perhaps it happened when I failed to confront the unsettling feeling Louie's gifts began to give. Why had he purchased the jewels and furs for me when I had more than enough? Kate had jested about the baptismal font, but could it have been a gift of contrition? Sometimes when Louie read his agricultural books or tomes on mining, his stories with a Russian flair, I'd stare and wonder if the new lines on his face arrived on remorse the same way as they did on mine.

Perhaps my failure occurred as I looked the other way at discomforting things, failed to mention what was bothering me for fear he would bring up something that might be irritating him. We still shared momentary passions, but each of us held back, it seemed, and so we lived as separate, distant beings who wore charming faces when together with a crowd. No one knew of our struggles, of our vacancy of spirit. Louie might not have even used such words of description, but I'd begun to.

I found no way to share my emptiness with him for it included him and my own lethargy failed to make it different. We didn't share our pain, and so sharing joys and laughter became strained too.

December brought a squall or two but stayed unseasonably warm. The unsettling of the weather might have forecast Harry's news, but we received it with surprise and once more faced new choices.

"You can say it in front of her," Louie told his brother. Harry'd stopped talking midsentence with my entrance from outside, poodles scampering at my feet. "She's known awhile now."

Harry glanced at me. "Louie's, ah, she's passed over." Harry turned back to his brother. "Tuesday, last. Dad said I should come tell you, in person."

"How?" Louie said.

"Tuberculosis."

"Was she alone?" Louie asked, and I saw a spasm cut across his face that made my own stomach lurch.

Harry shook his head. "She didn't know me, but I was there. Not an easy death, but she's at peace now."

Louie turned to the sideboard and poured himself a stiff shot of brandy. He kept his back to us, his wide shoulders dropped in sadness. He drank and refilled the glass again before he turned back to us and sat.

"Everything's been arranged and taken care of," Harry said. "Dad says to tell you this one's over."

How I wondered what the story was, how they had come to be, how they'd tilled their soil and what had made it sour. It took all my discipline not to ask. I watched Louie's eyes stare out to the bay. He reached absently to pat Rhodie who'd propped paws on his legs, longing eyes staring at him.

I reached across the table to touch Louie, to offer comfort to this man I loved. Almost imperceptibly, he pulled away. My hand looked exposed lying alone on the oak table. I brushed at imaginary crumbs and returned my hand to the empty hollow of my lap.

For any who asked, we'd said it was a shopping trip to the City. But once there, Louie took out the license, and we were married. It was Christmas Eve 1904. The judge read the words without emotion, anxious to return to his family, no doubt. With no fanfare, no gathering, no charming reception, just words of commitment, I became Mrs. Simpson.

We boarded the ship to return to Coos Bay, both of us lost to our thoughts. I was surprised mine carried such sadness. At the evening meal, an elaborate supper served on sterling greeted us. And when we finished with chocolate cake and iced cream, Louie went to his leather satchel and pulled from it a white silk scarf lettered with the word "love" in an elegant flower motif.

"Just something I picked up," he said tentatively.

"I didn't get anything for you."

"Not necessary. Becoming my wife is enough." He said it with a warmth I hadn't known I longed for.

I opened the scarf. Inside it was rolled a scroll of heavy paper.

"Had Charlie draw it up before we left, date it today."

It was a certificate for 450 shares of the Bank of Oregon and worth a small fortune.

"Don't want you ever to stay with me because you have to," Louie said. "I want your being with me to always be a choice."

"I could get out in style with 450 shares."

"Charlie cautioned my extravagance, but under the circumstances, it couldn't be enough. He had no way to know."

"You didn't tell him!"

"No, Cass. As far as anyone here knows, we've always been married, since the day we came. It's how I've thought of us, even when I couldn't tell you about…" He took a deep breath that could have turned into a sob. He swallowed instead, said: "Anyway, here it is, wrapped up in all the love I have, torn and tarnished as that's been."

On the legal document granting me a private fortune, Louie had also written what I treasured most. *"For love and affection and other valuable considerations I hereby transfer the within certificate of stock to my beloved wife, Cassie H. Simpson. December 24, 1904."* He'd signed his name with a flourish of large letters.

Back at the Old Town house on Christmas night, we admired the tree that stood nearly to the ceiling in the living room, all alight with candles and cranberries and silver ornaments shipped from Europe. The four dogs lay at our feet, BeeBee snoring loudly. A fire crackled in the fireplace, the light flickering against the strong lines of Louie's face. It was the same fireplace in the photograph with the poem I'd stumbled upon and chose not to mention.

"Have property of your own now, to dispose of as you wish," my husband said. He watched me look again at the certificate.

"I could buy a whole horse farm with that much."

"You wouldn't, though, would you?"

"I might."

"Like you to assume the value will only increase with Charlie as the manager, and not rid yourself of it for a thoroughbred or two. Think of it as insurance."

"Against what?" I asked. "Simpson's don't believe in insurance, I thought."

He didn't answer. He held me close instead, clinging almost, as though the joy of our being together after all this time was still as transitory as a daylily.

I tried to find fullness in my married state, a place where I no longer had to feel remorse. We were official now, as legal as Gus and Annie's union, Kate and Charlie's, Margaret and her Fred's. I could hold my head up higher.

I told Annie, thinking she would celebrate my joy.

"It's about time," was all she said. I knew she'd share the news with Margaret.

Kate and Charlie would have celebrated, had they known, if we could have told them without acknowledging all the lies that had gone before.

And so we celebrated the longed-for occasion alone, two partygoers accustomed to a crowd.

Louie continued to bring me gifts, especially when he traveled, which he did more. He backed an exhibit for the Lewis and Clark exposition in Portland planned for next year. Pushing Coos County, that was his plan. To redeem his absences, he brought the gifts. Silver brooches and garnet necklaces, earrings with amethysts set in the shape of ancient baskets and gold rings, slipped from his palm into mine with a kind of sheepish grin, an apology I took for his having spent so lavishly or for having left me behind. There were little presents, too, less personal but still clearly meant for me: a music box he'd have brought back from Paris or a china doll from Dresden.

He was tender and loving each time he returned, too, though oddly relieved when I accepted his gifts. I chose not to question the penitent look on his face.

Neither did I argue with him about the gift he gave to the Winsors' church, didn't say, "Why did you do such a thing?" He would have said it was just a gesture, something a mayor might want to do for the first church built in his new town.

I could have badgered him about it. I was tempted. I'd done it often enough before about his internal musings. A woman wants to know just what her man is thinking, what his thoughts are so she can feel she knows his soul and offer him good advice. Often I could cajole him into telling me things, and we would laugh together, though later I would wonder if he had simply charmed me once again and moved me back from any subject that might get too close to him. Curious as I was, I decided it was better just to let him be.

When Kate lost her baby, there was no need to speak more about the baptismal font. It would have been cruel to do so.

"Why couldn't Dr. Tower have saved it," I said to Kate more than asked. "Couldn't he see you were puffing up, gaining too much weight too quickly? You went all the way to Marshfield to see him. Think he'd notice."

I picked away dead blooms from the large azalea that stood beside the brass umbrella holder in the Winsor's hall. I'd come to comfort her but hadn't seemed to find the way.

"*Her,* Cassie. Our baby was a little girl. And there's no need to find fault." She lay resting on the couch, a sunflower-laden afghan draped across her legs. It seemed odd to see her not moving about.

"Why didn't you try Dr. Haydon? He might have offered something," I said. "He has all those herbs and things he uses in his practice. He's not quite such a barbarian."

"Some things just happen. I've heard that a miscarriage means the baby was damaged. Maybe some terrible trouble for the infant later on. We just don't know." She sighed and pressed a lace hanky to her eyes. "You see, none of us has the right to want something for ourselves at the expense of someone else."

"Aren't you angry?" I asked.

"At whom?"

"God. If He's so good and all-powerful, then why this? Why would God let such faithful servants falter? Certainly not for punishment. Only the foolish get that."

"Falter?" she said. "Oh, no, Cassie. I'll feel dreadful if you think we've lost faith or believe now that God uses loss as penance. You see, it was His gift to give and His to hold back, for a time, not a punishment. We'll try again."

"Too forgiving," I said. "That's what you are."

She turned back the afghan and patted the couch for me to come and sit beside her, which I did.

"Bad things happen for a purpose we just can't always see at first. That's what I believe. God and Job were the best of friends, you see, yet no one had a harder life than Job. For a time. And he learned so much during that hard time, about his friends and about God. No, this is an opportunity for Charlie and me to learn something, too, something we might never have learned without it."

It seemed simplistic thinking, and yet it granted her resiliency and reserve, a place of hopeful motion. She leaned to the tea service on the coffee table above spool-turned Victorian legs and squeezed lemon into her tea. She licked her fingers. My mouth watered.

"Who knows," she said, looking at me through pain-strained eyes, still red from her crying, "maybe there's something in this loss meant for our friends to learn too."

Louie and I didn't talk much about their misfortune. I asked that fresh flowers be brought on a Simpson ship each time one arrived and arranged huge bouquets for Kate that I delivered myself. Twice I spent the afternoon making horehound candy with her, wrapping the little pieces in colored paper while we talked across the table. The afternoons moved quickly, and I found a certain satisfaction in my acts of selfless giving.

Louie kept the Winsors in fresh fruit and, for Charlie, cigars. Neither of us knew how to talk about their grief with them. We lacked the words to speak of our own losses so had little practice for sharing with friends.

I did carry out my threat to Kate that I would attend a Mary Baker Eddy lecture, which I did. I didn't see it as challenging. I didn't see it as defiance to what Harry stood for, or Kate and Annie, or even Louie's philosophical doubts. I decided I was not opposed to religion nor did I favor it. *Indifference* described my thoughts.

No, I attended the lecture because I said I would.

It happened during one of the City visits I made with Louie, a rare one as I'd been so tired in recent months. This time, I pushed myself and convinced each of us that it would be a good time for me to travel. Louie had begun talking with railroad people and financiers about having the terminus for the transcontinental railroad be at North Bend. It would make the difference in the growth of our town, and visionary that he was, Louie began early to pursue it.

Several evenings found us dining with others, our heads bent to financiers. Louie was at his best during these affairs, bringing out admiring looks from women without offending their husbands. He said I did the same. I wondered that I still could turn a head or two, my face puffed up so and I'd added some pounds. The interchange of smiles and head-bobs, flirting forward then stepping back, reminded me of the whirling to the edge I always liked, and as usual, I minimized the danger.

Louie insisted that I wear the newest rage that exposed just the hint of high breast and forced my thickened waist inside a Gibson girl corset.

A mist of perspiration seemed to rise up from my skin. I smiled through the cigar smoke to make each man feel noticed and approved of, make him believe with my attention and my arm through his that he was the only one in the room. I became adept at pushing aside the threatening gnaw I felt when I watched Louie lean into perfumed curls of another to whisper words only she could hear. He was my husband now, nothing to worry over. He'd committed himself to me.

But something of the luster of the evenings in the City was missing. At times I stepped outside myself as though I dreamed. I watched me talking, leaning in to listen, to glide around a dance floor, taffeta skirts swirling, my hair piled high with shiny curls held with silver clips. I wondered who that woman was and what she lived for and who these people were and what they wanted here and would the world notice when either of them left.

In the morning following the third dinner event, my head was spinning, and I felt empty despite the lushness of the meals.

"Just drink champagne," Louie said. "It's much better for you despite what they say about those new California wines."

I wished then I could tell him about the gnawing that had nothing to do with what I ate or drank. I wished I could bring up subjects of the heart and carry them to completion, but I had no practice. Louie liked things spirited and fun and assumed I still did too. It made no sense, and I couldn't find a way to feed the gnawing that stood in my way of understanding.

So I didn't tell Louie when he left me at the Palace nursing a fluttering stomach and swollen ankles that I would later take a carriage to the lecture hall and hear the Eddys by myself.

They spoke of a new way of thinking, one they said matched the newness of our times: a new century, a new president, an expanding West that required new ideas, a world made closer through international wars and novel spiritual thinking. It was a time for introspection, fresh ways to withstand sin and sickness, to allow God to heal through my mind.

Back in Coos Bay, I found like-minded people who spurned medical doctors for healing, focused on discounting the flesh, rising above it and temptation. It was not about finding purpose, not about seeking peace or my place. It was about willing myself to wellness, that's what I thought of it. And only later, when I failed to overcome my weaknesses despite my practiced efforts, only then did I discover that my search was not for wellness after all.

It was 1905 and North Bend still boomed. The *Harbor* carried an article touting the beauty of Sunset Bay and the Seven Devils area. I clipped it and mailed it to Margaret with no response expected back. Louie saw possibilities north near two lovely lakes that could be developed for a growing leisure class, people who simply traveled to the coast for rest and the engaging views. Annie'd come to visit with the children while Gus took cowhides from his growing business to the wharf for shipment south and delivered lesser-grade hides for aprons and harness making to be done locally. Later, Gus would meet with Chauncey Byler about the purchase of a creamery he and Louie had looked at in the Lakeside district.

We spoke of babies—Annie fed baby Marvin at her breast—and flowers and new ideas for preserving vegetables and fruits. April played with old beads and baubles I kept in a basket in the corner. I hadn't seen much of Annie in recent months. Our paths didn't often cross.

Today she sat, eyes blinking, and I could tell she'd brought a subject she expected me to dislike.

"I don't believe it," I said when she was finished. I had wilted onto the ottoman while she talked, still holding a rose and the clippers and just listened to her, mouth open.

"Oh, he's a flirtatious one," I said at last, "but so am I. We've always been that way. Neither of us takes it seriously. You have to understand these things, Annie. It adds spice to our marriage, turns it up, like adding cayenne pepper to stew. Just like that time at the fights. Remember? He didn't even know the girl's name, it was that simple. It's innocent, whatever you think you saw. We're married now. He wouldn't harm that."

"I didn't see them," Annie said. "Gus did, when he was in San Francisco last. He's sure that Louie didn't notice him."

"Louie has a number of associates," I said, and began moving around the room, straightening books on the shelves, picking dog hair from the arm of the stuffed chair. I lifted a surprised Rhodie off the cushion and scooted her toward April, who sat mouth open staring at my movements or the look on my face.

"He often meets with businessmen and their wives."

"From what Gus described this was no business acquaintance." Annie's lips tightened into a sliver.

The dinner gatherings at our last trip came to mind, and I tried to recall any one woman who might have stood out, any one interchange that carried with it deeper meaning. Had I missed a scent of perfume or brushed powder on his suit?

"Any number of men from Louie's circle have bad habits," I said, stuffing the rose into a vase, then began batting at a pillow. "I can't understand what makes perfectly good goose-down pillows mat and stuff themselves to half their size."

"Cassie," Annie said, "we're not just talking about bad habits. We're talking about your marriage and Louie's very soul."

"Gus probably just *thought* he saw Louie."

My throat was dry and I pulled the bellpull for Ming Ho, who entered bowing low and out when I asked for fresh water. Annie waited for him to leave before proceeding.

"I'm sorry, Cassie. I've thought and thought about whether to say anything. It's so hard to know what to do with things like this. Is it gossip if I tell you? Am I being cruel if I don't? Should I say something to you or just Louie? I prayed and prayed about it."

Marvin squirmed at her breast, and I thought idly that medical doctors were wrong again saying that a woman could not get pregnant while she nursed.

"Gus thought you'd eventually discover it and it would be even more painful then, to hear it from someone other than family."

"What's to know?" I said. "If it's true, which I'm sure it isn't, there's little I can do about it. It doesn't mean Louie loves me any less. We're high-strung people. Intense. And if I'm not enough to make him happy, then it's good he's found another."

"Listen to yourself!"

My ears roared as though I held a shell up to them and I could feel my face grow hot. Where was Ming Ho with that water? I moved to open the French doors onto the bay and wondered why the blast of October air did nothing to reduce the heat I felt surging through my body.

Ming Ho returned with the filled pitcher and looked at me, an odd expression on his face. "What do you want?" I snapped. I couldn't find words to apologize before he retreated across the floor so shaken he still held the pitcher.

"You have to face it, Cassie," Annie said as though stating a fact about the price of sugar. "Just admit it."

"What would you have me do?" I hated my wail. "It's none of anyone's business what another's marriage is like!"

I thought about Joe those years before and wondered if he had known but kept it quiet, hadn't known how to talk with me, and what might have happened differently if he had.

Annie's intrusion into things she didn't understand angered me.

"I sat back once," Annie said interrupting my thought. "I watched you give away your world. I didn't have the courage to go to Joe or you when I first saw it happening. Didn't think it was my place. And look where it led."

"To a beautiful home with a fine husband," I said. My jaw ached from the clenching.

"And a lost daughter and a sister you never see and your bad heart and a husband stricken with—"

"You're not responsible for my choices."

"No," she said quietly, "only for my own. Which is why I'm telling you. I have to live with myself, and I decided that I couldn't if I didn't tell you. Of course, you'll do what you want, but I'd pull it out at the roots, Cassie. Otherwise it'll choke you both. You have such a way of stepping over things. If you do that now, you'll lose it all as sure as if you simply set a ship adrift on the bay without a captain. Worst of all, you'll never be satisfied, you'll always wonder."

I heard a grieving in her voice as though she reached her hands to a drowning person with little hope of having anyone reach back.

Marvin fussed at the activity, and she gentled him, then moved him to her other breast. She pulled an embroidered cloth over her shoulder and the child's face before looking up at me. Her eyes brimmed with tears.

A bottle of red wine sat decanted in crystal. I poured a glass, trying not to notice the trembling in my hand.

She shook her head. "That won't make it go away."

"You'd take all my crutches from me?"

"Can't begin to fix a thing until you know it's broken."

I felt the blood rise to my checks. "You've done your duty, Annie. Informed me of my misery, so not to worry." I swallowed the wine and waited for the warmth of it to ease through me.

"If what you say is true—and I don't believe it for a minute—then we'll work it out," I said. "A Simpson always works things out. It's what we do."

She could tell by my tone the subject was closed. I heard her sigh. "Just empty the feathers from their casings," she said nodding with her chin to the pillow I'd pounded earlier. "Have Lottie wash them up good with soap. Spread them in the cupola to dry, and they'll be as good as new. They just get heavy from age and want of proper preservation."

I stared, not sure she was speaking only of feathers.

Annie left me then, alone in my beautiful home overlooking the bay. I climbed the stairs, turning down the lights slowly. The moon glittered across the bay, promising quiet and sleep. Wakefulness always arrives, though, just as wind dries up the rain. When I awoke, my heart pounding from that familiar dream of melting ice, I couldn't remember what felt so heavy. Then with a spike of anguish like a rushing horse slamming to a stop, I remembered and was instantly alert.

Did I have to discredit all my husband's gifts to me? Did I have to wonder now if they were simply gifts of contrition, seeking penance for sins he'd committed but neglected to confess?

We had everything, led the most charming of lives, with wealth and adulation. Wasn't I the perfect mate for him, pushing myself as needed to be his companion and partner? We were married now, had gotten what we said we always wanted. It should have been the best of times. When had it slipped away?

I lay there in the morning light, staring at the sloped ceiling. A poodle slept beneath my cold fingers, three more breathing in the room. My fingers felt cold and stiff as I stroked the dog. The open window brought in scents of cedar and pines and the salty bay. As I lay there, I wondered for the first time where Louie really was, and if he awoke alone in San Francisco.

Lady Margaret died that morning.

Lottie found me digging with the spade in the corner of the garden, digging and digging, my fingers blistered, the webbing by my thumb rubbed raw. When she took the shovel from me, she placed her arm around my shoulder and the touch of it, so comforting and undemanding, gave permission to my tears.

"Oh, Lottie, I didn't know she was sick! How could I have missed it?"

"You were good to her. She lived a good life."

"I know she was only a dog, but I just loved her!"

Lottie let me cry until it felt my chest would break. She may have sensed the tears fell for more than the dog, but she said nothing. Instead she helped me lay the still form in the hole we'd dug and covered it.

"Ridiculous," I said wiping at my face. "Crying more over that dog than I did for my father almost. Just silly."

"Maybe you cry for failures," she said, "or having to live with unfinished things."

I glanced at her, always startled by the clarity of her vision.

Louie returned, but I chose not to discuss Annie's accusation.

My husband seemed so genuinely happy to see me, smiling and dropping to his knees as I sat at my writing desk, hugging me. He handed me then a sterling silver Dutch bride's box. Figures graced each of six sides. The engravings depicted trust, hope, prudence, love, and tenderness. He'd engraved our names on the sixth side of a box small enough to fit in the palm of my hand and had filled it with hard candies.

"Box a suitor gave his intended," he said, "in the 1600s. Filled it with gold ducats, but I couldn't find any. Candy'll have to do."

I turned the gift over in my hand feeling the tiny engravings beneath my fingertips. He watched me, his eyes dark and piercing as a raven's call.

There was something different about him. When had he begun parting his hair farther to the right or developed those circles beneath his eyes? When had little wrinkles begun winding their way from his eyes like rivers to a slough?

Louie cleared his throat and said, "Lottie says in her tradition, when a man courts, he splits a young fir tree to within a few feet of the ground. If two good trees grow from the single trunk, it's a good omen. If the tree dies, the marriage wasn't meant to be. Didn't think to do that when we wed. Thought you might like the Dutch tradition just as well."

"Am I being courted?" I said, feeling uneasy.

"Course not. Just saw it and liked its message. Knew your dad was Dutch."

I almost spoke then, telling him of the silly thing Annie had shared.

"Fine craftsmanship. Use it for your hair bobs or whatever," he said. He stood, kissed me on the top of my head, and turned his back. "I've something else for you too."

"Will I like it?" I asked.

He turned. "Would I give you something you didn't? What's bothering you?" He removed his cufflinks and pulled his tie from his neck.

"Nothing. I'm just tired. And I've missed Lady Margaret so much already."

He looked at me for a moment with a question on his face. "Sorry," he said. "I know the dog was special to you. We can plant the peach tree tomorrow. It's a special variety, from the Orient. Have no idea if it'll grow. Worth a try, though. Put it on the dog's grave if you like."

His next words spoke of business, telling me of his parents and sister, Edgar's planned visits. I set the marriage box down beside the bed and rose to hang his coat as he talked, then I caught the spine of one of the books on my shelf: Kate Greenway's *The Language Of Flowers.* I looked up "peach," half listening to him. It meant: "Here I fix my choice."

My moment for weed pulling had passed.

In the morning the two of us walked to the freshly turned mound of Lady Margaret's grave.

"We'll have to fence it or something," I said. "The deer are a fright to the new plantings."

"Harry says to hang potpourri in the leaves."

"Does he?"

"Strong scents deter them. Worth a try. Dry rose petals and lavender. Maybe put it closest to the quince. Barbs might push them off." We walked closer to the planted quince, and Louie pulled one of the leaves and crushed it with his wide fingers. "Won't be long and Belle'll use these to color her lips," he said. "Growing up fast."

"Cosmetics come in bottles now," I said.

Louie brought the small tree he'd set in the barn for the night and dug the hole just beyond the mound. He knelt to pull up dirt with his fingers, measuring to the right depth. The rootball on the tree held tight, wrapped with grape leaves and rope. It sent us the aroma of sweet earth from another land when we broke the rope and set the tree into dark North Bend soil.

My husband knelt and tapped the ground around the rootball. I carried a pitcher of water from the rain barrel and poured it over the roots until the tree sat in a soup of earth. When the water had soaked through, we pushed a bamboo stake into the ground beside it, careful not to damage the roots.

"Always thought that was the most tedious job," Louie said, brushing his hands together to knock off the dirt. "Staking things that already look perfectly straight and strong. Seems a useless thing to do. Until the first strong wind." He tied a thin leather thong to the small trunk and attached it to the bamboo.

"When did you stake plants so much as to find it boring?" I said. "Do you have another garden you've been tending, one that I don't know about?"

My husband continued tapping around the stake and didn't answer.

CHAPTER 17

ACQUISITIONS

❀

Louie grew busy with North Bend affairs, and he said certain things "demanded" my attention too. I made special efforts to accompany him, never letting a headache or tiredness turn down an invitation to lunch with him in Marshfield. If fluid pooled in my legs I ignored it and still shared a ship with him, north to Portland or Seattle to confer with railroad interests and those involved in land speculation. I didn't talk about my tiredness. I appeared full of vigor whenever he suggested a journey. It was my way of "staking up," and it kept my nightmares away.

North Bend grew. The school had to double shift in its October-to-May run. The Methodists dedicated their new church building (free land having been donated by my husband), and Louie helped Charlie Winsor pour his grief over their loss of the baby into the purchase of the Castle Building.

The building's three stories and upper floor had housed an early restaurant when new in 1904. Louie and Charlie and others soon took over the penthouse for offices. My husband decided that every growing town deserved a Commercial Club, too, for socializing and doing business. He believed the two went hand in hand.

"Let's you and me furnish the club," he said. "Whole third floor will be available for members. Lodges can use it too."

I thought wistfully about my father's lodge back in New York.

"Billiards?" I said.

"Room for two. One for ladies, one for men."

I laughed remembering a time when that had seemed so important. "We can order draperies and furnishings in Portland, I imagine." I decided that keeping him from San Francisco might just have some advantage.

He patted my hand in agreement. "Reading room, a card room and bar, a small dining room. A modern stool with a chain for convenience. We'll have a touch of our own little Hotel del Monte right here in North Bend."

"And carpeting. No pitching peanuts to the floor, agreed?"

"Agreed," he grinned.

I avoided Annie as much as I could. If she did stop by, I made sure Lottie remained in the room or I talked of her children, always turning a topic the way I wanted so I could paddle her from the foggy waters of my life.

In April, the earthquake struck San Francisco. The mill whistle blew at an unplanned time, so I knew something was terribly amiss.

The *Oregonian* newspaper had called the Coos Bay area "part of California" and it was never more real than April 6, 1906, when the Marshfield telegraph first received the news. Word spread across the bay like blood in water until everyone knew. It was as though we were a small town just down the road from the City with our aunties and uncles, grandparents and history now shattered by land wrenching itself violently beside the sea.

Hundreds of people jammed the telegraph stations. Simpson Lumber Company made Louie's contact easier, and we learned early on that there had been some business losses suffered at the harbor but no lives of those we closely knew. Still, Louie appeared distracted, saying, "Minimal losses to speak of," when I asked of any news he'd heard.

As word came back of the destruction and intense fires, we knew there'd be thousands lost, considered going there to help. I asked about his parents and family, left a space for any unnamed someone he might be worrying over.

"Mother and Dad are all right where they are, across the bay. Probably do more right here," he said, to my relief. "Harry's there. With his doctoring, he'll be in demand. Food'll be short and supplies. That might be something we can do."

Within days, the *Breakwater* left the harbor with eighteen hundred sacks of potatoes, two tons of live clams, and sixty-five hundred loaves of bread, several dozen baked in our kitchen with the help of my hands. Tons of butter and cheese were donated by the dairymen's association and the creameries. Louie began working on production schedules for other shipments of alder and fir needed to rebuild a once magnificent city even while the fires still raged day and night.

Kate invited me to help the churches raise money for the rescue work sending blankets and canvas tents to help house the City. I found the effort all-consuming in an invigorating sort of way. We spent long hours sorting through donations, labeling them, and talking with the box factory representatives about how to prepare the items for shipping on Simpson ships.

"I think of you as a sister," Kate said to me as she tied an armful of blankets with hemp rope and stacked it in the corner of the warehouse set up as collection site. We'd been working long hours together, swallowed by musty smells of dust and rope and warehouse. "You're a special friend to me, too, Kate," I said.

"So why do you hold back?"

"About what?"

"I don't know. Just that something's been a bother for some time, and it hurts me that you feel you can't share it with me."

I hadn't thought I'd changed myself with her, thought she was the person I could be most at home with.

"We've all had our share of troubles this year," I said. "It's just a little something I have to work out on my own."

"A little something," Kate said.

I stuffed some mullein into a section of old quilt before sewing it shut.

"It isn't a sign of weakness to share sorrow, you know," Kate persisted. "I find it's a way of giving. Allowing someone else to help carry a burden."

"You've your own," I said.

"Which you helped carry. Because you listened. I just want to do the same for you."

"I like getting things organized like this, don't you?" I said, my voice working at distraction. "Makes me feel, I don't know, valued, if that doesn't sound too strange."

She remained quiet for a time, folding and tying and stacking.

"Well, maybe that's what you always need to do then, Cass. See how you can give to others as a way to gift yourself."

I had reason to be in his office the day I found it. Gathering up information about shipments for relief, I let my fingers move across the names of files, slipping out one called "correspondence."

What I thought I'd find was not clear. Maybe to see if he had written to someone whose name I didn't recognize words I'd wish I'd never read. Maybe to discover a name of his first wife or confirm Annie's accusation, or perhaps a way to refute it, to be able to say to her, "Oh, that was Mrs. Wilson Gus saw my husband with. She's a friend of Edith's. Not to worry, Annie. Now the mystery's solved." Perhaps I sought some confirmation that if my husband once had a liaison that it was over, that with the planting of the peach tree, he had moved on.

So I was not prepared for the letter I found written in familiar script on the Simpson Lumber Company letterhead sent from Hoquiam. Some very distinctive double *es* stood out. I lifted the letter from its folder.

A business correspondence. A response to Louie about the purchase of a ship on behalf of the Simpson company. Joe Stearns had apparently been negotiating with someone in Hoquiam on Louie's behalf. The letter also contained a report on shipments of relief sent from Grays Harbor and ended with pleasantries about Joe's wife and Belle's new glasses Fanny had gotten for her in Tacoma. Nothing earth-shattering, nothing out of the ordinary for a letter. Still it bothered me that Louie knew something of my daughter and had any kind of relationship with my ex-husband that I knew nothing about.

If he could hide *that* relationship, he may well harbor others.

Perhaps it was time to tell him of Annie's accusation of betrayal, though I still feared that doing so might also open up a discussion of my own.

On a warm Sunday afternoon some days late in the summer, Louie planned an outing for just the two of us, telling our driver to drive us in our panel-boot Victoria buggy out to the lakes.

"Fish from the porch," he said, "if I can buy the land, find the time to build."

He held my hand in his as we walked along the sandy beach. One or two families picnicked nearby, their children splashing in the lake water, buckets and shovels scattered beside them. Two more little ones, their bare feet squishing soft sand between their toes, worked their way near the water's edge, picking up rocks they tossed then digging with sticks. Our three poodles were in seventh heaven, pacing along the shore, weaving in and out of the circle of shadow our umbrella made as we walked. Louie felt my fingers and commented again on how small my hand looked inside his and how cool it felt.

"Cold hands, warm heart," I said.

"That's a fact," he said and squeezed.

We stopped and chatted with other walkers. Several recognized Louie and me and they smiled as Louie recalled some detail about their previous encounter, made them feel special being held in his thoughts. A lip-chewing man with a sad-faced woman on his arm spoke of the creamery Louie had invested in, and I thought the warm afternoon might turn cool with business when we heard shouts near the water.

We turned to see behind us a woman running in the direction of the toddlers. She lifted her skirts to reveal men's brogans on her feet. Running, she raised one arm against the sun.

"Weren't there *two* children playing there?" I said.

Louie dropped my hand and started running, tossing his white jacket as he ran. Closer to the child than the woman, he reached the little girl and bent on one knee, gathering information in an instant. Before I could get my breath to say "Wait!" he had plunged into the icy water in the direction the child pointed.

The mother arrived breathless. "Where's Willie?" She grabbed at the child's shoulders and shook her. The girl couldn't have been more than four, and her eyes told everyone she was terrified.

"I told you not to let him from your sight!" the woman said.

"My husband's a good swimmer," I said, craning my neck to see if he had found the little boy. There'd been no splashing in the water when Louie entered it, and I feared the child had simply slipped under and away.

"She's a strong-willed one," the woman said of the child she released with a jerk and turned her back to. The little girl stood by herself, her fingers stuck in her mouth.

I pulled the child to me.

Together we watched Louie dive and come up, dive and come up. It wasn't very deep, though more than enough water to take a small boy. Louie moved about in the water as though he'd made a mental grid. Suddenly he stopped, waist deep. He shivered and stared, then pulled at a lifeless form.

Louie's body brought with it a cascade of water as he leapt, knees high, through the lake to bring the boy to shore. He laid him across his knees, cleared the boy's mouth with his fingers, and began pumping on the boy's back. He had already begun a rhythm by the time we reached them. Water dripped from his face and his clothes, and he shook with the cold.

The woman wailed and cried, held back by her companion. Others offered words of advice about laying the boy on his side or clearing his mouth.

"Maybe you can breathe into his lungs," I said.

Louie looked up, squinted, then laid the boy on his back and blew into his mouth. The action forced the boy's thin chest to fill, and Louie began another rhythm then, of breathing and pushing. Nothing dissuaded him. He worked alone on the beach. Every third or fourth pattern, he would put his cheek to the boy's as though hoping for some sign of life, a whisper of breath. The child's face was the color of cooked rice, pale even against the white sand.

"It's no use, Louie," I said, finally. I touched his shoulder lightly. "The boy was under too long. You've done all you could."

"Nothing more urgent to do," he said between breaths. "Do what we can."

A few people had actually started to walk away so uninteresting had this drama become, so sure were they that the boy was lost, that when the child lurched and a stream of water poured from his mouth like a break in the bilge, only a few watched it happen.

The woman sank to her knees in relief. "Willie!" she sobbed and wiped at the child's face now, lifting sea grass from his cheeks and combing his hair with her fingers. The man who'd held her shouted to those who had started away, and they hurried back, glad to be a part of the promise of a happy ending.

Someone had brought a carriage onto the sand, and the boy's mother and sister were lifted into it, their companion reaching to take the boy from Louie's arms.

"Head for Mercy," Louie said, and they drove off, all of them, leaving Louie and me at the end of the carriage trail left in the sand. I hoped the girl would not bear the guilt of her brother's near-death.

Our own Victoria took us slowly home. My husband sat across from me, knees wide apart, head resting on the leather back, his dry jacket draped around his shoulders. He half leaned into the side of the carriage. His hair was slicked close to his head, and his clothes, drying, began to wrinkle. He wore a soft smile on his face, one of satisfaction.

"My hero," I said and slipped up under his arm. "You could have drowned yourself."

He grunted and adjusted himself around me. "Not likely. Learned to swim when I was just a 'bit of a lad.' Shoot, we've even taken canoes out in the ocean, Edgar and I, we're so sure we could swim back if we needed to."

"You do like to take risks," I said.

He shook his head. "No risk in this one, Cass. Just a chance to do something good. Not many of us get to do that in a lifetime."

"The Chinese say once you save someone's life, they're responsible for you for the rest of their days."

"Hope the kid doesn't know who I am," Louie said and laughed. "Wouldn't want him to carry that weight around his whole life." He sat without speaking. I heard a finch sing as we passed by its perch. Our bodies bounced together on the bumpy road. "Nope. Helped a child who doesn't know my name." He kissed the top of my head. "Best way ever."

The *Coos Bay Harbor,* however, related the incident with names.

"They probably thought you'd be pleased," I said.

"Good deed is pleasure itself," he said, tossing the paper on the floor.

"Nothing wrong with letting others sing your praises. Someday you might want to be governor or president or who knows what. Then letting others know the kind of man you are will be important."

"Have a ways to go before I want folks knowing the kind of man I am," he said.

"What made you keep at it after it seemed sure the boy was dead?"

He was thoughtful. "No halfway markers. Just beginnings and ends. I couldn't feel the end so I kept on."

We sat quietly together.

"Something more, Cassie. Hard to describe. It was as if it was my boy I worked on." The photograph of the child inside Louie's book slipped into my mind. "Didn't feel that my hands were alone there, or my mouth or my breath. Felt like I was a part of something larger than myself, like I didn't really have a choice but to continue. Kind of crazy, isn't it?" he said and looked away.

> Despite frustrations, the finest gardeners always stake as necessary. The time to stake is not when the winds have already pushed and bent the stalk or pulled plants up by the roots but when stems appear upright and seemingly stalwart.

I read from one of the garden books given to the library collection accumulating at Kate's.

> Be wary of placing the stake. Do not damage the bulbs. If you pierce the root, disease and rot will set in.

Yes, I'd pulled some weeds, hadn't nagged when I might have. Even pruned back a bit, exerted myself to spend more time with Louie. But I hadn't shared myself with him, hadn't taken down the fence I'd let Annie's words build up. Exposed stems remained that needed healing from the piercing we'd done, the disease that had set in. I'd done little to keep my marriage from being bent or unsettled.

It was easy to ignore the staking. It required discipline, something I lacked.

Several days passed in the months ahead that made me wonder about Louie's discipline, too, what consumed his days. He made arrangements to be gone often during the day, not coming home for lunch, sometimes staying out until well into the night. "Business issues," he'd claimed when I asked. When he snuck into our room late, he'd swing his wool coat over the back of the slat-back rocker, and the scent of wet earth and a mixture of cedar and fir filled the room that brought back memories of a land hungry for trees. His body felt cool when he slipped in next to mine, and I wondered if he knew that I feigned sleep.

"Where have you been?" I asked him once when the wood smoke and earth scent were so strong I couldn't ignore them.

"Out," he'd said.

"Doing what?"

"Don't, Cassie."

"Don't? You come here hours after expected and I shouldn't ask you why or where you've been?"

"Don't need mothering," he said and turned over.

"You forget. Mothering's not one of my virtues."

He must have felt the frost that crossed between us like a swipe of cold paint, but he risked it and touched my face. "You can't know everything, Cassie. It would make your head explode. You just have to trust for some things."

He spoke in a way that would not let me press him more but my fears obsessed me. The day before Thanksgiving 1906, I followed Louie, taking my motored cycle and putt-putting right in public down the dirt road through town. But he'd outdistanced me on his machine as I waved through the misting rain at shopkeepers and a few startled matrons peering out beneath their umbrellas. I lost him along the trail somewhere in the tangled vines not far from the lighthouse. I rode instead to Sunset Beach and would have returned, but the rain stopped. So I sat there on the sandy shores, a blanket laid across ferns, listening to the waves roll gently into the cove.

I mentioned not a word to Annie or Kate of Louie's strange departures. I even found some odd response when Louie said once that the ferry driver had reported my having crossed riding the Harley.

"Got a special someone you go to see when I'm not around?" he said. His eyes sparkled in a tease.

"Certainly not!"

He didn't challenge me. I didn't challenge him.

The banking panic of '07 had not reached the western shores of Oregon, but the flurry of concern meant hours watching the bent heads of Louie and

Charlie as they considered the effects. Money came easily in a Simpson world, though we could lose it as fast as the men who played poker at the Englishman Thom's Saloon. Telegrams to and from San Francisco brought visits by Edgar with messages from Asa. I don't know how much my husband listened to his father. He had his own way of doing things that sometimes put the two at odds, though Louie rarely spoke ill of their disagreements. He always planned to please his father, feel the warmth of shared efforts, yet a fire burned between them that kept them distant.

When the launching of the *Lusitania* and its setting a transatlantic record was recorded in the *New York Times*, there was much rejoicing in the Simpson shipping clan. Business would keep booming, this first decade a small beginning to what would be ahead.

I found smaller articles inside the social page to be as fascinating. "The highest break ever in billiards goes to Tom Reece who played 499,135 in 85 hours and 49 minutes." And beyond, in fewer words still, the announcement that Philadelphians declared the second Sunday in May as "Mother's Day."

When Sophie, Louie's mother, died, we headed south to the City. I hadn't visited since the quake and while the rebuilding had been furious, the evidence of disaster remained in the freshly milled boards stacked beside piles of charred lumber and broken brick.

We returned from a funeral distinguished by Greek Orthodox chants—despite its New England, Protestant tone—and the number of people who gathered to pay their respects. They spoke of Sophie's graciousness and charity, her quiet strength and honor. With us came trunkloads of Sophie's paintings and many personal effects Edith said she'd have no room for in her apartment and Asa said he didn't want to look at now that Sophie wasn't there.

There were such a lot of things Sophie had acquired: jewels, furs, antiques, icons, and Ming Dynasty vases. "Whatever will we do with all of it?" I asked Louie, our own home already a clutter. He didn't answer, but it was clear he wanted us to take the pieces his mother had once touched.

"Dad gave her most of it," he said when we unpacked the trunks. "Every time he came back from a travel. Not sure she ever really found value in them."

"Perhaps she had her eyes set on higher things," I said and wished I'd taken time to know her better.

After that, Edgar often stayed when he brought messages from Asa. He and Louie'd ride off to some adventure now without the gentle interference of their mother to keep their impulses under check. They called Edgar "Captain," though I never did know why.

On Edgar's most recent trip, he brought news of motored autos, his latest interest.

"Imagine!" he'd said biting into the hard crust bread Lung Lem had baked just for him. "Speeds of twenty miles per hour!" With his finger Edgar stuffed the corner of his mouth full of the dark bread. He chewed, took a swirl of beer from North Bend's brewery, and nodded his approval to the Chinese cook still standing beside him. "Your best ever," he said.

"I give you much more?"

Edgar nodded, and Lem backed out for seconds with his bowing smile.

"Just think of how far we could go in a day in one of those! Wish Henry Ford would do more than form a company," he said. "People could drive up here from the City on their own. If there were roads."

The "Captain" had his own following of single men with nothing to spend their money on except whiskey, racehorses, and women. And now, it would be autos.

"Don't you think you're getting a little old for Edgar's shenanigans?" I asked my husband one evening as he dressed to go to the club.

"Too old? Never too old to have fun. Why, everyone, every day should have a little joy, something that says they're glad to be alive. Don't you have that Cassie? You used to."

I thought for a moment. "No, I don't. And I'm not sure it's all that important, either."

"You should," he said and kissed me on the forehead. "Sign that I've been neglecting you. Let's us plan an event."

"A picnic at the lighthouse?"

His hesitation caused a distance.

"Lakeside," he said. "Got something I want to show you there."

Chauncey and Louie had bought the creamery at Lakeside, then divided the surrounding land into plots touting them as "resort lands." He held back one place for us, and that's what he showed me the next weekend when we both rode our motored cycles out to the lakes. I loved riding through the canopy of trees with the brace of wind against my face and the tightness of the leather helmet molded to my head. The startled looks of those we passed added to the trip. Simpsons—who could afford to buy anything we wanted and ride in whatever vehicle we chose—had selected one that pushed the wind against our faces, wild in the open air.

We finished building the house on Trout Lake in June. Nestled near the sand dune, Louie did fish from the back porch as he had imagined the day he saved the boy's life. I played the piano he'd bought me on a trip to New York, brought out the silver flute from the attic, its soulful tones singing out across the water.

In the evenings, when the sunlight sent shadows across the still lake and birds twittered in the firs, Louie took photographs of blacktail deer drinking at the shoreline or of me, lounging in the bow of the boat with the setter panting happily between us.

"Frenchman named Lumière's developed a process for color photography," Louie said, his hands steady on the box Eastman. His eyes looked at me through the little lens. A lock of dark, shiny hair kept falling forward over his eyes causing him to push it back with one hand.

"Revolutionize what we capture on paper. Hold still now." He clicked the shutter and looked up to smile. "Imagine, having sunset reds and yellows in a photograph and not just from painting. Color photographs'll be stunning."

I couldn't imagine a more powerful image than the black and white one he'd created over the poem he'd written of his longing for a child.

Why did that poem and photo haunt me so? I'd been too frightened to lift the following pages and see what other longings might have waited there. Maybe it reminded me of my own child and how I'd let her image be a blur. I'd never had the courage to look at Louie's photograph again. Maybe if I had it would not have had such power. Not knowing about a thing seemed to wield more control than facing what was real.

The blur of a child sat there beside the fireplace, my husband staring, and I knew it was something I could have given him and didn't. I'd just turned thirty-six, not a decent age for birthing. Still, my mother had been in her late twenties when she gave birth to me and had Margaret three years later. Neither pregnancies had left a dent in her constitution, maybe even made her stronger, more disciplined.

That was, I suppose, the truth of it. I avoided the discipline. So my poodles lounged about the divans or curled wherever they pleased and still, after all these years, tried to enter Lem's kitchen every time he pushed open the door. I chose wine more often over walking to reduce my headaches. I'd pursued the Scientists' thinking with little vigor. I surrounded myself with people and made them laugh and feel lavished, yet did nothing to nurture alliances with true friends. I'd failed as a mother. As a wife, I had a list of lackings, greatest of all the discipline of dealing with difficult things.

The letter from Belle, written in her Episcopal-school hand, expressed her wish to see me. She had addressed it to me, her "Mother." "I do not know why you left us, Mother, but the time has come to move beyond, if you are willing. Please say you will not mind my coming for the summer."

Mind? I simply did not know if I deserved her invitation to forgiveness.

"People do that," Harry said on a visiting trip to the bay when I asked him why people deprived themselves of joy at times. "Hurt themselves rather than accept that they're worthy of something greater." He coughed. "I've watched experimental rats die rather than cross a chasm to food. The hole's covered with glass, but they don't know that, and they won't even try to cross, even to find something as basic as food. They just can't believe in some new way of seeing things, and so they die for lack of risk."

"Are you suggesting I take no risks?" I said.

He laughed. "No one would be so crazy."

I walked Harry out to his carriage, shading my eyes from the sun.

"Only that some people don't pursue what they need because they're numbed by drink," he said frankly, "if you don't mind my saying so." He tossed his medical bag into the boot. "Or filled with bad memories. Fearful, angry, can't forgive an old wound. Any number of reasons. They die without ever knowing their greatness."

He coughed. Through the years, he'd become as skinny as I was stocky. He cleared his chest often, and I thought the wet cool climate too much for him.

"The wood smoke," he said when I cautioned him that perhaps he studied and worked much too hard in discovering his greatness. "Doesn't happen as much during the summer."

"When it's drier and you're not both in school and doctoring," I said. "My very point."

"I really don't think it's the climate, Cass, or how I spend my time."

"It could be."

"Cassie," he said, stepping into the buggy. "You are as contentious as you are beautiful. Someday, if you're not careful, that will be your downfall."

"A person needs to be obstinate to come out on top in the Simpson litter," I said loudly as he snapped the reins on the mare's back.

"Cream always rises," he shouted back over his shoulder, "if you stop swirling long enough to let the milk settle."

"It takes a longer day to bring out a bloom," I shouted, my mouth cupped to send my homily to his ears. I covered mine then to avoid hearing his retort.

Lottie said my life lacked *naknuwisha*.

She said it following one of my observations about BeeBee chasing her tail. We were walking to the washroom beside the house.

"How futile," I said. "You'd think he'd know by now he can't catch it. Just keeps spinning around."

"Should look familiar," Lottie said as she dipped water from the rain barrel.

"I've seen it a dozen times," I said. I followed her into the washroom where she poured the water into the tub for heating. I found her presence soothing in its way. She was predictable and reliable, always honest. And she accepted me as I was.

Her insights were refreshing if not provocative at times, bordering on insult if I'd taken them that way. She always meant well, I thought. She had nothing to gain by bringing offense, and so I came to accept the directness of her observations as just her way.

"Think about it. Looks like what you do. Chasing here and there and never staying long. You need *naknuwisha*."

"Whatever is that? *Naknuwisha*? Is that a Coos word?"

"Sahaptin word," she answered. "A Yakima woman told me of it once when we displayed our baskets together at a gathering near Portland. We don't have a word that means exactly the same."

"What does it mean?"

"Caring for something precious, caring so much it swallows you."

"You sound like Harry," I said. "Only he'd probably call it commitment to duty."

"You swallow things to disappear."

"I don't," I said. I picked at a flaw on the pearl button of my blouse.

"Think about it," she said. She pounded the clothes in the tub with already heated water. Sweat dripped from her forehead. "Those who care for you worry."

I took the paddle from her. "I swallow only what tastes good and for no other reason," I said, turning my back on her. I patted my widening stomach. "It's my misery that everything tastes delicious." Lottie didn't smile. The clothes seemed especially in need of pounding.

"It's no one's business anyway what I do to myself. Or for myself."

"Some see it differently," she said. "That we are here for each other and for a reason. You are not honest with yourself. You do things to hide."

"Aren't you the Dr. Freud."

She took the paddle back and bent over to add bluing to the white laundry.

"It is our work to care for something precious," she said, "for each other. We won't feel the aches of age or disappointment then. Giving always gets. Won't spend time mixing up the past with the future, either." The smells of steam and body heat filled the little shed beside the kitchen. My skin began to crawl with the wet. "Like looking after little plants to make sure they grow, and being pleased to be a part of it when they bloom. Because it was what you were supposed to do."

"Are you suggesting I work more in the garden?" I said.

Her eyes lifted from the steaming water. Beads of sweat dotted her high forehead. She looked at me as though I were a slug she'd just stepped over.

"No, I don't suppose you speak of gardening."

Her words stayed with me when I walked outside, helped her hang the sheets and clothes on the line. The bay had a chop to it. Wind snapped the wet sheets into our faces. The scent of sawdust from the mill drifted over us, sent tiny fragments onto the sheets. I felt chilled when we finished and came into the living room. I curled beneath a quilt and closed my eyes.

I wondered if I should write to Belle and tell her yes, to come, that it was time I made the effort for her if not myself. But what had changed from when I'd left her behind before? Still so much uncertainty in our lives. Still no way for me to face it.

I wondered if the Scientists' studies could be consuming, could swallow me as Lottie proposed if I just committed to them. Maybe suffrage efforts, though I'd let those slip by without much effort. Not hobbies or passing interests such as decorating, they hadn't yet consumed me. Racing horses through the wind invigorated, but it didn't last. Consuming our French wine relieved, but only for a time. Even passionate moments with my husband I found wanting in the morning. Nothing consumed me. Not the lavish parties I planned nor even the rousing conversations with Kate and Charlie, the Bylers and the Loggies and others that lasted well into the night. Nothing consumed me except to think of Louie and what occupied his time.

When Louie invited me to take a ride with him, to show me something he'd been keeping secret, I thought at last I'd found my *naknuwisha*.

CHAPTER 18

ENCOUNTER

❁

He had purchased acreage in 1905 and made trips there as part of his work. It was a timber investment; I didn't expect it was more.

Then in April 1908, in the middle of the day, we rode our horses side by side to view the 900 acres on a site south of the lighthouse. He'd paid four thousand dollars for the original 320 acre land that had once been part of Jake Evans's Coos wife's allotment. He'd found it on a lumber cruising. Following a twisty trail, he and an employee of the mill came to Jake's tightly chinked log cabin hoping for a cup of coffee, which Jake gave them. And as they sat gazing out toward the ocean, Louie said the sunlight struck the water in such a way it formed a beacon for him that sparkled like a diamond. It lured him to the cliff's edge.

The vines were so dense and the timber so old and thick that he and his friend crawled on hands and knees, wet earth clinging to their knees, to the site where the sun hit the waves and spray of foam. Standing, they witnessed an incredible display of ocean surf pounding against rocks that jutted like buttresses from the ocean floor to slice the sky a hundred feet above the surface.

"It's a fabulous place, Cassie," he said as we rode toward the property that day, all excitement at having found both the promise of sunrises of new beginnings washed beside vibrant sunsets on the sea.

Finches flitted and chirped at us. The breeze lifted my hatless hair. We left our horses hobbled near the clearing above Sunset Beach and let the surviving poodles follow us, licking our faces as we crawled. Only Rhodie and BeeBee remained. The previous summer Beatrice, the victim of a delivery wagon's wheels, had been buried beside the Lady Margaret.

It turned into a glorious morning, and the ride alone would have buoyed my spirits. We neared the place where I'd once lost Louie's trail, which brought profound relief realizing this *place* rather than some other woman accounted for his absences. The road was muddy and showed signs of wagon use.

"Reminds me of the tropics," Louie said over his shoulder as we bent to enter a thickness of shrubs and ferns and vines that sucked the light from the sun. "There's a better trail now," he said. "On the other side. And we've put in thousands of feet of clay tile to drain the springs so it's not so wet. Get more water from a concrete reservoir in that east canyon." He pointed. "But I wanted you to see this as I did, the first time."

Wetness seeped beneath the trees, cooled my feet. "It'll be a challenge all right," I said, holding my arms to block a tendril of blackberry ready to snap as Louie eased through. He reached back to hold the branch so I could scoot beneath. Rhodie whined, following BeeBee, who lifted and shook each foot before stepping back into the mud.

"Told you I didn't think we should bring the dogs," Louie said.

"They'll get along," I assured him. "Poodles are bright."

Dark-trunked myrtle trees twisted themselves and branched out over the vines. The crawl through portions of the tangle took vigor and all my concentration. Eventually, the vines and trees opened, and we stood and walked the same path Lottie told me later had been used by her people as part of a main village that once thrived near there.

"The Collvers had a claim out here too," Louie said. "I remember Dad telling about Clara exchanging books at the lighthouse and coming somewhere through this way."

As we approached through the tall timbers, I saw milled lumber in a stack. Then beyond, through giant fir trees, I saw something more and gasped. A home rose there. No, a manor three stories tall with bay windows and shingles so new they lacked moss.

"How did you...when...?" I turned to see my husband beaming.

"It's not finished. Still lots to do. Need your help now, more than ever." He took my hand, then on impulse, I thought, he lifted me and swung me over the threshold, through the open door, the foyer, living room, and onto the massive porch that overlooked the ocean.

I heard the sea lions of Simpson Reef barking out their calls to each other. Now their sable-colored flesh became a part of a sight of rock and ocean and vastness of sky. Gulls dipped into their brown masses dotting the gray rock. Little birds hopped and flitted against the angular peak seeking treasures in the crevices and tidepools. Waves crashed and shot foam over stone, the white froth clinging like a vanishing hope only seconds before wind and water washed it away. The air smelled of driftwood and sea on the onshore breeze and dried the sweat on my face.

Louie set me down but kept his arm around my shoulder. He pulled little twigs from the hair knot that topped my head and brushed dirt and some wet leaves from my split skirt.

"Listen," Louie said. He raised his finger to the air.

A kind of stillness found itself inside me there, despite the bark of the lions and the crash of the surf, a stillness that comes with peace of rightness settled on its back, of knowing when you've found a place to be.

"However did you get Jake to sell?" I said.

"Told him it was too lonely in that cabin of his without Caroline. It's over that way. They separated some years back. He always looks forlorn." He pointed into a thickness of timber and vines. "Came to him on a hard day, I think. Said he never missed her more than in the fall when they used to hunt together, dry up venison and birds and gather up sea stuff, putting up stores for the winter. Showed me his little garden, what was left of it. Told me every man should put up larder with a woman he loves, in a place they live in, together.

"Told him I'd do just that with you if he'd sell the place to me. Think it was the thought of the two of us that made him do it, though suppose his pocket welcomed the visit of cash."

"It wouldn't be the money," I said. "Not with a place like this."

I'd never set my eyes on such a sight, not in all the tours of Europe nor on the trips from East to West. The vista, the rocks and sea lions (seals too), the ocean breakers, and the roar and the light blue of sea arriving unexpected through the tangled denseness. And now this home. No, estate really, almost finished.

"So will you put up larder with me, woman?" Louie said, pulling me in front of him and wrapping his arms about me like a wool sweater. "Pioneer with me just like they did of old, let me give you the gift of an ocean sunset every day of your life?"

"The question," I said, "will be if you're in this latest project for the long haul, not just the short ride over the bar."

"Surprised even you," he said.

"Any woman who loves you needs to keep that as a warning when you get some new idea." I laughed. "It's a sign her future is about to change."

I felt his arms tighten around me.

"There is only one woman now whose love matters," he said.

"And what does the *now* mean?"

A season could have filled the pause between my question and his answer, and when he gave it, sweetness held itself at bay.

"There was another," he said and squeezed me tighter. "One or two."

I felt my heart pound in my head.

"Before your first wife?" I asked.

He didn't answer.

Sound roared in my head, not the surf, not the gulls, but blood rushing, pumping against my temples. My chest felt tight. I struggled against him then, wanted to start circling, moving about, picking up dead leaves and sorting pebbles with my feet before picking up my skirts to run. He would not release me from his hold, though I pushed at his arms, fearful he might let me. I danced around words while feelings and their meanings thumped a rhythm in my head.

"I have always loved you. Always," he said. "But—"

"I can't hear this! I don't want to know this!" I tried to cover my ears but my arms were pinned.

"I've got to, Cass. Tell you once. Ask forgiveness. Hope you grant it. I hope you can. Just let me tell it!"

His arms crossed over my chest, and I could hear his heart beating though no louder than my own. My eyes stung, my breath came short. Waves sent spray up over us. I swallowed back nausea. I wanted to turn, to see his face in the telling, but I lacked the courage, not sure if I could hear it if I had to look into his eyes or watch his lips move, lips that touched others, lips that touched mine.

"Never a replacement for you, Cassie. You have to believe that. You were never out of my life." He held me against my struggle. "Please, Cass. Let me keep holding you while I tell this. Otherwise, I don't think I can."

I took deep breaths and stared out at the ocean, kept my eyes glued to the solid rock being hammered by the sea. Repeated beneath my breath, *you'll live, you'll live, you'll live.*

"Happened quickly, like it did with us, a fast-moving squall over the ocean. Don't know why exactly. Didn't even feel refreshed by it, like a storm does. Felt heavy knowing when I needed you most I couldn't come to you without bringing a shipload of grief."

"So why tell me?"

"Because it's over. And I want us to start again here, at Shore Acres."

"What's her name? Or names. What do they look like?"

"Cass, please."

"Just tell me!" His words seared like a branding iron against my skin. "Tell me the name of the latest woman who's replaced the wife you said you'd love forever."

A sharp intake of breath pushed his chest into my back and with it burst the odd sensation of being outside myself. Though he stood behind me, I saw the tight line of his jaw, the twitching of his skin near his ear, his hands flexed with tension. He held a woman I watched and judged. The knowledge of his infidelity burned against her, yet brought not just pain but an extraordinary intensity, a frenzy of indignation that shared a memory, deep and distant, of when I'd ached for immersion, longed to be consumed by something, someone, and had reached for risk and swirling, just to feel alive.

Had I driven him away, refused the things I knew would fill his life and even mine, just to experience this preoccupation, the consuming of betrayal? Had I wanted to feel that depth of rage, to punish both of us for what we'd done? Yet I'd denied it, stayed when I could have gone, never confronted, even lured him back, carrying the righteous knowledge with me that I had not sunk so deep as he. I had power and control, almost superiority, felt it throb through my veins like blood that kept me living, however vile the force.

I struggled against him. He held me firm, and I returned inside myself to feel the pain and know.

"Do they live here? Do I have to wonder about my friends and acquaintances? Keep my eyes peeled to the back of my head every time I see a woman smile at you, every time I see you bend your head to hear what a woman has to say?"

I felt him shake his head. "No. Far away. No excuse for it."

"Am I so wretched, so undesirable? What did they have?" I said wishing my voice hadn't broken.

"Failed you pure and simple, the one person I care about above all others."

He turned me toward him then, as though what he would say next must be spoken soul to soul to be accepted.

"That's why I stopped it," he said. "That, and suddenly realizing what I risked. Decided to start growing up instead of blaming you."

"Blaming me?" I leaned away from him.

"I don't, Cassie. But I did. For keeping from me the one thing I thought I couldn't live without. Until I realized that one thing was you. Not a child, not something I wanted to leave my future to. But you. I'm sorry. Not easy for a Simpson to say they're sorry and mean it. But I'll make the best of the next years of our marriage if you'll forgive me. Stay with me. I promise you that. With God as my witness, I promise you that."

Sharp words caught in my throat, things I wanted to say to make him burn.

"Where do we go from here?" I said, pushing myself against him and speaking my words to the wind more than him.

"Don't know, Cass. I don't know. I want to start over. With you."

I didn't know if I could set aside the image of the women he had turned to. I wasn't sure he could forgive me for the children I'd kept from him, for the irrevocable decisions we'd made that had hurt others, two people seeking selfish satisfaction.

"Start with forgiveness, I'd guess," he said. "Each other. Ourselves. Hope to cross over to something better after that. Build something we care about together."

I'd stopped struggling and let him contain me inside the circle of his arms.

"There's something more I want to share with you," he said.

"No, Louie," I said, starting to pull away. "I don't think I can." Tears burned behind my eyes.

"Trust me," he said, pulling me to him. "Please." I couldn't hold back the tears. "Just trust me." His hands, wide and firm, held my head while I cried into his chest.

I heard finches singing in the distance.

INTERLUDE

LOUIS

Nothing makes a man feel as helpless as holding a crying woman in his arms. Made the worse if he's done something to cause it, which I had. Still, no way to reclaim the past, even apologies and "I'm sorrys" don't. Just stood holding her, feeling as small as a slug. Something in the moment had made me want to confess, to get forgiveness, wash the beach clean even though I hadn't really planned to. Just took her to show her what I'd been doing these past months with the land, all the building, the making of my vision. But she could do that to me, make me forget what I'd planned and charge ahead, tell everything.

Words cracked between us and then she cried. Afterward, I didn't know if she'd stay. Finally, she let me take her hand and lead her away from the house through the timber. Grateful she came with me, didn't pull back or resist.

Pointed out the newly planted cypress trees nestled between cedar and fir. Pushed open a gate to a redwood fence and let her see how I'd worked on forgiveness turning the soil.

"Supposed to be a Christmas present," I said. Daffodils bobbed in the breeze. "Last year. Taking longer than I thought."

She gasped then, let go of my hand and walked past me. I started talking, pointing out plots we had put annuals in, for show, 'cause I knew she'd be seeing them. Had Lottie's boy start carnations, foxgloves, and delphiniums from seed hoping they'd mature and bloom. Talked 'cause I was afraid of her silence.

She walked like a wanderer in a dream, turning and looking at everything, not really spinning, fully engaged. Overhead, a canopy of wisteria vined over a white-pillared pergola not quite finished. Nothing was. Not the trellis, not the plotting, not the garden house though workmen hammered even as we walked beneath the wisteria, fluttered shadows washing our feet and the sandy path below.

I moved behind her and wondered if she felt my uncertainty. I wanted her to love this garden, to accept it as a confirmation that she could remain inside its future, but I had no way of making it happen.

"It's an Eden," she said, then. Her eyes caught the squares of roses and petunias and pansies. A dozen squares, lined with boxwood hedges marched around new seedlings, hydrangeas and azaleas. Beyond us, a variety of plantings formed individual gardens within the one. Had beach sand and pea gravel between each plot. Felt rock hard against my leather soles. I'd burned stumps and piles of slash along the perimeter of the several acres that had once been trees and brush. Months of work clearing a road, hauling material, building the main home before we even began to plant—months and an enormous commitment of resources, labor, and love. A commitment to a future, if she'd take it.

She reached back to take my hand.

Would've loved to've had an orchestra playing, Stravinsky's *Scherzo Fantastique* to immortalize the moment. We'd heard it in concert earlier that year, 1908.

She moved out from the end of the pergola, her rose-colored suit vibrant against green. Saw men bent over sawhorses. Still more hammered shingles on a small house. "Guesthouse," I said, "or the gardener's."

In the southern corner, men with teams of horses dug inside the half-acre crater that would become the oriental pond. "Kaiyu-shiki teien in Japanese," I said. "Tour garden, meant for walking. Detours and paths always unfolding. Have to walk through it to experience it fully." She nodded. "Polished agates'll go in the bottom. Have water drop from a bamboo spigot."

Beyond, separating all the flowered plots of pinks and reds and yellows, were patches of lush green not unlike the lawns at the Hotel del Monte. The poodles romped on the greens and rolled.

"The pond's not finished," I said, a catch in my voice. "Want to bring rocks from the bay." Rubbed my nose with the back of my palm. "Four acres takes a long time to turn into paradise. Flower house off there to the side." I pointed and gained control by talking of details and facts.

"Captains have a fit finding what I want. Keep cuttings alive on their ships. All of us keeping it to ourselves has been no easy task either. But it'll be worth it," I said staring at her, "if you like it."

Her silence cut me deeper than any words could've.

"I've got a dozen plans, Cass. Help me with them. Make this place worthy of starting over. Don't know if you can find it in your heart to put it aside, Cassie. Wouldn't blame you. But my life will end, all the joy gone from it, if you don't."

She looked at me then, her fingers brushed away the wetness on my face. She never said she forgave me, but I took her touch as answer.

Her liking the garden as I hoped gave me new drive to get it finished. House too. Meant scads of work and money. But what a showplace. We called it Shore Acres.

Logistics were a nightmare though Cassie's knowing of it made it easier. Talked about how to finish the myrtlewood for the front foyer interior or how we'd ship in the fireplace I wanted of European rock. With her, I could talk over ways to bring the ocean-smoothed boulders up over the cliff to surround the pond. Cassie analyzed things out and she had an eye for design. We made a good team. Wished I'd involved her sooner. Great adventures often die at sea for want of the right person to share them with. With Cassie by me, I knew this expedition would reach safe harbor.

The crew I hired included Benjamin, Lottie's boy. Good kid. Strong arms and back, good mind. He had a natural gift for earthy things and a way of going quiet when I suggested something he didn't think would work. Gave me a chance to reconsider without feeling challenged. Had enough challenges. Managing the Lillian Mine, helping with the Sash and Door

Company, and the hotel being planned at Ten Mile Lake. Had fires to put out too what with logging and shipbuilding and all. Real fires in Washington. Had to get the mill that burned there back up and running.

At Shore Acres, I felt a peace, but I could still throw myself into everything to experience it all, life being so short and full of twisty turns like a Seven Devils trail.

Giving Shore Acres to Cassie made it easier for me to devote my time to it. Didn't feel so selfish then, just doing something I enjoyed. Course, an act of contrition was needed for what I'd done to her, something large and equal to the crime. Foolish, maybe, young, "impulsive" my mother would have called it; "harebrained," Dad's word. But who hasn't at some point in their lives done things attached to those labels? Sinful is what it was, what we'd built our life on, and I wanted to start over, make Cass happy. Hoped she might even consent to giving me a child. Wanted that more than words could say.

How they treated their wives wasn't the sort of thing men spoke of to each other much. Ol' Harry knew our struggles, though he kept his observations about it to himself. Charlie Winsor said little either, but his looks told me I played with fire and risked being burnt before I ended my affairs. Felt my ears turn red with guilt. Mattered what Charlie thought of me a little more than others.

Chauncey, a worldly man, even he had made some comment. Cass and Laura had driven two fine black horses off to pick up a seasick Kate returning from the City, and Chauncey'd said as Cass slapped the reins, so tiny behind that team: "She's a fiery one, L. J. Don't do anything to break her spirit."

But none of them saw me sinking or if they did, didn't know how to send a lifeboat for my rescue. I didn't know how to ask.

Thought maybe Cass would come to know without my telling. Heart pounded at the possibility, but I did some things, got careless.

But Cassie didn't notice. Or if she did, I told myself she didn't care. If she had, she'd have spoken, and then I could have stopped it sooner. Know I could have. She was always stronger than me. Suppose I thought she'd pull me in before the tide went out. Not fair to make her do that, but I knew she could. Seen her make decisions and live through them that made my stomach ache. Like leaving Belle. Like sending her away to school.

Seeing Gus in San Francisco startled me. Brought my Coos Bay world and that one in San Francisco into the same picture. Didn't like them exposed there, together. Didn't like who I'd become in that pale image.

Gus still offered me advice on farming. Told me what he thought about Rhode Island Reds, the breed he thought'd be best for laying and for meat; plans for drying milk. We argued over Kierkegaard, his countryman, who said man needed to submit to the will of God to find authentic freedom. Said to avoid despair we had to take a leap of faith into religious life which was always wrought with mystery, incongruity, and risks. I countered with my views of Tolstoy, Turgenev, and the Russian poets, but our talks lacked enthusiasm after San Francisco. 'Bout the same time Cassie and Annie drifted apart.

So devoting myself to Cassie and Shore Acres proved a matched team. Engaged me. Kept me on course. Assured her and gave us something together.

It was always more mine, though. Cass developed other interests after that day in the garden. She read more, wrote more letters. Worked with Kate on raising funds not for suffrage things but for the work of Woodcraft women and families left fatherless by falling trees or wayward logs. Found out which kids had trouble seeing in their school and brought in an ophthalmologist. Paid for it herself, off the interest of her shares.

She still liked hearing of the garden's logistics, the work it took to bring the lumber. Had plenty of fir and western hemlock, some Sitka spruce all straight from the mill. Cedar for finish in the closets. But everything had to be brought by wagon till I sent the tug *Katy Cook* from North Bend with two scows over the bar onto Sunset Beach. Timing always mattered crossing the bar. Could lose whole loads of lumber sucked into surf. Had to have wagons and men to unload it and drive it up the ridge to the top of the cliff.

More than once the workmen brought their families, and after a hard day we'd picnic there at Sunset Beach amidst the strong smell of salt and seaweed, watch little kids hike their skirts and pant legs to tease the ocean with their toes. Cassie'd plunge in first, the bottom of her dress darkened with the wet. Best time of the day for me, watching Cassie and standing beside a child testing their courage at the breakers' edge.

Cass must have written to Joe, Belle too, because her daughter came to visit. Sixteen she was and as beautiful as her mother. The day Belle arrived I thought Cass would leave her skin, she was so jittery. The girl hesitated, then opened her arms, and I thought Cass would faint from the invitation. Think that's when her living really began.

Bought a thoroughbred for Belle and kept it at Old Town until we built the stable. Then she and her mother rode together, finding some settled comfort, maybe forgiveness, atop a leggy thoroughbred named King, stepping out in the early morning.

I could see right away that 320 acres along the Pacific would never be enough for all I wanted to do there, but it was a start. Added another 600 before I started to build. Wanted a circular drive, one with ample trees left standing so when people arrived, they'd come through a corridor of coastal denseness that would suddenly open up, like the curtains pulled back at the Metropolitan. Surprise them. Make them gasp with the grandeur. Loved the looks of admiration and surprise I could make happen.

Shore Acres gave me my best time with Dad that way too. Had made the ship captains keep quiet about the building going on, not tell him. When we had the mill fire, Dad came up, and as they sailed by Shore Acres, I guess he demanded to know what "imbecile" or "idiot" would build in a place where only an aeroplane could access. Captain just rolled his eyes. But when Dad arrived, he asked if I knew about that place, and I said I surely did. "You should see it, Dad," I said. "Let's go."

A little grin formed on his face.

Made the three-hour trip from Old Town to Shore Acres in a spring wagon, and when we came around the muddy drive and the estate appeared out of the trees and the mist, Dad said, "This is the finest place I ever saw and I congratulate you, Jerry." Was the finest moment between us.

Dad made arrangements to stay for almost ten days, and I can still see him throwing breadcrumbs to the gulls from the veranda and chopping wood for the fireplace. Only time I saw him really rested by something I had done.

Dad liked the garden too. Told me it would never be finished, that I'd always be out checking to see what came up, what needed to be torn out or reset. Always something more to do each year in that rich peat. Keep five, seven gardeners busy I imagined. Hard not to pull David Masterton and his help onto the house building crew though. I wanted it all done at once.

Mayoring took its toll too. Mrs. Larsen, a spindly woman so old she could remember the first Sengstackens, came weekly with her little canvas bag to complain about North Benders. Told me boys were shooting birds on their way to school and hiding the carcasses. That they cleaned them on their way home, stuck them in tubs of water to fluff them up, then sold them to shopkeepers as fresh.

"They'll be getting folks sick. You mark my words, less you do somethin' about it."

Lectured me about government doing little to serve the people. Only changed the subject once—that was after a special Commercial Club event. Lottie and Cass had dressed me like a German frau and named me "Gretchen." I had long yellow curls that hung down my ruffled chest. My waist was cinched in velvet making me all buxom on the top. Those girls giggled till their sides hurt, finding red stockings for my Dutch shoes, and skirts to show red pantalets. Cassie came as a senorita, flashed dark eyes behind a veil. Mrs. Larsen was speechless when she heard of that.

Cassie did a little civic fighting. Wrote a letter to the *Coos Bay Harbor* urging folks to be responsible for the condition of their community. Said any town that could have a grand saloon with water running in a terracotta channel beneath the foot rail of the bar could surely have dignity enough to put their garbage in one of the two city dumps. Or bury it themselves. Benders didn't need to let the dogs do it for them.

For two whole weeks after the letter appeared, Cassie smiled a lot. Went for walks with me in the morning, and the puffiness in her face and wrists went down. Shopkeepers nodded. She seemed pleased with her influence.

Those times made me forget when I'd seen the strained look on her face or when she gained attention by riding the Harley through town, maybe taking one of her thoroughbreds out at a fast pace. Color it brought to her face looked refreshing. But later, she needed to put her feet up while Lottie wrapped her in quilts and brought her hot wassail and wine. She'd be too tired to even smile, then. Can't tell how many photographs I have of her where she isn't smiling, something I noticed later, after she was gone. Worried me too her meetings with the Scientists. Not because I had a problem with her interest in faith questions. I didn't, like to argue them myself. But seemed she tried too hard to heal herself of what her sister'd told me years before was a condition known to flood the heart.

Kind of envied Charlie and Kate's lives some days. Didn't shout it at me or point their fingers at my guilt. Just lived their lives and mentioned once or twice they made it through by faith. Built a solid life together. Had one boy. Charlie said they still hoped for another but trusted God for whatever He provided. Admired that. I'd done my share of sinning, and if there was a God, He'd answered me by withholding the one thing in my life I really wanted. Watching Kate and Charlie made me pay more attention to what mattered, which in my mind was Cassie and finding refuge in Shore Acres.

Our three-story home at Shore Acres became real that Christmas of 1908. Brought a light plant in so we had all modern conveniences even though we never planned to live there permanent. Would be just a summer leisure palace. Had three dozen poinsettias pushed to bloom in the greenhouse. Set them in the foyer. Couldn't outshine the glow of myrtlewood that lined the entrance beneath the Tiffany chandelier. Two huge orchid plants graced the myrtlewood table. Brought the smell of wet freshness with them. Palm I'd ordered showed a little brown from the trip out through the cold in the exposed Victoria. Cassie strung holly and vines and tiny white lights run off the generator all the way down the winding staircase of the living room. Eighteen guests came to dinner. Each had a memory to write down in their journals. Men too. Know I did.

Cass furnished every room to stand alone. Be an event in itself as well as part of something more. Not unlike the garden.

"You're amazing, L. J.," Charlie said. He ran his hand over his thinning hair and shook his head as he gazed around the room. "It's a fine job you've done to make this grandeur appear out of the wilds."

Charlie and Kate had come early and walked through the decorated house. Cassie showed them the music room paneled with Circassian walnut, my office opposite with its bank of books. The kitchen at the north end, living room facing west. Bedrooms with private baths lined the second-floor hall.

"Louie'll be building plank roads by spring so everyone can make it here, even in the worst of weather. You didn't have any trouble coming out this afternoon, did you?"

"Sure didn't. Brings no small amount of class to South Slough," Charlie said.

"Didn't think they needed it," I said.

"They need a step above the floathouses," Kate said. She peered over her eyeglasses with an arched eyebrow.

"Still on that issue, are you?" I said.

"Maybe when women get the vote we'll take care of such things," Kate said.

"More likely when liquor's outlawed," Charlie said.

"Perish the thought!" I said.

That Christmas, as guests arrived, we took them into the finished fifty-six foot long living room lined with a bank of windows overlooking the Pacific, sharing our "view to the world." Like a tour guide, Cass commented about the house fashioned after one in Massachusetts, as guests twined their way across the Navajo rugs holding furniture of brand new rattan. That parrot came, too, older than Saint Seraphim and, fortunately, silent.

"Louie carved this home from a wilderness," Cass said, "and built it with love." Her smile lifted me.

She wore her hair brushed up high on her head. Ivy and white rosebuds woven into it. Dress as white as a lily kissed the floor. Her shoulders and neck were bare save the diamond necklace she wore. She swung open the doors and let a blast of cold air breeze in. People "oohed" with the chill and huddled a little closer.

"Come on now, don't be puny," she chided, cheeks flushed. "This is an experience of a lifetime, standing here overlooking a sea so black it might not exist except for the white foam edges and the sounds of it throwing itself against the rocks. Listen."

She talked flowery that way, as though she stood on stage. I sometimes wrote that vein of English, but I didn't speak it.

Dogs scampered out through the legs of guests spreading out along the veranda. Two wooden swings and two more rattan chairs hung from the rafters. Wind chimes clinked. Dr. Toye moved his ample bulk to sit, and I was glad we'd double-bolted the chairs. Most guests stood silently, some sipping on coffee and herb tea that Lung Lem and one of the newest cousins, Lee Ling, served on silver trays, moving like soft memories among the guests.

Electric lights glittered against sea mist looking like snow. Only the ocean's pounding against the reef broke the quiet. Stars twinkled in the sky.

Pleased me that even with the grandeur of this place, it was the ocean and the night and the heavens that held us spellbound.

Cassie's rich contralto voice broke into "Silent Night, Holy Night." Never heard Cass sing those words before. Stepped beside her, held her with one arm. Bare shoulders felt cool and she shivered. Before any other songs began, I urged us all back in.

Everyone spent the night, departing to bedrooms on the second floor furnished in fine oaks and bird's-eye maple from back East. Cass and I designed our own bedrooms. Places to be private and write. That night, following our first gathering and sharing of this place with others, she invited me to hers.

Russ Tower and his brother Jay opened "The Gunnery," an automotive supply and sporting goods store in '09. Cassie said getting a Harley-Davidson would be easier now that The Gunnery planned to carry them, though why we'd need more than the two we had was beyond me. Towers carried Buicks and some marine engines, too, and ammunition and hunting supplies. Spent a fair amount of time in The Gunnery. Issac, or Russ as his friends called him, was both sociable and honest. Invited him out to Shore Acres to hunt ducks. Said he'd like that. Imagine he knew how, having lived in the area his whole life.

Russ started coming even when hunting season wasn't in. Began that summer we were graced by Belle's presence. She came the next year, too, stepping across a space of wounded time to touch her mother.

Imagined her mother might have resembled Belle at seventeen, a striking beauty but without the sadness framed permanently on her face. Belle's shoulders drooped when she walked, as though she carried the weight of her world there. Maybe she did. She rivaled her mother for beauty and grace but not for presence. Cassie always had that over any woman, any setting, both sultry and forthright. She'd take Russ's or any man's attention from anything else he thought he fancied, and she often did. Not sure Cass knew she had that power or that Belle faded like a pale shadow when Cassie used it.

Belle had courage, though, to say with her presence that she wished to be there with us. Came to work something out about who she was that a mother could have left her behind. All Belle was yet, just a child wanting what we all want, to know we're loved and special in someone's eyes, to learn that being left says more about the one leaving than the one staying behind. Pretty sure she had some thoughts about my place in what had happened those years before. She never shared them with me. I couldn't find a way to talk of it with her.

Despite what happened between Belle and her mother, I envied my wife the rare connection she had with her child. Something I didn't have and knew I never would.

Charlie handed out cigars. After years of waiting, Kate delivered a little girl. Charlie Jr.—his dad called him Joe—was fifteen in 1910. Doted on his little sister as though she were his own. Couldn't have been happier for them. Asked us to be the sponsors when they baptized Helen.

"I'm not sure why they want us to do this," Cassie said.

We were dressing at the Old Town house where we still lived most of the year. She had changed her skirt three times, so I knew she didn't want to go. Helped slip a white linen jacket over her shoulders. Matched her skirt. I buttoned it at her waist as she held her arms out in surrender.

"Look at me. I'm ballooned up like a toad. I've had to get another new form brought in from Portland. Nothing fits."

"Look fine," I said. "Even have room at this button." I tugged at the center abalone one.

"Don't patronize me," she snapped.

Knew nothing I would say then would be heard for what I meant. Just kept quiet.

"Kate knows I don't see things the way she does. I'm happy for them, yes. Delighted." She smoothed the jacket out over her hips, circled before the mirror. "But promising to raise a child up the way they want if something should go wrong? I'm not sure I'm being honest."

She lifted a wide-brimmed hat from its box and pulled it over the thickness of chestnut hair on her head. A few white strands like cobwebs wisped at her temples. I handed her a silver hatpin.

"Not that one," she said. "The one with the heart shape at the end."

"Think of her as asking because of our civic status," I said.

The thought caused her to pause. I had been reelected in 1909 and for the first time, there'd actually been a challenge. Invigorated me. Major Kinney, who had donated land to build a new school, had led the charge for the opposition hoping his friend A. W. Meyers would unseat me. But Meyers used his religion as a club. Not that good morals aren't needed for public office. Not that folks didn't want the high road for their North Bend. But folks knew that any dry town would soon discourage investments in hotels and manufacturing, maybe even keep the railroad out. So I'd been re-elected.

"Don't be ridiculous," Cassie said.

I'd almost forgotten what I'd said to her.

"No, she wants us there because we're friends. I know that. It just makes me nervous. Maybe I won't be up to what she wants. She's such a good person and I'm, well…"

"Kate's got good judgment."

Cass didn't see herself the way I did. I saw her warmth and ways of embracing all the world, saw through her sharp edges that kept some at a distance. Couldn't penetrate what kept her thinking she was dirt and not the flower.

"You think so?" she asked. She turned her head sideways to get her profile in the mirror. "Oh, misery!" Sucked her stomach in and patted at it. Knew she didn't want an answer.

Well-wishers packed the church. The usual orchestra planned to play. Cass leaned over to me and said, "Hope Kate remembers to put her shoes back on when she finishes playing."

We held baby Helen. At least Cassie did. Long white embroidered gown flowed over my knees while we sat. Baby slept through Herb Sumner's cello solo. But when Will Simpson—no relation—lifted a cornet to his lips and Charles Worrel slipped his fingers on a smooth slide of his trombone and Kate and Charlie Jr. on drums chimed in, the baby woke. Wake the dead, the music they played. Celebration music, that's what it was.

She held my finger, Helen did. Her hand on mine felt light, almost not there until I tried to pull away. Thought then that some attachments are just like that, never know they're strong until you try to pull away.

Minister spoke, and we joined Charlie and Kate. Charlie Jr. stood there with us, too, circled around the silver baptismal font I'd given some years before.

"In baptism," the pastor began, "we die to what separates us from God and are raised to newness of life in Christ." The pastor emphasized each word with an s so that those words dragged out longer. Helen had fallen back asleep, her smooth face turned toward the lacy cap. Her pink mouth formed an O. Watched her in perfect peace, not a worry in her world.

"Baptism signifies the faithfulness of God, the washing away of sin and rebirth."

The minister said the words to the whole congregation, but he kept looking at me. Looked at Cassie, too, though she kept her eyes on Helen whom she still held in her arms.

"God's faithfulness signified in baptism is constant and sure," he said. "Even when human faithfulness to God is not. Baptism signifies the beginning of life in Christ, not its completion. Human faithfulness to God needs repeated renewal. Baptism calls for decision at every subsequent stage of life's way. The baptism of children," he said with emphasis, "witnesses to the truth that God's love claims people before they are able to respond in faith."

He asked people in the congregation to stand then. We all repeated some words together and made commitments on behalf of Helen. Then he lifted the baby from Cassie's arms. Saw a frantic look on my wife's face, as though she didn't want to give her up or something confused her for the moment. Wondered then if she had done this all with Belle. Must have. Belle's father would have insisted. Might have remembered a promise she didn't keep.

Just a moment in passing, a distraught look on her face, fleeting, then gone. Sunlight flashed against the silver font.

Kate leaned over to untie the satin bow beneath her daughter's double chin. Charlie slid the cap back to expose Helen's pale fuzz of hair. Pastor dipped his fingers in the font. Dribbled water onto her little head. Said words over her as he did it one, two, three times. Helen cried, her eyes and mouth open with the first feel of wetness. Felt my nose tickle and my eyes itch.

Pastor asked us, Helen's parents and Cass and me, Charlie Jr., too, if we were prepared to keep a promise. Put my arm around Charlie Jr.'s shoulder, Cass's too. Pulled them closer to the circle. To nurture and guide Helen until she made her own confession. Felt myself swallow and reached for Cass's hand. Cold. Held mine tight.

Helen's parents answered without hesitation. Took a minute then for me to say I would, wanting to be sure I could, promises being something I tend to take to heart, previous behaviors notwithstanding. I promised.

Wasn't sure if I heard Cass say anything. Thought her lips mouthed *yes*, thought I saw her head nod *yes*. Saw Kate and Charlie smile at her. Me too. Squeezed my wife's small hand and held her tight.

ANNIE

❁

I hadn't *intended* for my words to drive a wedge between us. It's just so difficult to know what to do when a friend's wounded and then wanders down a wrong path and seals the pain.

Remain quiet? I could have done that. Indeed. When I was silent back in Grays Harbor, Cassie *acted*, and look what *that* led to. My silence might even have encouraged it, let her think I condoned what actually horrified me. Well, maybe intrigued me, too, which made me feel all the more guilty, because her life fascinated me. I could never be so cheeky as to do the things she did.

Then later, after they moved to the Coos Bay and I learned they weren't married, then too, I said little. I hardly mentioned it except to say they *ought* to be. My visiting may have sent a message that I *accepted* what they were doing. I could have stayed away like Margaret did, but what would that have accomplished? I asked myself that and hoped the convenience their home afforded me for falling in love with Gus didn't cloud my judgment.

After she told me they *had* married, maybe I didn't rejoice enough. That she shared a secret with me in itself said she valued my friendship. Maybe I moved too quickly to try to encourage that they have a family at last, before Cassie got much older. That wasn't wise, I suppose. She'd always been sensitive about her age. I didn't realize she was born in '71 until Margaret said.

Showed me in the family Bible. There it was, Cass nearly six years older than her husband. Maybe it wasn't her age that made her petulant but the very mention of children. Maybe that was it.

Then had come that incident with Gus and Louie in San Francisco. Marvin was just a baby. He fussed and squirmed, and I suspect he felt my nervousness. Gus was quite sure of what he saw, and he was not a man to gossip. In fact, one of his great strengths is how he sees the good in everyone. Even that day when he related the story to me, he was kind in the telling, as though he could understand a man's waywardness though never condone it. "Ve all fall short," he'd said. Indeed.

So I told her.

I wish I could wipe out the memory of the look that flashed across her face before she caught herself and hid it. It was the look of an ailing dog just before it shivers with a seizure and falls.

She denied it. She was always good at that. Once when we were children and she'd been caught red-handed looking over Emmett Scott's shoulder on a Latin test, she swore she hadn't *seen* a thing. She was so clear about it the teacher began to wonder if he'd erred in charging her, but I had seen her do it. She received no punishment, she was so convincing.

I told her what Gus saw. And then I noticed a distance formed. The space between us left an ache. Cassie was my oldest friend, and I felt as though our roots wound together in the same soil.

I thought of myself as a sweet william within her shadow, indeed I did. My blossoms, such as they are, grow close to the ground in a tight cluster not fanning out very far. She'd changed that when she came back to give birth to Belle. I shouldn't have been surprised when she insisted I come west with them. I had secretly dreamed of it, wished and prayed. She knew my need even better than I did, and she was so generous about the offer, made it sound like I'd be helping her.

She could talk Joe into anything. He didn't even flinch when she told him I'd be going back with him. He just accepted, he adored her so.

"She'll be Belle's governess," she'd said, though I doubt I earned my keep, living as I did those years under the comfortable roof of Joe Stearns. My time with Belle was as much a gift as a chore.

Once Cassie put her mind to something, though, she was root bound in her efforts, like the way she spent her wedding night. And I'd thought loyalty one of her strengths too. My pointing up Louie's lack of such that day must have been too much.

I never knew if she confronted him or changed her ways to win him back. Didn't need to.

Louie still came out to see us, usually in the fall to hunt. Cassie seldom came along, even after Louie bought the Buick Runabout from Russ Tower's agency in 1911 and could have made the trip easy and in style, not even have to cross with the ferry since we had a bridge at Charleston Beach.

Things had picked up along the slough, probably because Louie and Cassie built Shore Acres there. By 1912, a planked road ran between Marshfield and North Bend, too, and Gorst and King ran an auto service between them that rivaled O'Kelly's "Boat King" water transport. Gorst's vehicles were faster and didn't get hung up on mud flats in the fog. So we took the auto service when we came in for the big celebration with the promise—at last—of a rail line to be completed that year.

Louie broke a bottle of Coos Bay Beer from North Bend onto the tracks, though the *Harbor*, in its teetotaling ways, reported it as "Coos Bay cream" that did the christening. Construction by the Willamette Pacific was to begin the swing bridge, and city boosters buried 125-pound "knockers hammers" for all those who'd ever disbelieved the railroad would arrive. Things looked likely for the rails and the region's future that day. I saw it as a time to chat with Cass. I hadn't meant to be *her* knocker.

The visit at their Old Town home was clouded with a dozen other people, so I did not clear the distance that hung between us like the tidal fog.

I took the boat service on my own a few days later. I planned to tell her how much she meant to me. And that I missed calling her my friend. Mrs. Winsor was there that day. As it happened, she and I *prattled* on about babies, she with her Helen now two, and me with my three-year-old Maddie. Cassie had planted sweet peas around the stable, and we walked there to check the strings and pick armfuls she later organized in huge vases around the house. The fragrance was heady and rich. Never forget how they smelled.

Cassie'd seemed pleasant enough. Said I'd have to come to one of the parties at Shore Acres that "are the bee's knees," whatever that meant. Even asked if I'd heard from Belle, which I had. We corresponded quite regularly, in fact. She was taking a European tour following graduation and sent me postcards from Athens and Milan. I didn't tell Cassie that, but she knew it, at least she asked if I knew Belle was traveling.

It was hard to know what might set Cass off. Even when I tried to couch every confrontation I had with her as being in her best interest, caring, as a sister would, she could go cold as ice. Once, when she and Joe still lived in Hoquiam, I'd commented on her brandy use.

"Medicinal," she said. "You're always telling me to rely on doctors. Campbell ordered brandy for my heart."

I'd taken a deep breath and challenged her about what I saw as an *alarming* trend, using brandy for pain. She let me talk and talk. I'd gathered deep within myself to share the care I had for her. I even tried to appeal to her generous nature and told her how powerful she was, that what she did affected others, that we worried about her wasting away, heart and soul.

She'd snorted at that, said something about not wasting away with hips carrying enough fat they could feed a family of four for a week. She looked puffy to me, not fat. When it was over, when I had said all I could to touch her, she gave me no indication that she understood how much I loved her nor heard a word I'd said. She was an ivy-covered, brick-solid wall I couldn't go over or through.

Instead the conversation turned to suffrage, and I knew the moment for speaking frankly about feelings had vanished. I'd always blamed the suffrage movement for giving credence to Cassie's strange behavior, leaving Joe and her child, but that isn't fair. She'd always been what my mother called a siren, long before suffrage or Joe. "That girl better learn to live with what she attracts," my mother had said. "Good thing they're sending her to that Episcopal college."

Cassie hadn't gone, of course, to the Episcopal campus. And I figured we *all* have to learn to live with what we call down on ourselves.

Mrs. Winsor was nothing like the typical suffrage woman I imagined. She was calm and stately, and the two of us had quite a lot in common, especially in our care for Cassie, though we didn't speak of it that day. Talk turned to that unfortunate Major Kinney who'd wanted to defeat Louie's mayoral reign. But then his investments failed, he lost his shirt and mind, both literally, launching himself down Virginia Street stark naked. They had to motor him off to the asylum in Salem. Kinney was the talk of the town for weeks. Always made me remember that unfortunate woman in Louie's life who lived her days in a haze.

Mrs. Winsor and Cassie spoke of raising money then, of charity auctions they were planning. Cass invited me to help and that surprised me. I didn't know she had an interest in the millworkers' children or in spending time with the Beautiful America Club, keeping our coast clean.

I was never sure that what I'd said to Cassie about her husband's infidelity that day was really within my place to speak. I hadn't meant to hurt her, but maybe some things are better left unsaid. Maybe I had tried to push a river to water a place that wasn't meant to grow a thing.

HARRY

❀

I'll tell you what I think. Cassie Simpson is a fast-flowing stream that some-times gets off course in its rush of fullness, especially in the spring. If you ask me, it's probably what my brother saw in her at first, that saturated speed brimming with vitality and promise. I wasn't sure if he really knew what he had when she moved with us to the river. I had Dad's eye for beauty and my mother's for brains and could see that Cassie had both, though her bursting beauty often overshadowed the latter.

When she became so ill and almost died, that's when I think my brother finally realized what he'd attracted and almost lost. I was glad he came to sense it. He'd messed up often in my father's eyes. He and Mother talked about my older brother in whispers, but I heard quite well. Especially about the "unfortunate incident" which is how my mother referred to his earlier marriage.

Cassie was sort of like a mother to me, enough older to make me think of that, anyway. Much different than my own, I must say, though now I've written it, that isn't really so. They both had great taste, especially in music and the arts. They both took over a crowd with their presence. They both endured men with quirks. Perhaps they even shared with silence their hus-bands' infidelities. At least I often wondered about the close relationship between Ellen, Lottie's mother, and my father and whether Dad was responsible in some way for that Coos family having an allotment in Lottie's mother's name. Lots of shenanigans during those early years when Father came here and left Mother and us in the City. When Mother died, she took all those secrets with her.

Cassie was a little bit my sister, too, sharing Edith's high spirit. Edith is a wonderful older sister; even now, with her marriage to Roy Pike, she's still wise yet fun loving, very protective yet willing to risk. She didn't visit Oregon all that much. Because I chose to live with Louie and Cass for the larger part of each year for more than ten, I lost touch with Edith after I turned seventeen or so. Cassie became my teacher, and I suppose I fell a little bit in love with her or at least under her spell. I was in good company. Most men did. It was difficult not to, if you ask me.

Cassie irritated me some, too, trying to be a big sister and a mother all in one when what I wanted most those years was a friend. She needed one, too, but she'd deny it as she did most things that touched her psyche.

Like any young lad, I knew how to annoy her, too, especially in those early years. Just bring up the subjects of her health or her soul, that would set her spinning!

Frankly, I worried over both. She took up with the Scientists that one summer while I was gone, and when I returned it was as though my life's work in medicine was a personal affront to her, said anyone could access God's spiritual power to heal. If you ask me, she was looking for someone or something to blame for her poor choices, and she never did want to look for the reasons close to home.

Freud's *Psychopathology of Everyday Life* revealed much about Cassie. When the book came out I devoured it. I was twenty-one at the time, and I confess, Cassie became somewhat of a project for me as I tried to analyze her behavior. I thought it fascinating that the unconscious could cause a person to avoid pain by taking strong drink, for example. Or create a view of themselves that was so totally different from the way others saw them. That fit for Cassie who was very bright, gifted in the arts, had the capacity to cause every head in a room to turn. She could mesmerize people into believing things about themselves they'd never considered before such as the virtue they'd discover by giving their wealth to a worthy cause. Yet she used words to describe herself that were demeaning. *Butterball* or *addle-minded*, words like that. Once she said she was unworthy of all my brother gave her and of her fine life.

"Nonsense!" I'd said. "You inspire him. Your inferior feelings come from some unresolved childhood trauma you have buried and choose not to reveal to your conscious mind. If you did, you could resolve such inadequacies. Confession is quite a catharsis."

She looked startled that she'd even shared a feeling with me, and I actually saw her heart close up behind a solemn face. She locked me out of any further exposure of that inner state. I cursed myself for speaking instead of listening, I tell you. For plunging ahead as though I held the reins of that horse when it was she who did. She had invited me along for the ride, and I had tried to take over. A nasty Simpson trait.

She was right to accuse me of treating her like a specimen, too, no different than pinning the tern's wings to the board, except that this specimen was alive, with feelings. She quoted Voltaire once in the midst of one of our arguments and said medicine "consists of amusing the patient while nature cures the disease." Her charge humbled me. Not because I believed Voltaire's version for a minute, but because I saw the flash of pain cross her face as she said it, as quick as regret and as piercing. I vowed to see her as a person not a patient after that, quite sorry that anything I did might hurt another.

The year I began my own practice in the San Francisco area, I remembered what she'd said. I believe I was a better doctor because I saw my patients as people first, with their symptoms second. Cassie led me to that. And of course I later learned that confession without Christ is merely cathartic, lacking the healing that brings on new life.

How I wished I could have changed her mind about medicine! The year she almost died of typhoid pneumonia I was only nineteen. I was so grateful Louie listened to me when her breathing became raspy. Cassie was white and clammy and looked not unlike the finches I chloroformed just before they died. Nothing to trifle with.

She could be so adamant, so stubborn of a thing, and even when she could barely speak she told Louie not to take her to the hospital. Thank God he didn't listen! He was usually not strong enough to resist her demands. Maybe it was the thought of his first wife, whom he'd lost in another way, that made him stand firm then with Cass.

Wish he'd stood firm with her about the Scientists. Of course she claimed his Masonic Lodge and Elks were just the same. "You meet with your cronies and gather strength together, seek after God in a little different venue from ours, that's all," she told him once. She'd just gotten back from one of her meetings and pulled the hatpins with gusto as she spoke. She jabbed the silver back into the felt as if she were stabbing something else. They could really spar, those two, and I learned much about unfair fighting by watching. Never knew when a simple discussion would explode into war.

"Entirely different," my brother had said, calm that day. "Masons surely don't prevent good treatment if it's needed. Don't claim to have men replace the power of God, either."

"If it's a God-made mind, I see no problem," she'd said, and it had been my experience that there was no arguing with her when she used that tone of voice.

I wondered then if it wasn't a desire to be an "independent woman" that propelled her to those meetings, a belief that a person couldn't be strong if she latched onto medicine or faith in something larger than herself. Healing would be a sign of strength if one could claim it as her success; "doctoring" a sign of weakness.

If you ask me, faith beyond herself was the very thing she needed. I favored Kierkegaard in that kind of thinking, though I may have lost something in understanding with the Swedish translated into German. I disagreed, though, with his belief that we are called to God by dread. Love can call us, too, and that was what I wished for Cassie.

After Louie and Cass built the resort at Sunset Beach, we'd sometimes go there for a lunch and some of Pauline Wasson's seafood specials. There were always fascinating people vacationing from California, Washington, even places back East. They rented tents at fifty cents a day or a cabin by the week. The ocean is exquisite within that peaceful cove, and I watched with envy my brother and his wife walk hand in hand along the sandy beach, her narrow silk-striped skirt keeping her steps tiny and close together. She leaned into his waist, his stride shortened for her. From a distance they appeared to have everything, and maybe, with prosperity coming to North Bend with the railroad (as Louie had long ago predicted), with Cassie seeming to have found a peace in her civic work and time with young Belle, maybe at last they would have everything.

Once several of the railroad executives joined Cass and Louie at Sunset

Beach, then motored up to Shore Acres. They were celebrating the new construction of the Southern Pacific and the swing bridge to be built across the Coos Bay not far from the Old Town house. It was a loud and raucous crowd, just the way my brother liked it, and Cass was the star, as always.

But when we got to Shore Acres and the grandeur of that place, something came over Cass, and I saw her settle her guests in and then slip away. I happened by the wicker chair she'd been sitting in at the farthest edge of the veranda, though, where the view is of the slanted rocks and the sea lions most vocal. The heavy shades were drawn expecting wind. There I noticed a book. She had marked several passages in her Scientists' text she left lying on the side table. The wind riffled the pages but the markers held.

I suppose I shouldn't have peeked. But it was as though she meant for me to see it. After all, Freud says we make no mistakes, that what we label as such are really unconscious desires reaching up through the ooze of our guilt and unconscious to take us into the light of day. Anyway, all the passages spoke of overcoming the seduction of sin, of "willing" oneself free of fleshly compulsions.

After I contracted tuberculosis, I turned to the biblical texts on healing. I moved to Riverside, California, then, hoping the climate would improve my health. I wrote to Cassie of how I thought of healing, what part I believed divinity played. She wrote back to me of light things, the way the red-chested finches came to water in the garden the same time each day, the sound of the surf against rock, the heady scent of lilies in the spring. She even wrote of the farm, how Louie had expanded Shore Acres by purchasing the adjoining Collver Ranch. They'd added more staff houses and had to hire a full-time couple to handle the herd of dairy cows and make the hay. She wrote about the hum of the generator that ran the vacuum cups to expedite the milking, the fragrance of roses. She wrote of many things, but almost conspicuously absent, never of her spirit.

I knew Cass had a Bible, too, and scads of books on philosophy and religion, all to broaden her perspective. But she'd left her Bible lying on the entryway table at Shore Acres, too, sometime in 1913. It must have been fairly new because few pages were dog-eared. She'd claimed it as her own, though, and had written her name in bold script with "Shore Acres" below it, as though that place was her most prominent address. Later, I wrote to her of the passages in that text that comforted me. I suppose I found some succor from remembering the verses myself and imagined that she might have looked for them and found solace in them too.

KATE

❀

I have been constantly blessed by a good husband who was my childhood sweetheart and by two lovely children, longed for and delivered fifteen years apart. They all shared my love of music and of faith, and I couldn't imagine a richer life. And yet it had been made richer by Charlie's investments and his shrewd legal handling of other men's affairs. When the Bank of Oregon merged with First National, Charlie became the primary stockholder and vice president, and he celebrated by a contribution to the church and the purchase of a Pathfinder Self-start automobile with Gray and Davis electric lights and isinglass curtains. It was in 1914, and it was the judge's gavel and the envy of our friends and foes alike.

Except for Louie. Though he was as competitive as a champion race-horse, he had no envy. Louie was as happy for our good fortune as he could be. He saw another man's affluence as signs of progress and always cele-brated it even if it meant his own fortunes might be shadowed in the process. Several of Charlie's ventures involved Louie, including the proposed Simpson Hotel. Louie had pledged ten thousand dollars to it along with sev-eral others who wanted the county wet if they were to make good on their money. Charlie said it was part of business, and I wondered how he kept his integrity sometimes, but I believe he did.

Louie's generosity knew no limits. Cassie's either, especially in later years.

We did have the most wonderful times together, even after Helen was born. My daughter challenged Cassie, I know, brought back memories. I know Cassie didn't always understand why I'd decide against attending an event because of my child.

"Is she ill?" Cass would wonder. "Can't you leave her with Rachel?" Lottie's daughter helped out at our home and was adored by Helen, but no, I thought a mother's place was with her child when illness struck.

I'd tell her. "I can see by the way she's pulling at her ear and how fussy she is that she's not feeling well. Probably one of those ear infections starting up again. I can't bear the thought of her being in pain like that and me not here to comfort her or call the doctor."

Later on, after Louie gave her the garden and built the estate, I saw a change in her. She was softer, more giving in her own way. Her time with Belle seemed to nourish her, especially their morning rides. I thought then that Cassie behaved like a mother who had finally become her daughter's friend.

Cassie didn't think anything should really get in the way of an event she'd planned, whether it was the lot of us gathering at the Star Theater to watch eight reels of *Quo Vadis* or some celebration at the Grand Restaurant. And of course, those elaborate parties at Shore Acres that were the envy of every Bender, she believed nothing should keep the Winsors from one of those.

"At least with the Pathfinder you can come and leave early if you want," she said.

"Provided the roads aren't a river of muck," I answered.

And they were, often, though once Louie got the twelve miles planked, driving there or to the resort was a breeze. Their driveway could still be a trial, though, and more than once our departure was delayed by muck even with the back tires chained.

Of course by 1914 there were lots of vehicles motoring around North Bend. So many that Louie's younger brother, Edgar, bought a place and built a garage in our fair city. He and C. H. Burritt did, actually, calling it the Terminal Garage. I always thought that a funny name, as though it spoke of a lethal place for cars rather than a destination. Edgar imported a Simplex Roadster that year, one of only six supposedly in all the West, a real extravagance what with the war looming and no one sure when we'd be pulled in.

The Roadster weighed forty-eight hundred pounds. All the men kept repeating the weight as though it was truly something. Even when the *Harbor* covered the story of a bet between Edgar and Burritt about traversing thirty-two miles of mud to Bullard's ferry in less than six hours, the men talked about the weight. Burritt's Hupmobile had gotten stuck while Edgar's Ford made the journey in less than four hours "despite the weight." How the men raved about it, so excited about the prospects of the future these new machines would bring to the region.

They said only a little less the next week when the *Harbor* reported Edgar's accident: "Capt. Simpson Has Bad Accident with New Car: Strikes Stump Tearing Front Wheels Off His $6,500 Roadster"—that weighed forty-eight hundred pounds. Then the men talked about how money was never a problem for a Simpson.

Charlie and Louie spent a fair amount of time together planning the latest of Louie's dreams—"The Simpson," a hotel to rival any in the West. Both men still seemed to think that development would continue, with another big boom as had started it those ten, twelve years before. They were counting, of course, on the railroad being completed and on Prohibition being defeated.

There was the crux of the thing. People wouldn't pledge money toward the hotel unless the railroad came and the locals voted to keep North Bend wet with whiskey flowing. What a terrible price to pay for progress. Charlie and I had no small number of debates about the issue. The four of us as well, though I was the only holdout for Prohibition. I had no doubt that drink was the downfall of the masses and that it was eating its way into the soul of my good friends. Once we'd watched the sunset over the ocean at Shore Acres, and Cassie had announced that she no longer needed brandy or wine, was filled up with the grandeur of the sea.

"Oh?" said the parrot.

We'd laughed until our sides hurt.

Something more than drink ate into Cassie's soul. What it was she never said. I felt it when I walked the dogs at the beach with her or when we strolled with Helen beneath the wisteria surrounding the pergolas or sat with our knees to our chins overlooking the Japanese pond. Even then, when she was quiet, I sensed a yearning in her.

Once she astonished me by asking what I thought was the difference between the Christian Scientists and Dr. Freud's work and my Christian faith. We'd donned gloves and aprons and headed to our yard, which was where the question was posed.

"The Scientists, well, don't emphasize, after having studied and read about them, what I believe is so important, and that's the compassion and truth of Christianity," I said. "The understanding that none of us is perfect and can't make ourselves be without faith in Christ. I suppose I see Freud's work as fascinating and insightful of the human condition...and he is Jewish, which I think explains his emphasis on guilt and shame, on the role of the unconscious, his Superego and Id, which to me is a version of good and evil, judgment and sin."

"Christianity seems as caught up in rights and wrongs and details as any other belief system," she said.

We were kneeling together in my vegetable garden by then, thinning early plantings of onions and carrots and peas. The May morning was spectacular, as warm and inviting as a child's first kiss. Helen sat beyond us with her beach pail and shovel. Her faded bonnet hung by its bows at her neck. An egret eased its wings over the tips of the trees.

"That surely happens, that judgment part," I said. "But knowing we're so fallible, that we make so many mistakes, and yet are still loved, that's what sustains me. I was raised in the church, Cass, but I chose my Christian faith. All of us choose something, even if we think we don't."

Three Easter lilies sat waiting to be planted at the end of the row. Louie'd had them shipped in from Japan and had given to the church for Easter. The ground was moist and warm, good earth for lilies. I reached for a plant and Cassie, without words, began digging with her trowel, the scent of wet soil lifting with dignity to my nose. She pulled the soft earth back around the roots and tapped the soil around the lily. She dug and set the plant, and we moved our knees as one to dig the final hole.

"Think these'll bloom again this season?" Cassie asked.

"Uh-huh," I said. "And many more years after. All those over there were set out after each Easter sunrise service. My favorite time of year. Promises renewal and the hope of resurrection." A whiff of blooming lilac arrived on the wind.

PART II

CHAPTER 19

PASSAGES

❁

Everyone agreed the Christmas weather had been glorious, and January 10, 1915, appeared to be just another calm and balmy day extending a holiday season that saw temperatures sometimes rise into the tepid sixties. Whales swam south, and we had a series of telescopes set on the porch at Shore Acres permanently fixed on the sea. When not in use, binoculars were discarded on the wide rattan chair arms or on the low veranda wall. Shouts rose up as someone spied the big gray mammals breaching and diving or captured with the naked eye their blow of water shooting up like geysers from the sea. Edgar and Louie still knocked knuckles to announce their complicity in spying the mammals without the use of telescopes. They both had exceptional eyesight.

I had forgiven my husband. And slowly, I was choosing to forget. "After all I've done!" a voice inside my head would say, "look what he did. After all I've done!" And so my demands, my shoulds for how he should have behaved could fill whole days if I would let them.

Whatever the impetus, I came to accept. Louie too might say as he gazed tenderly at children not his own: "After all I've done for her, she betrayed me too."

On my weaker days, when I felt low and insignificant, I wallowed in his duplicity, his impulsiveness, his flirt with my affections, and told myself we were very different spirits, he and I. I found it a great effort to trust him then, though he assured me with his presence and his generosity that his motives now were pure. Still, I scanned his person each time he'd return from an extended trip, warily accepting his presents.

But the gift of the garden and my tears began to heal me. With risk, I began exposing myself like a new shoot pushing up through snow. I reached out a bit to others, found some satisfaction in watching a child put spectacles on her face and see the world in a different way. It was my task to do as well, see the world through clearer eyes. I shared a little more with Kate and found I liked the feelings our ladies' nights delivered.

Kate's strong fingers pounded out the latest piano beat, enough to make the fans move like fish tails before the flushed faces of the elders. Secretly, people loved to give their money, I decided, felt flattered to be asked. Together, Kate and I would have them bobbing apples as though they were children, playing hopscotch for dollars. We'd send them off making sure they'd be coming back again, full of fond memories, not the money they'd lost.

It seemed no small skill that we could convince total strangers to part with their well-earned money for an important social cause. It proved to be a different kind of passion, one that left a longer glow and warmer.

I even invited Annie to Shore Acres on a January day in 1915, not just for a party with dozens about but for a small gathering of family. While the men discussed Rhode Island Reds and their laying practices, the Marines' landing at Tampico, and the Trade Commission's ruling to police interstate business practices, Annie and I put on light sweaters and, behind the active children, walked the gravel path to the pergolas. Even in the dead of winter, Donald James, the new head gardener, had prepared a feast for the eyes mixing the colors of leaves and grasses and branches with dormant perennial plants so it seemed we stepped on a foliage arrangement instead of our feet. The changing light of the day promised new vistas whenever we walked.

"Who'd have thought a garden in winter could be so interesting?" I said, taking in a deep breath of the pine-scented morning and exhaling slowly. The pampas grass and stand of bamboo reflected in the pool.

"I see why you like it here," Annie said. "It's grand, yes, indeed." Annie motioned Marvin on when he turned to wait for us to catch up. "Go over to the park area. See if you can find the deer." April looked like she might like to eavesdrop on her elders, but Annie motioned her on too.

"You can learn something here even from planting a seed too deep or discovering that certain flowers grow better next to others. And of course pruning has its epiphanies," I said.

"Terribly philosophical, Cassie. My vegetables are just a garden for me. But then, you always did get more out of things than anyone else I ever knew. Margaret said she thought you had more fun in life than anyone."

"More misery, too, I bet she said. I've made more unfortunate choices, that's for sure." I spoke it lightly, already deeper into a discussion than I'd planned to go.

A breeze moved Annie's fiery hair coiled loosely around her head in shiny twists. I pulled my sweater tighter around my shoulders. The wool nubbins against my skin felt comforting and warm. I couldn't afford the sniffles or a cold now. Both took me down so.

Annie said, "Cass, there's something I want to say. Have wanted to for a time now. About what *happened*, that day, when I came with Marvin and talked with you about…what Gus saw?"

"I'd rather forget," I said.

"Yes, but I didn't mean to hurt you. I never meant that." Her words tumbled out, and I could see she'd been storing them, waiting to say something that would clear the path that had grown rocky between us.

"It's past, Annie. And I'm trying to keep the past where it belongs. Not here, not now."

"Still—"

"Still is what you need to be," I said and touched my fingers to her lips. Her eyes moistened.

"I thought you were drowning," she said. Her voice caught. "So wrapped up in looking the other way. I *couldn't* let you sink in, I just *couldn't*. But I never meant it to divide us or for you to think I didn't care."

"You took a risk, Annie," I said and took her hand, swinging it as we walked. "When no one else would. That there was pain in that touch is not your fault." Then quickly, before she could respond, I released her hand and said, "Oh look, there's Belle and Russ. Aren't they just the handsomest pair?" My feet propelled me toward them.

From the look on their faces they wouldn't welcome my intrusion or appreciate this act of rescue, but I didn't want to give Annie details. I couldn't tell anyone what happened because I didn't want people condemning my husband or me. I didn't want them judging me as the kind of woman who couldn't keep her husband happy, or worse, the kind of woman who drove her man away. People think their observations useful, but I would have been content to live without ever knowing what he'd done. Of course, healing would have been delayed, then, maybe never come. There was that to think about.

Annie joined our threesome, wiping her eyes with the back of her hand.

Belle had come for the season. We'd found a kind of peace together, mostly when we stepped out to ride horses. She'd even come to my defense once, against Louie. I can't remember what my husband and I were arguing about, but he had sharp words for me at the very moment Belle strode in from outdoors. Classic in her riding pants and tall Italian leather boots, blond hair pulled back into a snood, she'd been headed for the stairway. Instead she strode across the Navajo rugs to where Louie stood beside the fireplace, her shoulders straight and true. And before anyone knew what she intended to do or say, she slapped Louie's face with her riding crop.

"Mother doesn't deserve that now or ever," she'd said and turned on her heels and walked away, her eyes ablaze and her cheeks flushed.

How I wish I could remember what we were arguing about!

Louie stood stunned, rubbing the welt on his cheek, staring after her as she stomped up the winding staircase to her rooms.

"Has her mother's temper," he said.

I could have retorted, said something hateful though true. Instead, I marveled that Belle had called me "Mother" and had come to my defense.

On that January day when Annie and I walked in the garden, Belle looked regal, shoulders a little straighter, seeming younger than her years. She carried a pink parasol against the sun, and her pointed-toe shoes with French Louis heels poked out beneath her straight pink-and-red-striped skirt. She wore a long-sleeved linen blouse and fiddled with the feather boa around her neck as she walked.

Perhaps because of the fabulous weather or more likely due to Russ Tower's frequent visits, Belle wore a smile, though as I approached it diminished some, as tentative now as toes in the ocean. She was almost as tall as

Russ, and though they may not have known it yet, connection arced between them.

"You don't mind if we walk with you, do you?" I asked and slipped my arm in the crook of Russ's elbow.

He looked startled. "Not at all. What could be finer for a thorn than to be surrounded by roses?"

Annie caught up, and the four of us walked abreast down the wide gravel path to the sunken oriental garden. There we sat on the concrete steps and talked of general things: Russ's purchase of the Ford agency with his promise to bring in eighty Fords during the year; the planned replacement of the Commercial Club by the North Bend Club, with Fred Hollister as president.

"Always politics operating in our little North Bend," I said.

"Might be operating even farther if your Louie has his way," Russ said, still talking politics.

"He's doing enough as mayor," I said. I scratched at Rhodie's old poodle ears.

"Best hold on to your feather hat because I think he's destined for greater things."

"A Simpson always is," Edith said walking up behind us, her husband, Roy, close behind.

We spoke of Alpha, our housegirl, and her romance with a Norwegian sailor, of whale watching from the ocean porch, the price of tuna sold now in cans, and how many boats could fit in the boathouse just built beside the cove.

"I miss Lottie," Annie said then, looking around. "Haven't seen her for ages."

"Looks after the Old Town house," Louie said, he and Gus joining us.

"She's getting on in years. We just couldn't ask her to look after this big place too," I said. "And Alpha's been a dear at both houses."

"Old indeed," Annie said. "She's younger than you."

"Well of course *Alpha* is," I said.

"No," Annie persisted, "I meant Lottie. She's much younger than you."

Gus coughed into the silence that followed, then said, "Ve check the vhales, ya?" He steered his wife to the veranda.

We had lunch and adjourned to the front lawn where Louie could show off the trick he'd taught Ulysses, one of Edgar's two boxer dogs.

"Will he jump as far as the birdbath?" Edgar shouted when the dog had leaped on command through a hoop and landed on a stool covered in velvet the color of sunset. The dog landed with ease, and we applauded. Ulysses bounded toward me. His movement brought the other dogs, who barked and pushed for position. So I heard before I actually saw the motor of Charlie Winsor's Pathfinder making its way through the trees toward the champagne circle, past the marble birdbath, and stop at the front of the house.

I looked to see if Kate and Helen had come, but he'd driven out alone. He stepped out, his face serious, and walked straight to Louie and touched his shoulder.

"It's your dad," I heard him say. "He's had a heart attack. He's gone."

The tycoon of the West and master of my husband's heart had died. He'd been working in the office in Oakland though he was ninety years old, writing payroll checks of all things. Just collapsed over his books and died. No lingering for him. He left as he lived: no nonsense.

I ached for my husband, knowing how it was to have unfinished business with a parent and never having said or heard the things you wished you had.

"Harry phoned," Charlie said. "He's motoring up to Oakland from Riverside and will begin taking care of things."

Louie looked at Charlie as though he hadn't spoken.

"Dad?" he said as Charlie walked over to Edith and motioned Edgar in. "Get Alpha to help pack up, Cass. We're leaving."

There's always so much to do when a parent dies: siblings to suffer with, lawyers to haggle with, effects to go through, old suppressed hurts worked to the surface. A million memories run like movie reels through your head.

We all boarded a Simpson ship and met Harry in San Francisco. Along with Asa's business associates, we mourned a man who had been a giant, even larger in my husband's eyes.

Edith decided that Louie and I should have the bulk of household things, paintings and furniture and a marvelous marble statue the lawyers valued at forty thousand dollars. Linens from the house in Oakland and some from the place in Stockton came to us as well, along with oriental rugs and exquisite Chinese lanterns. "You've plenty of wall space at Shore Acres," Edith said.

She was such a vibrant woman, in her early thirties, and so self-assured, knowing just what she wanted and choosing to have it. I envied her that, and the way she grieved for her father: face flushed, genuine tears during the service, shaking lip at the graveside where we each threw in handfuls of dirt. Edith was fifty plus years younger than her father, and he doted on her, the way a grandfather might. I suspect she would miss him the most.

We rode back from the graveside in a hired car, and Louie leaned his head back against the leather. Tears pooled at his eyes. "One time Dad sent me to South Africa to handle a cargo. Did a stupid thing. Sold everything including the schooner and made my way to London. Blew it all." He smiled a sad and wistful smile. "I think he might have forgiven me that. Wasn't the first time. Simpson money I squandered, and families are known to indulge. But on a Sunday afternoon in London, I saw this tie. Lusted after it. Cold sober at the time. Thought it the prettiest thing. Picked up a brick and broke the window, reached inside and took it. Easier than taking clams from the sand." He closed his eyes. "Didn't mean a thing once I had it. Just wanted it." He sighed. "Never saw Dad so angry. He said I'd never amount to a 'hill of beans' if I couldn't resist stealing what wasn't mine. Said he was sorry he'd sired me. Actually said that, 'Sorry I sired you.'"

Tears made tiny streams like the beginning of spring freshets from his eyes. "Scared me. Words like *stealing* scared me too. Paid him back the lawyers' fees and all. Never cheated in business. Thought I contained myself, even after my wife…" He swallowed. "Then I met you."

I felt my heart throb in my neck, push against the tight collar of my black dress. "And did I lose value, once you had me?"

He reached for my fingers, ran his thumb over my nails. "Didn't know how many it would hurt."

"Undisciplined desire," I said. "I chose it too."

"Reap what we sow. Mother used to say that." He picked at lint on his pants. "Only hope is to plant better seeds. Late for that. Always thought the moment was what mattered. Might have been right once, not sure now."

"Did you ever tell your Dad you were sorry? For the tie or…"

"Never did." He sat forward and thumbed his eyes of wetness. "Don't know if he'd have forgiven me if I had. Not in his nature. Simpsons rarely say they're sorry."

"You have," I said. He squeezed my fingers.

"Except for Shore Acres," Louie said, "I never heard him say I'd done anything worthy, nothing I can recall."

"He put you in charge of everything. He'd never have done that if he hadn't believed in you."

The hum of the car engine filled the silence. "It was Shore Acres though that made him say it."

"At least you have that," I said. "At least you have that."

We stayed in California for a few weeks dealing with the reading of the will and the sorting. We didn't worry about Shore Acres. Donald James and his wife, Helen, looked after things, along with Alpha. Mike Bastendorff, a Luxembourg man, managed the farm.

The addition of the Collver acres, building the barn and milk house and a small apartment above, made Shore Acres a working farm, with dairy cows grazing on a point south of the house and beyond the garden. Large Belgian workhorses with the white-tufted hocks pulled the plows and seeders across nearly two hundred acres under cultivation. A good dozen thoroughbreds startled across the pastures, tails to the wind, then rested their heads over wide board fences. Chickens and goats and hogs competed with the sea lions for noise at the sea.

Louie, the ranchman—I marveled when I thought of it, remembering a night when we'd done the "choresing" for Annie and Gus, and Louie had put forth this plan. "Be careful what you wish for, for you may get it," someone had said. And so he had.

One could restore themselves at Shore Acres, surrounded by sentient beings of flora and fauna and mammals of the sea. It welcomed us back from the City along with the grandeur of a violent storm rolling into shore. It was all I'd ever hoped for, all I'd thought one day my world could be.

So I found my malaise in the weeks that followed confusing. I sighed as I walked around the grounds, pointing out some overgrowth Donald might want to take a look at, suggesting the garden house needed railings renailed, or the lily pads on the pond thinned and given away. My occupation was "at home," as we women of leisure called it. "At home" as though nothing else would command me.

When Asa's extensive book collection arrived, we gave the books to Kate for the North Bend Public Library. She wouldn't accept them. "Unless you come with them," she laughed. "We need help with the collection and you'd be perfect for it. We have over six hundred books, and Mrs. Hollister has donated the use of the house, the heat, and the lights. Even the janitor's service. And the basement billiard room. I'm sure I can count on you now!"

It was another challenge, organizing the collection, getting the books available for lending and securing their return, and I accepted it with enthusiasm. I wondered why I hadn't paid that much attention in the years before. I became so busy reading, writing, stacking shelves, I even forgot to eat.

Louie resigned as mayor of North Bend as soon as we returned from California and began the expansion at Shore Acres.

"Why?" I said. The planned remodeling seemed dissolute, decadent almost. I thought his efforts might be considered ostentatious, high-flown perhaps, invite ridicule instead of admiration. "We have the most fabulous estate south of Portland and north of the City. There's no need for more."

"Shore Acres will be our permanent home someday," he said. "Needs to look like it."

"What about our Old Town house?" I said. "I like living here, actually."

"Got other plans for that when the time comes."

He would have a swimming pool put in at Shore Acres, twenty-six by fifty-two feet, inside a Roman bath room that rivaled the barn in length. A pool, heated, with either fresh water or sea water—guests could order what they wanted a day ahead. In between the pool and the living room, he'd build a palm room where green foliage would flourish in air always steamy and sultry like the South. A ballroom, too, would appear on the third floor with only side lighting so it could be converted for billiards. Several bedrooms were added to the second floor, including a master suite with a fireplace above the Roman bath. Louie said we may as well pour a tennis court north of the house so people could compete with a view of the sea. It would be the best available, everything he did, no expense spared, costly concrete where cedar would do.

It was a monument, I decided, to his father. Something that would be unparalleled, extraordinarily sublime. A finely designed estate set upon a rocky ledge dotted with foliage and color not unlike a city's arboretum.

Louie'd hired the architects the year before and had begun some changes to Shore Acres even while Asa lived. With his father's death, there came a frenzy about the work, as though he had wasted time in considering what he wanted. Now he would have this fine estate almost double in size, be even more glorious, to prove to the world he was a man of substance and not just the reputation of frolic and fun who had once been such a trial to his father. He had a quarter share of twelve million dollars to work with, if the lawyers' figures proved true.

Realizing what his father left him and that he had none to pass it on to, made me wonder if he intended to use it up before he died. His behavior felt vaguely familiar to me, that delirium of activity, of making something happen, getting in deeper as though spinning through trees.

Whatever it was, it consumed him, and he spent days at Shore Acres, watching and directing, living in the midst of plaster and sawdust of renovation. Sometimes when the pounding and disruption got too much, he'd spend the night out there, telling me when he returned to our Old Town house of progress.

Even at the Old Town house, where we still lived, his efforts shifted. There, he occupied himself with the carnival planned for the swing bridge completion. It was a new experience for him not to be the leader of an event and only a participant in the planning for dignitaries and food and celebration.

"Think they're making a mistake," Louie said as he lifted barbells in Harry's old room now converted to an exercise space. Harry couldn't visit much. His tuberculin troubles kept him in dry climates. That acrid, medicine smell that came from Ol' Harry's room still hung faintly in the air, permeated into the lumber over the years. Sweat dribbled off Louie's forehead as he strained. He was still a handsome man though he had some pinking across his nose. He'd grown fuller across his shoulders, added weight to his middle, but despite my puffy figure, he could still swing me off my feet.

"What kind of mistakes?" I said.

"Only letting the *Tide* know about the events, shutting out the *Coos Bay Harbor*. Cutting off their noses to spite their faces," he said. "Two good papers could make this town prosper. Show the comprehensive nature of our community. Tolerate differences of opinion." He squatted and stood, squatted and stood. He laid the weights on their holders. I handed him the towel. "Remind me," he said and leaned to kiss my nose. "If I ever run for office again, to let all the papers in the state know at the same time."

"Are you?"

"Not this year," he said and laughed.

In September we received another phone call from California, this time not from Harry but about him.

"Harry's dead," Edith said, crying into the telephone. I'd never heard her lose control, and at first I couldn't make out her words. "He fell," she said. "At that hotel he was staying at. Down some blasted twisting backstairs. A family he'd promised to spend time with after church found him. You've got to come," she said, and hung up before I could say that we would.

I thought of Margaret and the distance between us as I watched my husband mourn his brother. There is so little time, and while we tell ourselves we'll write or extend words we've always meant to say, we don't. Then they're gone, and we've no one to blame but ourselves.

It was one thing to lose Asa. He'd lived a long life. But Harry had just turned thirty-three.

He'd spent all those years learning medicine and caring for others, and became ill himself. Yet with the simplest act of living, walking down stairs, he'd died. No chance to say good-bye, no occasion for expression of fond farewells. Just gone, within an instant without a wife or heir.

We boarded the *Breakwater* and steamed south to San Francisco to pick up Edith and Roy and Edgar and then on to Riverside to bring Harry back to Oakland for services and another reading of a will. I thought about words I would have said to him, could have written to him. He was always so good about writing to me.

I'd saved the letters Harry'd sent when he'd been hospitalized for tuberculosis and had brought them with me, wondering if Edith might like to read them, or even Louie.

My husband shook his head when I offered. Harry'd identified Scriptures on healing, and I wondered if they had continued to comfort him after his recovery or if, as I was tempted to, they were relied upon only when in peril. I'd dismissed the references when his letters had first arrived. Now I found them speaking to me in a new and different way.

It was standing-room-only at Harry's funeral. People from all walks of life squeezed into pews and later told us stories of Harry's generosity and selflessness, his altruistic bent. The small church held the smells of butchers and farmers and seamen and matrons and businessmen too. But most stunning were the children. Dozens of them carrying carnations they trotted forward to place on the shiny cedar casket.

Harry had planned ahead for his funeral and even selected what verses to read. It was an odd selection, I thought at first, about Peter being chastised by Christ before that disciple denied him at the cross.

"Christ knew what Peter would become," the minister said, "and he confronted him because he knew. In love, he corrected him, knowing something better lay ahead. His words offered hope and the promise that healing is possible in each of us, through Christ, regardless of our past."

Louie thought the selection unusual too. "Remember hearing it as a boy," he said. "Peter failed Christ, and then followed a mountaintop experience where his disciples are told about the future. How good it'll be once they've dealt with the loss."

"Maybe Harry knew his future," I said. "He planned his service, which is odd for someone only thirty-three."

"Can't see how," Louie said. "Would have avoided the stairs if he had known."

"I was thinking more about his believing in the goodness of the future and not letting the miseries of today get in the way of hoping for something more."

The more I thought about Harry's deep abiding care for others, it was as though he had written me another letter. He'd always said I denied important feelings, stuffed them deep and did not let others close. Perhaps he still wished to confront me about my life, my ways, yet saw some hope in me I could not see myself.

Aside from bequests to a San Francisco asylum and a tuberculosis hospital, Harry left everything to his brothers and his sister, no small amount since that included his portion of Asa's estate as well.

It was after our return that the gnawing of my life began to cease, and I found the filling I had longed for. It came connected to the European War.

We were not in it yet, but I devoured the newspapers, gathering details about airship bombs and battles. At first I wasn't sure why I was moved to scrounge through newspapers, converse with Louie and our friends for what they heard from relatives and contacts in Germany and Russia, France and Italy. It had been bad enough with the assassination in Sarajevo by a Serbian nationalist. Then right after, the nationalistic spirit pitted Europe against Russia. Now it seemed as if the world was mad, had been waiting for this moment to sear old wounds, stage battles to conquer former neighbors, not just enemies, but friends.

Then I began to see the pictures of refugees in flight. So many were women and children, displaced not by their choosing, but by the poor decisions of others.

"I want to gather funds for them," I told Louie. "Relief. Food, blankets. We'll be in it next, won't we?"

"We can hope not," he said. "Do what we can from here."

But I knew. War would come to us, affect our future.

I set about my work, channeled my experiences now for innocents. I thought of Harry's charity to patients, his caring well for others. The refugees became my *naknuwisha*, my caring for something precious, and through them, I received permission to finally appreciate myself.

CHAPTER 20

LOST
CHANCES

❁

My efforts had to stop for celebration.

The Big Bridge Carnival began October 7 and ended on the 9th. It would be a splendid event culminating past hopes with new ones for the future. Huge tents with food and music and beer gardens appeared like goose bumps along Virginia and Sherman Streets and out near the beachfront. Speeches washed down by North Bend Brewery products filled the days along with music. Prohibition had come to North Bend but would not go into effect until the year's last night. Dancing went on through the day on planks laid out not far from our Old Town house. The swing railroad bridge permitted tall ships to still sail the bay but allowed the railroad to cross the water as well.

Bunting of red and white and blue spread across the speakers stand where Louie sat along with the current mayor, Southern Pacific dignitaries, and members of the organizing committee. We wives with our yellows and greens and silks of red were included too. A sea of faces bobbed before the stands. Well-wishers waved hankies and men threw their straw hats into the air at the appointed time for an engine to cross over the bridge linking the northern half of the state to us North Benders. Only eight dollars and ninety-five cents and a bridge across the Umpqua River kept Coos Bay from connection with Portland.

On Sunday of the three-day festivities, following church services, another gathering formed with music minus ale, and certainly no one bet the horses where anyone could see. The day waned and all would have closed down for the night when Dick Rogers, a local entrepreneur, noticed a large tent not yet struck. He rented it and rounded up the dancing band for one more glorious evening of the Bunnie Hug or Texas Tommie.

We danced the Lame Duck and Grizzly Bear and Panama Pacific too. Dancing was outlawed on Sunday, just as liquor and gambling were, but the fifty-year-old Sunday closing statute was ignored for dancers and especially on such a festive occasion.

One hundred couples crowded the floor beneath the Virginia Street tent, and we'd just begun the Bunny Hop, our dresses flouncing just a tad above our high-topped shoes, sweaty hands on the waist of a gentleman or gentlewoman just in front. When the laughter was at its most feverish pitch, the Methodist minister appeared looking all fiery-eyed and hot. He took his life in his own hands, I thought, by shouting down the band and yelling the protests into silence. He demanded we all go home, and the local constable concurred.

Louie and I walked home, waving at people and nodding as we made our way beneath the gaslights, all like chastised children.

At the Old Town house, Louie suggested the cupola. "Haven't been for a long time."

The cupola corralled the stars that night. They popped out like waited-for thoughts, soft and sure and inspiring too.

"Want to close the house down," Louie said. "Take a trip to Europe before things get worse there. Take a honeymoon of sorts. Come back to Shore Acres with a new home, new everything. Make it our permanent place."

"You'd leave North Bend?"

"Never leave it in my heart. But at Shore Acres, can be active to the end, like Dad.

"I didn't think this was a downhill slide for you," I said, teasing.

"Got lots of living yet to do before I die. You too, Cassie, you too."

I remained quiet, surprised by the thought of death expressed in the same breath as my name.

"Wish Harry were here," I said. "You know, I don't ever think I saw him dance. He didn't have much fun, not like you and Edgar."

"Short but sweet," Louie said.

"That's a word for it, yes, *sweet*," I said. "His life was sweet. And yet I think he left more behind him in a way than I ever will. At least seeing how people grieved for him makes me think his life was full."

"Shore Acres and the garden'll be your legacy," Louie said.

"Yours, not mine," I said. An owl hooted in one of the fir trees. "I've not done much with my life. Except take my time learning."

"Let's don't talk about death tonight," Louie said. He pulled me down to the narrow cot he sometimes slept on when he wrote so late.

"Careful," I said. "This bed may not hold both you and your butterball wife."

"Butterball?" He held me back away from him for examination, moving his head left, then right. "Voluptuous, I'd call you. Alluring, inviting, desirable. All those. What you've always been for me."

"Flattery will accomplish what honesty will not," I said.

"What I was hoping," he said and pulled me to him.

The three-week trip included Sweden with its large stands of timber and declared neutrality; Belgium, for yards of white embroidery and lace; and France, for fine wine and champagne. But our tour lacked luster. Strain of war showed on the faces of waiters and porters, shopkeepers and maids. Border authorities were terse and tense, pawing through our papers, staring at us to see if we really were Americans or spies. We returned through Stockholm and listened helplessly as a Montana man argued unsuccessfully that he was an American citizen. Frustration lined his wide forehead and sizzled in his eyes. Though we offered, we could do nothing to help. Faces of refugees came back to me, and I felt embarrassed by the bulges in our bags. I urged Louie home.

A week after we returned, we held the warming party for Shore Acres' expansion. But I negotiated with my husband: He would match the party costs and make donations. "To the Red Cross?" Louie asked.

"Whichever—the YMCA, library, just so our abundance reaches well beyond us."

Even Lottie and Gus and Annie joined the affair. Belle, too, along with Russ, his sister Nellie, and Edgar and his latest date. Kate and Charlie dropped in for a moment. We kept the parrot in my bedroom so no guests would be surprised by Annabelle's insights. "Whoever could have taught her?" Belle asked during the party. Gus rolled his eyes to the heavens.

Louie brought in a photographer named Streeter from the City, and he took a panoramic view of our Shore Acres, stunning in its grandeur.

We danced all we wished, adding the waltz and the Grapevine to the dances the Methodists disliked. Children lay like cordwood around the edge of the floor asleep while we adults Texas Tommy-ed on.

Everyone brought their bathing clothes, and at the stroke of midnight, with Alpha, Helen, and Rachel left to watch after children, the rest of us received glasses of Louie's famous champagne and made our way down the winding staircase, through the living room and the steamy palm room to the expansive Roman bath.

He'd saved the pool to show till last with its choice of pure water or sea, natural or warmed.

My husband delighted in their praises, of the clear water and the warmth dripping from their wet fingers, the view of the crashing surf through the tall windows. Palms and marble statues sat around the edges making the room feel more like a European hotel than a wing of a home on an isolated Oregon cliff. Candlelight flickered for effect across the water with Edison's soft lights for vision.

"To my dad," Louie said, raising his glass. "Who always loved a fabulous adventure and saw Shore Acres for what it was. Just that." Louie's eyes glistened.

The men murmured approval, and we all raised our glasses in kind.

"And to my wife," he said, his eyes finding me in the gathering. "Who is my inspiration. Can't say anything that means more to me. To Cassie," he said raising his glass, "as important to my living as my very breath."

His accolade suited someone admirable and giving. I felt a warmth inside me, almost a blush which I hadn't felt in years. Perhaps I had inspired some greatness in another, contributed, just because I stood beside him.

"Here, here!" Charlie said. We sipped, the moment passed, though I savored its sweetness.

"Bring out your bathin' suits, ladies," Louie ordered. "You too, Red." Annie giggled like a girl. He led us women to the dressing rooms that arched with elaborate French burgundy silk for curtains across the south end of the pool.

We'd just finished dressing and stood as though we were all lined up for some kind of beauty contest, our little ruffled skirts flouncing. I had gotten us into a chorus line of horizontal stripes when I noticed some rustling going on behind my husband. He stood admiring us as though we were a bouquet of tiger lilies. He still wore his white suit and his white leather shoes. He stood with one foot forward, head cocked, glass filled, and was about to speak, I know he was, to say something witty to us women.

But the men lifted my unsuspecting husband, champagne glass, white shoes, and all, and dropped him shouting into his own grand pool.

He went under. We rushed to the edge of the concrete. His dark hair floated to the surface followed by his face, shoulders, and hands still holding his glass. Amidst the shouts and splash and laughter and enthusiastic applause, he tipped it to us all in one grand Simpson toast.

A triumphant smile filled his face, water dripping from his chin: for the pure pleasure of a thing, for the gathering of friends inside the mansion of his dreams, and, I like to think, for me, the woman he said later God had made and then thrown the mold away.

Bruce Evans, the evangelist, did his work in 1916. He brought every church in North Bend and some in Marshfield, too, to the Star Theater in May, and with them Prohibition became a reality. It had already been, of course, but not everyone in North Bend took the 1914 vote seriously.

We didn't attend. Kate did and Annie told us of it later while we lounged at Sunset Beach. Soft waves curled into sand before us.

"Too bad he didn't make that speech a couple of years ago," I said. I pulled my Irish sweater against the easy breeze. "Might have done away with the Star's apartments and its rooms of 'negotiable affections.'"

Kate called to Helen and insisted she wear her straw hat to guard against the sun. "There are plans to paint it before the railroad jubilee in August," Kate said.

"Be the only thing to celebrate," Louie said dropping down next to us on the sand. He leaned on one elbow, picked up a tiny pebble and tossed it, aiming for some unseen target toward the sea.

"The railroad'll come, won't it?" Annie asked.

"Yup. Southern Pacific is scheduled to make its debut come August, but think it's past its prime. Waited too long to have it to be the boost I thought it'd be. Thom's pledge of ten thousand dollars for the hotel'll never come through now. No brewery owner's going to invest in a place that can't serve his beer even if the railroad brings folks to it."

"Be a strange jubilee without whiskey," Kate said. "Might allow us to enjoy the music, finally."

"Not to worry," Louie said. "Edgar knows a man who makes his own."

"Music?" I said, and they laughed.

"We hear you're going to lose your Alpha," Kate said then.

"Yup. She finally set the date," Louie said. "Her Norwegian sailor plans to take her to Garibaldi, and who knows how long it'll be before we see her again. Miss her. She's been a good help."

"Seems young to me," I said, "to be marrying."

"Everyone seems young to me these days," Annie offered.

"It's nice you've brought your Portland seamstress in to do her dress," Kate said.

"Belle and Russ play their marriage cards tight to their chests so my daughter may never need imported hand-embroidery," I said. "Alpha's ready. She can hardly contain herself at the fittings."

"It's a kind gesture, your gift," Kate said. A gull screeched across a sky streaked with high spring clouds. "I remember you had all those flowers sent, when we lost our daughter. It was so generous." With her fingers she drew a design in the sand and appeared pensive. "Generosity's always returned."

Alpha Wicklund and her beau, Iver Johannesen, did marry and the white embroidered dress draped the bride's body in a perfect pattern with her matching hat. I thought it the wedding of the season and was pleased to play my part.

I hoped Louie erred, that the railroad at last would open things up in North Bend. I wanted it to, for his sake. He'd put so much of himself into that town, wanting it to be the San Francisco of the north. If goodwill and the giving away of Simpson money could have done it, it would have happened years ago.

The festivities brought Annie and Gus out from the Winchester arm in time for the jubilant wedding. A reporter from Eugene had written a poem about the union of "Mr. Eugene Lane (County) to Miss Coos" and a mock wedding including bride and groom and flower girls took center stage. The two cities were joined. We wanted it to be a "Boost for Coos" just as the banner over the specialty gates read.

"Better than 'Let 'er toot' or 'Choo! Choo! Here you come!' Annie mused about the discarded booster themes.

While more than ten thousand attended the railroad jubilee, when they all left, permanent North Bend residents numbered barely two thousand, nowhere near the City's.

"Wish we could have convinced half to stay," Louie said when he heard the figures.

We motored back to Shore Acres after the big event, and a kind of lull eased into our lives. Something we'd been waiting for had been accomplished. The railroad had arrived; celebrations planned and completed. The joy of anticipation vanished. It was a Simpson's most dangerous time.

Not that Shore Acres didn't have much to consume us. No ranchman will ever tell you his life is boring. The soil, "humus," spoke of humbling, but it failed to sustain in the way an anticipated event could, one holding both risk and the promise of consuming passion.

When I felt well, when my legs did not puff up to the size of my thighs, I drove the old Buick runabout myself in to meet with Kate and Laura Byler and her girls. Not for socializing but to organize campaigns for Europe. None of us said what we knew: that some of our own would be needing our help if fears of America's role in the war loomed true.

Louie busied himself with his ranchland, and sometimes on quiet ocean days, he'd take the canoe out of Simpson Beach onto the ocean. Edgar and poor Gus had been talked into it too. From the garden, looking over the cliff to the sea, we photographed the canoes like locust pods on water. The sea looked like a lake that day, a camouflage of ocean, not a power that could take an entire ship and thrust it onto the rocks or foul it up against the jetty. When the *Santa Clara* wrecked at the bar the previous year, we'd all believed her lost and her passengers too. But the seas were calm, and the U.S. Life-saving crews had rescued everyone. The state of the sea matters in rescues, more than the ship or her crew.

Belle had moved with us and had her own suite of rooms on the second floor. Privacy was her middle name, and I know of at least one whole week in which she never exchanged a word with a single human being, not even to shout close to Lung Lem's good ear to ask for buttered buns. She read voraciously and loved to ride, and our closest times were when we found ourselves at the stable in the early morning, neither having spoken to the other of our plans to ride.

Belle helped me saddle up, gave me a hand to hold my foot to mount. I felt the warmth and rareness of her touch. She didn't often look at me, but sensed when I tired and turned her horse back toward the stable before I became exhausted. Once after we'd ridden farther than planned and my chest hurt, I caught her glancing when she didn't know I noticed. Her slender face wore a look I couldn't place. Only later, just before I fell asleep, did I recognize it as fondness and affection, maybe even love.

Belle rarely brought up the past. She didn't ask why I'd left her behind or didn't fight more for her presence. Harry's death reminded me that life so quickly changes, and if I ever wished to speak contrition with my daughter there was no time like the present. But I didn't, too afraid, I suppose, of hearing words I didn't wish to or too frightened to discover the depth of pain I'd caused another.

My daughter seldom spoke of Hoquiam either nor said much of her Minnesota school. In the class picture, she sat in front, definite space between her and her friends on either side. Her face stared into the camera but lacked a smile. She could live within herself, that child of mine, and do it better than her mother.

Occasionally we rode together past Edgar's place at Big Creek, a farm he'd bought for the timber and visited sometimes when he came north. He kept a mean-spirited palomino corralled there. Edgar'd married and had a son and a growing collection of vehicles. Sometimes he'd ride his big palomino to Shore Acres instead of using his car. I always hated that. The horse lacked discipline, much like Edgar. A kind of glee crossed his face when my mare sidestepped to avoid his mount, and he'd laugh and slap his horse's neck as we rode away.

"I have little regard for riders who're as unpredictable as their horse," Belle said. I knew he heard it.

"You're quite the spirited one," I said when we'd ridden away.

She straightened on her mount and her chin jerked toward her chest. "I…I didn't realize I'd spoken."

"How would you describe me, my riding?" I said.

She hesitated, seeking words as the horses clopped together into the silence. I wondered at the throbbing of my heart as I waited for her words. "You're volcanic and high spirited," she said then. "But deep feeling and tenacious too." Belle looked at me, her blue eyes shadowed beneath her riding hat but bringing me to her just the same. "What I have of those qualities, Mother, were gifts from you."

"Penny for your thoughts," Louie said one dusky evening as he and I rode out together. He didn't often ride with me, having a preference for cars. He'd lost his Simplex Roadster when the *Shasta* rammed the Simpson steamer *Hardy* near the bridge at Golden Gate. It was the last ship in the fleet, and we'd lost tons of hay meant for the dairy too. Mowed grass lay drying for hay, and old Doc and King stomped quietly in the barn. A warm sea-breeze brushed the evening. Louie said he felt like a ranchman, and ranchmen rode out with their wives.

"Just about the peacefulness of this place," I said. "That's what I'm thinking of. I didn't think I'd like it way out here."

"We're not isolated." Louie said.

"I'm not complaining. It's just that I always liked being surrounded by people. It's where my thoughts grow from, like billiard balls bouncing off each other. I didn't expect to find musing outside a crowd, and now I have."

"Suppose that's part of why I still keep my ties with my lodges," he said. "Invigorating in a way that's different from the land." We rode without talking, then he said, "We're bound to get into the war, you know, Cass. There'll be things to know about statewide, and do."

"We've already talked about it, Kate and I. The Red Cross will need support too."

"Are you up to it?" he asked. "Noticed that edema."

"I'm drinking more water. Lottie said my body needed it. But I still puff up." I lifted my leg from the stirrup and held it straight out. "Looks like a sausage."

Louie frowned. "Wish you'd see a doctor. I know, I know. 'No time for 'em.' But maybe for me. Would you go for my sake, just to be sure there isn't something someone could do?"

"It doesn't really matter now," I said, and at that moment I realized it didn't.

We'd ridden back along the hawthorn trees that lined the drive toward the garden. Louie tied the horses near one of the staff houses then offered me his hand.

"Let's walk," he said and we did, beneath the pergolas hung with vibrant magenta fuchsias. "Depends on what you want from life," he said as though in the middle of a conversation with himself. "Figure everyone needs something to consume them, something to stay healthy for."

He stopped along the gravel path and pulled out his knife. Swallows dipped and winged their way over us picking mud for their nests on the side of the gardener's house. Louie cut at the stem of a Rosa Alba for me, white as ocean foam. "Only blooms once a season," he said and handed it to me. "Maybe that's what you were missing all these years. A dream of your own that wasn't in someone else's shadow."

"More likely doing for others," I said. "So Lottie tells me, in that way she has, humming and whatnot. Then jabs me with her insights and says I should put my feet up in early evening, drink more fluids, and sleep well, but in the days, to spend less time in retrospection and more time in servitude and dispatch."

"Lottie said that?"

"Not those words exactly, but that's what she meant. And I think she's right, though I'd never let her know that."

"What did you tell her?"

"That I'd think about it."

Louie and I closed Shore Acres, left the farm in the able hands of Mike and Donald, and moved to Portland. We had good reason to rent a house in that inland port city. The Red Cross was gearing up for statewide drives for blood and money, ways to help our doughboys who would soon be called to war. Louie needed to bend his head with men of influence, and Portland promised enthusiasm and intensity, gatherings and events, treats too sweet for Simpsons to resist.

After we'd gotten settled and I'd begun my work with the Red Cross, I wrote to Margaret to see if she could meet me halfway.

Margaret arrived by train, then hired a cab to our door, her little square feet emerging first. She stepped down wearing an ivory linen suit that snuggled her ankles, eased out at her thickened hips and back in at her cinched waist, though like me I suspected she wore the latest in Bon Ton corsets. She placed a closed parasol before her and rested her gloved hands on top, surveying. The sun glinted off a locket hung around her neck. She took in several deep breaths before stepping forward. A broad-brimmed hat with a single dark feather shaded her face, so I couldn't see her expression as she walked up the steps to the screened porch. I watched from the window.

It had been more than fifteen years since I'd seen her. She'd never set her little feet on Shore Acres. When she rang the bell and the maid opened it, I saw a woman as beautiful as ever, her skin without powder, soft and clear of lines. Margaret had given birth to one child, a son, Fred Jr., whose arrival may have spread her waist a bit. But beyond that, she could have been twenty-four instead of just turning forty-three. She was still the Lady Margaret to me, well coiffured and crisp.

She opened her arms to me and I sank into their invitation.

"I'd have given *anything* to have a dozen," Margaret said when I asked after her son. We sat at the round luncheon table, and she fondled the locket between her fingers. "Fortunately, both Fred and I are honorary aunt and uncle to the Soule children, and Joe's wife is like a sister."

"I'm glad you had one close by," I said.

"I *know* she's not my sister, but Fred adores her, too, and there isn't a struggle about seeing them." She spooned sugar into her tea, didn't hold my eyes. "Not the way there is with you, or was, what with your 'arrangement' and all."

"We married as soon as we could."

"I'm sure."

I sat with my back tight against the Queen Anne chair while Margaret stared at the cup as though looking for a hidden message in the tea leaves.

"It's all right, Margaret," I said. "I didn't expect you to understand."

"Who could have?" she said so quickly. "I mean I never *said* a word about it, not to anyone." Her precise pronunciation of *ts* and *ds* made her words crisp. "But it grieved me so, to see you making choices that caused such suffering."

"I've had to make my peace with it," I said.

"Have you? I wouldn't have guessed it."

"I can't imagine you could recognize the state of my soul from your distance."

"I'd have come to nurse you when you were ill, Cassie. I would have done that, despite your situation. I just didn't know."

"It didn't matter." I shrugged my shoulders. "I hardly knew, and when I discovered I was in a hospital, those around me wished they'd stayed away." I laughed to make light of it.

"Neither of us came, though. Not mother, nor I. When we learned you'd almost died, I felt dreadful about it." She looked away, but she must have seen the tears in my eyes that appeared before I could stop them.

"I never meant to desert you, Cass. I ached for you and wished more than anything I could have intervened. I could see the dangers down the road, and I couldn't understand why you didn't. I felt so powerless."

"So did I," I said. My heart beat a faster pace, unprepared for the emotion her words sent coursing through me.

She shook her head as though she'd itemized my actions a dozen times without me present and never found a way to make it different.

"It wasn't about you, Margaret," I said, blinking. "It never was. You didn't make me do a thing and you didn't fail me. It was about me, my decisions and choices. And I'm the one who's had to live with them. Besides, I remember the one and only time you came to see me, you asked for my forgiveness. And I gave it. That makes it all right, doesn't it?"

"Cassie. Please." She took a shallow breath.

"I never thought I needed forgiveness," I continued. "I imagined myself wounded enough by Louie's decisions to punish me for what I did to you and Joe and Mama. And to Belle."

"You could be as thick as a fir log," she said.

"Then Belle reached out to me," I said, "when I didn't ask or deserve it. And I saw then, through her, that I needed forgiveness. God's forgiveness. Because of it, I knew what to do for Louie too."

"Have you wanted to get even?"

Her question startled me. "With whom?"

"Louie. Or me or Mama or anyone you might have envied or resented. One of the oldest emotions, revenge. It keeps healing at bay."

The maid removed the dishes and brought bowls of fresh fruit heaped high in clear, thin-stemmed dishes.

"It might have been worse for Belle if she'd come with me, considering everything. But I never meant to hurt her. I never meant that. I'm not a mean-spirited person, Margaret, truly I'm not. Thoughtless. Self-centered, but I never meant meanness. And I've mellowed with age."

"Why didn't you ever have another child?"

"The doctors said…"

"Nonsense!" She threw her napkin in a wad next to her strawberries. The tone of her voice brought the serving girl, but I motioned her back into the kitchen.

"They never said you *shouldn't* have children. You inferred that, from how you felt. Yes, it's a heart condition, but that isn't why. Not having them just *satisfied* you." She adjusted her glasses and dabbed with an ivory hanky at the moisture appearing above her lip. "Satisfying Cassie, who was insatiable, that's what it was always about."

Her words rattled me coming so quickly from a calm.

"Let's not fight, Margaret," I said. "It's the first time in years we've had together. It may be our last."

"Oh, don't be theatrical. I have a heart problem, too, you know. They treat it as they can. But I'd have risked my death to have another child. We did, in fact." Her voice dropped and she blinked behind her spectacles. Then she reached across the table and held my hand. "You deprived yourself, and Louie, too, of something wonderful. I have wished that for you both, to have had the connection of a child. It might have softened Louie in my eyes, to think he would have liked a family."

"He did," I said. Her eyebrows arched in surprise. "It's one more thing I have to find forgiveness for."

Our desserts finished, we walked around the backyard lawn Louie puttered with his golf clubs in and sat on the wrought-iron bench beneath a
shady elm. Rows of peonies marked the paths. We discussed fashion and the
fancy plaids of Particular skirts, of Louis Banks speaking on Prohibition in
the City, and the popularity of the chatauqua speakers way out here in the
West. Then our words turned to the war, the unrest in Russia, and the
rationing of meat and bread in London. And of the deaths, all those women
and children's deaths.

"It seems we always come back to sad things," Margaret said. Her fingers
swirled the open parasol moving the air of the still day. "The world is able to
dredge up so many bad things it's hard to stay on the upper deck."

"Doubly sad when we've had so much," I said.

"'Whatever does it profiteth a man if he gains the world but loses his
soul?'"

"So what consumes your soul?" I asked.

"Besides my Freds? My church, I suppose, and the Red Cross. And the
refugees in Europe."

"We have something more in common," I said, surprised at our affilia-
tions.

Margaret took the train back to Hoquiam. She didn't even spend the
night. I wrote often to her, after that, filled her in on our news. But a loss
lived where our relationship had been, a bossy older sister and her sibling.

I did think of Margaret and her heart when I visited the doctor a few
weeks later. The size of my ankles and shortness of breath made me go. I
couldn't lace up my shoes and had worn my slippers instead. I heard the bell
ring over the door as I shuffled through, announcing my change of heart.
Perhaps I came to satisfy a curiosity or confirm a suspicion; perhaps to admit
defeat.

Like Lottie, the doctor said I should drink four pitchers of spring water
daily, to flush my system. "To reduce fluid in your ankles, hands, and face."
He reminded me of a pitchfork, rigid with purpose. "Sleep at an angle, thirty
degrees. Almost sitting up. Put away your corset. Stay away from known
places of illness. You're susceptible to pneumonia and there's a wretched flu
said to be starting."

"So what's causing it?" I said.

"You have an enlarged heart." He stared at me. "I suspect you've known.

And your kidneys are not functioning properly. Accounts for your puffiness. Possibly your liver as well. Have you been treated? Anyone advised a brandy snifter before bed?" I shook my head. "Well don't do it. Liquor has no medicinal value, except as an anesthetic, of course. You've had one child? Did this happen during your pregnancy? The swelling? I thought so," he said when I nodded. "Well, you won't like my prescription," he said, washing his hands in the porcelain bowl. "Rest, rest, rest. Plan nothing strenuous. Your heart'll be compromised by excessive efforts either physical or mental. And do yourself a favor: Have a wider pair of shoes cobbled, for comfort."

His news was nothing new, really, and surely did not need sharing with Louie.

I spent my days working on philanthropic issues, thinking about starving faces, thin European children weeping and hurting and hungry for more. When they became individuals to me, not just a mass of childhood, my days went more quickly. I didn't notice the long hours of meetings with Portland's elite. I could mesmerize potential donors, so complete was my passion. My days began early with breakfasts and teas, and then in pairs we matrons approached the business establishments and requested donations. All the charm I had to offer I handed over, with such a rush of joy when we convinced them, matched their need correctly with our own. We'd plan elaborate auctions, create large, exciting gatherings that gave people a joy, a bit of social adventure while being separated from their hard-earned money for a worthy cause.

Once donations were committed, we arranged for pickup and delivery. Then came the events themselves and the invitations and the preparations of the food and music and service for the evenings and delivery again of exchanged items and then the cleanup. Every detail needed tending. Keep my feet up? Not an opportunity for it, though the nights lasted long with the weight of my ankles and the pinched dryness of my eyes and my labored breathing.

We moved back to Shore Acres not too long after, deciding our statewide work could be carried on now from home. I wrote dozens of letters seeking donations, raised money, helped with the local Red Cross chapter to do the same. I even marveled about God's sense of humor that I should spend my days now passionately helping children.

Louie worked on increasing spruce production for Britain's burgeoning aeroplane industry and mounted a Liberty Loan campaign with his employees too. In February, Benjamin left to serve in Europe. Lottie and I prepared boxes of dried fruit and tiny seashells and even some of Louie's Sunset Milk, condensed, to remind him we held him in our minds. It became a new cause, sending gifts from our Coos country to those boys serving us across the sea and keeping them daily in prayers.

Giving, to my surprise, satisfied me. The view from the cliff at Shore Acres held me straight as I stood on the veranda, the salt spray on my face. The scent of roses and iris and a hundred flowering plants filled my head. Horses ripped at grass beneath a gathering of finches. The sea and garden and my efforts at care formed a melody that healed, not my heart, but my spirit.

LAST
RIDES

❀

Louie decided to run for governor. He'd bring newspaper editors from around the state to Shore Acres to showcase the region and introduce himself to them.

"Governor Withycombe will run again," I warned. I wasn't sure why I wanted to talk him out of this. Perhaps the fatigue I had noticed came calling. "Incumbents always have the advantage."

"He'll be challenged by six or seven in the primary, folks say. Open up the election so a newcomer, someone with fresh ideas, can win."

"Someone's been feeding you," I said.

"Hope so," he said patting his widening middle. "Already formed an election league when we were in Portland last year."

"And you've just now chosen to tell me?"

"Don't be testy, Cass."

"It'll take you from Shore Acres."

"Why I want to bring the press association here this year. Course then we'll announce the campaign after that, to all the papers at the same time. Early January. Have a whole four months for planning, most of it taken care of from right here."

My thoughts on it were irrelevant, I knew that as soon as I saw the light shine in his eyes. It was as though someone had said "build North Bend" or "bring the railroad in" or "expand Shore Acres." If adventure lived in it, the whip of fame and risk, duty and contribution, then there he'd be, one more time, regardless of my reservations.

"You'll look fabulous up on the stage with me, the perfect backdrop to a political man." He kissed my nose to punctuate the sentiment.

The press association, editors from newspapers around the state, did arrive with their pads and pens and Cuban cigars. In between business meetings, they lounged on the veranda and played billiards on the third floor. Louie said my presence charmed them, those writing men. It wasn't my intent. Instead, I saw the time as opportunity to twist an arm or two for refugees and Red Cross campaigns.

The coast accommodated us by offering up one of its spectacular storms that rolled like purple velvet toward the cliff pushing spray and saltwater into sandstone, crashing surf higher than the spruce trees, and sending thunderous breakers against our cliff. Wind whistled through the trees and pushed against the house with whipping, explosive sounds. Candlelight flickered in the bedrooms. Froth and the memory of swells shattered against the veranda leaving the redwood floor slick and wet. Men scurried for the comfort of the living room. Appearing humbled, they watched in awe through the windows. Once experienced, a coastal storm is driven into memory, impossible to forget.

In January, when Louie announced his intent to challenge the sitting Republican governor in the primary, the statewide papers treated him kindly, calling him the "handsome stranger" from the south. They praised his platform promoting Oregon development and applauded his business successes and marveled at his good relationships with the working man. They didn't even criticize his more nationalistic note, about extending Oregon's progressive view on women's suffrage to the whole country. Kate adored him for that, but Louie saw the time had come. Women, after all, might decide to vote en masse for him.

He had five months to run, but the endorsement of the American Federation of Labor and its twenty-one thousand members, the Eagles, and the DAR promised to serve him well. His contacts with the Shriners and leadership in the Masons and the YMCA were all positive and brought his good name forward.

Before the May 17 election, he crisscrossed the state visiting cities such as Portland and Clackamas and then to out-of-the-way places he understood well. Towns such as The Dalles and Moro and little Grass Valley that felt disenfranchised by their distance from power.

Louie's letters arrived with his flowery scroll filling pages of description and excitement, about the state and the people he'd met. In Lakeview he apparently became so excited by the crowd's response that he donated his Ford at a dance scheduled to raise money for Red Cross. I heard about it later and told Kate, "That county just met their quota!"

I didn't go with him. My own Red Cross work and helping flu victims at Mercy Hospital occupied my energy, but more, I didn't think I had the stamina for such a lengthy tour. Louie looked askance at first when I said I wouldn't go. "I've an occupation at home," I said. An occupation with a purpose outside myself.

He might have thought it a lie if he had seen me as I saw myself the morning after he left, catching my image in the hall mirror as I descended the stairs. I didn't recognize the bloated face staring back or the lips that were thin and white as fear.

I handled correspondence that came from Louie's speeches and the ads placed to put his name before the public. People wrote kind letters, one from a Portland physician who said Louie'd helped a patient of his once, a total stranger, and that a man like Louie, with such humane and Republican principles, would serve us well in the governor's chair.

He would have, but Withycombe won.

Louie sent a letter the next day to the chief executive, who praised my husband. "He is a gracious man," the governor said, "who can lose one day and offer kind assistance on the next." I thought he might have hoped for an appointment in Withycomb's cabinet, but tragedy struck shortly after the election, and the governor died to be replaced by a man who had little knowledge of Louie.

"Are you sorry you lost?" I asked him one evening as we strolled through the garden. Donald had been working on a new variety of rose and told us he worried that he grew as many kinds of rose diseases in the soil as blooms. The sheepdog licked at Louie's hands as we walked.

"I'd have done a lot of good for our state. But the campaign itself was rousing. You know me, Cass. Always like something that stirs the blood."

After the election, Louie renewed with vigor his interest in Shore Acres. He studied food experiments and increasing production related to his famous Rhode Island reds. He expanded the deer park. Lottie's boy returned with tales of France and some seeds he shared with Louie. Benjamin still helped his father in the cranberry bogs. He'd escaped injury in the war and the flu and come home. The young veteran acted content to plant flowers and keep our pond clear of debris.

Louie corresponded with Thomas Edison that year. The famous inventor kept a botanical garden in Fort Myers, Florida. They exchanged information about species propagation and lilies.

I admired how he kept himself engaged with life. I'd see my husband often with the dogs, walking across the meadows, his head leaned toward big Mike's as they discussed some new way to monitor butterfat, or staring out toward the sea fading at sunset. But I noticed Louie had circles beneath his eyes, too, and he walked with a stoop added to his shoulders. Ten years or more we'd been building on Shore Acres, five since we'd moved here permanently. And while we were still both within our forties, still with so much promise and resource, I felt a shadow falling.

"Thought I'd find you here," Louie said as I watched him approach along the squares of roses toward the oriental pond where I sat. The copper herons placed in the west end of the water looked almost real, and I'd been gazing at the light shimmering against them. Two sheepdogs lay like rag mops at our feet. "What's on your pretty mind sitting here so quiet? You cold?" He warmed my hands in his.

"Just feeling old," I said.

"Aren't."

"Nearly half a century."

He shivered, exaggerated the horror. "Lots of time yet, Cass, lots to do. Think the new aeroplane industry has some potential. And Simpson Heights will take off, you wait and see. Got some ideas for another development company." He stretched his long legs out before him and leaned back on his elbows staring out over the pond. "Development. Always land to be claimed and sold. They're not making any more of that. Looking at selling some of the ships," he said avoiding my eyes. "Maybe even the shipbuilding."

"Nine hundred acres is more than enough," I said.

"Suppose it is."

"All the deaths," I said. "Nothing to stop this epidemic."

"Wish you wouldn't go there. Funny, me hoping you stay away from the hospital now. Just worry over you getting ill too."

"'Thick as a fir log,' Margaret would say. As tough, too. I doubt I'll get sick. Tending those boys and now children and grandparents, it's all so humbling."

"We've had our share of good and done it too."

"Will you marry again after I die?" I asked him.

He cocked his head to stare and wrinkled his brow. "Don't even think like that."

He sat up and pulled me into his side. His calloused fingers brushed some tendrils of hair that had fallen against my face. "You're getting morbid in your old age." He smiled. When I didn't respond, a worried look crossed his face. "Do you know something you haven't told me? Have you seen a doctor?"

"Am I the doctoring kind?"

He turned back to gaze at the pond. "Probably not. Teddy Roosevelt said it was a sign of weakness for a public man to marry after the death of a wife. Tragic he lost his in childbirth. I'd be strong." He squeezed my shoulder. "Besides, you'll outlive me."

"T. R. remarried. To Edith Carow."

"Did he? That's right, he did."

"Rather quickly after his wife's death, as grieving men are prone to."

"Not a subject I wish to pursue," he said pushing himself to standing. He reached to pull me up. "Especially with my wife."

Belle and Russ were married later that year, and at my request, Louie gave the Old Town house to them as a wedding gift. "I know it's yours to give, but…"

"Splendid idea," he said. "Should have thought of it myself. Just like Dad gave us, but without Ol' Harry hangin' around to bother them."

"Wish he still was," I said.

"We'll give them the parrot instead."

The wedding itself was catered and quiet. People seemed pleased that a fine family like the Towers should be teamed up with someone connected to a Simpson. Belle made a fine choice of a caring young man who had that quality children of physicians often have, noticing the ills of others and wanting to relieve them.

Best of all, the marriage meant Belle would remain in the area, and I hoped we'd widen our truce into more chosen acts of caring.

I meant to spend more time with my daughter, to share stories of a former life and marriage. But I didn't act to do it. Maybe if I hadn't been so tired, I told myself. Too tired to plan "volcanic" parties, too tired to ride, and too tired to confront my past. I was gaining vigor to make peace with my future.

Despite fatigue, the 1920s had to be announced with some extravagant event. So of course we held a New Year's Eve party at Shore Acres, one that began on a Saturday at dusk and would not end until Sunday, late.

Ice sculptures adorned the champagne circle to welcome admiring guests who arrived through a December drizzle. Inside, smaller replicas of fountains and flying birds and oversized ice mums became centerpieces on the long oak table surrounded by platters of the finest cuisine the San Francisco chef we'd imported for the event could imagine. Once again Louie agreed to send a donation to the charity of my choice equal to the party's expense.

A four-piece chamber group played Mozart from the music room while guests grazed on delicacies. Upstairs, the Victrola sang out familiar dance tunes, and the dozens of guests gave their best efforts to the movements.

"Rachel's wearing a rather risqué skirt," Annie said, standing beside me.

"Somewhat uplifting," I said.

"You need glasses," Annie said.

Some guests had chosen to go swimming, and I could hear them splashing from the Roman bath. A game with a ball bounced from hand to hand brought shouts. Other guests walked the grounds beneath umbrellas, their capes turning dark from the drizzle. Several guests walked with lanterns to look for deer in the fenced park. Lights were strung from the garden house along the pergolas toward the pond with smaller white lights dotting the translucent lunaria and poinsettias set beside the paths. Guests walked in a fairyland, and I'd been pleased with Donald James's rendition of my plan to light the leaves. The evening had a chill to it, but the food, friends, fire, and bootleg wine warmed everyone.

We were all to assemble in the living room an hour or so before midnight to toast the end of 1919 and the beginning of 1920. That was the plan. Louie would narrate a version of Wister's *The Virginian,* and we'd have a little play with cowboys and the like.

I looked around for Edgar's wife. The two had come north from California, and this was her first event at Shore Acres. I spotted her talking to Kate and Charlie Winsor in the music room. Her bobbed hair gleamed in the light, and her hands drew designs in the air as she spoke.

Louie was nowhere in sight. Neither, now that I noticed it, was Edgar. A prickling began up the back of my neck, remembering an Advent season some years back, and I wondered if Louie and I might begin the twenties with another rousing fight. I hoped not. I had become accustomed to peacefulness of companionship rather than the rush of angry passion. But old habits die hard, and despite myself, my eyes scanned the room to see if any women were absent among the guests.

"Have you seen Louie?" I asked.

Lottie stood beside the door, her arms crossed over her plump chest. She looked awkward as the guest I'd insisted she attend as rather than the maid. "Maybe he gets ready."

I shook my head. "He's been dressed in his jeans and spurs for hours. Don't know what those things'll do to the floor."

I started through the entry to see if Louie had taken a stroll in the garden when a loud roar rose up from the ocean side. It did not come from the sea.

I turned to see what made the racket.

Edgar's yellow palomino charged in first, Edgar astride, arms waving, spurs digging in. Behind came Louie, mounted, the riders shouting and whooping like madmen. They ducked their heads as they urged their mounts across the veranda and through the French doors on into the living room.

The animals clopped across the wood floors, stumbled on the Navajo Rugs, scuttled people and chairs to the perimeter like cockroaches leaving light.

Edgar's wild and unpredictable stallion flared its nostrils, and his eyes showed more white than brown as it twisted and turned, flicking its white tail, then bunched itself together in the middle as though it would leap. Louie's gelding pranced near the fireplace catching the iron poker by its back leg and scaring itself and the rest of us when the metal clattered against the hearth. Both men looked perfectly pleased with themselves.

Edgar kept shouting and pressing the reins against the palomino's neck, and I could see the animal, frightened and confused, ready to bolt but for the too-tight bit. I had visions of him dumping Edgar in the man's intoxicated state, and terrified, charging people in the room, maybe even killing someone seeking escape.

"Happy New Year!" Edgar shouted oblivious to the lack of joy his entrance brought. He swirled one of J. B. Stetson's finest just inches beneath the chandelier.

Someone had to act, I could see that, someone with some height and strength, someone able to step across their fears to try to settle the horse. No one moved.

So I did.

I stepped in front of Edgar's stallion. With both hands, I reached for the bridle now lathered at the mouth. Foam and spittle splattered the front of my satin dress. The horse lifted me from the floor as it raised its head, and I had the briefest sensation of floating before letting go. Grounded, I reached again, wrenching my fingers near the bit.

"Easy boy. Easy." I spoke with as controlled a voice as I could both to gentle the horse and to calm my heart pounding like a driven surf. Behind me I could hear a man's voice shouting at Louie, but I kept my eyes on the bridle and the horse. I could smell the horses' fright.

Edgar's animal sidestepped, bringing its hindquarters to crash against the myrtlewood table, which startled him anew. He lunged forward now, knocking me to the side. Still hanging on to the bridle with but one hand, I shouted, "Someone! Cover his eyes!"

Benjamin tore off his coat and grabbed the other side of the bridle, higher up on the leather. He dropped his jacket over the horse's head with his other hand. I cupped my palm over the horse's nostril and got beneath its neck, my back to its sweaty chest, the thrust of his legs moving against my back. "Easy," I said. "Easy, now. Easy, now."

"Hey!" Edgar complained, aware of a shift as his horse quieted. "Who stopped the merry-go-round?"

Louie must have come to his senses then too and seen the terror in people's eyes and the danger their antics entertained. He dismounted, and I saw that Charlie circled around Benjamin and me now. The stallion had calmed some, but a wary fear emanated through its heaving chest.

"Looks like the ride's over," Louie said, pulling Edgar to the floor.

Edgar stood with a sappy grin pasted on his face as his wife moved up beside him, her mouth open in amazement.

Edgar glared at me, then, standing with my hands on his horse. "Why didn't you just tell me you wanted to ride? I'd o' let you have him."

"Not even the devil could tell you anything and hope to have you hear it," I said.

Edgar's wife grabbed at him as though he were a wayward boy and led him toward the music room despite his protests and people's muted, tension-lessened chuckles.

Both horses had quieted enough that Benjamin led the palomino out, stroking his nose as they walked. Charlie took Louie's gelding from him, said something to his friend. They both looked over at me. My jaw clenched and I brushed the smudge from my dress. Charlie led the horse out.

Our guests moved toward the center, and the giddiness that follows fear conquered began to sparkle around the room. Chairs were righted. Broken glass picked up and discarded. Lottie rushed in to settle rugs and soothe still-ruffled guests. Already people began to tell each other the stories I knew would be legend.

"You always were a fine horsewoman, Cass," Louie said as he approached me. He looked sheepish. "Last ride I ever take in the living room, I promise."

"It was an incredibly foolish thing for you to do."

"More crazy for you, of all people, to try to stop us." He wiped some of the horse's spittle mixed with my sweat from the side of my face. "I am sorry." He wore his Labrador eyes, then took me in his arms. People clapped so they couldn't hear him say, "Would've been a poor way to begin the twenties, without you in them."

I was never afraid of Edgar's horse after that. The animal had taught me something, that all my impulses weren't just to please myself, just to "satisfy

Cass" as Margaret contended. I could act for others, even in an instant when I hadn't planned a thing and had mere seconds to choose. That night I had chosen well, and I was pleased to have the memory.

The smell of smoke routed Belle and Russ from the Old Town house that September morning of 1920. That and their poodle's insistent barking and Annabelle's elderly screech. Flames already engulfed the south side of the house, the side with the wisteria climbing the fence blocking out the mill whose sparks from the burner probably started the fire.

Belle stood shivering in the fall night that attracted neighbors with blankets to wrap around them. Others rushed inside as best they dared beside Russ who dragged out photographs and papers and whatever treasured gifts that might be spared. They survived with the clothes on their backs and the dogs safe and the parrot, opinionated, beside them.

Smoldering wood and the smell of damp ash drifted over the town along with a sadness that a house that had been a part of the history of the river region had vanished.

"We'll build again," Russ told us. And they would stay with us while they did.

Russ graciously allowed Louie to review the plans and offer suggestions as only a Simpson can.

"Daddy never got to see that house," Belle said.

"Never took the time," I said. "The house was there."

"He always called Shore Acres 'Louie's Castle.' Everyone in Hoquiam did."

"Louie's castle! Louie's castle."

Louie laughed along with the bird.

"Think we should plan a party while you're here," Louie said. "A grand bash to celebrate elk season or duck hunting or the 1920s we're already ten months into. Call in a band and have people dress up as sheiks and Arabian girls. Doesn't that sound promising?"

"What does that have to do with hunting?" I said.

"The girls'll look better sporting navel jewels 'stead of Winchesters," he said. He wiggled his cigar at me and grinned.

I watched Russ and Belle exchange glances, but they said nothing to discourage their host's newfound excitement. For myself, I noticed that the thought of a gathering painted weariness over zest.

It was a fine dance. And people did come dressed in costumes with veils of flowing gossamer and filmy pants and men wearing fezzes and hats with plumes and others wrapped like sultans of the sand. Swords were worn at waists, and sometime in the night it was decided Louie's guns should be donned instead. It was, after all, a hunting party. A Tiffany chandelier in the ballroom became an unfortunate target along with the plaster ceiling.

In the morning, there'd be achy heads and wild tales to tell, and Louie'd call the plasterers in for repairs and the stories would be told for months, maybe years to come. At least he'd imported no camels for the event.

I did not enjoy the party much, though it added to the refugee coffers. It took all I had to greet people and wear the face they expected of me, gracious and vivacious when what I felt in my chest was a weight as great as the new refrigerator we'd purchased for the kitchen. I thought Belle watched me with wary eyes. Annie came over to me once and suggested I rest a bit, but I prattled on instead about the new furnishings I'd designed for a guest suite.

Annie and Gus left early. Annie kissed me on the check as she was leaving and said something about how cool I felt. "You take care," she warned. "You'll catch your *death* in those flimsy pants." She still reminded me of Margaret.

Lottie, too, serving Lem's parfait in tall glasses, wove her way in and out among the guests, but paused by me and said with hushed but anchored words: "Think about it. You should go upstairs."

"That's why you want to serve rather than be a guest," I said. "So you can boss me."

She just smiled, revealing that gap between her teeth. "I don't trust your electric buzzer to call for help," she said.

"As soon as everyone is settled."

Kate came over after Lottie stopped to talk with her and with a gentle hand beneath my elbow said, "I'm a frazzle with all these people. Let's go up to your rooms and just rest."

She didn't look a bit frazzled with her greyhound frame dressed in pink gossamer over her sequined naval jewel. But I agreed and we wound our way up the stairs, pausing on each step. The wood of the banister felt smooth and firm beneath my palm.

I don't remember much about her helping me undress except her light touch as she removed the arm bracelets and tugged at the hat that held my long veil. She smelled of lilies and lemon. But the cool sheets against my face and the salty ocean scent through the open bay window soothed me as nothing had. If the parrot spoke, I didn't hear her.

When I awoke, Louie was sitting at my writing desk, and the sunrise, not content to stay in the East, sent its pink into the western sky, causing the ocean to blush. Sea lions barked and that was probably what woke me, that and the sound of the sea.

"Feeling better?" he asked. He looked tired but clearheaded. He walked to stand over me, and his hand was cool on my forehead.

"Just needed some rest," I said. "What are you working on?"

My chin pointed to the writing desk and the photograph album I recognized as the one with the picture and poem of the child. It lay open to another page, the black paper covered with silver script from his hand.

"Want me to read it to you?" he asked.

If it was sad, like the one longing for a child, I wasn't sure I did. "I read the first one. A long time ago. About a child."

"Did you? You never said."

I hesitated. "I felt so, well…guilty, I guess. For depriving you."

"Maybe you couldn't have," he said.

"Maybe. But I might have tried. For your sake.

"Over and done, Cass. No use lamenting."

"Will it make me cry? Your new poem?"

He laughed without joy. "Can only count one time I think I saw you cry. Me the cause of it too. Maybe two, not counting when the dogs died. Always thought you grieved dogs better than people."

"They love unconditionally. A difficult thing to lose."

"Doubt I'll make you cry with this one," he said, "unless it's the wretched grammar."

"Go ahead then." I pulled on the satin bedjacket I guessed Lottie'd left beside the pillow.

"Legend of the Shore Acres Cave-Man," he began.

"When you were a cave-man
In days of old

And dwelt in your cavern deep
And the ocean beat relentlessly
And wild winds sang you to sleep,
Sometimes a note—sweeter far than the wind—
Called you forth to your wave-hewn door,
And you looked in vain thro' the mist and rain
All up and down the shore
To find a trace of the singer sweet
Who awakened an indistinct dream
That a spirit of strife and a wild weird
Life
Had never given a gleam...

"There's more," he said. His face held the look of a small boy awaiting some recognition for having done his lessons well.

"I'm listening." I couldn't decide if I was the singer sweet or some distant dream he harbored. Or did he lament our "strife and wild weird life?"

The poem went on to talk about being haunted by the melody and how he then saw the singer, a mermaid, beautiful and desirable that he wished he could pull to his side so she'd never go away.

She gave in answer a smile so sweet
And came in nearer shore.
"My home" she said, "is down deep in the sea
You've heard the legend and lore,
How a mermaid never can love a
Man
Who lives upon the earth,
He never would understand her well
You must long in Vain with lonely pain
O, you wild man of the cave."

"Who's it about?" I asked. I wondered if he'd written an ode to another long-lost love, one I'd never been privy to.

"Me," he said. "Mistakes and longing and grabbing and hurting the people I loved most."

The poem went on to talk of his capturing her, the mermaid, luring her into his cave and breaking the taboos, kissing her and holding her close and then taking a last gaze at her. But when he looked, nothing but seaweed and ocean spray remained because he'd broken the rule.

And with saddened heart you saw depart
The soul of "What might have been"
And never again to your cavern home
Came the song of the love now gone.

"It isn't finished," he said.

He'd never read a poem to me he'd written and he acted almost embarrassed.

"You still have fame and fortune," I said. "What do you long for you think you can't have?"

"You," he said surprising me. "I've never really had you."

"Me?"

He swallowed. "I have your company, have that. And your attention, often. But you've always kept a part of you from me. Never really... Always found a way to avoid difficult things, and I let you. Then did foolish things to make you not trust me, go farther inside, so deep I think you never will come out, not really."

"What might have been, in your poem?"

"The greatest love ever," he said. "Between a man and a woman and the children they bring into the world. Had all the money a man could ask for, all the adventure and even some fame. Never had that, though. Never that.

"You couldn't trust me, and I did things to confirm your judgment. I couldn't love you enough to make up for your fears, and you did things to push me away when I tried. Kind of pathetic, for all our wealth and grandeur."

He spread his arm around the room, as exquisite as any hotel suite in Europe. "Believe Red and Gus and Kate and Charlie have more. I envy them. At least, their peace."

He was quiet a time and then he said, "Maybe that's all I wanted, peace." He flipped the pen back and forth between two fingers, his thoughts sent out to the sea. "Something I couldn't finesse or demand or use Dad's money or power to make happen." He walked over to the side of the bed and sat down. "Might be unfair to assume you kept me from it. You didn't. Choice a person has to make by himself."

"How to live and how to die," I said. "Two things we're forced to do alone." I shivered. "Terrifying, isn't it? For two people who've always kept a crowd around."

"I do love you Cassie and I always thought it would be enough."

"But it isn't."

"Full of regret," he said. "For what we did to each other and Belle. And...others."

"For our sins," I said, spitting out the last word.

"Not sure I really know what sin is. Breaking the rules?"

"Being separated from God, I think, and letting the distance fill with longing and emptiness instead of loving someone, no matter what, and allowing grace to take the pain."

He picked up the edge of the pillowslip and wiped the wetness that threatened my eyes and dribbled down to my ears.

"Never meant to make you sad, Cass. Nor blame you for a thing. Just seeing you lying here this morning, so still, so pale. Walked over to see if you were breathing. Had this panicked feeling you might be gone." He shook his head. "Silly of me. Didn't expect to read you the poem or have it end with tears."

I stopped his hand from dabbing at my face and gently tapped his knuckles with my own. Then I kissed the back of his fingers. "I'm just so very sorry," I said, "that you've never gotten what you wanted."

He dragged the back of his palm across my forehead. "You get some more sleep," he said and bent to kiss me. He held his face next to mine for a time.

"Finish your poem," I said. "You can read it to me when I wake up."

Louie did work on his poem, and he promised to read it to me several times later in the year. Something else always needed tending: the Old Town house rebuilding, the ranch and the dairy.

It wasn't until January of 1921 that he pulled the black-covered album from the luggage and sat beside me in our stateroom to read.

"Keep your mind off the bar," he said. "Going to be a rough crossing. Sea's growling today."

We were sailing out from Charleston Beach, and south, to see if specialists could help my labored breathing and the slowing of my heart. Lottie traveled with us in another room. Belle had planned to join us if it looked like I'd have to stay. It wasn't the plan I wanted, but I had my suspicions sponging on the fluid of my face, the pinched shoes on my swollen ankles.

"You remember," Louie said, summarizing the poem. "The caveman had just made a poor decision and tried to hang on to the mermaid."

"And she'd disappeared, the very thing he longed for most in his life was gone. I remember." The sea was rougher than I'd remembered and I felt a little sick. "And you longed for something you can't have."

"Right. None of us can have it. Only one thing is really lasting," he said, not telling me what he thought that was. "So here's the ending:

"And all the waves that lashed your caves
Hummed out in a monotone:
'You may take what you want, you
Man from the cave,
But your memory will always be haunted.
Muscle and vim will sometimes win
But *not keep the thing you wanted.*'"

"You don't say what that is," I said. I took a deep breath, admitting at last that these times with him were numbered now, as they always really were. "It's not just me, as you said before, is it?"

"Different for different people," Louie said.

"I think that isn't so. The only things that are lasting are decisions that feed the soul. They're the same choices, for all of us. The ones that let you keep what you *really* want and need."

"Getting theological on me in your old age?" he said. He smiled from his mouth to his eyes, and I felt of rush of love for him that spread through me like a flooding stream in spring.

"Better late than never," I said.

"It's still you, Cass. That's what I always want to keep."

"You know you can't."

"Well, sure, I know we'll all die sometime," he said, almost annoyed that the discussion was turning to life and death. "Sorry I read this now. Read you something lighter."

"No, Louie. I've avoided it as best I could, but now, acknowledging it, will be a gift."

He closed the photo album and looked at me. "What are you talking about?"

"I'm dying, Louie."

"Don't be a goose," he said and stood. "We'll get you to this specialist and everything'll be fine. Should have insisted years ago. You wait and see."

I shook my head. "Not this time."

His eyes looked frightened for an instant, the way Edgar's horse had the night of the decade party.

"Time to tie up loose ends," I said. "Knowing about your death can be a treasure, if you don't deny it."

He paced around the room. "I don't like talking about this, Cass. You make it sound hopeless. Medicine has all kinds of cures."

"Hopeful, Louie. Because I can say to you all the things I always wished I had. Or write them down. Not leave any unfinished words before I die. Not to those I love. Not to you or Belle or Kate or others."

He stared at me as though seeing me for the first time.

"Think we've crossed the bar," he said then. He set the photo album on the bedside table, tapped his fingers against the black silk cover. He stared out at the sea. "How long have you known?"

"Awhile. I visited a doctor in Portland the year I saw Margaret. He told me there was nothing to be done. My heart will just wear out. I think that's what it's doing now."

My husband never did do well with pain and disappointment, and I could see him struggling to defend against them, against a thing he couldn't buy or tame or charm away.

"Feel like walking on deck?" I said. "I'll bundle up."

He sniffed, his back still to me. "Pretty windy."

"Oh, come on. Let's look at Shore Acres, from this angle."

He nodded then and turned to help me stand. His eyes were red, and they didn't meet mine as he helped me pull on a heavy wool coat. Then arm in arm we walked to the port side of the ship just as we approached Gregory Point and the lighthouse and then began the breathtaking sight of Shore Acres.

"I was the happiest there," I said, "even though I loved the Old Town house."

"Don't talk in the past tense," Louie said. "You'll come back here, after we see the doctor."

The estate seemed to move across the screen of our eyes, dipping in the swells: the tennis court, the barn, the house. Our little Simpson Beach cove and then the barn and milk house and home of the old Collver farm. The rocks and sea lions watched as we eased by.

Louie bent to kiss me, then pulled my shoulder into his chest, staking me like a young peach tree.

Beyond the rocks and buildings stood the trees that marked the opening to the garden, that wonderful garden that couldn't be seen from the sea.

I said, "You can't tell that garden's there. Can't see it or smell it or touch it or hear it or taste it."

"It's there, all right," Louie said. "If you were standing beneath those trees, you'd smell wet earth and feel the cool breeze on your face. Hear finches and sea gulls and watch Donald digging in dirt."

"I know. But from here, I can only imagine it. I have no evidence. That's the part I never wanted to believe. I always thought I had to experience it myself to know a thing was true. And if I couldn't feel it or will it so, then I didn't believe in it."

"We're not talking gardens anymore, are we, Cass?"

"No," I said. "We're talking about choosing to trust that something's really so. And then acting that way, even if you can't see it or be sure."

"It's so that I love you," he said.

"I know."

Shore Acres drifted away behind us, cedars and firs like slender feathers against the sky. I heard the sea lions barking in the distance. I sighed and leaned into this man who had taken me places inside myself and in this world further than I'd dreamed I'd go.

"I thought it was independence and pleasure and adventure that I wanted, and the rush of spinning in trees. And standing out in a crowd."

"And?" he said, listening without rushing me, waiting for me to finish.

"But I got all that, and 1 still felt hungry. I didn't feel filled up until I stopped thinking about myself, started giving away to others. It was so late, though, in my life. I regret that."

"Takes the longer days to bring on the bloom," Louie said. "Whether it's a single blooming plant like a century cactus or those columbines that show up year after year. Won't bloom until the light's enough."

"Columbines: 'I will not let you go.'"

He squeezed my shoulder. I felt the spray on my face and heard the swoosh of our ship slicing the sea. I'd grown up on the Pacific though I'd started late in my years.

"Can water and stake and prune, but what you have to have in order to bring forth a glorious flower is more light," Louie said. "It's what every gardener knows."

"More light and love," I said. "Guess that's what I always hoped for. I just never knew how to ask."

EPILOGUE

LOTTIE

Louie Simpson took his wife to San Francisco. I sailed along, in January 1921. Another *wit-litz*, she called it, a going-over place. Strong winds tried to push us back. I held her hand when Louie wasn't by her and told her many times this ship had crossed the ocean and would again. She would too, though I did not know then this was a lie.

"I've always been a fraidy-cat, about some things," she said. I served her unbuttered toast and tea while Louie talked cargo with the captain.

"Not true," I told her. "I remember you with your big feather hat and your little waist and you stood up in my cedar canoe. You were no fraidy-cat then!"

She smiled. "Who would've thought it would end this way?"

Her tone was as sad as a lone goose calling for its mate. I felt tears burn behind my nose. She looked like a milkweed pod, so fragile and all puffed up. Not at all the woman who could make men's heads turn while their wives longed to come to one of her parties.

I said, "Just going to the doctor, that's all we're doing today. Think about it. We'll come back." I patted her hand.

"No, Lottie," she said. "You and I were always honest with each other. Well, at least you were with me."

I nodded 'cause I knew she spoke the truth then. We were not just going to the doctor. We were going south for her to die.

Louie came back. Later, I saw them watching their Shore Acres disappear from sight.

We took a suite, she called it, in the Palace Hotel. More like several houses held together by an alley and a roof. We stayed there two months with Louie sitting by her side, rubbing her legs, wiping her forehead until he looked ragged too. She got frailer and more peaked-looking. The doctors came and checked her and said no hospital would help her heart. Her waterworks wanted to shut down.

Her sister came once and told her their mother had gone before them, in February.

"She'll be waiting for you," Margaret said. "Just went on *ahead* to get things ready."

"Will she be setting her clocks?" She had a twinkle in her eye. Margaret saw it too so knew she teased. She was still well enough to tease. The two cried together later. I saw that, Margaret holding her sister's hand.

Belle came too and stayed the month of March, and they talked quietlike seeming to be pleased to be in each other's presence.

Louie's wife had endocarditis and nephritis, Dr. Rothschild called it. An illness around her heart, which was bigger than it should have been, or so he said. Didn't seem anyone could have too big a heart, but Louie's wife did.

In early April, a decision came. By private train, Louie moved us all from the Palace to a furnished house, south, to Burlingame, California, on Easton Drive. She loved the ride down the peninsula, all wooded and the sea. It made her talk of her first trip west from New York.

We stayed on a street with big houses and old trees in the yards and flowers in bloom. Rows and rows of old eucalyptus kept off the breeze. The hospital nearby once treated tuberculosis patients, like Harry.

I wondered why she didn't want to die at home with family and friends around? Must have said my thoughts out loud 'cause she said once, "I want no memories of my illness at Shore Acres. It should always be a place of joy and fun. Nothing sad or negative. Nothing to overshadow the love that built it and the gardens."

Louie had his Hudson coupe driven to Eugene and then shipped south. He drove her around in it one day to see the flowers when she felt well enough and insisted. They were like children. Excited over an outing. Louie especially. I think he thought it meant she might get better. I knew she wouldn't. You could see her illness crowding out who she was and had ever been, even though I applied the powder and lip rouge as she asked.

Louie carried her to the Hudson and wrapped her lap in a Pendleton blanket, though it wasn't cold that day. She waved and smiled through her hat veil and wore high color on her cheeks. I think about it! They had such a good time!

When they came back I overheard them while I puttered about her room. Louie held her small hand in his and sat beside her on the white bedspread.

"I love you, Cassie," he said.

She was still a long time, then said, "I believe you truly do. I might never have believed that if it hadn't been for this, the way you've been here for my dying."

"Maybe I wouldn't have been so noble if I hadn't known. I might even have betrayed you again," Louie said.

She shook her head and ran her fingers though his gray-streaked hair. "You would've been there, loving me. I just wouldn't have noticed, always so wrapped up in myself."

After that she slept more. Breathed so I could hear her in the night, had trouble swallowing. Two nurses came to tend her. Not sure what I added. Bathed her, washed her fingers, and rubbed oil on her tiny hands with tapered nails. Hoped she felt precious as I cared for her. Spooned her blackberry tea and told her of the old days along the Coos Bay and the Slough.

I listened, too, as she told it all, what she remembered of her choices and her life. She'd smile sometimes and look far away, and I suppose I gave her that, a chance to remember what had been, with favor. Friends give each other that. Both ways.

Louie held her hand most times, and I watched him wipe often at eyes that looked worn, like old walnuts left in white sand.

Kate Winsor stayed four or five days. I heard them talking, about solitary journeys. Mrs. Winsor'd gone to Shore Acres before coming south. She brought both the Scientist's book and a Bible, as requested. Not wearing any shoes, she read from the Big Book. Curled her feet under her and sat at the corner of her friend's bed and wrote letters as she was asked to.

They laughed together, too, and I was pleased that in her dying days Louie's wife had the sound of joy in her damaged heart. Everyone should have the privilege of knowing when their time is short so they can grieve and smile and touch the ones they love and each feel settled in their soul before one leaves the others behind.

Louis Simpson's wife died on April 30, 1921. The services the following week, May 3, took an hour in the morning. Louie sent word back to North Bend. Benjamin told me later that all the businesses but one or two closed down at 9:30 A.M., and flags were lowered at City Hall when Louis Simpson's wife was laid to rest. People said she gave her all for causes that helped others. Some say her work made her die fast. I think they helped her live.

Louie put me on the train back to North Bend, gave me a slow time to think and remember all she said. He drove his Hudson back. His brother Edgar met him and drove his new Maxwell just shipped in from Roseburg, but there were no antics on that trip. A sober two, they were, they said.

Redheaded Annie came by my home some weeks later. We talked of family and friends and then, her fingers drawing imaginary pictures on my tablecloth, she asked if I thought our friend would go on to heaven. I am not sure why she asked me. I could not even say her name. It is the custom of my people that once a soul has left its earthly body, we do not speak their name out loud, not until a mourning time is passed. It is a sign of respect and of letting the person leave, not calling her back through the sound of her name spoken by someone she loved. I had set myself a half a year from the time that she was buried until I would speak her name again.

"Who knows the ways of another person's heart?" I told Annie.

She blinked her eyes fast like a hummingbird's wings. "Well I know it's not possible to be *sure* about anyone. Not ours to judge. But I thought she might have said something. In her last days. That would be a clue."

I thought of words we'd exchanged.

"After Mrs. Winsor visited, she lost her fears," I said. "Her eyes were not flighty like little finches moving from branch to branch. Not even at night or when the pain would rake itself across her body like a slow breaker. Never knew when one of those waves would be a sneaker come to take her away. But after Mrs. Winsor came, she slept better and looked peaceful, even with the pain. Like sunset over a dead-calm sea.

"Mrs. Winsor bowed her head sometimes," I continued, "and said words over her. She was never told to stop. She said once, just a day or so before she crossed over, that she was glad she would not go alone. Thought she heard someone singing over her. Said it sounded like a mermaid or something even prettier."

"Did she?" Annie asked. Her eyes leaked but had brightness too.

"I did not ask what she meant. The book that had pages folded over was the King James one, though," I said, remembering.

"Perhaps she did choose well, then," Annie said.

Edgar stayed with Louie at Shore Acres when they returned. Louie mourned there, his grief exposed like a snag in a sand dune. He told me Belle would come to visit in a month or two to select special things of her mother's. "Anything she wants," he said, "Belle can have it. Know Cass would have wanted that."

But Belle did not come before the tragedy, the second of that year.

Friends stayed with Louie at Shore Acres. It was a gathering place even without a party. Someone said a Fourth of July event would be good for Louie, to bring him from his sadness as though such actions can shorten a grieving time.

Benjamin and I helped Lem set up for events the day before, July 3. Then my son drove our buggy home following the midnight fireworks.

When everyone else had retired, Louie walked down to Simpson Beach. He wrote there for a time until he saw the glow, he said. About 2:00 A.M.

That's what the paper reported, that he was reading and writing poetry on the beach when he saw it, the glow from the fire that swallowed Shore Acres.

By sunrise, only the flagpole, the fireplace, concrete urns, and steps overlooking the sea still stood.

Everyone escaped. Mr. and Mrs. Ede noticed smoke first and set the alarm. Mr. Ede climbed up to the second floor to let Edgar escape. Lem couldn't save a thing. The Byler girls, Alice and Dorothy, and their mother just back from Berkeley, lost all their trunks and clothes, and neighbors bought blankets and things for warmth. Edgar crawled out an upstairs window and said later he'd lost one hundred dollars in gold he kept hidden in a drawer. He found it three days later. Melted. One of his prized boxer dogs died too.

Louie placed an ad of regrets in the *Harbor* telling those who mailed him statements or correspondence or bills to send again as all was lost. All the fine furnishings. All the paintings and even some of the jewelry Belle was to have gotten from her mother. Eaten by flames. All but the memories gone.

None of it insured, something that was of no surprise to me but seemed to startle those who heard it. Insurance is a frail thing I thought shows lack of faith.

It was a sad time after that for Louie. He did not mourn well, had no family to tell him when to stop. He broke his leg while surveying the new Coos Hotel and had to stay a time at Winsors. His Simpson Heights did not take off as he wished.

But he never lost hope.

When six months had passed, I came to visit Louie at Shore Acres. He was staying in one of the staff houses, but that day he worked in the garden digging out lily pads from the pond by himself. The little fountain sounded like spring, though it was fall.

"It suits you," I said, "from where I stand."

"Nothing humbles a man more than doing dirty work." He grinned up at me. "How do you think the urns look?"

"Good place for them." He'd had them set at the entrance to the Japanese pool. "I came to plant a locust tree. For Cassie."

"Did you?" He acted pleased. "Remember right, locusts have something to do with 'affection beyond the grave.' Don't know how well it'll do in this climate."

"I just like the looks of them," I said.

"Thinking about planting some lilies for her, myself. Did you notice the height of those pines?" He pointed toward the sea. "Really took off this year. Well, let's do it then," he said and stepped out of the muck.

Not far from the garden house, we dug together and gentled the small tree into the peat, pressing the loamy earth around its roots. I liked the smell. It was a windy October morning, and few blooms were hardy enough to still offer up color.

"I have a gift for you," I said when we finished. I walked back to the buggy and returned, handing him a basket.

"Cassie tried her hand at one and honored our custom by giving her first basket away. She gave it to me. The basket teacher often gets the student's first. I give it to you now," I said and placed the melon-sized gift in his open hands. "Giving heals."

"I'll remember that," he said. He turned the cedar-root-and-fern basket around in his hands. "I never knew she made something like this. Not half bad," he said, surprise in his voice.

"She had many sides to her and a hard time choosing which would be first."

"Don't we all," Louie said. "Don't we all."

I asked him that day what he was writing the night Shore Acres burned. He wiped his hands and asked me to wait while he went to the house, then brought an album filled with photographs and poems. We sat on the cement steps overlooking the pond and looked at them.

The first photo was of a child whose face could not be told, and in the picture Louie gazed at him from a distance. Other black and white pictures showed his sister and brothers in the garden and one of Cassie on horseback wearing a feather hat and not a sidesaddle. That one took up one whole page. Another was of Annie with binoculars staring at the sea. Louie and Cassie were together in several, and Belle and Russ stood in one photo, Edgar too.

"Sure miss Cassie's dogs around," he said when I turned to several small photos of my friend with her poodles and setters and boxer dogs. "Never could spoil them the way she did. Thanks for taking the sheepdogs, Lottie."

"It is a likeable thing for me."

In one photograph, several people lounged on the lawn in Arabian costumes and must have been snapped when they were rehearsing for that party.

Louie'd written things beneath each image, and in between was a long poem he said was about a mermaid.

"Nice you save these," I said.

He nodded. "All I've left of her except the memories." He looked wistful. "People ask if I'll rebuild, and I might if I can pull the funds together. I just might. Every man has to have a dream, right, Lottie? Another Shore Acres may as well be mine."

I turned to a picture of a gravesite. Beneath it, Louie had written, "Consider the lilies how they grow; they toil not, they spin not."

"After Kate visited, she wanted me to read that verse and others around it," he said. "Marked three other places in the New Testament. About Peter speaking repentance at Pentecost, and a verse in Hebrews about expecting better of a person and hope being the anchor of a soul. Toward the end, she made me find one in James and mark it too. Said it was to remind her of the uncertainty of this life and committing ourselves and our affairs to God's providence."

"Annie would be pleased to know this," I said.

"Would she? I'll stop out and tell her."

The last picture in the book was one of Cassie. She was wearing a dark robe, wrapped, as she sat on one of the wicker lounges on the veranda. Most of the wind shades were drawn to block the breeze. Her face was already puffy, and she did not smile. She gazed off toward the sea.

"Took this the day before we sailed south," he said. He swallowed. "Last one I ever took of her."

Next to it he'd written another poem and titled it "The *Last* Day."

The sun is setting o'er the sea
Now at the close of day.
Tomorrow it will rise again
But I will be away.

"It is always hardest to be the one left behind," I said, "on any *wit-litz*."

"Suppose you're right. Guess she's saved from that misery, anyway. He put his arm around me to walk me back to my buggy. "She always hated to be last."

When the huckleberries popped out the following year, Louie discovered, too, that healing comes from giving, and he gave his heart away again. He married, and he and his wife, Lela, adopted two children, little girls.

For a time they lived in one of the staff houses near the garden. Then one day in 1923 the schooner *Brush* wrecked on Simpson Reef. Boards of Simpson lumber washed up on Simpson Beach and at Cape Arago. Louie took it as a sign and dreamed again: of an estate, built on the cliffs.

He rescued what he could and hired an architect and rebuilt. Not quite as grand as the first. Only two stories, but still longer than a giant fir tree. It overlooked the sea right where the first had with the big gardens still lush and hidden beyond the Monterey pines.

In 1927, with tulips "bobbing in the breeze and daffodils dotting green," as Cassie would describe it, the Simpson family moved into their Shore Acres overlooking the sea: Louie, his wife, and their children.

Louie still dreams. If I think about it, next to remembering his Cass, I would say he most of all loves watching his children play in the shade of the cypress trees.

Gardeners still look after Cassie's roses and rhododendrons and hundreds of lilies and columbine. I still imagine her walking there, bending to smell a rose.

AUTHOR'S NOTE

Cassie Hendrick Stearns Simpson interested me from the first time I stepped beneath the cypress trees at Shore Acres. What kind of woman inspired a legendary garden and fueled the passion for a great estate? Where did she come from? How did she make her choices?

The journey to my version of the answers traversed a path with twists and swift surprises not unlike a stroll through Louie Simpson's garden laid out with hints of hidden coves and the promise of crashing seas. The lives of Cassie and Louie were not always as they seemed and inspired the title, *A Gathering of Finches*, which is derived from the multiple meanings for *charming*: "the power or quality of pleasing," "confused voices or bird calls," and "a gathering of finches."

With few exceptions, the accounting of events as portrayed is factual. Pages from the Hendrick family Bible document Cassie's birth in 1871, that of her sister, Margaret, three years later, and her parents' wedding date. A copy of Cassie and Josiah Stearns's marriage certificate from New York confirmed where the journey began. Cassie's great-nephew (Margaret's grandson), Fred G. Foster, living in Aberdeen, Washington, noted that when Cassie came from Corning the second time following the birth of Belle, a friend named Anne or Annie came with them. A woman named Annie living on the Oregon coast was remembered in Cassie's will. Whether she married a farmer is unknown.

Fred Foster also related the reason for the delay in the Simpsons' marriage, an event later confirmed by other family members. Pages from newspaper accounts from the *Grays Harbor Washingtonian* dated 1892 through 1902 indicate when Cassie and Louis likely encountered each other in Hoquiam, Washington, and when they left. Their paths must have crossed at gala parties, gatherings of lumber barons, or when Louie built an apartment complex within sight of the Stearnses' home. The press even recorded the nature of theatrical events, illnesses of Louie and Cassie, visits by Louie's mother, and the tragic encounter with Robert Hunt.

The nature of Cassie's first husband, Josiah Stearns, his role in the development of the Grays Harbor area, and his kind, meticulous, and sometimes quirky nature, and the dates of his marriages were confirmed by newspaper reports and from family anecdotes shared by Mr. Foster, Bud and Peg Day, and Elizabeth Lambie of Mendocino, California (granddaughter of George Emerson and John Soule and great-niece of Josiah Stearns's second wife). Photos of Josiah were located by Elizabeth Lambie. The date of Margaret's marriage was recorded in local newspapers. Most newspaper accounts about Washington were provided through the diligent and generous efforts of Hoquiam residents and historians Harold Schmidtke and Cecil Herrington. The story of Louie's penchant for a London tie was first noted in a memoir by Frank Lamb published in 1948 as *Fifty Years in Hoquiam*.

Confirmation of Louie and Cassie's actual wedding date could not be found in part because of the San Francisco earthquake, which destroyed all records prior to 1906, and because the place of marriage, though believed to be San Francisco, is unknown. Record checks in San Mateo, San Joaquin, San Francisco, and Alameda Counties proved negative. Census records (with Cassie giving a variety of ages for herself) record that she and Louie and Harry all lived together in the Coos River region in 1900 and still in 1910. The gift Louis gave to Cassie in 1904 with the inscription, "For love and affection and other valuable considerations," is on a legal document of bank records observed by North Bend author Dick Wagner and first noted in his book *Louie Simpson's North Bend*. That it became a wedding present is speculation, though studied, given the information from Cassie's sister's family interviewed for this book.

Cassie's search for meaning is documented by her personal books, newspaper letters she wrote, and interviews with descendants. The intensity of living, the emotional attachments and betrayals, the partying and extravagance were drawn from anecdotal information, interviews, and photographs from Louie's album.

L. T. "Bud" Day (Belle's nephew), and his wife, Peg Day, still live in North Bend on the site of the Old Town home. They graciously shared with me Louie Simpson's album which included the photographs described and the poetry as written. The poem Louie wrote of his longing and of Cassie's last day were included in their entirety. The album was one of few items saved from the fire and may well have been what Louie worked on the evening Shore Acres burned. Additional photographs of Cassie with her horses and dogs and Belle at Shore Acres were located by the Days. In addition, the Days permitted me access to family papers, newspaper accounts about the Stearns family history, as well as anecdotal stories of relationships, Josiah Stearns's interest in inventions, photography, and trains, and Cassie and Louie's life and love.

Interviews were graciously granted by Ann Koppy of the Coos Historical Society, Dan Collver (whose family farm expanded Shore Acres and whose ancestor, Clara Collver, took treks to the lighthouse to exchange books as recorded in an 1890 journal), Irene Pittam (daughter of Alpha Wicklund, who worked for the Simpsons at Shore Acres), Anna Beckham (who lived as a child at Shore Acres during the rebuilding), Mrs. Bastendorff (who lived at the farm), and authors Dow Beckham, Melody Caldera, and Dick Wagner. Historian Stephen Dow Beckham, author of *The Simpsons of Shore Acres*, provided invaluable information.

Dates of the development of North Bend, the arrival of the railroad, the modes of travel along South Slough, the Lakeside and Sunset Beach developments, Louie's rescue of a child, his run for governor, his gifts to the Presbyterian church, the interrupted dance, the Chinese cooks, Cassie's work during World War I at great cost to her health, and her generosity, including Alpha's wedding dress (worn since by several brides) are based on fact. The Winsors were real. Harry's illness and medical interests were real. Edgar's, Louie's, and Cassie's wild and dramatic sides were legendary.

The life and times of coastal residents at the turn of the century are portrayed as authentically as possible. Marshfield is now named Coos Bay. North Bend still flourishes. A description of the estate and the fire came from the local press, which also recounted the story of Louie's father's acceptance of Shore Acres. Photographs of the original estate, inside rooms, and outside on the champagne circle were provided by the Days.

The date of Cassie's death in Burlingame, California, as April 30, 1921, is accurate despite several printed works to the contrary. Both the newspaper accounts from the *Coos Bay Harbor* of May 6, 1921, and the certified copy of the death certificate verify the date and the cause of death as portrayed in the story despite some speculation about the effect of the fast living the Simpsons were known for. Cassie's personal maid and two nurses tended her during the time of her illness in a furnished home on Easton Drive. It is unknown if her maid was a Coos woman from the Miluk band. Cassie's sister died in 1937, also of a heart condition.

Like Cassie's friends, I came to care for her despite her flaws and choices. Several interviewers reported hearing her described as "fabulously beautiful," a "siren and a mankiller," "a lover of fast living." What appeared on the surface as a charmed life I believe hid scars of pain and guilt and disappointment as evidenced by her personal books with her own bookmarks.

Remembrances of Belle, or Izzy as her father called her, the relationship with her mother, especially in the later years, their shared love of horses and riding, and her intensely private life were shared by descendants of Cassie and Margaret and through family photographs. Belle resided in the Old Town house until her death in 1988. She was the owner of one of the oldest Ford dealerships in the United States.

Prior to his death in 1949, Louis Simpson continued his tradition of generosity and of encouraging Oregon development as well as his interest in and care for native coastal people. In later years, according to historian Stephen Dow Beckham in a letter to me, Louie and his partner, William Robertson, "gave 6.1 acres in 'trust' to the United States for the reservation of the Confederated Tribes of Coos, Lower Umpqua and Siuslaw Indians." The site is in the heart of the Empire District, and Louis hoped it would assist the tribes as well as bring new development to the region.

Louie built the second mansion in 1927; he and his third wife later sold it, along with several hundred acres, at well below its value to the state to be used for the people of Oregon. During World War II, it served as an army barracks. The mansion was razed in 1949 due to insufficient funds for maintenance, according to the park service, and also due to political considerations at the time. Louis Simpson died the following month.

While most of the Simpson fortune was lost during the Depression, I believe he found the treasure he longed for most reflected in the eyes of his children.

In 1974, after Shore Acres had been almost forgotten, the Oregon State Parks Department launched an effort to restore the grounds and garden. In September 1975, the garden, with its Japanese pond and "rooms" of flowers, was rededicated. Included on the dais that day were state officials and dignitaries including Louis Simpson's youngest daughter. Plans are under way for the possible rebuilding of the grand mansion.

Today, the state of Oregon operates Shore Acres as a state park. In the summer months, several gardeners create daily displays of spectacular floral events with nine hundred rose bushes, five thousand tulips and flowering annuals. Finches flit among the cypress trees making a visit memorable any day of the year. During the Advent season, however, a spectacular event occurs. A show of more than 150,000 lights strung by volunteers of the Friends of Shore Acres lures thousands of visitors to the garden. Guests wander past decades-old flora, imagine life as Cassie and Louis Simpson lived it, and warm themselves on hot apple cider in the gardener's home, not far from the Japanese pond and blast of the Shore Acres' waves against rock. It is a place that honors a tragic and passionate love. The garden inspires both contemplation of decisions and the launching of great dreams.